Breckkan

Breckkan's mind raced. The terror was like that he'd felt when his father had died. Total helplessness. He could feel sweat running down his spine.

Von Stein's excited, albino eyes seemed to possess a disconcerting ability to simultaneously stare at Breckkan and yet focus on the entire scene. Suddenly, Von Stein flicked his wrist, but Breckkan felt just a touch. No pain. Then numbness in his left cheek. A warm sensation spread down his face to his jaw. Warm drops fell onto his white lab coat. A pungent, sweet odour flooded his nostrils; he knew he was bleeding heavily. The first sensations of pain broke through the numbness.

"Just a nick. The beginning. I repeat again...the data books?"

"I don't have them in here. For God's sake, do you think I'd keep them here? They're in the central safe."

"Oh, come now. You expect me to believe that?"

Breckkan cupped his right hand under his jaw to catch the blood streaming from the wound. "I tell you, Stein," the scientist insisted, "rules here demand central storage. Ask any of my technicians. Everyone knows this is a secured area."

"You have one minute, Breckkan. Then I'll carve out your tongue through the wall of your cheek."

A paroxysm of stimuli exploded in Breckkan's brain, demanding action. No plan, just manic impulse. He knew he had to act NOW to prevent the Nazis from obtaining his atomic research... And to rescue Bonnie from their soon-to-be invaded homeland, Norway.

Breckkan

by

Kent F. Jacobs

Commonwealth
Publications

A Commonwealth Publications Paperback
BRECKKAN

This edition published 1997
by Commonwealth Publications
9764 - 45th Avenue,
Edmonton, AB, CANADA T6E 5C5
All rights reserved
Copyright © 1995 by Kent F. Jacobs

ISBN: 1-55197-062-7

Designed by: Jennnifer Brolsma

Printed in Canada

To my Sallie

Note from the author:

I wish to credit the poem in chapter sixteen to
my great-grandfather, Olof Blomgren.
I found it in a letter he had written March 27,
1847, postmarked Ørje, Norway.

PROLOGUE

September 1, 1920

Skatøy, Norway

Heavy-eyed, Olav Breckkan waited for his brain to wind down, to relax. His mind was exhausted, crowded with images of the inferno on the wharf— innocent men burning, the screams. He felt a flood of emotion sweep over him, a mixture of regret and guilt. He closed his eyes, but the giant fireballs would not go away. He wrapped his arms around his sides and shivered. Guilt. The trawler shuddered, rose and fell as a sudden swell opened and closed. His neck muscles tightened and he began yielding to a feeling of overwhelming sorrow. Whether he was blameless or not, his self-condemnation was total.

Another heavy wave tossed the boat; this time his mind played a trick. The old nightmare returned once more with vivid intensity. He was back in his childhood, in the dark coastal waters of Norway, heading again for the terror. He fought the memory, but it engulfed him, becoming as fresh and agonizing as that late summer day.

They had been a family intent upon wasting none of the remaining hours of that summer at their island retreat. It was located on the small island of Skatøy, part of a land-hugging archipelago accessible only by private boat or the rare passenger ferry. From the white-fenced boatdock, a path worn into smooth granite rocks led up from the rocky cove to the simple dwelling. It wasn't humble, but unpretentious— a whitewashed, wooden house with a steep, tiled roof.

Though he had been born in America, the island pervaded his every childhood memory. His

American mother's love for her adopted country was almost fanatically evident in the home. The walls were whitewashed, the scrubbed pine floors covered by traditional Norwegian runners made of rough cotton.

He remembered wild blackberries, bare feet and crayfish parties during the long evening twilight—simple pleasures.

Olav Breckkan was at his favorite spot in the house, his seat at the kitchen table, where his view to the sea was framed by red geraniums in a window box with a sheer white valance above. His mother, Dora, and their manservant, Petter, were bickering good-naturedly in front of the black iron stove.

It had rained for a week.

Looking toward the rock-studded waters, Olav could see swirling wisps of clouds hugging the distant mainland. The quiet fog had lifted. The water was ruffled by a light wind and he could see occasional patches of brilliant-blue water as the light changed.

Nic Breckkan entered the kitchen, walked over to his son, and placed his hands on Olav's shoulders. "Finally, a chance for a sail."

"Nic, it's late," called Dora.

"There's plenty of time. Not many days of summer left for us. Petter, what do you think?"

"Perhaps a short one, sir."

"Well, what are we waiting for?" grinned Nic. "Ole, grab your sweater."

Olav joined his father at the gate and followed his gaze all the way down to the water. The rocky hillside sloped sharply away to a natural bay. Side by side, they looked out at the seascape and their boat below. He was too young to know of his father's fame, his brilliant developments in mining. He was too young to understand or even care, but as they stared out at the sparkling water, he understood he was living a privileged life.

They began walking down the steep path. Nic looked at his son and said, "Ole, how many steps to the dock?"

"Fifty-four, sir!"

"Right! So how about you taking her out this time."

"Really?"

"You bet! Just let me check your straps." Nic bent down and adjusted the life jacket on the boy. "Okay, on you go." He grinned and boosted Ole onto the sleek, twenty-two foot, single-masted sloop.

While Petter and Nic cast off the lines and unfurled the jib, Olav ceremoniously attached the red and blue flag of Norway to the fantail of the *Northwind.* Soon they were running before the wind, the water flashing with tiny whitecaps. A breeze was picking up, the velocity increasing as it squeezed through the narrow channel between the mainland and the archipelago.

Petter broke out the slickers, but Nic tossed his aside. "Nothing like the northern wind," said Nic. He took a deep breath and called to his son. "Remember this day, always."

Olav nodded and concentrated on holding tight to the wheel. The prow sliced cleanly through the waves. Glancing up at the mast, his face radiated with reflected light from the billowing sails above him. He watched Nic reach to set the spinnaker in place and leaned forward, bracing himself for the burst of speed.

Suddenly, an explosive blast of wind caught the sails, causing the boat to jibe violently. The mainsail ripped. The boom swung out of control and swept across the deck, catching Nic in the chest, splintering his right clavicle and rib cage.

The brutal force of the boom carried him overboard into the frigid water. Instinctively, Nic fought his way to the surface. His head broke through the water; he frantically gasped for air. He gagged and floundered. With each movement bone fragments acted as serrated knives. His right lung collapsed as the jagged-edged ribs punctured again and again, cutting the spongy tissue into useless pulp.

Just as Petter bolted into action, the *Northwind* lurched with the sudden change in weight and broached, veering headlong into a deep trough. The mast crashed near Nic as the sloop rolled, the heavy canvas and dangling ropes engulfed him. The sail quickly saturated with water.

The *Northwind* slid terrifyingly and took a sickening dip. The boat shuddered and rose on the knife edge of the next wave and flipped, throwing Petter and Olav into a black wall of water. The freezing water swallowed the boy instantly. He felt the water sucking at him, pulling him down in vicious circles. He clawed upward, pushing and kicking with all his strength. As his head broke through the surface, his ears were blasted by a surging, hollow roar. He screamed as he was suddenly lifted high on a wave.

A brilliant whiteness flashed around him and he heard the crack explode nearby. In the eerie light, he saw the boat breaking up fifteen feet away. He felt a powerful push from behind. "Swim!" screamed Petter.

They scrambled up onto the hull, gasping for air. Olav frantically searched the blackness for his father. Another wave blasted the boat, the water hitting his shoulders. The wind was a frozen, constant roar; the air vibrated with lightning. There was no horizon; everything seemed tilted. Olav lost all sense of up and down. He swallowed more water. Petter moved close to him, clapping him on the back and brushing the hair from his eyes. His waterlogged sweater hung from his shoulders. Olav shivered uncontrollably, his teeth chattered, unable to speak.

Nodding at the boy, Petter jerked off his slicker and yelled, "I'm going after him. Stay here! Hold on tight!" He slipped off the hull and disappeared under the dark water.

With powerful strokes, he dove deep and found the sail, clawing at it in search of Nic. An arm. Nic was caught and twisted like a corkscrew, wrapped in all the lines. Petter pulled and kicked, trying desperately to free the contorted body.

Petter felt a crushing pain in his chest and broke through the surface, gasping for breath. The 45 degree water was exacting its toll.

"Papa!" screamed Olav. Nic's head broke the surface. His face was strangely blue.

Nic coughed and choked, trying to breathe. There was a gurgling sound and pink bubbles flowed from his nostrils. His head slipped into the foam and darkness, disappearing below the surface.

Wrenching his knife from deep in his clinging trousers, Petter breathed deeply and dove under again. He frantically hacked at the tangled sail. No! Don't give up! Not now! Push! He grabbed Nic under his shoulders and, with all his remaining strength, brought him to the surface.

Colorless eyes rolled back, the dying man was trying feebly to fill his blood-soaked lungs with air. The frigid water, the rupture of the tissue, and the weight of the sail combined destructively. Nic slipped from Petter's arms and slid below the surface.

Gasping, Petter lunged for the body. A vicious spasm contracted in his legs as he fought the churning water. He pushed back toward the boat.

"Papa!" Olav screamed hysterically. Water and tears ran down his face. "Where's Papa? Find him!"

Spitting more frigid water, Petter breathed, "I can't. He's gone." He pulled himself onto the hull, numb with cold. Olav huddled motionless, unbelieving.

The wind died down. A veil of mist moved in, gray and silent.

Olav shivered. He had never felt so cold, so empty.

PART I

CHAPTER 1

April 1, 1940

Berlin

The Mercedes crunched down the dark, empty streets, the headlights illuminating piles of black ice at the base of the streetlamps. No new snow had fallen to cover the ugliness of old winter. Turning onto Dahlemstrasse, the car pulled to the curb before an imposing stone building— imposing only because of its sheer mass; certainly no architectural effort had been made to give the viewer pleasure. The solitary ornamentation was a tower at the northeast corner, crowned with a curious round dome topped by a sharp spire reminiscent of the Kaiser's helmet. Only the plumage was missing.

The carved words, "Kaiser-Wilhelm Institute of Physics," were barely visible above the main entrance. Emblazoned with black swastikas, two blood-red banners, three stories high, rippled in the pre-dawn breeze. These, unlike the carved name, were floodlit.

The two officers stepped from the brittle cold into what seemed an even colder entry hall. The Lieutenant pulled open a door with a frosted glass pane and the Colonel walked ahead into a small anteroom. A corporal standing behind a counter glanced up and asked, "Are you expected?"

The Lieutenant stepped forward and slid a large envelope across the counter. The Corporal snapped to attention as he focused on the seal of the Abwehr above the signature of Admiral Canaris. After reading the single sheet of orders, the Corporal saluted. "A few moments, Colonel Richter. Follow me."

The only sound was the clacking of boot heels on the white tile floor. Entering a small room at the end of the corridor, the Corporal thumped his knuckles against a metal locker. "Please remove your uniforms and hang them in here." He picked up two sealed packages from a bench below and said, "Don't let the smell bother you. Traces of nitrous oxide. Harmless. Put on these surgical gowns and cloth boots. Don't forget the cap and mask. When you're ready, go to the elevator." He pointed to the door on the opposite wall.

Richter and the Lieutenant were suddenly alone as the Corporal left the room, slamming the door behind him. Surveying the gray-walled cubicle, Richter noted there were no chairs, papers, photographs, emblems— nothing to hint of the business carried on in the place. Bothersome was the fact the exit door had automatically locked upon closing.

To the Lieutenant's surprise, the Colonel suddenly let out a burst of throaty laughter. I'm impressed, the bastard already has us at a disadvantage, he thought to himself. And we are supposed to be the experts at intimidation. How appropriate it is to nickname this place "Virus House," run by this malignant son-of-a-bitch.

"Do you know Major von Stein?" asked the Lieutenant.

"Only by rumor." Richter unbuttoned his great coat. "He seems to have enough clout to drag us here before dawn." He handed his tunic to his aide and sat on the bench, putting his right-booted foot on the Lieutenant's back. The Colonel's boots fell to the floor; the Lieutenant turned his attention to the paper-wrapped packages.

Just as both men shrugged into the pale green gowns, the lock turned and the inner door swung open to reveal the elevator doors ten feet away. A red light glowed above a black and yellow sign that read in German:"DANGER! RADIATION!" They entered the cage-like elevator and the doors clanged shut. A voice crackled from a speaker in the ceiling: "Slide the lever to the left." Just as the Lieutenant did so, the elevator began slowly descending.

Closing his eyes to the harsh light in the elevator, the Colonel cursed under his breath, wondering if the voice on the speaker was picking up his every sound. The door opened—Level C. A hooded figure stood in a far corner of the brightly lit, white-tiled room.

Colonel Richter glanced at his aide and waited to be acknowledged by von Stein. The elevator doors clanged behind them. Despite the chill in the laboratory, he could feel his face flush with anger at the impudence of the scientist.

The arrangement of the lab was impressive, crowded with equipment, but immaculate. There were two screened windows on the north wall, red warning lights glowing above each. On the opposite wall, a scurrying sound emanated from stacks of metal cages. Von Stein stood at a long steel necropsy table. He tossed another lump of matter on the work table and murmured almost as if to himself, "Good morning, gentlemen. Sorry for the early hour. Time is critical in my work; my experiments set the schedule."

His tone was pleasant enough, Richter noticed, but the hint of cynicism seemed deliberate.

"Let me show you something." Von Stein reached down, picked up one of the amorphous lumps, and said, "The coat easily separates from the epidermis. Intriguing? The changes in hair pigmentation: a result of radium exposure. You are familiar with Mme. Curie?"

"How many rats do you have in this laboratory?" interrupted Colonel Richter.

"At the moment, we're low on supplies, Colonel.

It's really rather difficult to judge radiation exposure dosages. This laboratory is currently studying the alterations induced by different levels of radiation. Unfortunately, there are deaths, but back to your question. I would guess..." Von Stein pointed to the cages and answered, "Probably five thousand."

The Lieutenant audibly gasped, fighting off the nausea rising with his panic.

"Do they bother you, Lieutenant? Not fond of rodents?" asked von Stein as he picked up the most recent specimen, sliced the head off, and tossed the carcass onto the pile. Smiling behind his mask, he held up the rat's decapitated head. "I need to finish this last one." He released the base of the neck and watched the blood drain. The rat's eyes turned gray.

What is he trying to prove with this vulgar display, wondered Richter. He watched von Stein closely, appraising him like a country gentlemen buying a stallion for breeding purposes. He knew the bastard was indulging himself in a bit of repulsive harassment, though his obvious lack of remorse could make him an excellent agent. "In the end, just what is the purpose of all this?" asked the Colonel, an icy stillness in his voice.

Von Stein laid down his engraved pocket knife and slowly turned toward him. "You, of all people, should know. Genetics. Some of us feel that radiation, used properly, can change the genetics of an animal for the better. What an opportunity...a perfect race." He wiped off the knife blade, put it in his pocket, and snapped off his surgical gloves.

Without another word, he ushered the officers into the elevator and took them up to Level B. As they stepped into a large tiled room, von Stein instructed them to remove their surgical gowns and masks. He undressed quickly beside them, then pressed a button on the tiled wall. Torrents of steaming water flooded from high-pressure shower heads. Watching von Stein methodically scrub himself, Richter spoke out, "And what diseases are we protecting ourselves from? Or radiation exposure, Doctor?"

"We're not, Colonel," von Stein said as the showers turned off automatically. "We're protecting the rats from us. Radiation severely alters their resistance to infection. Here at the Virus House, we don't ever have accidents. If there's to be infection, we create it."

Jesus Christ, thought Richter. We've suited up for a damn rat.

Von Stein pointed the way through a narrow door resembling the hatch of a ship, heavy bolts at six points. He pulled the door shut and threw the six latches, locking them into the dim, red-lit chamber. At first there was a silence, then a gradual whirring began, a low hiss that built in intensity until it was nearly deafening. Hot air blasted around their bodies until they were dry and red-tinged from the heat. Suddenly, the sound stopped and the oscillating air subsided.

"Partial to Dante, von Stein?" the Colonel said sarcastically. The damned son-of-a-bitch.

Von Stein ignored the comment and opened the exit door. "You'll find your clothes in the cubicles, gentlemen. I'll meet you in the stairwell."

As they ascended the metal stairs to the main level, Richter was able for the first time to observe von Stein clearly. He was dressed in a well-cut, dark suit, a subtle tie at his throat. But Richter immediately noticed that the skin of his hands and face appeared unnaturally white, almost bloodless. Von Stein's face was narrow but strong-jawed— even oddly handsome—and his hair appeared to be bleached, glistening as he passed under the conical lights along the stairwell. Richter couldn't really evaluate his eyes because they were shaded by tinted, silver-rimmed glasses.

At the top of the stairs, von Stein motioned toward a set of double doors. "My office, Colonel. You, too, Lieutenant. I have to make a call to Leipzig. If you don't mind waiting..."

Richter pushed past the Major and entered the private office.

Von Stein acknowledged him with a vague smile and motioned toward the side chairs. Speaking quietly into the phone, he turned away, his body partially hidden by the highback chair.

The walls were paneled in dark mahogany and, as his eyes adjusted to the subdued light, Richter noticed the antique walnut desk. He recognized it as Italian: severe lines and panels carved in austere but perfect geometric diamonds and triangles. The two matching side chairs had richly carved legs and pale ivory leather seats and backs. He scanned the shelves covering two walls. They were filled with books and journals along with a collection of bottles containing unidentifiable specimens. He could feel the curious juxtaposition of specimens and carefully chosen antiques adding to the unnerving aura surrounding von Stein.

The Colonel also noticed the conspicuous absence of a portrait of Hitler. Instead, there was a candid photograph of Admiral Canaris in a silver frame. So we were correct, he thought. Von Stein really did want to join the Abwehr.

The phone clicked in the cradle and Richter looked up at von Stein. Running his hand along the desk, he said, "A perfect example. Sixteenth century. A favorite period of mine. I'm surprised to find it here."

"Speer and I've been friends for a long time," said von Stein. "He has the sources, and the clout.

Since I seem to spend my life in this building, I asked him for a few of his finds. There seem to be so many people choosing to relocate lately. Besides, I'm rarely at my apartment."

Richter knew all too well about the "relocations," but said nothing. Instead he walked away from the scientist, his eyes drawn to a small picture hanging on the wall opposite the desk. The chalk drawing on faded cream paper was spectacular, restrained in color, with only glints of silver and russet across deep shadows. "Titian. Correct?" Von Stein nodded. "You're certainly partial to the Italian Renaissance. Did Speer find this for you too?"

"Titian, yes, but not from Speer."

"I've always found it strange," commented the Colonel, hoping to provoke an argument. "The combination of paganism and Christianity that flourished side by side during the Renaissance. Though, as always," he continued, "their consuming preoccupation seemed to be with worldly goods, rather than religious values."

"An amusing simplification, Colonel, but their worldliness brought Italy out of the Middle Ages and produced the consummate artist, Michelangelo."

Turning to face von Stein, Richter said, "It also produced Machiavelli."

Von Stein shrugged. "Both great Florentines." He pointed to the chairs, asking them to be seated.

With a grunt of disgust, Richter leaned forward, took a pouch from the hand of his aide and removed a leather binder. Richter distrusted something in von Stein's make-up, not just his arrogance. There was the possibility of the unpredictable buried in his scholarly achievements. He had seen it in upper-crust Germans before. Von Stein would have to be carefully controlled. Holding the bound folder and tapping it on his knee, Richter stared unblinkingly at him.

Von Stein shifted in his chair. Only the ticking of the wall clock and a growl from his stomach broke the silence.

"First, Doctor von Stein," the Colonel finally began, "we know you're a linguist and an authority on Scandinavia. We also know your professional expertise. You're only thirty-four and you've already published twenty papers under your name. Three years with Professor Bohr in Copenhagen and, I think, one of his star pupils."

"I was the best Bohr ever had."

Richter paused and then asked, "So why didn't you accompany him to Princeton in the United States?"

Von Stein smiled thinly, and said nothing. The Colonel turned several pages.

"Well then, Doctor, do you recall any problems?" asked Richter, crossing his legs, focusing on his shiny black boots.

The muscles in von Stein's neck stood out like taut cables. "Certainly," he replied, drawing a deep breath, "part of the profession." He watched Richter, waiting for his next move.

"The incident isn't important to the Reich. It's just that if you have, or rather had, some personal problem with a Doctor Breckkan..." Again von Stein said nothing, his tinted lenses masking his thoughts. What drives him, the Colonel wondered. If jealousy was the route, then he had the answer. He knew von Stein's dossier by heart.

Richter began a strategic course of destructive analysis. "Your funding is dependent on the General Staff, so you could hardly hold the position you have here as *Provisional* Head without our knowing a great deal about you. For example, it hasn't slipped our attention that you desperately wanted to join the Abwehr. Apparently you think we enjoy a certain unassailable prestige. Your kind of mind admires such professionalism. Am I correct so far?" Von Stein remained silent.

The deft handling of a potential agent was not new to Richter. It was his job to take this man's innate genius and weaknesses and use them. "So, Doctor, you were refused membership in the Abwehr, weren't you? Of course, you are Aryan." The Colonel looked away, as if studying the Titian for a moment, then said slowly, "You were tripped up by your own genes. Your mother was an albino. You are an albino. I understand you insisted, medically speaking, it is a trivial genetic defect, except for your failing eyesight. But really now, isn't the whole idea of the Super Race perfection, especially genetic perfection?" He sensed von Stein's attention harden. He uncrossed his legs and stared at the pale face before him. "Perhaps there's some discrepancy in our files? Perhaps you would like to set things straight?"

"That's enough, Colonel," von Stein snapped, rising to his feet.

"Shut up, Doctor, and sit down. I've had enough of you. Now you're going to be a good soldier. I have accommodated your damn schedule and have tolerated your insolence long enough." Clinching his teeth, von Stein sat.

Richter walked over to the bookcase, intentionally turning his back on von Stein, and took down a specimen jar. He looked at the tissue sample with disgust, placing it back on the shelf. Then he strolled across the room to the photograph of Canaris. After a pause, he clasped his hands behind his back and said, "They say truth is virtue, don't they? Well, isn't it true that Doctor Breckkan asked you to donate blood for one of his experiments? And didn't you refuse and then lose your temper?"

Von Stein slammed his hands down on the desk. "That's a lie!"

Richter suddenly crossed to the desk. The Lieutenant flinched as the Colonel brushed past him, but the abrupt movement didn't stop von Stein.

"As to that 'incident' you refer to, the woman who registered the complaint is a bitch," snapped von Stein. "She would never have been with Bohr if her father wasn't head of some second-rate institute in Norway." He took a deep breath to calm himself. "Colonel, you're not a scientist. You don't know about the politics that go on. Both the woman and Breckkan were trying to discredit me in front of Bohr."

Ending his tirade, von Stein whipped off his glasses and glared at the Colonel. From where he stood, Richter could clearly see von Stein's eyes. The right one was pink, with gray striae radiating from the pupil. The other was clouded, opalescent— unearthly eyes. He signalled for von Stein to be seated and backed slowly into his own chair. The Lieutenant sat motionless but at attention. Reopening the folder, Richter said, "Doctor Breckkan apparently volunteered to testify against you, but the woman dropped the charges. The inquiry ended 'In question— No disciplinary action taken.' The report doesn't mention you were asked to leave Copenhagen shortly thereafter. You were fired, weren't you?"

Von Stein replaced his glasses then lit a cigarette. A coldness swept over him. "Assuming the incident will be expunged from my record," he paused, drawing on the cigarette, "and being assured there will be no impediments to my future career here at the Kaiser-Wilhelm, what can I do for you, Colonel?"

"As you very well know, at this moment the Reich has the ability to dominate the world in the field of nuclear physics. Soon we'll take Denmark, and Professor Bohr's Institute with it, then France and their cyclotron. We already have Norway, though they don't know it yet— eventually England."

"What about the United States? They're experimenting, you know."

"They're halfhearted, besides they are years behind."

Von Stein nodded affirmatively, knowing not to question the section chief of Military Intelligence.

"We know Bohr is in Oslo right now. Breckkan saw to it that Bohr was the keynote speaker for the European Physics Society Conference. Our contact tells us Bohr has been heard openly speaking out against the relationship between Norway and Germany."

Grinding out his cigarette, von Stein said, "Bohr was doing that in '38. At the International Congress he delivered a vehemently anti-Nazi speech." He leaned forward. "A lot of the delegates walked out, including myself, but then you probably have that in your records, too."

"What about Breckkan?"

"He wasn't there. What's so important about him anyway?"

"Both Breckkan and his wife, I believe her name is Bonnie, know the significance of Bohr's theories. Our contact tells us Breckkan is working on a secret project at the Norsk-Hydro Heavy Water Plant. Somehow he's tied to the work in Bohr's lab." Von Stein suddenly stood and walked to the windows. He jerked back the drapes. The pale early morning light filtered across the oriental rug.

Richter made a guess. "What's the matter, Doctor, didn't you know they were married?"

Looking out at the park, von Stein asked, "What does any of this have to do with me?"

"You're a scientist, one of our country's best, a

genius in nuclear physics. Canaris personally picked you for this project. We need everything they know, everything they're thinking. Lieutenant, the tickets." Holding up the packet, he continued. "A private dinner party is being given at the Royal Palace in Oslo honoring Professor Bohr tomorrow night. Dr. Breckkan will be there. Our contact has arranged an invitation for you, Major von Stein. Perfectly logical, with your background. Get their data. We have to know how far along they are in this nuclear business." He tossed the packet on the desk. "Get Professor Kittleson's data, too."

"Why Kittleson? The old Norwegian hasn't published for years."

"Get it all. Understand? And if you meet with resistance...well, use your judgment." Richter polished the bill of the hat on his tunic sleeve, then added, "Maybe you'll return as Permanent Head here."

Everything in his life had been fine until Breckkan, thought von Stein. A career blighted by the charges. Since leaving Copenhagen, he had felt like a terminally ill man, his only alternative death, and with it, freedom from the stigma. Suddenly he smiled to himself. The irony of it: a reprieve. The Colonel had just given him a chance to get back at Breckkan, to clear his own name. The weak sunlight glinted off his white hair as he looked up and asked, "If I need back-up in Norway?"

"Help will be available, but they will contact you. That's all you need to know. The Director of Intelligence expects total success."

Descending the steps of the Institute, the bitter cold enveloped them. Richter shrugged on his great coat. "I need air, Lieutenant. Let's walk." They crossed the street into the park, the black Mercedes followed at a crawl, the tires crunching through the ice.

The chestnut and lime trees were barren, their

branches standing black against the gray sky. A soft yellow light hovered behind the swiftly moving clouds. He'll do it, thought Richter. Not out of duty or commitment; no, there's a much deeper motive.

CHAPTER 2

Berlin

Major von Stein was suddenly ravenous and realized he hadn't eaten since the day before. He pushed the call button on his desk. Immediately, there was a knock at the door.

"You called, sir?" asked the Corporal, snapping to attention.

"Scrambled eggs, with cream, stirred slowly, low heat."

"Yes, sir. Would you like anything— "

Von Stein cut him off. "Coffee, black, lots of it." As the Corporal backed out the door, von Stein withdrew to a side chair to wait. He closed his eyes, and in an orderly way allowed his mind to wander, and like pulling a file from a cabinet, he chose to recall his summers in Italy. Suddenly he looked up at the Titian, impulsively strode across the room and removed it from the wall.

Kurt von Stein had no recollection of his mother; she had died when he was still an infant. His father never mentioned her albinism. She was an exquisite pale beauty. Baron von Stein was an elegant man with a captivating presence, a man who had mastered leisure. The Baron loved Italy, as had his own mother, and had managed to achieve the respect of Italians, including the upper crust of Florence. He was a clever statesman, but a disinterested administrator, a patron of the arts and a devout cultivator of that which the Medici admired most: power. Like them, he bought, borrowed, bribed for and stole whenever he could.

In such an atmosphere of greedy acquisition, it was ironic that the von Steins' summer home, situated above Florence in the small village of Fiesole, was originally a convent. An exquisite example of

Renaissance style, the villa was equally prized for its outdoor dining terrace overlooking the Arno, the scene of luxurious meals where the Baron orchestrated conversations ranging from the benefits of aromatic herbs to Puccini's *Madama Butterfly*.

Often, when the Baron was out of hearing range, guests gossiped about his past and his pale, beautiful wife, now buried in the floor of the villa's chapel. Idle talk in the village mentioned her insanity. The onset apparently had been insidious; during the last years, she lost all contact with reality. Albinism rarely progresses to that end, but in a few instances, the mind surrenders to the disease.

The Baron had sequestered her in the villa. Indeed, for several years prior to her death, no one recalled seeing her. After an appropriate period of mourning, Kurt von Stein's father earnestly rededicated himself to amusement.

Major von Stein lowered his head and rubbed his brow roughly with the back of his hand, as though to avoid having to look at something that wouldn't go away.

The summer of 1923 was to be his last in the Tuscan hills. Like so many in Germany, the von Stein family fortune was in jeopardy. The total financial collapse of Germany ushered in an era of turmoil, allowing Hitler and his Nazi gang to take over. That indelible summer terminated suddenly. Just days after the communication from Berlin, his father summarily dismissed the servants, closed the villa and left the farm and vineyards to the care of the local tenants. He had the chapel sealed shut by a local mason. The Baron and his son returned immediately to Berlin to face the confiscation of the von Stein industries. Kurt was sent to a private boarding school, and went on to graduate with honors from the University of Cologne.

With such a stellar background, he was invited to continue his graduate training in Copenhagen under Dr. Niels Bohr.

The von Stein family never returned to Italy.

The final insult from his father came in 1933 when he received the telegram notifying him of Baron von Stein's suicide. Hitler's hatred for the baronial system had triggered its destruction. Returning to Berlin, where his lawyer read the will, he discovered that the Baron, to maintain his life-style and still support his son's education, had sold the remainder of the von Stein Estate and most of the family possessions. Kurt von Stein's great inheritance from a once powerful and wealthy family had been reduced to an antique Italian desk, two side chairs, and a Titian drawing.

No matter how wrong his father had been, how self-centered, materialistic, or hedonistic, he would always remember the early years of travel, the exposure to the rich life in Italy, in a world surrounded by great art. And his superior education allowed him to aspire to the great worlds which great men seem to appreciate. His soul still yearned for this. He still needed to be like the families who live on private estates, stay in the great hotels, whose lives and thoughts are occupied with pleasure and elegance.

He long ago had forgotten the sealed crypt.

His father had lived the life of a dilettante, leaving him only furniture and a token masterpiece. Strange how war can give a man a new beginning. He shuddered and warned himself to be very thorough, very careful.

CHAPTER 3

APRIL 2, 1940

Oslo, Norway

Breckkan turned hard left at 41 Ankir and drove down the stone-paved private drive past the stable house into the darkness of the first garage. He left the car running, enjoying the warmth of the heater, and switched on the overhead light. He rarely rechecked his agenda, once was enough, but he wanted to make sure his list of Professor Bohr's guests for the dinner at the Royal Palace had passed the security check. Opening the single sheet on the seat beside him, his eyes ran down the names. Added to the august group of scientific luminaries were King Haakon's chosen political attendees. Beside the name of the head of the German Trade Delegation was a scribbled notation, "and guest." It wasn't Bohr's handwriting; perhaps the secretary at the physics department was informed of the addition—forty-five names and their positions. Breckkan memorized them in less than one minute.

Nic Breckkan had suspected that, even at the age of five, his son had recognized the powers of his own photographic memory. Young Breckkan could recall incidents with near completeness and accuracy. Faces, the nuances. Conversations. Colors. A whiz at dates, numbers, facts.

Breckkan folded the sheet of paper and tucked it into his overcoat and snapped off the light. As he pulled the garage doors shut and locked the crossbar in place, the freezing Norwegian air blasted him; the wind chill from the Oslofjord brought the temperature to 15 degrees. His oversized coat caught the wind, turning with him toward the stone house, the Breckkan Estate. Smoke was streaming from the five chimneys; his American mother's penchant for comfort was obvious. Could she live with the coming austerity?

Nic Breckkan had never mentioned Olav's photographic memory to his wife, knowing Olav would someday realize that total recall could be a curse, remembering the bad with the good, the superfluous with the vital. It wasn't until Olav was in his early twenties that his mother, Dora, recognized his unique faculty. Graduating early from the University in Oslo, Breckkan had gone straight from academics into full-time training with the Norwegian Olympic team for the Winter Games in February of 1932. Cross-country skiing was his love, and the coach was also pushing him toward the Biathlon, a combination of skiing and shooting. Since the first Winter Games in 1924 at Chamonix, France, the Norwegians held the event dear to their hearts, and were intent on taking the medal. But Dora Breckkan had other ideas for her son. The coach was extremely upset when she interrupted his training at the austere training camp above Trondheim.

She had him on a train with her to the Continent before Breckkan realized the full intent of her plan. He was to escort a young American student, Katherine Wakefield, to the Opera Ball in Vienna. Baroque, rococo architecture, the music of Strauss, all background for the social whirl. Dora loved it. She made certain Breckkan stayed in the right circles and it was at one those proper events, a soiree at the Schönbrunn Palace, that Dora realized Breckkan's amazing capacity for visual observation and retention.

A valet in the finest livery escorted a group of the guests through the immense reception halls of the Imperial Summer Palace, pointing out the hidden passageways behind the walls where servants would stoke the huge porcelain stoves or attend to any royal needs. As a child prodigy, Mozart himself had been escorted through the passageways to appear for his performances. At one point in the tour, the guide had asked if the guests would please look carefully at the next two ballrooms; he would have a question for them. The ballrooms appeared to be exactly identical, approximately forty-five feet long, lavishly decorated with gold leaf upon gold leaf. When the valet turned to the group with the inquiry as to the singular difference between the two rooms, only Breckkan raised a hand. "The pattern in the parquet floors is the exact reverse in this ballroom. The light woods versus dark woods have been interchanged," was his answer.

Katherine Wakefield had stood beside him that evening and although Breckkan literally saw nothing unusual in the Austrian's question, he suddenly realized Katherine was in love with him. A cable from Copenhagen announcing the acceptance of his appointment for a fellowship with Professor Niels Bohr saved him. When Breckkan left for Denmark, Dora knew her son had seen the trap. Katherine Wakefield never forgave him for leaving her without an escort and neither had her wealthy father.

Breckkan jogged across the courtyard and before he made it up the steps, a uniformed butler opened the door.

"Welcome home, Dr. Breckkan!" Petter pumped his hand vigorously. "You look tired. Your research, too much work?"

"Work? Work's easy compared to living with that redhead of mine. It's that Scottish blood of hers—great stamina," Breckkan said, rolling the R's in a Scottish burr.

He slapped the slight, white-haired butler soundly on the back. "Where's Mother?"

"Upstairs, in the drawing room. I believe she's still on the phone."

"Another suitor?" asked Breckkan, handing Petter his overcoat and homburg.

"I believe it's Mr. Wakefield."

"I want to talk to her, and I don't have much time," he called, hurrying up the burnished wooden staircase. He hesitated at the landing, making sure nothing had changed. He spotted the large bouquet of daffodils on the credenza and smiled as he slid the double drawing room doors open with one quick motion.

His American-born mother was passionately addicted to Norwegian antiques. The darkness of the paneled walls was partially relieved by several large tapestries, their muted richness lending an illusion of warmth. In a corner, a commode with deep-cast gilt pulls and escutcheons boasted a collection of sepia-toned photographs. At the center of the grouping was a large picture of Breckkan's father standing next to King Haakon with two small, towheaded boys kneeling at their feet. The older boy was Crown Prince Olav, the younger was his namesake, Olav Breckkan.

The only light in the room came from a reading lamp with a green shade, looking strangely businesslike in the elegant setting. Dora was seated at her desk, her frailty due to a long respiratory illness all but hidden by a fur throw over her lap. She hung up the phone and looked at him. She seemed smaller than he remembered, but her expression was the same, both stern and affectionate. Her white hair was pulled into a bun at the nape of her neck. Her face was still sublimely regal, opalescent in the dim light.

"Mother, the daffodils are beautiful. It's still so cold. Where did you find them?"

"You're late, Olav. Bohr has you working too hard. You're not his lackey anymore," she said, closing the ledger.

He tossed several logs on the fire, warmed his hands then turned to her. "Bonnie sends her love."

"Come, give me a kiss."

He placed a newspaper on her desk, knelt at her side, and gently kissed her on each cheek. She looks so pale, he thought. "I've missed you."

She smiled and reached for a cigarette. Breckkan lit it with a heavy gold lighter, then set it down next to the package of Lucky Strikes. "Still partial to American cigarettes?"

Ignoring his comment she inhaled deeply. As smoke curled around her words, she said, "Ole, what's in the news today?" Starting to reach for the newspaper, she stiffened. "Why do you insist on reading *Dagbladet*? Damn! You know your father hated that paper!" Her voice rose a key with the mention of Nic Breckkan.

"Mother, surely you're listening to the radio? Oslo still looks like its orderly self, but you can feel the tension. Poland's gone; that outragcous pact he made with Stalin allowed the bastard to invade Finland. My God, Finland! Is Norway going to be next? How would you like Hitler or Stalin or any of their ilk right here in this house?"

Putting out her cigarette, she said, "Calm down, Olav. You and I always have so little time, besides, don't worry, Gustave keeps me up to date. He's in a position to be well-informed, you'll recall. More important though, I just finished speaking with Bill Wakefield. You remember him from Vienna? I think he's quite concerned about you. Whatever you and your Professor Bohr are up to must be very dangerous."

"I'm not so sure that Mr. Wakefield thinks much about me at all."

"He just asked about your work!"

Like his father, Wakefield was a self-made man. Tough. Maybe it was the way he approached subjects: "Even you, Mother, will agree Americans are so straightforward, blunt, if you ask me." Or was it the way he lived: "He's used to getting what he wants. WKW is a powerful company." That was it, power. "I can't help but feel he doesn't have anyone's concern at heart but his own." Breckkan checked his watch. "I've got to change; Roald Duun is picking me up. Remember him? We used to ski together."

"How can I forget? He brought you down the mountain." She grimaced, her face filled with concern. "At least Bonnie has tamed some of the daredevil in you."

"Roald's been promoted. Secretary of the Navy, no less."

"I read." She shifted the fur blanket. "The King has intensified security at the Palace this week. Bill's right. You are in danger. Why don't you quit that research business and come home?"

"Let's not get into that now."

"Ole, listen to me. Our iron mines are at full production with your Uncle Gustave at the helm of Breckkan Mining and Manufacturing. He's making us money, but if you were running the company I would feel much more comfortable. And, you could help keep Norway neutral."

Breckkan didn't want to argue. His mother had the infuriating talent of a born debater, able to balance both sides of an argument and still sound logical. Her logic. "I've got to get dressed. After Bonnie's cooking, I hope I can still get into my waistcoat." He patted his stomach.

She chuckled. "Curse of the newlywed. But I won't

let you get away without having a drink with me. When you're ready, ask Petter to bring our drinks."

He closed the double doors, pausing a moment to admire the daffodils once more. She is such an enigma, he thought. Never misses a chance. He walked into his room and tossed his tweed jacket on the bed, noticing his formal evening wear had been carefully laid out.

Petter hadn't missed any detail; the medals were on the dressing table. He had received the gold one to commemorate his appointment to the Norwegian Storting's Nobel Committee for the Peace Prize. A particularly sweet appointment, Dr. Nobel's fellow Swedes had never quite forgiven him for entrusting the Peace Prize selection to the Norwegians.

"Your bath is ready, Dr. Breckkan," Petter called from the bathroom. "Leave your suit. I'll tend to it."

As he eased into the water, Breckkan thought back on the endless number of unsettling encounters he'd had with his mother. Tonight was no different. Within minutes, she could first demand then flatter, coerce then condescend, bully then appease. But she was still the doyenne of the family and she had heaped on him the wealth of her fortune.

According to stories told him, his father had first seen her at a concert in Chicago. Nic Breckkan was transfixed by the fragile young American with the crystal-clear blue eyes. The concert had been in December. In February, Nic had said, "I would like to have a son by you."

The wedding took place after Easter. They sailed to Europe and went on to Venice for their honeymoon. Nic was older and already famous outside of Norway. He knew where he was going and his business was expanding rapidly. But it was Dora who was his prize and he jealously guarded his jewel. It didn't particularly bother her to be protected and spoiled; on the contrary, she loved her new life and adopted country. She became more Norwegian than most Norwegians. She was a source of stability for him, until in 1913, at the age of forty-eight, he died so tragically. Dora was only twenty-eight years old with a young son, but she resolved to take over the management of the company. She learned to use her fragility with cleverness and as a consummate pragmatist, she became an extremely independent and dynamic businesswoman. Yet she seemed to have never understood why her son abandoned the family business for a career in theoretic physics.

Olav Breckkan did not know just why, whether it was her disappointment in his choice of careers, or some kind of her own personal crisis but while he was at the Institute in Copenhagen, she suddenly stepped down from active control of the company. Dora spent the next several years traveling the world.

Returning to Norway in 1938, Dora Breckkan settled back into the estate situated high on a hillside overlooking the Oslofjord. The drawing room was filled with even more antiques, surrounded by music and photographs of Nic and her son. One memento never changed: a sequined mask on the table beside her chair, a memory of her honeymoon in Venice in 1905.

"Not much time, sir," called Petter from the bedroom. "The Commodore just rang. He wants to be at the Palace a little early."

Breckkan got out of the tub, reached for a towel from the heated towel rack and wrapped it around his waist. He put on the starched white pique shirt and stood patiently while Petter fastened the pearl studs in place. White tie and waistcoat, black tails.

"The medals," Petter reminded him. "You should pay more attention to these details. I'm not always going to be around to do it for you."

"Petter, has Mother mentioned leaving Oslo?"

"If you mean Skatøy, no, sir. I assume once the ice has broken and the weather is safe, we'll go down as usual for the summer."

The mention of the island to Breckkan brought images, images all in shades of ochre, sienna, blue-black. Waves of black water crashing on to the rocks, pure white froth surging over the granite like ribbons of lace. A flash of red, red geraniums in a windowsill.

"Just another six weeks, Dr. Breckkan. I'll let you know when she plans to leave. Maybe you and Mrs. Breckkan can join us later in the summer. You're ready, sir. I'll be up with the acquavit right away."

Breckkan walked across the room for a final check in the mirror. He shut his eyes and stood quietly for several moments. He had no intention of telling her about Bohr's stubbornness, that he refused to leave Copenhagen. The Germans were poised like a hair trigger, ready to take Denmark and probably all of Scandinavia. No matter what Bohr's reason was for refusing asylum, Breckkan knew he and Bonnie would have to make a decision right away. His eyes were dark with worry. He knew he would have no luck convincing his mother to leave Norway. Certainly not tonight. "Christ, why doesn't she go home, back to America?" he muttered. He checked his watch and walked briskly to the drawing room.

"Very handsome," said Dora. "Your father's cologne... There you are, Petter, please serve." She was addressing the butler, but her eyes didn't leave Breckkan.

They accepted the small, frozen glasses of clear alcohol. Breckkan sat across from her and raised his glass. "Skoal."

Breckkan's face was framed by the darkness of the tapestry-covered walls. There was a flush on his cheeks, his forehead pale, his strong jaw set as if his teeth were clenched. He seemed to be on the brink of something, something critical, explosive, and his indecisiveness bothered Dora. Olav Breckkan was known as a man who took risks, but tonight his entire being was full of caution. Had his meetings with Professor Bohr brought him secrets so dangerous, information so vital, that her son seemed paralyzed? Or was it Breckkan's other side taking control, the genuine sensitivity he took pains to hide, the complete devotion Dora knew that he gave totally to anyone he loved.

Her words were softly spoken when she finally asked, "What is it that's bothering you?" He raised his hand in denial, but she continued, "I may be getting old, but I haven't missed that dark look in your face. What is it?"

"Vemork. The heavy water project is taking up more and more of my time. I got a call this morning asking me to get back as soon as possible. They didn't say why, but..." He looked at his mother, trying to decide whether to tell her more.

"Go on," she said.

"It's all mathematical, but the implications are terrifying." He turned away, his last words barely audible.

Dora watched him pace in front of the fireplace, allowing him time to sort things out in his mind. Suddenly, he spun around. "A number of countries...people would like to have our work." He paused and looked away, then returned his gaze to her. "An unimaginable amount of energy can be released." He sat heavily, staring at the flames of the fire.

Dora waited, not sure what had prompted his comments: apprehension or justification.

"Our work proves..." He emptied his glass, then spoke loudly as if trying to convince himself, "When an atom is split, the energy produced is beyond belief." He let his head fall back against the sofa and looked at the ceiling. "That energy must be controlled...protected."

When he was launched into the fellowship in Copenhagen, he had no idea where the hours of pacing in a sweat-soaked shirt before a blackboard would take him. Bohr had known better, and sitting on a park bench in the bitter cold earlier that afternoon, the Professor had warned Breckkan of the consequences of his secret research. He was silent for a moment; what he wanted to say was locked inside him. He was afraid he was going to lose her, to lose another parent, and there wasn't a thing he could do about it.

Desperately trying to leaven the moment, she said, "Before you go, open this." Dora handed him a small black satin box, then nervously fingered the antique Italian cameo centered in a triple strand of pearls at her throat. "Happy Anniversary."

"You remembered," he said, slowly opening the box. Inside was the Medal of Merit. Though Breckkan knew what the medal represented, he read the engraving on the back: "To Nic Breckkan. An Engineering Feat: The Modernization of Mining in Norway." He felt a confused emotion sweep over him, certain doubt.

"I know how respected you are; even our King speaks about you. You should have the medal." He didn't answer. "For goodness sake, Olav, let your Norwegian pride show. Now, let me pin it on."

As he straightened up, he heard the bell at the front door ring. "Mother, consider leaving here, for my sake," he said quietly. "Time is short. You should let Petter take you down to the island right away." She opened her mouth to protest, but he anticipated her. "I know, it's still cold, but get away from Oslo."

"Dr. Breckkan," Petter said from the doorway, "Commodore Duun has arrived. His driver is waiting."

Breckkan stood, leaned over and kissed his mother softly on the forehead. "Think about it. Please leave."

She turned toward the fire and rearranged the fur blanket. "You're going to be late, Olav."

CHAPTER 4

As he descended the stone steps of the estate, Breckkan felt more than just the bitter cold of Norway engulf his being. Accompanying the chill on the back of his neck was his very real fear that he would never see that grand woman again.

Breckkan ducked and slid into the back seat next to Commodore Duun. The car topped out from the steep drive and headed into the slick street. Ice glimmered on the pewter pavement. The Commodore shut the glass panel, separating them from the driver, then said to Breckkan, "He's okay. My personal attache. He's cleared, but I've got something personal to tell you. For starters, Breckkan Mining sure as hell is in the middle of things."

"What's that supposed to mean?"

"We did some simple background checks. I.G. Farben's got stock in Norsk Hydro. In fact, between the Banque de Paris and them, they financially control the Plant. Farben just took out 50 gallons of heavy water from the Vemork installation."

"I already know that, Roald. As far as I can tell, the Germans are trying to get all our output. We're not stupid; we secretly shipped a huge load of heavy water to Paris to get it out of their reach. But what has Breckkan Mining got to do with anything?"

"You ought to know, Breckkan Mining is selling most of their production to Germany."

"They're what?"

"You heard me, Breckkan. I know, Norway is *technically neutral* at this point, but in my book, your family is selling to the enemy."

For a split second Breckkan thought his life-long friend was trying to provoke him, but he realized Roald's words were meant to be a warning. It was a murky sea out there for international businesses. Fortunes were made during wartime, and Nic Breckkan had tied up some of Norway's richest natural resources, just the kind of basic ingredients a tyrant would need to stock his munitions and armament factories. The coldness that had swept over him on the steps of the Breckkan Estate intensified; he sat extremely still.

The Commodore waited patiently. The silence wasn't awkward; he knew Breckkan would mentally turn the corner and be back with him momentarily.

Finally Breckkan spoke. "Thank you for telling me. I'm sure there's more."

"The Germans aren't satisfied with buying all the heavy water, iron ore and oil we can produce. Now they want the whole goddamn country."

"You're talking invasion?"

"In the next twenty-four to forty-eight hours."

"Good God!" Breckkan stared intently at Roald. "What's going to happen to Mother"?

"Our sources tell us the Nazis are assembling a huge armada at their northern ports. There's suddenly no movement of German ships in our harbors. Churchill's decided to take action; England has a flotilla of warships sailing toward us right now. We verified that just this morning."

"Then why hasn't the King canceled the banquet? This is ridiculous; it doesn't make sense."

"He's totally aware of what's going on and we all know the risks. In our opinion, canceling the banquet would tip off the Germans, letting them know...without question...that we know they're coming, even know their timetable. The King has purposely included Germans on the guest list."

They were now in the city proper. Traffic quickly became a problem as they tried to avoid darting bicycles and clanging tramcars. The Commodore opened the panel and ordered the driver to turn onto a side street. Midway down the block, he pointed to a nondescript building. "The new German Trade Council Building. And our city fathers welcomed them with open arms."

The official car turned off Victoria Terrasse and onto Karl Johans Gate. As they passed the Grand Hotel, a sudden gust of frigid air blew swirls of dry snow off the steeply pitched rooftops, showering down onto the boulevard.

"Breckkan, tell me more about that work of yours at Vemork." The Commodore kept his eyes on the road. "Is it so important, to the Germans, I mean?"

"Most of the applications are theoretical right now."

"Come on, make it simple."

Breckkan leaned back, wondering how he could explain something he had trouble coming to grips with himself. Bohr, Fermi, and all the other experts argue constantly: "Will it work or won't it?" Is it a doomsday project or will it be of value to the world? Was it time for grim predictions or spectacular revelations? Breckkan drew in his breath and spoke quickly, "Okay, number one: we think the energy inside an atom can be released. Number two: if that energy is released slowly by using heavy water to act as a regulator, we have a new source of power. But, here's the catch, if the energy isn't regulated but is released all at once, there will be one hell of an explosion."

"A new weapon," the Commodore said quietly. Breckkan nodded. "How powerful?"

"A hundred tons of TNT equivalent."

"A hundred tons! Do the Germans know this?"

"Hell yes, they do. Most of us think they're way ahead." Inside his gloves, his hands were wet with perspiration.

"Jesus, Breckkan, that alone will give them justification to invade us. Tell me more about this heavy water. Exactly what does it do?"

"Professor Bohr believes that a neutron from heavy water can split an atom of uranium, like sparking a fire."

"And this heavy water, what is it exactly?"

"Heavy water is just that. Heavier than regular water, because an extra neutron has been added that gives it the added weight, but doesn't change the electrical charge of the water molecule. The extra neutron's not supposed to be there, so the heavy water molecule will give it up easily."

The Commodore couldn't claim to fully understand the process, but he understood the simple part: a horrendous weapon. "I think you understand that we Norwegians are kind of on our own right now." He cleared his throat. "Prime Minister Chamberlain and Churchill just returned from Paris. The French echelon agrees with the Brits. The Germans desperately need our fjords and ports. They're critical for the German expansion; they could gain domination of the entire Atlantic. So the British have promised to take the initiative. They are going to mine our coastal waters."

"Mines! Off Bergen? What about our so-called neutrality? Wouldn't that be an act of war?"

"The British are all too aware of that. Churchill is adamant, but there's a furious argument raging behind closed doors all over Whitehall. We really have no choice...it's either the Germans or the British who grab the advantage. That's why Churchill is willing to commit a flotilla. They're not waiting to see what Hitler does. That flotilla is built around their battleship WARSPITE. That's heavy artillery, Doctor. Churchill means business. Right now, as we sit here, they're steaming up the

West Coast to Bergen. They're determined to stop any ship from trading with Germany. Now, can you see how your family's business is right square in the middle of it?"

The driver braked; the car slid on the ice, veering to the right. "What's going on?" snapped the Commodore.

"Sorry, sir. Look ahead."

They were directly in front of the grounds of the Royal Palace. As the car drew closer, the blur of frosted light gradually defined itself, illuminating temporary wood guard towers along the entire perimeter of the Palace. From each tower, powerful spotlights with intense beams raked down across the grounds. Two soldiers were stationed in each tower; one watched the streets, the other carefully scanned the path of the tracking lights. Large X's, constructed of razor-edged steel rods, were at twenty foot intervals between the towers; coils of barbed wire added to the defense. As they pulled up to the temporary gate, two guards approached the car. Against the brilliant white light, their faces were darkened silhouettes; only the clouds of their breath gave them life.

The driver pulled into the vaulted entry passage of the Palace. Breckkan followed Commodore Duun through the right side door and up the stairs where two servants received their credentials. A member of the Honor Guard escorted them down the length of the main hallway toward the Grand Salon. Crystal chandeliers illuminated the paneled walls and the rows of heraldic flags.

They took their place in the receiving line awaiting formal introduction to King Haakon VII. Looking ahead, Breckkan could see the King quietly acknowledging the greetings of each guest, and just beyond the entrance to the Grand Salon, others visiting in small groups, their voices mingling with the music of Edvard Grieg. The Commodore leaned close to Breckkan, "I'm sure you recognize those men near the door, just beyond the King?" Breckkan nodded. "Notice the Germans are in full uniform. That's new."

"Why? What's unusual about that?"

"The military full dress...instead of tails, especially for a scientific reception. Isn't that your uncle with the King?"

"Yes," said Breckkan. "Of course Gustave would be able to attend." He would delay his own funeral not to miss a party, he thought with a smile. His attention returned to the receiving line. "I had hoped he'd be here. I've got to talk to him about getting Mother out after what you just told me." He thought, God, the King looks haggard. He's always been thin for such a tall man, but tonight, he really looks gaunt.

They were next to greet the King; the Commodore placed his calling card on the small silver tray held by the aide.

"Your Majesty, may I present Commodore Roald Duun," the aide said quietly.

"Your Majesty," responded Breckkan respectfully, as he bowed to the King.

"Doctor, it's always good to see you. An auspicious occasion you've organized tonight. The guest of honor is already here," said the King, stepping forward and placing his hands on Breckkan's shoulders, embracing him warmly. "I'm pleased to see the Breckkan medal on your chest. Your father...I surely miss him. Norway could certainly use him right now. I hear you're doing a fine job in your new position. We must talk about it."

"At your pleasure. Is the Crown Prince here tonight?"

"No, Olav, and Princess Martha and the children are at the Skaugum Estate in Asker." Looking at Commodore Duun, he added, "We feel the family shouldn't be in the same location at the same time."

Breckkan could see the fatigue in the man's eyes. "Mother asked me to extend her greetings."

"Please give my warmest regards to Dora. I hope her plans include leaving Oslo very soon."

"She'll appreciate your concern, sir." Breckkan stepped back, bowed stiffly and entered the Grand Salon. He immediately spotted the guest of honor, Professor Niels Bohr, at the far end of the room.

On this occasion, the guests were all men. Waiters in black cutaway jackets and white leggings circulated among them offering glasses of champagne. The mood was completely masculine: low-pitched voices, mingled with cigar smoke, drifted toward the elegant gold and crystal chandeliers.

The ambiance of the room was set by two mammoth fireplaces located at either end. Heavy, waist-high black andirons held four foot-long logs, burning brightly, crackling and snapping. The light was subdued, only hints of past monarchs' faces in the life-size portraits were visible.

Roald touched his elbow and they walked toward Bohr. Breckkan felt a tap on the shoulder and turned to face a familiar figure. A massive hand swallowed Breckkan's. "Dora said you'd be here. You look like marriage is agreeing with you." William K. Wakefield's eyes were hooded, watching everything.

"Roald, this is Mr. Bill Wakefield." Breckkan searched the man's face for a hint of his thoughts. He analyzed his every body movement for a signal.

Wakefield stepped close to Breckkan and placed a hand on his shoulder. "I know the Commodore. Good to see you, Roald. Satisfied with our last contracts?"

"Came through ahead of schedule. Impressive for as big a company as WKW, especially when it's run by an ex-professional baseball player that even toured Europe with Babe Ruth!"

Wakefield laughed as he shifted his weight to his other foot. "Remember, I was a great fielder, but a rotten hitter. A short career. But I've got two grandsons headed for the diamond. Gave them both baseball gloves on their first birthdays."

"How is Katherine?" asked Breckkan.

"More beautiful than ever," answered Wakefield. "Her husband is making an obscene amount of money in the radio business, of all things. She seems to love New York. I'll be sure to tell her that you asked about her."

"What brings you to Oslo?" asked the Commodore, reaching for a glass of champagne and a canape offered by a passing waiter.

"I'm here informally, at Roosevelt's request. He needs time and some solid facts to build a case that will wake up Congress." Wakefield lowered his voice. "Churchill's been putting on the pressure, wants the US in this deal. If a crisis comes, FDR firmly believes that American aid must already be committed, not stuck in Congress like it was in Finland's case."

Breckkan scanned the room, fully recognizing the importance of the American's statement. He paused and took a step backward, holding up his palm in a gesture of submission. "Bill, I'm just a scientist with a healthy skeptic's eye. Diabolical world plots, I don't understand," said Breckkan, picking his words carefully. The others realized he had the presence to forestall their conversation. It was not the proper setting. When he spoke again, his tone was brisk, but pleasant. He knew Wakefield was a pro and would say no more. "More champagne, gentlemen?" he asked.

"Of course," said the Commodore, standing to his full 5'4" height and signaling to a waiter. He had always used his girth to make his presence known. He wasn't obese...more like a bulldog. Tough. He had thick, dark hair, graying at the temples, and his recently acquired beard was immaculately trimmed. Exchanging his empty glass for a full one and taking one more canape, he said, "Breckkan, it's your uncle." A round of applause came from across the room, drawing their attention to a tall, heavy-set, distinguished-looking man. "Probably quoting Ibsen," replied Breckkan.

Wakefield laughed. "I can remember him getting fired up at a dinner one night and mesmerizing the entire party. He was a favorite of my late wife."

"Greetings, Uncle."

"Ah, my favorite nephew. Spotted you when you came in. Good evening, Commodore. Don't you look robust these days. Must be the sea air."

"You're looking fit yourself, Mr. Breckkan. I've been wanting to talk to you. Perhaps lunch tomorrow. How about Blom's?"

"Fine, Commodore. I've got to leave Oslo by tomorrow evening, so lunch would be perfect. Before I seem too impolite, may I welcome you back to Norway, Mr. Wakefield."

"Thanks, Gustave. How's Breckkan Mining these days? You know, Nic was always way ahead of his time."

"Olav's father was a stubborn man," said Gustave, running his hand smoothly through his thick white hair. "He often spoke of the advice you gave him. The technical data you provided for that hydroelectric generating plant."

"No need to flatter me," replied Wakefield. He turned briefly and looked at the group of Germans now visiting with Professor Bohr, leveled his eyes on Gustave, and said quietly, "You do realize it would be a catastrophe if your company's output of raw iron ore were to end up in Hitler's hands."

"Did I hear someone mention the Fuhrer's name? Good evening, Dr. Breckkan," said von Stein, as he tapped him on the back. A grin crossed the Major's face; clearly he was loving the moment.

Breckkan turned to face a uniformed German. A slight hesitation. "Major von Stein," he said, looking at the Ritterkreuz, the Knight's Cross, at von Stein's throat.

"An astute observation, Dr. Breckkan. Almost as clever as your work in Denmark."

It was all coming back to Breckkan. He recalled the gray corridors of the university, his fellow students leaning over their experiment tables, white lab coats in a row, and the resonant voice of Professor Bohr. He heard the peal of the bells coming from the myriad of towers and spires over Copenhagen. It was not a pleasant reminiscence.

"That was a long time ago," he said with great control.

"Old history, of course," von Stein agreed. "Although I'm relocated in Berlin, I've kept in touch with Bohr's research. And yours." His comment was acid, barely concealing his hatred.

A wave of warning crossed Breckkan's mind. His eyes seemed sadder than ever. Don't react, he told himself as he asked, "Your laboratories? Where are they?"

"I'm not at liberty to say."

Breckkan nodded, unaffected by the German's impudence. "Tell me, Stein, just who's speaking here? Is this the arrogant intellectual I knew in Copenhagen or is it the Reich?"

Von Stein laughed. "Both," he said. "I understand you're married. When did you finally decide to make her legal?"

"Careful, Stein." Whatever the German's motive for coming here, merely the fact of his presence, especially tonight, was wrong, very wrong. He felt a mixture of disdain and revulsion. He'd forgotten just how white von Stein's skin was; more than that, the gray-tinted glasses didn't completely camouflage the piercing glare.

As if reading Breckkan's mind, von Stein abruptly leaned forward and removed his glasses. His right pupil was scarred with a dull-gray opacity. The other eye nervously darted back and forth, doing the work of both.

"Don't stare. You know the genetic progression." Von Stein slowly replaced his glasses and continued, "We have so much to talk about. I remember how you bragged about the art collection here at the Royal Palace. So, what do you say, how about the grand tour?"

"Fine." Breckkan shot a look back at the Commodore, then touched the German's arm to indicate the direction.

Von Stein jerked his arm away. "Lead the way."

They walked into the wide corridor and turned left. Reaching the base of the staircase, Breckkan, trying to remain civil, said, "You're about to see some of the finest engravings and woodblocks of Durer, each selected by a personal friend of King Haakon, who now I believe is the curator of the Albertina in Vienna. Personally, the woodblocks are my favorites."

"Seems like I recall your questionable taste from our Copenhagen debates. I far prefer Italian Renaissance."

"I remember. You spent your childhood in Italy. Florence...correct?"

"Good memory."

"Wait until you see these. They may sway your opinion."

They reached the first landing of the triple-wide staircase and were met by a member of the Palace Guard. "Good evening, Captain Breckkan."

"I didn't know you had military rank," von Stein said, turning to Breckkan.

"Not really. Purely honorary," Breckkan said, tapping the medal on his chest. "Corporal, Major von Stein and I will be in the library."

Reaching the top of the stairs, he ushered von Stein through the double doors. An enormous Agra carpet covered the floor, its warm, deep colors and soft texture setting an intimate mood in the dimly lit room. The bookcases were filled with leather-bound books with burnished patinas, suggesting frequent use. There was a minimum of furniture. Several carved walnut chairs faced the fireplace, and an oversized pillow covered with an antique kilim carpet was near the hearth. A Norwegian elkhound sprawled on the pillow, enjoying the warmth. He raised his head and wagged his tail at the sight of Breckkan.

Breckkan moved to the paneled wall near the door and flipped on a bank of soft lights over a row of framed pictures. As von Stein walked over to the treasures, Breckkan casually half-sat on the corner of the large walnut desk, his right hip taking most of his weight. He watched von Stein closely. The light on the engravings reflected onto von Stein's white hair and skin, washing out all color. To Breckkan, he resembled a piece of carved white marble. His tinted glasses gave the illusion of two dark bore holes...defects in the marble.

"From the 'Apocalypse Series?'" asked von Stein, taking a seat opposite Breckkan.

"Correct. The draftsmanship, exquisite!"

"Agreed, but you realize Durer copied Leonardo's system of proportion."

Irritated, Breckkan said, "Stein, you're a paradox. Here you are sniping at a German master, who, in your mind, is staid, not progressive, and yet your modern day German art, or should I say your Hitlerian art, is about as static and contrived a phenomenon as I can imagine. It's a kind of galumphing realism, intended, I guess, to portray Germany as a nation of jolly extroverts, all bursting with health, not a neurosis to their names." He stopped for a moment, despising the smile on von Stein's face. He felt his stomach roll and cautioned himself to slow down.

He walked to the door and, with a quick motion, flipped on another set of lights, illuminating six pictures behind the desk. "Ever heard of our contemporary Norwegian genius, Edvard Münch? Even Goya would've been overwhelmed by his work. Münch managed to expose the inhumane, brutal world of Europe today. Did you know all of his work has been confiscated in Germany?" Von Stein looked at the woodcuts. "Or are you afraid of truth? Are you afraid your happy, beer-drinking society isn't quite what it's portrayed to be? Goddamn it, man, there've been mass murders in your country! We've heard you scientists are carrying on unimaginable experiments. Totally inhumane!"

The accusation brought von Stein furiously to his feet. "You bigot. You haven't changed since Copenhagen!"

With extraordinary control, Breckkan spread his hands on the desk. "You chose to resign. No one was trying to sabotage you or your work. And though you made accusations, no one was stealing from you. I'm no psychiatrist, but you brought everything on yourself. It's your paranoia. You're sick! Thank God Bonnie realized it even before I did. You've wrecked every relationship you've ever touched."

Von Stein's response was calm, laced with icy contempt. "I feel nothing but revulsion for you, and I've wasted too much energy tolerating you. You were always impulsive, volatile, but Bohr seemed to relish your ability to manipulate. You are his tool, able to infect an entire group." A contemptuous sneer crossed his face.

Breckkan fought to keep the fury he felt from exploding. In a whisper, he said, "How little you know, how little you understand, Stein. You're despicable. I'm not the one who tried to rape someone!"

With pure menace, von Stein began, "Is that what she..." He stopped as he heard voices at the door.

Commodore Duun entered the library with Professor Bohr and Bill Wakefield. "Here you are, Breckkan," Duun said, not missing Breckkan's dark expression.

Bohr, seeming to ignore the circumstances, was drawn immediately to the Münch woodcuts. "Amazing! This one, 'The Cry.' The head, the contorted torso, a picture of terror."

"Another lecture, Professor?" prodded von Stein. "Or are you, in your usual tangential way, editorializing on political affairs?"

No longer able to contain his feelings, Bohr replied, "You haven't changed, have you, von Stein? Still walking the edge. You know, I've never been sure if you're being insulting or just plain stupid."

Von Stein removed his glasses, his good eye shifting back and forth between Bohr and Breckkan. "You're the professor, you decide."

"That's enough, Stein." Breckkan walked to the door and motioned to the German. "I suggest you leave the Palace now. You're not welcome here."

"You'll regret this, Breckkan." All were distracted by the low, menacing growl of the elkhound, obviously reacting to the sinister timbre of the German's voice. Breckkan quietly raised his hand, palm outstretched, to calm the dog. The growling stopped, but the elkhound remained alert. Von Stein left the four men in disquieting silence.

Bohr put his hand on Breckkan's shoulder. "Do you realize that former pupil of mine is acting director of the Kaiser-Wilhelm Institute?"

"Von Stein?" asked Breckkan.

"Where else do you think those horrific experiments are taking place?"

"That son-of-a-bitch!" Breckkan said, hammering his fist on the desk.

"I saw him when I came in," said Wakefield. "Intimidating bastard. Breckkan, what the hell went on up here? You know that guy?" Breckkan looked away as if he hadn't heard the question. Wakefield's eyes narrowed.

"They're announcing dinner," said Commodore Duun.

Breckkan patted the elkhound gently and turned off the bank of lights. "The Cry" was again alone.

King Haakon's aide was directing the guests to the dining room. Breckkan spotted the German at the door. Von Stein caught Breckkan's stare and tapped the rim of his hat with his index finger, turned and left.

King Haakon and Professor Bohr led the way, crossing the hall and entering the state banquet room through an arched doorway. The banquet room was long and narrow, warmed by a huge fireplace at one end. Four tall windows were aligned on the long side opposite the entrance. Tonight the heavy velvet drapes were drawn; the usual spectacular view across the Palace grounds, and the lights of Oslo, was lost.

When the guests were seated, Professor Bohr was ushered to the seat of honor at the right of King Haakon. Olav was seated directly across from Bohr.

"Good evening, honored guests," began the King. "Tonight I have the sincere pleasure of asking Prince Olav's closest friend, the son of a great Norwegian patriot and the director of this countries atomic research, to introduce our esteemed guest."

Breckkan had not expected this honor, but though his thoughts still tumbled with the confrontation in the upstairs library, he rose, spoke softly and with conviction of his mentor and the role Bohr played in current world events.

Breckkan shrugged into his overcoat and joined the line of men awaiting their cars at the Palace door.

"Going down to Vemork tomorrow?" asked Gustave, signalling for his car.

"No, I've got to get back to Bergen." Breckkan turned to look for the Commodore's car in the long line of vehicles. "Roald is taking the Professor and me to the train station."

Roald, too, was looking for the official car and suggested Bohr step back into the entry to wait.

"Roald, I still can't understand how von Stein got in here. It had to have been a mistake. Security was as tight as I've ever seen it," said Breckkan.

"No mistake. He was a last minute addition to the German Trade delegation. Damn the driver. Hell, let's walk."

They started for the parked car. Approaching the sedan, both men could see the driver behind the wheel. Yet the driver made no apparent effort to start the engine. The Commodore grabbed the door handle and jerked it open. The attache's body fell forward against the steering wheel, touching off the horn.

Breckkan grabbed the man and pulled him back against the seat, immediately spotting the trickle of blood running from his left ear. A sharp instrument had obviously been plunged into the ear and ground into his brain. He glanced up at the nearest guard tower and back to the dead man's face, then looked around the empty lot. "Where are the Germans? Von Stein?"

"Breckkan! Stop Gustave; we need his car."

"I'll get Bohr to the train. You've got to take care of this."

"I'm not supposed to leave your side. Get going!"

Breckkan ran toward the covered entry of the Palace, calling out to Gustave. "What the hell is going on? Where's your driver?" Gustave watched the men push into the rear seat.

The Commodore cut him off. "Car trouble. Let's get to the station."

Gustave headed the Mercedes down through the royal grounds. In the field of searchlights, needle-like ice crystals reflected against the blackness. "We're barely going to make the Copenhagen Train. The road is slick, solid black ice." It took them nearly twenty minutes to travel the mile straight down Karl Johans Gate. No one said a word.

Pulling into the East Station, Gustave spotted an empty slot and quickly parked. Their mood of shock was broken by the cacophony of hissing steam, scurrying crowds in the freezing station and the drone of arrival and departure announcements. The platform was bathed in bright light, exposing piles of soot-covered ice along the tracks. The final boarding call for the Copenhagen Train was announced: "Track 4." Commodore Duun and Breckkan pressed through the crowded aisles, guiding the Professor to his sleeping compartment.

Breckkan tossed the Professor's luggage onto the overhead rack. "Still won't stay? The King's offer of asylum stands. We can get your family out at a moment's notice."

"No, Breckkan. It's my home."

"Then for God's sake, be careful, Professor Bohr." The car lurched; Bohr gave a small wave with a gloved hand.

Retreating down the steps behind Roald's bulky frame, Breckkan said, "Roald, please call Bonnie and tell her I'll be in on the Bergensbanan early in the morning. Take care of yourself, my friend."

Hurriedly purchasing a ticket, Breckkan ran toward the Oslo-Bergen Express on Track 3. In the background, he heard screeching steel as the Copenhagen Train gathered speed and labored from the station. Jumping on board, he walked midway down the narrow passageway and found his seat in the first class compartment. He brushed off the sleet clinging to the damp wool of his over-coat and turned up the collar against the cold.

The cabin lights dimmed and he wiped the condensation from the window. A sudden jolt and the train slowly emerged from the station. The sleet had turned to snow. He leaned back, closed his eyes and rubbed them roughly. Erratic flashes of light darted across his visual field. The vicious encounter with von Stein, the murder. A coincidence? The memory nagged at him relentlessly. Like a patient testing a wounded limb, flexing the tender muscles, Breckkan probed his own mind, cautiously exploring the disconcerting possibilities. He tried to settle into the darkness; he would need the sleep.

Five hours later, the train suddenly slowed,

jolting Breckkan awake. Vaksdal. Two more stops before Bergen. He looked up at the second floor of the station and saw a mother holding her child to the window, the glow of light behind her.

His mother had let him go, had let him go to Bonnie. But would she get out of Oslo? Damn! Would Dora and Petter make it to safety?

The stationmaster waved the train on.

CHAPTER 5

April 3, 1940

Bergen, Norway

A glimmer of light glanced off the glass window of the cabin door and reflected onto the ceiling. Breckkan leaned forward and pulled back the curtain. The train left Vaksdal and followed the South bank of the Osterfjord, roaring through tunnel after tunnel down the steep hillside, continuing to gather speed as the tracks leveled out. He stretched and massaged his neck, cursing the stiff collar of his formal shirt. Station lights glowed dimly; fog mixed with steam swirled across the platform. With a sudden forward lurch, they came to a stop. Nearly losing his balance, he stood at the window searching for her.

He quickly spotted the handsome redhead wrapped in a stunning gray fox coat. Her features were almost aristocratic, a perfect foil for her abundant long hair. The mists of Scotland and Bergen accounted for her clear, fine complexion. Her eyes were an extraordinary shade of liquid green, all too often sparkling with a mischievous glint. She was her own woman.

Over the public address system, the conductor announced the arrival of the overnight Oslo-Bergen Express. Breckkan saw Bonnie moving toward the rear cars and pressed through the crowd after her. Just when he caught up, she spun around and enveloped him in her coat. He immediately realized she was completely naked.

"Happy anniversary, darling."

He pulled her close and could feel the hardness of her nipples. "You are incredible!" He tried to ignore the rasp in his voice.

"Want to know the real reason I married you?" she asked.

"My photographic memory." He entwined his hands around her neck and stroked her hair. With an open mouth, he kissed her deeply.

"Come on, let's get home. I can't wait any longer." She grabbed his arm and, holding her coat tightly closed, headed for the exit gates.

Turning again up the steep hill on the narrow street, they passed a milkman on his rounds. She cut around his white van, driving up on the sidewalk, and turned right onto Fjeldsgaten, stopping at Number 4. A young, towheaded boy sped by on a bicycle, bouncing on the cobblestones and carefully raised one hand in a brief wave. The rest of the street was empty.

They shared the Kittleson home with her father, Knut. Professor Kittleson had gladly divided the early nineteenth-century wooden house into two living areas. He took the bottom floor for himself, complete with library and garden room. The eccentric wooden home provided a spacious second floor apartment for Bonnie and Breckkan. Their studies were cater-cornered off the upstairs hallway. Hers was bright yellow, small and sunny, his was white, slightly larger and austere.

During the hurried twenty-minute drive home, the sky had lightened. Moderate breezes blew inland from the North Sea. The air was sweet with a mix of salt air just cleaned by sporadic showers.

Breckkan breathed deeply of the fresh air and pulled her tightly against him. "I love you." She smiled, then hurried upstairs to their bedroom.

He was right behind her.

White lace draped the windows, matching the white eyelet bedspread and pillows piled against the inlaid mahogany headboard. Undressing as he walked into the bathroom, he heard her boots crash to the wooden floor. He splashed water on himself and rubbed his chest and face roughly with a towel then looked back into the bedroom.

She was waiting for him, her pale face encircled by thick tasseled red hair set against the mounds of pillows.

"Beautiful." He slid under the eiderdown and propped his head against the headboard.

"Things are bad in Oslo, aren't they, Ole?" she said, unconsciously running her hand through her hair. The sash of her pale green silk robe slackened at her waist.

"I'll tell you about it later. When I look at you..."

He leaned toward her and, one hand on her shoulder, pulled her gently into the bed. With his right hand, he separated her robe and slid his hand over her body, exploring her as though for the first time. He slipped the sash loose and let the robe fall open. He leaned down and kissed her first on the cheek, nose, and then mouth. His hand gently found its way down her body. He luxuriated in her female wetness.

Bonnie pushed the eiderdown away, saw his erection and took him in her hands. He moved onto her. Their lovemaking was intense, fast, and selfish. They each took what they needed. Lying quietly, both with eyes closed, breathing deeply, they drifted into a transient twilight sleep. A blast of rain against the windowpanes awakened them. Breckkan rolled over and looked at her.

"Happy anniversary."

Her fingers lightly traced the round scar under his chin and she wondered how he ever survived childhood. She reached up and pulled him onto her.

They held each other tightly, feeling the pounding of each other's heart. She loved him. She wanted him. This time their lovemaking was slow and for each other.

When he awakened, she was dressed, sitting cross-legged in the large armchair against the window combing her hair straight back and braiding it quickly into a bun. She smiled at him and said, "You need to get dressed. It's almost noon and Father will be home for lunch."

"You're braiding your hair. You're getting serious on me."

Smoothing back errant wisps of hair, she shifted in her chair and turned toward the window. Despite the muted gray sky, she could look past the twin towers of St. Mary's to the mouth of the harbor, and the old fortress, the Bergenhus. She knew the docks would be crowded with the afternoon boats leaving for Lerwick, Newcastle, and Denmark.

"I guess we're going to have to get out of Norway."

Sitting up, he said, "Do you realize what you've just said? What made you say that?"

"Ole, I'm not stupid," she said quietly. "Everyone says the Germans are coming. And little gets past Knut." She crossed to the bed, kissed him, and held his head to her side, stroking his hair. "I hope you've come up with something. We've got to talk him into leaving too."

"When the time comes, I promise, Bonnie." He patted her bottom and said, "I'm famished. All that exercise."

"Right." She kissed him affectionately on the top of his head and walked to the stairs. "Hurry up. I don't want to face him alone."

Ten minutes later, Breckkan found her in the kitchen stirring a fish soup on the stove. Without looking at him, she said, "How much time do we have? Weeks? Months?"

He described the Palace security, then repeated part of Roald's conversation. "He's sure Hitler's going to make his first global move, not just expand his own borders." He couldn't bring himself to tell her about the preparations for war. "From what he says, I think we only have weeks...probably just days."

"Days?"

"Right." He buttered a slice of dark bread and bit into it. "Bonnie, I'm worried about Knut. How's he been feeling? Escape, even if everything goes perfectly, could be damn hard on him."

"What about you? Can you leave your mother here?"

"God, Bonnie, you know how many letters, calls, and conversations I've had with her. She absolutely refuses to leave. It's killing me."

"I know, Ole, I know. Let's concentrate on Father. Since Mother died, his life has been the Institute. I honestly believe it's his only reason for living." Her eyes filled with tears. "At least we have each other, no matter where we are."

He pulled her close, wrapping his arms around her. "You're the only person I really care about."

"Ah, that's good to hear," interrupted a gravelly voice at the kitchen door.

Breckkan winked at Knut. "You know I'm partial to redheads."

"An honest man. Now that's a rarity...one a father wants his only daughter to wed."

Professor Kittleson slowly unbuttoned his heavy loden coat, removed his felt hat, and hung them by the door. He had white hair that grew like wild grass and a permanently creased, ruddy complexion, the face of an ancient warrior. He was of a generation that regarded winter as a minor inconvenience; on occasion he grudgingly wore gloves.

But despite his well-known tendency to be pigheaded and stubborn, he was a profound romantic and had overseen Bonnie's free-spirited upbringing with complete affection. Lacking the heart for harsh discipline, he had allowed her to strike out independently, alert to her particular compulsions but had restrained from smothering her enthusiasm. His balanced permissiveness had created an extraordinary bond of trust and love between them.

He walked over to the table and sat down stiffly. Breckkan was struck by how stooped he was, moving with a leaden gait. His usual style was that of an academic tyrant, stiff-backed with a crisp jaw, unnerving his students. What was weighing so heavily on him, he wondered.

Facing him across the table, Breckkan said, "You've been putting in some long hours, I'm told. Breakthrough in the lab?"

"Wish that were the case," Knut answered. "No, I've been advised to finish up my current work and sterilize the lab. Word is the Germans want all our data and us too."

"So you've closed down the lab?"

"Almost, I'm still trying to finish the graphite experiments. Breckkan, the data is suggesting it's a pretty efficient nuclear fission regulator and physically easy to manage." Breckkan nodded, absorbing the positive tone. "I've got Bonnie setting up some sham experiments. Don't want to cause any unwanted curiosity."

"Are your data books in a safe place, Father?"

"Why do you care? You two don't believe in the graphite theories." He glanced at her, his face taut. "It's the heavy water experiments. Isn't that all that's important?" he snapped, his eyes flashing at Breckkan.

"Not true," said Breckkan. "Someday there will be a place."

"But this is no time to argue. Where's your data now?"

"Here. I've brought them home a few at a time."

"Why didn't you tell me?"

"It wasn't necessary."

"The soup is hot," Bonnie said, carrying a tureen to the table. "The collaborative paper, too?"

Nodding and taking a piece of bread and passing the basket, Knut answered, "Yes, the collaborative papers. How is Professor Bohr, Breckkan?"

"His usual stubborn self. We received word at the conference that Germany is likely to move on the Low Countries. I tried to convince Bohr to get out. The King offered asylum for his family, a place to work, everything."

"And?" asked Knut, his bushy white eyebrows lifting slightly.

"He refused. Left on the train to Copenhagen last night. Damn! Why couldn't he listen to reason just once? Stubborn old fool."

"Jesus Christ!" Knut slammed his fist on the table. "I suppose you think I should run, too? Well, by God, I'm not running. I'm old. This is my home."

"Father, please..."

"No! Don't you dare Father me, Bonnie. I'm not leaving and that's final. You both know all too well that we're not prepared to fight a war. Our beloved, ancient Bergen, built of wood will need me, all of us to take care of her. So far the only air raid protection our illustrious city fathers have come up with is to dump sand at the end of each block. Didn't you notice it? It's the duty of each homeowner to sprinkle sand on their roof in case of incendiary bombs. While we sit here waiting to be attacked, the sand is being used by children, and of course, dogs and cats. No, Norway will damn-well need all her people."

Bonnie looked at Breckkan, her eyes glazed with tears. She started to speak, but the monstrous ridiculousness of the situation left her speechless. Breckkan looked down, following Knut's lead and concentrated on eating. No one spoke until Bonnie took away her untouched soup and the men's empty bowls. She smoothed her hair back with both hands and stood behind her husband.

"Knut," Breckkan began softly, "the last few months have been terrible for all of us. While I was in Oslo, I saw firsthand evidence that Norway will not be ours for long. I know I'm being harsh, but that's the truth. You've already prepared the Institute for takeover. Why the hell do that if you're not in danger?"

"Don't you lecture me. I've seen a lot of this world, and I've survived it all. By God, I'll survive this, too."

"But for how long, Knut? A year? A month? A week? It would kill you. Your work is your life... What good is it if you can't work freely? You're a man of integrity. You won't work for people you don't respect. That's why they listen to you." He paused, and took a swallow of coffee. "Besides, your leaving will signal your colleagues in the strongest way. Leave nothing for the Nazis."

"I can't leave, just divorce myself from my life. Everything for me is here. Breckkan, don't you understand?"

"Please, Father. Listen to Olav."

"No! I'm going to the greenhouse. I've neglected my orchids." He pushed back from the table, head-ing to his habitual hideout when distracted or upset. Bonnie stood behind Breckkan and dug her fingers into his shoulders.

The old professor pushed open the glass door to

the greenhouse, welcoming the immediate fragrance of the rich damp soil and healthy plants. The window panes were partially fogged with the excessive moisture. The room was a steady 60 degrees, ideal for growing his preferred species of orchids.

Despite his heavy sweater-vest, he shivered and reached up to the rack by the potting sink for his gardener's smock and pulled it on. Next to the smock was an old tweed hunting jacket, leather patches at the elbows and a padded leather insert on the right chest. Bonnie had bought it for him in Edinburgh, on a trip back to her mother's homeland. He took the tattered coat, held it out in from of him, then laid it on the work table. As he fingered the horn buttons, his mind played with long ago memories.

His beloved daughter. How many times had he prayed he would never stultify her intelligence, or make her cling to him? Raising a daughter without a mother had certainly proved far from boring. He recalled that, at age six, besides sailing through her studies, she was already extremely competitive. She consistently beat adults at bridge games and destroyed learned professors at chess. The same men, his contemporaries, hooted while she fired her shotgun at the Royal Gun Club. Knut rubbed the shoulder patch gently, thinking they were probably quite the sight: he in is tweed hunting jacket and Scottish tam beside his young daughter, she with her red hair in braids. Her shooting stance wide and secure, she pumped shells in the chambers, then raised the gun to her narrow shoulder and fired away, rarely missing a clay pigeon. Her hand-knit sweaters often smelled more of gun powder than of perfume, but Knut realized the active mind of the young girl had to have powerful persuasions to round out her personality.

He had pitied the man who would try to court

her. She was so independent— happily independent. Suddenly he heard a loud bang, a series of
harsh loud cracks coming from the street. He
ducked instinctively. The engine of an old truck
coughed and backfired again. He sighed, stood to
his full height and leaned against the worktable,
then spun around and opened the greenhouse door.

Breckkan absentmindedly tapped the table
with his fingers. Bonnie turned from the sink. "Do
you think I should go and check on him?"

"No. Give him some more time. He knows
what's right."

Clearing his throat in the doorway, Knut said,
"Come see my lilac-throated cymbidium." They
looked at each other and followed to the greenhouse without a word.

The pale afternoon sun glimmered through
broken clouds. Rivulets of rain ran down the panes,
catching the sunlight. The only sound was the occasional cry of a gull swooping up from the bay.

"Your flowers have never looked so beautiful.
It seems neglect serves them well," said Breckkan.

Knut picked a pair of clippers, snipped off the
prized orchid, and let it drop to the floor. "Since
we'll have to travel by sea, I guess we'd better look
for a boat." A thin smile crossed his drawn face and
quickly faded. "Unless you have a better idea." His
decision set, his eyes became fixed on a point beyond the windows. There was an awkward silence.

"Who's the best captain?" Breckkan asked finally.

The old man's mind seemed suddenly to
refocus. He spoke up briskly. "No question. Ron
Larsen. You know him."

"I don't think so."

"Leif's son. You know," Knut said impatiently,
"the janitor at the Institute. He owns a trawler. I'm

positive he will take us to England or Scotland, though the weather probably is vicious this time of year. Not the best time to be sailing on the North Sea."

Breckkan looked at Bonnie and said quietly, "You and Knut make the arrangements. I have to leave for Rjukan tonight. My papers are still at Vemork. I've got to get them out."

"Can't someone else do that?" she pleaded.

"No, Bonnie, I've hidden my data."

"Breckkan, all you've been saying is we have to get away. Things here are too dangerous," argued Knut, seeing the fear in his daughter's eyes. "You can't travel across the country and back without expecting—"

"I have to; there's just too much to lose."

"Have you forgotten? Your photographic memory. You know everything in those papers, Olav. It can all be reconstructed. It's not worth the risk."

"No! I have to get the hard copy. The Germans would love to get their hands on it." He shook his head as he stepped behind her and began massaging the tension from her neck, always knowing where she had knots of tightness. He held a constant pressure on it, kneading it gently. Her head leaned forward, her shoulders relaxed and dropped. Thinking out loud, he continued, "I'll need two days. Should get back here the morning of the fifth. Will that give you two enough time to get us a boat?"

"I'll find it," Knut said firmly.

"We'll need warm clothes and food, and money."

Breckkan nodded and said to Bonnie, "Please don't meet me at the train." In an attempt to soften the moment, he explained, "That red hair draws too much attention." He planted a light kiss on her hair. "I'll make it on either the express or the afternoon local." He paused, still massaging her shoulders. "If for some reason I don't make either train, you go on to the Tracteursted Tavern the evening of the fifth. Have dinner as usual. You can slip onto the boat during the night."

"We'll wait," Bonnie insisted.

Turning her around to face him, he said quietly, "Bonnie, get out before daylight on the sixth. Understand? Have Larsen tell his father where you're heading. He'll probably choose Lerwick or Newcastle. I'll catch up if I miss you here." He glanced away, momentarily lost in thought, then suddenly spoke quickly to Knut, "Who do you trust the most in London? You lectured there last year."

"Chadwick. James Chadwick."

"The Nobel Prize winner?" Knut nodded. "Okay. I'll have Roald use diplomatic channels to advise him that the three of us will be in London in, let's say two weeks, three at the most."

"How can you be sure he can get a message through?" asked Bonnie.

"Roald is clever, very clever. He'll get it done."

Knut took off the smock and returned the clippers to the rack of meticulously arranged tools. He seemed to have more energy now, as if the decision had recharged his old muscles. He stooped to pick up the orchid blossom lying on the brick floor. He slapped Breckkan soundly on the shoulder. "Get those papers of yours, Breckkan. Don't leave a thing for the bastards. That work is too important. They'll use it against us. Don't worry about us," he said in a louder voice. "You be careful, son." Breckkan nodded. "We'll see you in two days." Knut twirled the orchid in his hand and left the greenhouse, closing the glass door quietly.

Bonnie walked through the greenery to the windows. The moist smell of earth somehow seemed comforting, yet the cold of Norway seeped through the brick floor. The harbor below was dark. The overcast sky reminded her of a Canaletto painting, mauve clouds tinged with a ribbon of yellow at the horizon. The bay had never looked so beautiful; it was as though all of Bergen were showing off. The light failed quickly. She turned to Olav and said, "It's getting late; you'd better go."

CHAPTER 6

April 4, 1940

Oslo, Norway

Exhausted, Breckkan walked slowly down the platform of Oslo's East Station. He had had little rest on the train; his mind had constantly jolted him awake with disturbing dreams. He exhaled, realizing just how close he was to being out of control. Walking through the packed station and past the office of the stationmaster, he crossed to the main ticket-counter. Through red-rimmed eyes, he looked up at the schedule board and noticed newly added Oslo-Kongsberg departures. Just as he joined the line, he heard someone shouting his name. He stiffened and turned quickly, spotting a bulky uniform passing by a young couple pushing a pram.

"Thank God I caught you," Commodore Duun puffed.

"What are you doing here?"

Roald edged Breckkan out of the line. "Bonnie rang up your mother after you left last night to tell her you were coming. Luckily, Gustave was there. He sent keys for a company truck to my office early this morning. He's on his way back to the mines or he would have brought them himself. Might interest you to know that he told me during our lunch yesterday, that he plans to stop shipments to I.G. Farben."

"That makes me feel better. Your driver? Any leads?"

"No one saw anything, but the investigation pretty well rules out a personal vendetta. And our people don't feel that anyone breached security. It had to be someone on the guest list. My Petty Officer parked your truck just down the way."

"Thanks, Roald. I'm sure being an errand boy is all you had to do this morning." Breckkan felt his skittishness disappearing, hearing the apology in his own voice.

"Don't worry about it. I was relieved to know I would see you again," he said, steering them toward the exit. They moved silently with the crowd out of the station onto the steps. "We don't want you taking any trains."

"Why not?" Breckkan asked, staring at the bearded man walking briskly beside him.

Roald spoke curtly and unemotionally, a military habit. "The Germans are watching everyone traveling to Rjukan. All Norwegian employees of either Norsk-Hydro or the Vemork High-Concentration Plant are under surveillance as well as the German engineering staff already stationed down there. Their interest certainly isn't completely scientific."

"What exactly do you mean? It was a cooperative arrangement from the start. I've known those men for years. Some of their families are my friends. Hell, Rjukan's been their home since we built the place in 1934."

"Breckkan, they're informers. All of them." He motioned to his left, moving with quick strides, his overcoat cinched tightly around his girth. "The truck is just down this side street. Has Professor Kittleson agreed to leave?"

"Yes, but I'm worried about him." Breckkan turned up the collar of his trench coat and shifted the weight of his rucksack to the other shoulder. Stopping beside the truck, he rubbed his gloved hands and stamped his boot-clad feet on the ancient cobblestones. The early morning Arctic chill was numbing. Black ice lined the gutters and clung to the warehouses. The pale light of the streetlamps vaguely pierced the freezing mist, emphasizing the bleakness of the empty street and the fatigue in his face.

The Commodore rocked back on his heels. "Anything I can do to help? It's not going to be easy to get out of port. There're German sailors reported all over Bergen and Trondheim, in fact, the whole damn West coast."

"I think we'll be okay using a fishing trawler by a Captain Larsen." Breckkan tossed his rucksack into the cab. "Can you get through to London...more precisely, Cambridge?"

"I have connections."

"We're planning on staying in London until it's safe to come home." Roald nodded, settling his beard further into his white muffler. "Could you get word to a Professor James Chadwick. He's a friend of Knut's. Tell him we'll be at the Savoy."

"Be more specific. Give me a time."

"What port should we head for?"

"Lerwick. The Shetland Islands. The Scots are very cooperative. I believe your mother's ships docked regularly there. The dockmaster will recognize your name. He can help."

"Good. I plan to be back in Bergen tomorrow night. Late. If everything is set, we should be at sea the next morning, the sixth. How long will it take us to get to Lerwick?"

The Commodore leaned with both arms on the truck bed, his head turned, looking down the dreary street toward the harbor. The morning ferry from Denmark was arriving. "Hard to estimate, not knowing what to expect; the weather could be real bad. Even with the sun at your back, I'd say a day and a half, maybe two."

"And from there to London? We should be able to get a car on the Mainland." Breckkan's voice actually sounded more optimistic. A schedule was comforting. It made the escape plan seem possible.

"Driving? Even day and night, the best you could hope for would be three to four days, probably more. You'll have to stop sometime. Remember the Professor."

Breckkan's breath fogged in the crystalline air. "So we're estimating anywhere from a week to possibly two." The frigid cold of the cobblestones began to seep through the soles of his high-laced boots.

"Okay. I'll notify Professor Chadwick and suggest he have someone watch for you beginning in a week at the Savoy. If you're not there in three weeks, there will be reason to worry."

"Worry? Who's worried?" Breckkan actually smiled as he climbed into the freezing truck cab. He turned the key; there was only a dull groan and then silence.

"Oh," laughed Roald, the visible part of his chunky face flushed from the cold. "I forgot something." He pulled a pewter flask from his overcoat. "The old dear, she's a drinker."

"What?"

"She needs a bit of acetone in the carburetor and she'll purr like a kitten. The Petty Officer figured her out this morning." Roald opened the hood, and moments later shouted, "Give her a try."

Breckkan turned the ignition. With an explosive bang, followed by a gigantic expulsion of exhaust, the motor caught and settled into a rough rumble.

Slamming the hood of the old truck, he handed the flask to Breckkan. "Keep your chin down."

Breckkan picked up the beat and chimed in, "And your eyes straight ahead." He ran his finger across the round scar under his chin and feigned a duck into his coat.

"It was a good lesson for both of us. Just be careful, Breckkan."

Breckkan silently cursed the long drive and hairpin turns as he rolled down the window to let in a blast of fresh air. The narrow road was bordered by dense stands of birch and pine. Ahead he saw the perfect hill, just the right incline: 45 degrees and a bowl of powder at the bottom. He and Roald. Two daredevils. Roald wasn't so heavy then, he remembered, but just as determined. And Gustave was there to chaperone their shenanigans at the ski jump.

It was perfect weather. Cold and bright. Roald had just finished a beautiful jump, leaning out over his tips, arms against his body, his landing timed perfectly. Clean and beautiful, even generating some applause at the base of the jump. Then Breckkan had a great idea. He looked at his uncle. Sure, why not, Gustave answered. Gustave was in superb shape and easily hoisted young Breckkan onto his shoulders and, after three or four rocks in the gate, pushed off with tremendous speed.

If only he'd remembered to drop his poles.

Breckkan winced, grinding the gears of the truck, and spun out of a curve spewing ice and rocks to the side.

He was balanced perfectly on his uncle's shoulders. The crowd cheered the pair down the steep jump. He sensed the landing when Gustave began to crouch. Then they landed. The pole glanced off the hard-packed ice and shot upward, straight through Breckkan's jaw and into his mouth.

Gustave had broken his collarbone. Roald had carried Breckkan down the mountain.

"Who's worried?" he said out loud.

Rjukan, Norway

The truck made the final groaning climb before entering the canyon. Ahead the road began snaking its way down the precipitous route, Breckkan stopped the truck. He exhaled through tight lips, whistling low. There was a whipping wind coming up from the deep gorge. The canyon was a long slice in the earth with a river at its heart.

He could never look casually at the awesome natural setting of the Heavy Water Plant, which totally dominated the landscape. The seven-story main building was a colossus, rising like a medieval castle, built in this most inaccessible location. Angling down the steep slope were giant pipes that supplied hundreds of tons of water per minute to the massive plant. The equipment was so mammoth, the men tending it looked Lilliputian. Compared to the natural site, in a valley plowed out by some primeval sheet of ice, even this monumental effort of man seemed fragile, inconsequential.

Though the wind was blowing furiously, he could still hear the hum of the machinery reverberating from the steep-sided gorge. "This isn't going to be easy," he said aloud, hardly recognizing his own voice. His throat was tight, but his mind was suddenly clear.

He headed the truck down the canyon in a hairpin swing and stopped at the check-in gate. He pressed the buzzer for the guard. He looked up, prepared to show his papers, then froze. It wasn't the usual Norwegian guard. Instead, a man with a familiar face scowled through the truck window.

A friend, an engineer wearing a German uniform, held his hand on a Luger still partially in its holster. In German, he said icily, "Identification papers." The German casually perused Breckkan's papers, knowing full well who he was.

Breckkan sat motionless, remembering the Germans' neurotic love of paper: forms, passes, anything written and appearing official, much like the Norwegian obsession with statistics, data. Watching the guard, he felt his inappropriate focus of attention was like people who visit museums and devote their time to labels adjacent to the paintings, ignoring the paintings themselves. The German was about to admit a dedicated saboteur.

Without making eye contact, the guard returned his papers and said tersely, "Proceed to security."

Breckkan drove the truck into the parking area and chose a spot near a small grove of trees. He hoisted his rucksack to his shoulder and walked to the building located a hundred feet from the massive cable-supported bridge. Threading his way behind the sandbag emplacement, he entered the security area and immediately noted triple the usual number of guards, mostly German. He walked to a desk where a familiar-faced clerk sat typing.

The Norwegian looked up and smiled. "Welcome back, Dr. Breckkan. It's been several weeks since you've been here."

"Yes," answered Breckkan, reaching out to shake his hand. "I've been in Oslo. Everything okay?"

"Yes, sir. A little more security," said the clerk, his eyes moving around the clearance area. "If you'll sign the register, Doctor, I'll give you your badge." Breckkan looked oddly at the clerk then signed in. "Sir, before you take the tram, you'll have to show your identification and sign again over there."

"Why? What's that all about?"

"The Germans don't seem to trust us any more."

Breckkan muttered a curse under his breath then turned to cross the room. So Roald was right about the German engineering staff. A young guard looked up at him and abruptly stuck out his hand, palm up.

In response to the silent command, Breckkan unblinkingly stared back into the German's eyes. With calculated precision, purposely allowing several moments to pass, he withdrew his identification papers. He talked straight through him. "I am Dr. Breckkan. If you're thinking of staying around, you'd damn well better get to know who I am."

"Of course, Doctor, you're one of the designers of the installation," replied the Oberlieutenant. "Your papers are in order. You may proceed to the tram. The 12:00 is just leaving."

This sudden change. Who ordered the build-up in security? Just who's in charge now?

Breckkan walked out of the clearance area and over to the electric tramcar. The engineer was standing beside the door, dressed in the regulation gray jumpsuit required in the security area. Seeing Breckkan approaching, he waved and quickly slid open the side door to the car. Breckkan climbed in and greeted him warmly but formally. He needed time to think and hoped today the driver was not his normal loquacious self. Spotting an empty seat in the last row, he walked quickly to the back of the tram. With a quiet whoosh, the tram began the bridge crossing.

Breckkan felt his mind sharpening while he surveyed the narrow valley enclosed by the snow-tipped mountains. Stark in the crystalline air, their black pinnacles were etched by snow and ice, leaving narrow ledges covered by small outcroppings of spruce and pine. Tiny streams ran down the steep-sided gorge to the half-frozen river below. Updraft winds buffeted the suspension bridge. A bank of heavy snow clouds was pressing from the

Northeast. His mind was in complete focus; his scientific acumen cataloging every detail.

His pulse quickened when the tram lurched as it left the suspension bridge and moved onto the curving track leading down to the entrance of the Vemork Plant. He noticed several new wooden barracks, presumably housing the added contingent of German guards. Then the roar of the giant turbines from deep within the building reached his ears.

The engineer stopped the tram and sat back while the passengers disembarked. The last to leave, Breckkan stopped for a moment by the driver and said, "Sorry we didn't have our usual visit. I've been on the train all night and I'm exhausted."

"No apologies necessary, sir. Glad to see you're back. We're all a bit tired. Triple shifts the last few days."

"Triple shifts? When did that start?"

"After the German Major arrived. Didn't you know?"

Questions raced through his mind as he heard himself mumble a reply. "Aren't the extra guards getting in the way?"

"Not really, sir, same number on the night shift. The extras are only here during the day. Seems the Major thinks the most crucial time is when all you scientists are on duty."

Typical neurotic German mistrust, he thought. "Well, I'll call you when I'm ready to leave. I won't be late."

"Sorry, sir. The major's ordered a new tram schedule, too. I'm afraid I'll have to take you with the rest at 5:30."

Breckkan shrugged, as though the new schedule was little more than an inconvenience. He felt trapped. Too many changes too fast. Adjusting his rucksack, he headed for the building, flashing his pass once more. He walked quickly to the entrance, though in his mind he felt conspicuously slow.

He crossed the polished wood floor to the bank of elevators. He needed time. His heart skipped a beat when the elevator door opened. A German guard at the controls.

Eyeing the civilian clothes, the guard snapped, "Where's your visitor's badge?"

With an icy stare, Breckkan spoke with a sharp upper-class edge. "I'm Dr. Breckkan, the senior consultant for this place. I built the goddamn thing." Breckkan sensed the guard was the sort of man comfortable only with one small job, a job he intended to keep.

The guard nervously moistened his lips and dropped his eyes. "Excuse me, sir. What floor, sir?"

"Seven. The top."

As the elevator ascended, Breckkan considered his first lesson learned: keep the initiative. The door opened and, without speaking, he stepped out. Everything appeared normal. He stopped at Room 706. The sign on the door read "Cryogenics."

Little did Faraday and Davy realize what door they were opening when they pioneered low temperature physics. The theories for forming such cold substances were simple: the combination of two conditions reduced gas temperatures in the presence of increased pressure. These conditions forced gases to liquify and those liquids, when exposed to normal pressure, evaporate rapidly, causing a cooling of anything in contact with them. The state of the art was a coalition of gases, each cooling the next gas in succession, ultimately achieving an immense coldness, -130 degrees and even lower. Breckkan's team dubbed the process "cascading." All his early work with Bohr dealt with extreme low-temperature physics. Indeed, his professor had depended on him for this arena of knowledge. It was crucial to work in nuclear physics. Under the auspices of Bohr's Institute in Copenhagen, Breckkan initially had been welcomed at national and international societies to deliver papers on his work. Now things were changed, the brilliance of the young physicist had been recognized and he was looked upon as an equal by the senior scientists. Often he was consulted by laboratories all over Europe when data didn't fit pre-fixed theory.

Opening the laboratory door, his first glance took in everything. He casually slipped off his trench coat and donned his white lab coat. The laboratory was rowed with steel experiment benches, each experiment set-up looking like a plumber's nightmare. Five-foot tall steel canisters were aligned against the side wall, chained in place to protect them against accidental jarring, protecting their ultra-sensitive valve systems. Every employee at Vemork knew a sudden release of the super cold liquid could result in a violent explosion.

Walking toward his private office which adjoined the lab, each of his technicians deferentially acknowledged him. They were all intent on their respective tasks, ear plugs in place. He made no effort at conversation; the roar of the turbines below prohibited casual exchange.

Breckkan removed a key case from his pocket and slid a key into the lock, opening the door to his windowless office. It was pitch black. He knew the room by heart: twelve feet by twenty feet, two walls of bookshelves, overflow of supplies from the lab, files, and a large, old scarred desk.

He closed the door and immediately sensed a presence in the room. Cigarette smoke. Like a blind man, his sense of smell was sharpened by the darkness. He dropped his rucksack and stepped to his right, reaching for the light switch. His fingers touched leather. His mind soared to hyperalertness as the blue-tinged fluorescent light flickered on.

His pupils, dilated by the few seconds of complete darkness, focused on the uniformed man seated on the corner of his desk. Under the unflattering fluorescent light, the intruder's skin looked overexposed and bruised.

Von Stein smiled and leaned against the wall. With a black-booted foot, he kicked the desk chair across the room. "Dr. Breckkan. Sit."

Breckkan clenched his teeth. "What the hell are you doing here?"

"Now, Breckkan, is that any way to greet an old friend?"

"More to the point, is this any way to intrude on an old friend?" retorted Breckkan.

"I'm surprised at you. Such an inhospitable welcome. After all the years we worked together..." Von Stein paused, leaned forward and spoke intently, "From now on, we're partners."

Breckkan stepped toward the table and felt the blood rising to his face. "I'll say it again. What the hell are you doing in my office!"

"Whether you like it or not, we're partners. I'm here to see your progress." His tone barely concealed his malevolence.

"This is my laboratory, my people, my country, not yours. You're trespassing. Now, get the hell out!" snapped Breckkan.

Lighting a cigarette and watching the flame inch closer to his fingers, von Stein focused his shaded eyes on Breckkan. "Careful, Breckkan, you're this match. We can either let you burn or save you. Understand?"

"You bet I understand!" exploded Breckkan. "Get your black-booted ass out of here or..."

"Or what?"

"I'll have security in here in seconds!"

"Why don't you do that, Doctor. In fact, let me do it for you." Von Stein pushed off the table, walked to the door and jerked it open. "Guards! In here. Now!"

Two Germans immediately emerged from the hall and took positions on each side of the laboratory entrance.

Von Stein's eyes darted toward the lab technicians. "Watch them," he said curtly. He stepped back into the office as a third guard entered and pointed his gun straight at Breckkan. Von Stein threw the dead bolt on the door. "Well, Dr. Breckkan, now throw me out!"

He ground out his cigarette on the floor and stood inches from Breckkan. "Anything to say?" Breckkan didn't speak. "Well then, Doctor, I suggest you put that tight butt of yours in that chair!"

"I've nothing to say to you."

"Oh, I'm sure you do." Von Stein blended cynicism and contempt with his demand. "To begin with, let's see your data. All of it. I assume it's of some value."

Breckkan could feel his blood pressure rising and a roaring in his ears. The tinnitus, like crackling bacon, momentarily ground out the sound of the turbines rumbling deep below. With intense mental effort, he brought himself under control. When he spoke, it was as if he heard his own voice from far away. "And what data would that be?"

"Come now. You're no idiot. Your equations!" said von Stein furiously. "I'm prepared to wait in this room, which you have so conveniently supplied, until you hand them to me."

"Cut the crap, Stein. Unpublished data is privileged information. I can't imagine it being of value to you."

"Privileged?" He laughed—a ragged, disgusted laugh. "That sounds just like you."

"That's right, privileged, confidential. Got it?"

"No. But now you'll catch on," grinned von Stein. He slowly walked over to Breckkan, whipped off his tinted glasses and stared down at Breckkan. "I'm not leaving here without your equations. Where are they?"

"They're not here."

"All results and calculations are either in this room or...perhaps you just brought them with you."

Von stein turned, grabbed Breckkan's rucksack, unbuckled it, and dumped the contents on the floor. He removed his pocketknife and snapped it open, exposing the razor-sharp blade. Quick slices through the rucksack. Nothing. He tossed the mutilated bag to the corner. With deliberateness, he moved closer to Breckkan, pointed the knife blade at the Norwegian's eyes. "It is very easy for me to kill. I am extremely well-trained." He paused, then said, "Perhaps you remember your driver the night of the banquet?"

"Now. The data books," von Stein repeated. "Where are they? One more minute and you'll have no tongue. Then you'll show me like a dog, pointing with your fucking nose." The guard snickered, enjoying the ridicule.

Breckkan's mind raced. The terror was like that he'd experienced when his father had died. Total helplessness. He could feel sweat running down his spine.

Von Stein's excited, gray-pink eyes seemed to possess a disconcerting ability to simultaneously stare at Breckkan and yet focus on the entire scene. Suddenly, von Stein flicked his wrist, but Breckkan felt just a touch. No pain. Then numbness in his left cheek. A warm sensation spread down his face to his jaw. Warm drops fell on his white lab coat. A pungent, sweet odor flooded his nostrils; he knew he was bleeding heavily. The first sensations of pain broke through the numbness.

"Just a nick. The beginning. I repeat again...the data books?"

"I don't have them in here. For God's sake, do you think I'd keep them here? They're in the central safe."

"Oh, come now. You expect me to believe that?"

Breckkan cupped his right hand under his jaw to catch the blood streaming from the wound. "I tell you, Stein, rules here demand central storage. Ask any of my technicians. Everyone knows this is a secured area."

"You have one minute, Breckkan. Then I'll carve out your tongue through the wall of your cheek."

A paroxysm of stimuli exploded in Breckkan's brain, demanding action. No plan, just manic impulse. He suddenly shoved his hand full of clotting, sweet blood into von Stein's eyes. The violent, irritating properties of the blood acted quickly on the hypersensitive eyes. Von Stein swung his knife blindly at Breckkan's neck, snarling gutturally. Breckkan jerked to his left. The knife flew from von Stein's hand, landing in the far corner of the room.

The guard instinctively moved toward the Major. Breckkan bolted from the chair, grabbed it and fiercely swung it at the Germans, sending them both sprawling against the wall. Maintaining pivotal momentum, he swivelled around and snapped off the light. In the dark, he grabbed for the doorknob, his bloody hand slipped.

From the blackness, von Stein's voice bellowed, "Goddamn you!" Breckkan slammed the door.

Stunned by the blood-stained coat and face of their director, the two technicians stood frozen while Breckkan pushed a heavy steel table against the office door. "Get down!"

He knew he had only moments before the hall guards would respond to the situation. He swung around, grabbed a two-gallon canister of liquid nitrogen and ran toward the main door. The guards rushed into the lab simultaneously. Breckkan spun the relief valve on the steel canister, stopping the guards immediately as the stream of liquid nitrogen struck their faces. Both screamed when the initial super-cold sensation evaporated and a violent burning sensation took control.

The technician nearest the door quickly grabbed a steel beaker stand and, with two violent blows, struck their heads at the base of the neck. Their bodies collapsed, their faces skewed and marmoreal.

"Lock the hall door!" Breckkan yelled. He turned his attention to the pounding noise coming from his office.

Running across the room, dodging laboratory apparatus, he yanked a steel rod from an experimental setup. He inserted it in the chain linkage holding a nitrogen canister against the wall and broke it cleanly. Breathing heavily and wincing, he watched the office door edge open. Immediately he saw von Stein's gloved hand straining at the door frame.

He carefully lowered the long, heavy canister to the floor and rolled it under the steel table. Moving rapidly, he pawed through an equipment drawer looking for an elbow connector with a universal threading.

He hunched down and crawled under the table. Wedging himself parallel to the tank, he screwed the pipe onto the control valve. Groaning with effort, he pulled his body and the tank closer to the door. His mind was remarkably clear. He turned the valve, releasing a fine spay of freezing nitrogen.

Von Stein never heard the hissing of the escaping cold gas as he edged his boot through the door and, with one final shove, pushed into the laboratory. His boots were inches from Breckkan's head, but the table top hid the Norwegian's body.

Breckkan turned the connector pipe straight up and, with a final lunge, pushed the canister between von Stein's legs, spinning the valve to full open.

The jet of super-cold liquid found its target; only seconds were required to convert von Stein's boots and breeches to hoarfrost. Silence. Breckkan felt his heart beat three times.

Von Stein screamed and fell backward into the office. Breckkan slithered from under the table and slammed the door shut.

The two lab crewmen immediately helped Breckkan force heavy steel benches against the door, barricading it securely. The muffled screams of the Major were subsiding. The liquid cold had turned gracious; it had not only neutered the man, but had also destroyed the nerve endings reporting the catastrophe to his brain.

Pointing across the room, he motioned toward the crumpled guards. "Get them into the storage closet. Hurry!"

Wasting no time, Breckkan dropped to the floor near the cryogenic tanks. He carefully tugged at the base of the last canister, working it away from the wall, reached behind the tank into the space just large enough for his hand, and felt for the register grate. His finger touched the cold metal and slid between the metal grate and the wall, trying to loosen it. Grabbing a steel beaker stand, he used the narrow rod to pry the grate open. He strained and groped for the familiar leather data books. Both were there.

He stood up, placed the books on a lab table, and ripped off his blood-stained coat. Leaning over the sink, he turned the water on full; the cold water gushed over his head and face. The senior lab tech gently helped wipe off the blood. He kept both hands on the edge of the sink, gritting his teeth. "Harder!"

"Easy, sir, easy. You're not a pretty picture," said the gray-headed tech. The pain should have been intolerable when the towel dug into the two-inch long wound, but in his current mental state, the pain served only to heighten his concentration.

"You handled them well, sir. Best get this stitched up right away," the older man murmured.

Breckkan nodded and said, "Get the first aid kit and bring me a burn bandage." I need pressure, stop the bleeding, he thought, squinting to check his eyesight. Blood still oozing from the wound, he quickly applied the dressing with the help of the technician, packing a thick pad of gauze over the gaping wound and taping it tightly to his forehead and right cheek.

Holding his hand against the pressure dressing, Breckkan looked at the two Norwegians. "Listen! No heroes now. When the Germans get here, blame everything on me." The senior technician lifted his brows as if to object, but the meaning of the words was understood. "Just try to avoid retribution."

"God help you," said the lab tech.

Breckkan was already cramming the data books into the outside pockets of his tweed jacket as he pulled on a fresh white lab coat. He raised his arm in a brief wave, then reached for a twelve liter canister of liquid oxygen and quickly closed the door behind him. Hurriedly walking to the elevators, he methodically reviewed the steps he took entering the Plant. Each step was now an obstacle.

He exhaled, breathed in deeply and pushed the elevator button. In moments, the doors opened; there was the same guard.

Taking the initiative again, he touched the dressing. "An accident. Damn clumsy. Hope there's no scar. Second floor."

"Yes, Doctor." The guard snapped to attention and concentrated on the controls. The elevator stopped and Breckkan stepped out. He picked up the tank and said nothing.

The second floor housed storage, general supplies, and a cafeteria. He slipped into a storeroom and went straight to the window.

Surveying the entrance to the installation, he saw the tramcar parked at the end of the track just beyond the building. Perfect. From his vantage point, he surveyed the wooden barracks and could see no activity within the wire perimeter. He wiped the perspiration from his forehead and stood motionless. The floor plan of the Plant clicked through his mind.

A light snow was falling and the surrounding mountains were shrouded in dense clouds. The clumps of pines on the grounds bent intermittently in the strong gusts of wind. Already the overcast sky was closing in on the canyon.

Leaving the storage room, he grabbed the oxygen tank by the rectangular handle and headed down the hall. He stopped beside the cafeteria door. Through the frosted glass he could make out the figure of the tram driver, coffee cup in hand, gossiping with a small group of fellow Norwegians.

He continued to the end of the hall and pressed the crossbar on the stairwell door. The stairwell was dark, but manageable. In the gloom he passed the first floor, avoiding the guards at the building entrance, and stopped his descent in the basement, the heart of the heavy water facility.

He entered the vast underground chamber where heavy water was being made. It contained the vital electrolysis tanks, each four feet high, twelve inches in diameter, protected by stainless steel jackets. The rumble of the gigantic water pumps was deafening. He wished he could sabotage the tanks, but told himself to move on. He would have to do that another time.

Shouting over the roar of the machinery as if to a deaf man, he greeted the guard. The single gray-uniformed Norwegian guard on duty merely smiled and nodded at the familiar white-coated scientist and turned back to his check list. Exhaling with relief, Breckkan headed for the far southwest corner of the gigantic room. He knew the major cable intake tunnel was located behind the massive holding tanks.

Though he was involved from the beginning with the construction of the building, he had forgotten the narrow diameter of the tunnel. He realized he would have to push the canister of potentially explosive oxygen ahead of him. He hesitated for a moment, hoping the outlet valve would not snag on the maze of ring fittings and cable connectors. Seventeen feet of tight space, intricately woven with a network of wiring lay ahead. He pushed the tank into the opening and wormed in behind it.

As he slowly worked his way through the duct, he felt warm fresh blood seeping through the dressing. He stopped several times to catch his breath. He knew he was beginning to weaken and wondered if he would make it to the outside entrance when suddenly the tank began to pitch forward toward the ground. He lunged forward, banging his head on the duct and frantically grabbed the tank with both hands. Exhaling, he gingerly pulled it back against his chest. He rested his sweaty cheek against the cold steel tank.

"Jesus, the goddamn thing almost fell out!" he breathed to himself. Damn it, I can't remember, how far is it to the ground. The passage was too dark and too narrow to see beyond the tank, so at best, he knew anything he did would be risky.

Laying his chin on the handle and keeping the canister stable with one hand, he reached inside his lab coat inside his tweed jacket, and squirmed to remove his belt. Pulling the belt up past his ribs, he twisted to his left and slid it around the handle and back through the buckle, forming a noose. He held the end of the belt tightly and gingerly pushed the oxygen tank forward. As it started to tip again, he wrapped the belt around his hand, keeping it taut. In unison, his body and the canister inched forward toward the failing daylight.

Suddenly, the belt went taut when the tank abruptly popped out into open space. With his free hand, Breckkan quickly grabbed the freezing rim of the tunnel to maintain his balance. Simultaneously, his right arm took the full impact of the dead weight of the dangling canister. Then came the dreaded thud when the tank struck the side of the building. Involuntarily, he ducked his head in anticipation of the violent explosion.

Nothing.

The sweet smell of cold air and fresh snow poured into the tunnel, cooling his sweating face. He inched forward, hearing the tank scrape against the wall with each move. The torturous strain on his right shoulder slackened as the tank slipped mercifully into a bank of soft snow.

He carefully released the belt and, with both hands, vaulted his body out of the tunnel into the snow bank next to the canister. He sank back in the drift, stared at the tank and slowly massaged his right shoulder. He sat silently, thankful the lab coat blended into the snow.

Thirty feet in front of him was the unguarded tram. From his angle, he could see the side door was open just enough to allow the driver to manually push it open.

Breckkan felt both pockets. The data books were there. He picked up the canister and climbed out of the drift. He cautiously approached the waiting tram. He slid the door open, laid the canister across the nearest seat, and climbed up and in. Quietly, he slid the door shut. He looked at his watch. Two o'clock. Still three and a half hours before the next shuttle. Suddenly he was aware of boots crunching to his right, brisk and vigorous. Muffled voices. Two guards were nearing the main entrance, talking animatedly, one clapping his hands together for warmth and gesturing broadly. Breckkan crouched down. Then he heard the scuffling sound of boots stamping at the entrance. The main door banged shut.

In a crouch, he edged toward the driver's seat. Hunching over the instrument panel, he could see it was simple: a speedometer and a toggle starter switch. A warning sign on the panel read: "DO NOT EXCEED 20 kph." He wiped his hand on his coat, knowing he had no choice. He switched on the motor, released the brake, and engaged the small hand lever. With a soft whir, the tram slowly began moving forward and gradually picked up speed. He gently pulled back on the gear and the speed settled at 10 kph.

The tram passed the barracks where the only activity was the curling of smoke from the tin chimneys mixing quickly with the blowing snow. The few small windows were glazed with frost. He turned and looked behind but saw no one.

The great building blurred as the falling snow veiled the facade. The wind and the eternal roar of the turbines covered any sounds made by the tram. He remembered that the cafeteria windows faced the rear of the building; no one could see the tram curving toward the suspension bridge.

He adjusted the throttle, slowing to a mere 8 kph, when the tram moved onto the span. Icy blasts of wind, funneling up from deep in the gorge, buffeted the bridge causing it to swing perceptibly. Time to move, he thought.

Walking back to the oxygen tank, he was thrown against the side door and grabbed frantically for a seat back. Regaining his balance and bracing himself, he pushed the tank under the seat and wedged it tightly against the wall of the tram. He carefully turned the release valve. The odorless gas began filling the compartment.

From a crouched position, he looked out the window, gauging the midpoint of the bridge. He twisted the valve full open and crawled back to the driver's seat. Reaching for the throttle, he edged it forward to the stop position.

When the tram slowed, he carefully opened the side door and felt the freezing wind blast his face. Now! He slipped out onto the narrow crawlspace and slid the door until he felt it click shut. Down on his hands and knees, he crawled to the blind side of the track, his lab coat billowing in the violent updraft. He heard the suspension cables groaning in the wind.

He crawled along against the guard rails and suddenly felt light-headed, momentarily confused. He slipped and nearly lost his balance. Had he lost that much blood or was it the swaying of the bridge? The track seemed to ripple as the bridge swayed again, and he felt like he could fall into the swirling white void. Calm down, easy, he told himself. It had to be the motion, the violent wind; the snow was actually blowing up from the gorge. The world seemed quite upside down. He realized he had to pace himself.

Reaching the end of the bridge, he stopped, his breath whistling thinly through his teeth. No time to slow down now. He tore off the bandage. Fresh blood ran down his cheek. Move, man, move!

He jumped up and ran toward the security building, yelling, "Help! Help!"

The German guards bolted out of the door, weapons in hand, aimed down at Breckkan. Gesturing wildly, he pointed to the tram on the bridge.

"Help! In the tram! He tried to escape! Top-secret files! I tried to stop him," he yelled, touching his face.

While the guards ran ahead, a sergeant forced Breckkan to the ground to shield him and asked, "Where is he?"

"On the floor, near the driver's seat. He's got a gun. The bastard! Do something!" he yelled hysterically.

The German thrust a handkerchief at him and snapped, "Stay down!" The Sergeant joined his men and moved toward the bridge, their dark uniforms obscured by the blizzard.

Wasting no time, Breckkan got up and ran across the parking area to the truck. He slammed the door shut and inserted the key, then remembered the acetone. "Damn!" He clicked open the glove compartment and groped for the flask. There it was, laying on a clump of oily rags. Grabbing for it, his hand touched a small wooden box. He knew immediately: dynamite caps. Opening it hurriedly, he saw it was half-filled with mercury fulminate caps. For once, Breckkan Mining is worth something to me, he thought.

He climbed down from the truck and opened the hood. He pulled off the distributor cap, placed five caps inside and then partially filled it with acetone. He snapped the cap back on, slammed down the hood and ran toward the security building.

Looking past the hut toward the gorge, he could make out the vague outlines of the Germans moving along the bridge toward the silent tram. From his position, he could see only the roof of the car; the geometric construction of support cables blocked the cab from view. The towers were virtually lost from view in the storm. Damn! Why don't those trigger happy bastards shoot at it?

He turned and burst into the security building. It was empty except for the Norwegian clerk. In a taut but clear voice, Breckkan instructed him, "Call the guard at the entry gate. Tell him I've been injured and need a driver." The Norwegian nodded and thrust out a handkerchief. Breckkan daubed at the wound. "The keys are in my truck. Tell him to bring it over here."

"Yes, sir."

"Are there any guns around?"

"No. The Germans have all of them."

Breckkan searched the room for any sort of weapon, while the clerk telephoned the main entry guardhouse. No weapons. Think! He threw off the lab coat and nervously patted his jacket pockets. He felt the box of caps and moved to the window, looking out at the bridge. "How many guards at the gatehouse?"

"Usually two," answered the clerk.

Breckkan stepped behind the counter and began drumming his fingers on the desk. Then he noticed the telegraph key and the attendant wires. Reaching around the green gooseneck lamp, he yanked the wires and broke them at the connection box on the floor.

The telephone was his next target. "The only one?" he asked, pointing to the phone.

"Yes, sir. They've planned a switchboard, but haven't installed it yet."

Breckkan removed the receiver from the cradle, jerked loose the cord between the two, and replaced the receiver.

Now the fireworks...Father would love this, he thought, reaching for the lamp. He unscrewed the bulb and carefully placed two caps in the base of the empty socket, then gently screwed the bulb back in. His sense of touch was acute. At the moment of first resistance, he stopped. One more turn and his arm and hand would be blown off.

Motioning to the clerk, he said, "Bring me a chair. Hurry!" The Norwegian scooted a chair to the middle of the room and Breckkan quickly jumped onto it. Using the bloody handkerchief, he loosened three of the four bulbs in the overhead fixture, stepped down, and pushed the chair to the wall.

He noticed a heavy, hooded overcoat on the coat rack. "Yours?" he asked.

"Yes. Take it."

"You'll never know how much you've helped," Breckkan said, pulling on the coat. "You're going to have hell to pay when the Germans get back." The man shrugged. "It's my turn to help you. Check the window and watch for my truck."

The clerk walked to the window and peered into the virtual whiteout. Breckkan went to the desk and picked up a metal embossing stamp. With a single motion, he caught the clerk on the back of the head. There was a sudden release of air from the man's mouth as he crumpled to the floor. Blood began flowing from a small gash at the base of his skull.

Breckkan stooped and felt for the carotid pulses. They were strong. Good. That will save his life when the Germans get here, he thought. He smeared blood from his own face onto the clerk.

A loud crack, followed by muffled thuds came from across the parking area. A second, larger explosion followed immediately. Breckkan raced out the door. The first explosion was activated when the guard turned the ignition; the second had to be the auxiliary fuel tank. The flames, fed by high winds, seared the nearby stand of pine trees.

His attention was turned to the muffled reports of several rifles. He spun to look at the bridge. There was an enormous flare, a suspended, glowing ball of ill-defined pink and gold pulsing through the white curtain of snow. Simultaneously, a hollow deep-throated roar reached his ears.

The tram! he thought giddily. The bastards finally shot at it. His self-congratulation was short-lived as chunks of metal showered around him. He ducked and ran for the entrance gate.

He heard a shout. His heart stopped. A German yelled, running toward him through the blizzard. Breckkan dove into a snow bank on his left, rolled over into the scrub oak, stopped and lay silent. The guard ran past his field of vision and disappeared into the storm.

He cautiously crept out of the brush on his hands and knees and moved in a crouched run toward the gate. Reaching the guard hut, he warily glanced through the frosted pane. The hut was empty.

Ducking under the wooden entrance gate, his eye caught a shape covered by a tarp leaning against the guard shack. He pushed up the bar and ran back to the hut. He brushed through the snow. A motorcycle. No locks, just a starter switch. He quickly checked the gas tank, and finding it half-full, pushed it onto the road and through the open gate.

Just as he mounted the motorcycle and kicked it to life, a sharp crack-like sound reverberated from the security building. Breckkan knew a poor bastard must have tried to turn on the desk lamp. If he survived, his career was over. No army takes men with no arms.

The engine sputtered to life, then suddenly he heard shouts. Goddamn it, he thought, the bridge isn't out. He ground the gears and roared up the hairpin road, slipping and sliding all the way.

CHAPTER 7

April 4, 1940

Bergen, Norway

The ticking of the clock was unnerving. The bedroom suddenly seemed too lonely, too confining, and the blankets too heavy. Bonnie dressed quickly, then brushed her hair back, cursing the length as she braided, wrapped, and pinned it into a bun. She snapped out the light and hurried downstairs to the kitchen.

Walking down the darkened hall, she spotted a thin line of light under the kitchen door. Knut, his thick white hair in disarray, sat at the kitchen table, preoccupied with the contents of a thin volume.

She refilled his coffee cup and placed it before him. "What in the world are you doing up so early?" she asked softly.

"I couldn't sleep."

"What are you reading?"

"Just some poems I wrote a long time ago. I wrote them for your mother. I feel so close to her in this house. Her kitchen, her greenhouse. I just needed time to say goodbye."

She sensed his feelings of profound loss, not just melancholia. "We'll be back sooner than you think." Swallowing hard, she fought the tightness in her own throat. "How about a big breakfast? We've got a long day ahead."

"Whatever you want."

It was a simple breakfast: a large platter of smoked herring, boiled eggs, and cheese. Bonnie watched him carefully, but his expression revealed nothing more than a vague preoccupation. He occasionally looked up with a distracted smile. They both ate dutifully, making disjointed conversation.

"Don't forget the cash for Lief," she said.

"Right." His voice seemed stronger. "Let me help you clean up."

"No, I'll take care of it, then I'll drive you to the Institute. I've got to take care of some business. Think you can wrap up things in the lab by yourself?"

He patted the volume of poetry with his slender hand. "You know, I've always dreaded moving all my junk out of that old office. Now I can just walk out. Leave it for someone else to do." Bonnie forced a smile, unable to reply.

The Institute of Nuclear Physics was in the northern outskirts of Bergen, housed in a cluster of white wooden buildings. Knut had founded the engineering department. The main building, in fact the oldest, was a simple two-story structure situated on a hill, providing a spectacular view of the harbor when weather allowed.

Bonnie swung the car into the director's space and pulled her gray cloche down around her ears. They slowly walked toward the building, comfortable in each other's silence. A light rain was falling from the pale northern sky; a soft mist merged the horizon with the sea. Lights on either side of the etched glass doors reflected two stripes of cool yellow on the wet steps.

The custodian saw them at the door and left his sweeping to unlock. "Good morning, old man, and a good morning to you, Bonnie. Didn't expect you so early," he said affectionately, taking their umbrella and shaking the rain from it.

"Good morning yourself, you old goat," said Knut. The janitor laughed and his teeth rattled.

Bonnie withdrew an envelope from her satchel and handed it to Lief. "We're grateful for your help."

"My son, Ron, he's a fine captain."

Bonnie headed for her father's office. He was

already seated at his desk in a battered leather chair, shoulders screwed up around his ears, fingers clasped at the bridge of his nose. For a moment, she was afraid he was going to burst into tears, but laughter began shaking through him. "What's so funny?" she asked.

"Your experiments in the lab. They're ridiculous. I'd love to see the Germans' faces when they try to figure them out. In no time the Reich will either think we Norwegians are either the smartest or most stupid people on the face of the earth."

Ignoring his comments, she said, "Make sure you've got everything."

"Of course," he said gruffly. "Take care of your own business and stop hovering over me." He gave her an imperious glare and thrust the umbrella at her.

It was nearly 10:30 when she arrived back at the Institute. Mentally running down the list of supplies needed for the trip, she suddenly spun around, verifying what her subconscious had registered: a caduceus in the window of a car at the entrance.

She ran into the building and down the hall to his office. A stranger sat unsmiling in Knut's chair.

The Professor was lying on the time-marred leather sofa, a stack of journals pushed to one end. His secretary was kneeling by the couch, holding a wet cloth on his ashen forehead, grumbling half-heartedly about the mess on the floor. Road maps, journals and tins of old ski wax, the clutter of years, lay heaped on the floor.

"What's wrong?" Bonnie asked, trying to hide the palpable fear in her voice.

"He's had a heart seizure, but seems better now." The physician folded a stethoscope and placed it in his pocket. "He needs to slow down. Rest for a month or so and he should be all right."

She stood over her father and asked, "How are you?" Bonnie waited, trying to ignore the rasp of his breathing.

Watching her, the Doctor repeated, "Lots of rest. That arrhythmia could kill him. I've given him Quinidine, but we need time to adjust the dosage."

"Well," interrupted Knut in a weak voice, "it had better not take more than a day or two. I've got things to do." He paused, his heart felt as if it were going to jump out of his chest. I need room, space, he thought. Overworked. Too many memories. Old memories. "All of you," he weakly waved them away, "I need privacy. Leave me alone."

"Don't push yourself. I'm serious," said the physician.

"Later," Knut said hoarsely, closing his eyes and turning away.

Bonnie stood at the entrance doors struggling not to cry; she traced the raindrops on the glass. Olav's on his way. I know it. We can handle this. She turned and walked slowly down the hall and back into the office. Knut appeared to be asleep. She sat at his desk, knowing he was comfortable with her presence.

She had often seen him slip into a state of detachment. His mind was capable of wandering off through libraries, laboratories, solving problems, formulating theories, listening to a string quartet, or creating poetry. He dismissed the uniqueness of his concentrative powers, but once called his disappearances "an escape into greater reality." He obviously enjoyed the little diversions.

He stirred. She looked up at him. "Do you want anything?"

"I'm hungry."

"Chicken broth?"

"No, some caraway rye and blood sausage. And sour pickles."

"You're kidding."

"Hell, no. I need my strength." Shutting his eyes, he said, "I'm all right. I can rest in London."

Rjukan, Norway

The infirmary was on the first floor at the Vemork Plant. The threat of accidental injury was constant, considering the presence of potentially dangerous gases, chemicals, and high voltage generators. Though the infirmary was small, it was superbly equipped.

Major Kurt von Stein was the sole patient. His condition serious, consisting of seared and blistered legs, groin, and lower abdomen from the extreme cold of the liquid nitrogen. His penis and scrotum were joined, a bulbous, deep purple mass of flesh. His mind couldn't distinguish between cold and hot. Because of all the destruction and pain, in conjunction with the intravenous morphine, he was experiencing a twilight mental status. Burning, intense burning.

Von Stein had been severely burned another time, that time by the Italian sun. He was sixteen years old.

German guests filled Baron von Stein's Renaissance villa above Florence in the hills of Fiesole. Loving the heat, they persistently ignored the sweltering afternoons of July and August when the heat-filled haze of the Tuscan hills forced the local population indoors behind shuttered windows. Occasionally, when young von Stein was invited to join his father and the guests, the Baron would effusively compliment his son's mathematical genius. He would also just as easily shout without provocation, belittling him: "You can't compete with the other boys. You're like your mother, anemic, wandering around at night." These outbursts always seemed to be in front of guests, usually late in the day after hours of drinking.

He tried to ignore his father, excusing the unpredictable tirades, but they left him devastated. He too had heard the village gossip and secretly spent hours in the chapel sitting on the cool marble floor, gently rubbing his hand across his mother's name chiseled in the top of the crypt. Did father murder you? How much of you does he see in me?

Neither the Baron, nor anyone else, could guess the state of apprehension smoldering in young von Stein. He considered his father to be ruthless, a well-bred drunk, a connoisseur of dissipation, and he detested his every weakness. He vowed to endure the sloth until he himself would control the von Stein fortune.

His favorite time of day had always been the long evenings when he could avoid the devastating sun and heat. He had coveted his late-night swim in the enormous pool, surrounded by the quiet grounds of the estate. Floating in the cool water, a rare sense of well-being settled over him. He was suspended in time, surrounded by vaulted porticoes and colonnaded arches aligned in delicate precision. As he walked through the courtyards in the moonlight, he felt only contempt for German architecture: what was there to enjoy in Berlin? Compared to Florence, Berlin seemed functional, brutally masculine.

Brutal. The word rang in von Stein's seared mind. Grudgingly, he gave in, his brain walling off the present wave of nauseating pain and the calamitous physical destruction, turning the years backward, focussing on one particular experience. A terrible, physical price had been then paid as well, but he had learned much about himself.

The white buildings shimmered in the sun, the red tile roofs baked in the heat. A Sunday afternoon in August. The usual mix of people lounged around the pool: among them Signore Enrico Polo, a shrewd banker who shared the Baron's appetite for sports: "The only time I'm truly alive is when I'm competing," Polo had often reminded his host. That afternoon he had brought his son, Danieli, a tall, darkly handsome specimen of the Roman male. Danieli, in a tight black bathing suit, was thoroughly enjoying the pool.

"Enrico," Baron von Stein said, "Your son's quite a swimmer, a natural."

"The best," Polo said, watching his son. "Soon he'll take over my bank, but before then he'll win many contests and make many conquests." Polo smiled at the thought. "But Baron, you must be proud of Kurt...very intelligent, eh?" He tapped von Stein on the arm.

The Baron jerked his arm out of range, reacting as though burned, startling Polo by the abrupt, almost menacing reaction. Slowly he replied, "Kurt's a genius. However, you've never had the privilege of watching him swim, my dear friend. He's the most powerful swimmer in Italy."

"Is that so?" He took a sip of wine. "How about having the boys do a little race? Perhaps a little side bet, Baron?"

"Name it!" Polo fell silent. The Baron continued with an amused smirk. "It seems you can't, or won't come up with a proper wager, Enrico, so how about the winner selecting a rifle from the loser's collection?"

"Perfect." Polo slapped his hand on the table.

The Baron stood, straightening the crease of his white flannels and buttoned his navy blazer. Looking around the terrace for his housekeeper, he brushed off the already immaculate monogram on his breast pocket, the von Stein family crest. With a snap of his fingers, he motioned for Maria Louisa.

"Do you wish lunch served now, Signore?" The housekeeper folded her hands across the white apron covering her ample waist.

"No. Go find Kurt. Send him out here."

She scurried across the terrace, up the steps and into the villa, going directly to the young von Stein's private suite. Kurt was looking down through the louvers at the pool, feeling utter disgust as he took in the considerable quantity of flesh baking in the sun. Guests were lounging near the shallow end, drinking and laughing raucously. He couldn't help thinking of how the water would smell by evening, when he would swim. He could see few guests were in any real physical shape and he suspected even fewer could form a single intelligent thought.

"Your father wants you at the pool right away," interrupted Maria.

"What does he want? He knows I hate his drunken friends."

"I don't know, Signore Kurt."

"And that Danieli. I've been watching him strut around. He swims great, but I'll bet in a marathon he'd have to use his prick for an oar."

"Don't talk that way, I'll have to go to confession twice today."

Putting on a wide-brimmed straw hat, he said, "Your saying, 'Costa quella che costa,' usually means more than just money, Maria." She nodded and handed his dark glasses to him.

He left the suite after her and started down the circular staircase, running his hand along the marble banister, absorbing the coolness of the stone. Despite his irritation, he couldn't resist winking at his favorite pair of cherubs gazing down at him from the fresco covering the cathedral-like cupola. He wondered if anyone else ever noticed the two cupids fondling each other.

Villa San Domenico had been in his family for three generations. His grandmother, affectionately known as Lilli, had spent decades restoring it. From its southern portico, it overlooked the villa's chapel. The architect had positioned the porticoes and windows to take advantage of the sunlight and cooling winds, and had used graceful, arched loggias to connect the main dwelling with the outbuildings that housed the hired help, livestock, and granaries. Lilli wisely had made large scale investments, creating a prosperous farm, orchard and vineyard, assuring a healthy bank account for her son. Thus Baron von Stein could exude the easy confidence of one whose power was a simple matter of inheritance.

Kurt crossed the reception hall and exited through the ten-foot-high, glass-paneled doors and stepped out from under the portico into the brilliant sun. His eyes constricted painfully as he looked into the brightness. He went straight down the terraced garden steps to the pool.

"Finally," said Baron von Stein, gesturing expansively, "Signore Polo and I have a slight disagreement and we've decided that the solution to our problem is a little race in the pool. Shouldn't take long at all. Here, join us."

Even though they were sitting under an umbrella, Kurt was increasingly uncomfortable as his sensitive skin absorbed the heat. He shaded his eyes with his hand and watched his father empty another glass of wine.

"Enrico here feels Danieli is the best swimmer in all of Italy. I told him he hasn't seen anything until he sees you. I've bet you can outlast him."

"Wait," interrupted Polo, "I prefer a sprint."

"Come now, Polo. For the best in Italy? What better way to test them than by all-out endurance? Are you afraid Danieli will give up...too much pasta? Or is it losing that new shotgun, that Purdey 12 bore you just picked up in London?"

"Hell, no. Okay, endurance it is...at matched pace. The last man to swim a full lap wins. Danieli can swim all day, so let's get started."

"You're on, but you'd better make plans to spend the night. Go change, Kurt. Let's show these people just what we von Steins are made of." The Baron stood and shouted to his guests, "Hey, the rest of you fine Italians, how about reaching into your cassepanches—those deep coffers you brag about. A race is on! Let's have some bets."

Back in the cool, semidarkness of his room, Kurt's eyes still flashed from the scintillating light. He grimaced as he thought how much he hated him—Father, with his friends, already drunk and sweating like pigs. They'll get their laughs, but I'll be in agony for days. To hell with it, I'll give them a real show.

He pulled on a simple black maillot, snug, like a competitive swimmer's. He caught a glimpse of himself in the mirror. Though his skin was abnormally pale, it covered a well-proportioned, taut, hard-muscled physique, which showed a certain disciplined agility as he walked from the dressing room. He put on a cap and a terry cloth robe with the von Stein crest, the red initials woven in intricate stitches around the stylized black eagles of the German State.

He stepped out of the villa, slammed the glass doors and paused to put on his dark glasses. Looking toward the pool, he saw Danieli standing halfway out on the diving board. He watched him somersault and straighten out cleanly into the water.

Kurt smiled thinly. How ironic life seemed to him, even at the age of sixteen. He was certain he could outswim the cocky Italian, but he also knew the sun would fry his skin. He winced, picturing his body, cracked and blackened, turning slowly on a spit. So much for the predicament. He intended no one to know the price he was about to pay. He had learned early in life that endurance was a great power against any adversary. His pallor, combined with the dark glasses, gave the illusion of weakness. The glasses, however, served to give him a sense of invisibility—an invisibility that protected him from the jeers of his contemporaries.

Kurt focused on the statuary at the end of the pool, unaware of the guests crowding around. Danieli splashed water on his shoulders.

"Ready?" asked the Baron. "Remember, swim at the same pace, but swim until you drop. Go!"

The race was on.

Kurt immediately realized the Italian was setting a quick pace. Careful, careful, he cautioned himself.

Each had powerful arms and used them in long, overhead strokes—their legs kicking rhythmically, propelling them through the water—but while Danieli executed each turn with lyrical precision, Kurt attacked each new lap with an explosive kick off the wall.

The first thirty minutes were uneventful with both swimmers easily maintaining stride. The onlookers, money in hand, stood at the pool's edge cheering them on yet waiting for a hint of fatigue. Kurt's white skin stood out starkly against the azure water; but Danieli, with his deep tan, was a mere shadow, small silver splashes glittering around him. Forty minutes passed: it was a standoff. Neither swimmer showed signs of tiring. The guests, now bored and lulled by the heat, wandered from the pool's edge to the shade of the umbrellas, calling to the servants for fresh bottles of wine.

The blistering Italian sun was directly overhead. Kurt ignored the pins-and-needles sensation beginning on his shoulders and upper back. He knew he was burning.

The race went on.

An hour and ten minutes. Kurt's brain refused to heed the screaming fatigue of his muscles, but was consumed by the acute pulling and burning of the skin on his shoulders and back, and now the back of his legs. The scorched skin over the calves felt like it was going to split. The strain and fatigue were causing nausea. All he wanted was to get away, to lie down naked in a snowbank, sucking on mouthfuls of snow and ice. On the verge of giving up, he fought to remain conscious. Suddenly he became aware of cheering.

"Kurt, stop! You can stop! Danieli quit four laps ago," the Baron shouted at him. "Damn good race. Damn good," he added, ignoring Danieli's choked efforts to breathe. The young Italian vomited uncontrollably and sat wearily in the grass, gasping for air. Polo gently rubbed his son's shoulders with a towel.

Kurt slowly began to lift himself out of the pool. The Baron crouched down and grabbed his son by the shoulders. Kurt screamed involuntarily. The sudden grab felt as though his skin and muscles were separating from the bones. Waiting until the intense pain subsided, Kurt slowly pulled himself onto the deck, this time spitting at his father, "I'll get out by myself." He waved away the towel Maria offered and, with incredible self-control, walked toward the villa. Each step was agony. The bottoms of his feet were seared and swelling. Every inch of his skin emanated a red sheen.

By late evening the full effects of the sun were obvious. Parts of his body were covered with myriads of tiny water blisters arising from violatious skin. His shoulders, neck, and the backs of his legs had large, some giant, water blisters. His right calf was a single huge blister, purple-gray, tense and shiny. His eyes were bloodshot, the eyelids red, pillow-like puffs. He could barely see. He felt he looked like some rare form of aquatic life which resides deep in the ocean, its body blending with gyrated surfaces of brain coral.

He grimaced when he shifted position on the lounge. "You didn't have any choice," said Maria, handing him a cold compress. "I remember your mother suffered terribly. Once, just because she refused to go sailing..." Her voice trailed off. "But her sight was still okay when she..." She sighed sadly and looked up at the star-filled sky.

He knew in his mother the syndrome was complete. The doctors in Berlin had explained it all too graphically. At least his mind was untouched. The sun was his great enemy. Too much direct exposure and he would be blinded. And the chance of cancer...

"Kurt, let's go inside and try to eat something."

"I don't think I can keep anything down." He swung his legs off the lounge and rose slowly to his full height. The loose cotton slacks clung to the seeping sores on his calves.

Maria resisted the urge to help, knowing she dare not touch him. Just then the bell at the entrance rang, breaking the silence. They watched from the darkened reception hall as the Baron accepted a package, then rudely slammed the door. He stood in the foyer for several moments, looking at the large manila envelope; then, obviously preoccupied, turned and walked slowly back into the library, closing the door behind him.

Major von Stein jerked awake. Italy, Florence, vanished from his thoughts. The white walls and lights of the infirmary forced him to consciousness. He tried to sit up but the searing pain in his groin immediately returned. The tugging movement jerked the intravenous needle in his vein. He tested the resistance, not fully understanding where he was or why. Suddenly he felt the need to scream and the one word that came roaring into his conscious was BRECKKAN!

Telemark, Norway

Breckkan downshifted the motorcycle as he approached the fork to Oslo. With no premeditation, he suddenly turned away and headed west. Increasing speed, he pulled the hood of the coat over his head.

The snow had stopped; the thrust of the storm lay behind him. The mountain summits of Telemark were obscured by the thick cloud cover. He passed Lake Møstvatn along the southern shore near the dam. Across the lake lay the wild and forbidding Hardanger plateau, the largest and loneliest mountain area in northern Europe.

The road soon entered the forest; black walls of pine edged the snow-covered track. A slow moving truck labored down the center of the road toward him. Veering to miss it, he drove onto the ice-encrusted shoulder and nearly lost control. It's going to be a very long drive, he thought to himself, swerving back onto the narrow track.

Time ground by, and early evening descended. The northern sky darkened; clouds swirled lower, enclosing the man and his motorcycle. He switched on the head lamp and leaned forward to chip the ice off with his nearly frozen fingers. He was alone, a muffled shape bent into the frigid wind, surrounded by the high-pitched roar of the motor. I've got to stop. I need gas, food and rest.

Rjukan, Norway

The antiseptic calm of the Vemork infirmary was interrupted as the entrance doors burst open. Three officers entered, their black uniforms emblazoned with Waffen SS insignias.

"Where's the Major?" the Senior Officer demanded.

"Through those doors, room on the right," answered the orderly, pointing.

"Wait a minute," called the infirmary physician from the chart room. "What do you want with him? He's already been questioned."

"What I want, Doctor, is none of your business," snapped the Captain.

"Captain," began the doctor, assuming a dictatorial tone inherent in many physicians, "the Major isn't going anywhere. He's receiving intravenous fluids and morphine for the pain. The burns have caused severe swelling of his genitals— can't even relieve his bladder without a catheter. There will be permanent scarring. Let him rest, for now. He will have a great many adjustments to make in his life."

"Thank you for your medical report, Doctor," said the SS Officer as he swept into the white-tiled hall and turned into von Stein's room.

The bed was empty.

"Where is he?" shouted the Captain.

"Check the closet," said the SS Captain.

"Gone. Boots, everything."

Pointing to the smashed drug cabinet, the Lieutenant said, "Look!"

"What's missing?" demanded the Captain.

"Morphine. Bandages. Needles."

"Your security is marvelous, Doctor," said the Captain.

"I can't believe he's gone. Too sick, too badly burned," muttered the physician, staring at the empty bed.

Turning to his Lieutenant, the SS Captain said, "Notify Reichsfuhrer Himmler that von Stein has broken protocol. He'll want to notify Canaris about his agent immediately."

Telemark, Norway

He stopped the motorcycle at the top of a hill above a small village. He could make out a dozen or so small wooden buildings clustered together. Pushing off, he gunned the motor and the cycle crunched forward. In the beam of the motorcycle lamp, he spotted the sign of a small inn. Two front windows were lit. He stopped by a stand of birches behind the building and pushed the bike into the trees.

Shuddering from the cold, he clasped his shoulders with his arms and exhaled loudly through his lips. His breath crystallized in the night air. I must look like hell, he realized. He reached down, scooped up a handful of snow and rubbed it on his face, wincing from the pain.

He stepped onto the wooden porch and tried the door. It was locked. Through the window, he saw a small woman seated behind the simple reception desk. He tapped on the pane to attract her attention. She peered out at him. Breckkan pushed back the hood of his coat and stepped back into the full porch light, waiting in the cold.

He held out his hands and mouthed the words, "I need a room." The door opened. The woman coolly appraised him. "I'm sorry. It's late, but I've had an accident. The storm...the roads were icy. I need a room to rest and clean up."

"Are you badly hurt? Your face..."

"It just looks bad, but it's really just a scratch." His voice seemed to reverberate inside his head.

"Come in. I've banked the fire, but I guess I can stoke it up." She stirred the fire, pushing the logs against each other, starting the flames.

He stood dumbly for a moment, then remembered to remove his coat. He sat down in the worn, overstuffed chair near the fire.

"Are you hungry? I can get you something. Nothing fancy."

"Thanks." He rubbed his hands vigorously, blowing on them to regain feeling. The leather laces of his boots were stiff. He tried to untie the frozen knots. Chips of ice fell from his clothing onto the wooden floor and slowly melted.

He looked up to see the woman standing beside him, holding a wooden tray covered with an embroidered towel. He gulped the hot venison stew, scooping up the last bit with a chunk of bread, then realized she was still standing next to him.

"Your face. The bandage is soaked through. This bandage is all I have. Hold still." Breckkan quietly accepted her help. "I have brandy. It'll quiet the pain."

He leaned back, staring into the fire, and when he next looked up, a decanter of brandy and a glass were on the table to his side. He poured a full glass and drank. As the tension eased in his body, he was struck by the dead weight of his exhaustion.

From the doorway, she said, "Your room is at the end of the hall. The door is unlocked."

He groped in his pocket to pay her. When he turned, he caught a glimpse of the back of her slight figure and heard the tread of her footsteps on the stairs.

He bolted awake, blinking in the pitch blackness. Where am I, he wondered, completely disoriented. Sitting up, he fought to get his bearings. Heavy drapes blocked out the first tinges of the frozen dawn.

He stood up too quickly and immediately experienced vertigo. His face throbbed. Images of the Vemork Plant flooded his mind. Then he remembered the pale, watery eyes of the innkeeper. Touching his bandage cautiously, his hands felt puffy, as though wrapped in velvet. With the headache came a sick flood of apprehension. He stiffened and cocked his head like a curious dog. The sounds were wheels crunching in the ice, a car motor idling. Feeling his way toward the window, he searched for the separation in the drapes, pulled them back and stood in the shadows. The engine switched off.

Two figures stood silhouetted against the glow of the porch light. He could barely see the outline of another figure at the wheel of the car. His attention returned to the men on the porch, drawn to the bulk of their overcoats. Greatcoats...black greatcoats. With a rush of adrenaline his mind was fully alert. Dear God, I don't have any more strength.

He moved cautiously to the door and cracked it open. Voices came from the reception desk down the hall. My God, they're all speaking German, he realized. He heard the woman reply in German. Painfully slipping on the brown overcoat, he checked his jacket pockets for the data books. He bent to tighten the laces on his boots; blood pounded in his head. In the shaft of light from the hall, he could see a sink in the corner of his room and, beside it, a stack of towels. He stuffed one in his coat and moved down the hall, away from the voices, now a mingle of German accents.

He twisted the handle on the back door; it was

locked. He took the towel from his coat, folded it once, and draped it over the handle. Kicking the door open, the towel muffled the sound of his boot heel. He caught the door in a rush, stopping it from striking the wall, stuffed the towel back into his coat, and quietly closed the door behind him.

In a shed behind the hotel, he found a jumble of woodworking tools. Something, anything for a weapon, he thought. He snatched an awl, blunt from use but still deadly, and slipped it into his pocket. Checking the inn again, all seemed quiet. In a crouch, he ran toward the thicket, the only sound his own boots crunching through the ice-glazed snow.

Pushing the motorcycle to the side of the inn, he leaned it against the wall and cautiously looked around the corner at the car. The driver was gone.

Breckkan moved in a crawl toward the car. He glanced in the rear window and saw two steel helmets. Cautiously opening the door, he grabbed a helmet and then closed the door with a soft click. He moved to the rear of the car and crawled under headfirst, squirming under the caked snow and frozen mud on the steel frame.

The gas tank of the old Mercedes was enormous. Taking the awl from his pocket, he braced it against the tank and, with his fist, hammered the tool repeatedly. Working furiously, he finally perforated the metal wall of the tank. Gasoline sprayed onto the snow and his face. He rolled to the side and shoved the helmet under the tank. Jerking out the awl, the helmet filled quickly.

He topped off both the main and auxiliary tanks on his motorcycle with the gasoline in the helmet. Gritting his teeth from the pain, he wiped the gasoline from his face and for a second watched the gasoline pool under the car and stream onto the edge of the icy road.

She can't keep them occupied much longer, he thought. He realized he didn't know the inn-keeper's name.

Mile after mile of winding, forest-lined road lay behind him. He braked to a stop as the road crested at the top of a steep hill. Below him lay a spec-tacular glacial mountain lake. In the failing after-noon light, the low-hanging clouds against the tow-ering cliffs reminded him of a Chinese watercolor. Voss can't be too far now, he thought, checking his watch. Eighty-five miles to Bergen. He might just make the connection. Keep moving!

He roared into a tunnel of deep emerald-green, curving sharply to the left, his vision confined to the lonely, ice-rutted road. His right leg began to cramp and he shifted his weight in an effort to relieve the pain. The motorcycle slid out of con-trol, skidding across the ruts, and sent him sprawl-ing on the ice. The bike landed in a snow bank, the wheels spinning in the air; the motor choked to a stop; the gas line flooded. Silence, broken only by the wind in the pines, engulfed him.

He stiffly rose to his knees, flexed his arms and arched his back. "Nothing broken," he said aloud, brushing ice crystals from the dirty brown coat. Limping to the dead motorcycle, his ears caught the sound of a train whistle coming from deep in the forest. He grabbed for the cycle and, after sev-eral vicious kicks, brought the motor to life. Move!

He threaded the bike back into the ruts and gunned the motor. Five minutes. He broke into a clearing. Railroad tracks. A bridge. A gorge. The road turned sharply at a right angle. A thicket of pine stood like sentinels in the middle of the open-ing, guarding the bridge. With infinite clarity, the site registered in his mind. He increased speed.

Suddenly, the train burst from the forest. Recognizing his inexorable choice, he opened the throttle completely and pushed the machine beyond tolerance. The violent torque of the engine convulsed through his body.

He knew his only chance was to jump to the train at the edge of the pines just before the bridge. The road abruptly began a hairpin turn to the left, snaking its way down into the gorge. At this speed, he could never make the turn. He skidded to the edge of the road bordering the tracks parallel with the train. Frosted birch branches whipped and sliced at his face. With the motorcycle engine whining at full throttle, the train lumbering past, the bridge racing toward him, he twisted the cycle straight at the train and sprang from the bike, clawing and grabbing for the ladder on the last car.

His hands froze to the raw steel, his overcoat and body fluttering behind him like laundry on a line. He fought to catch a rung with his feet. The rhythmic reverberation of the train changed when it sped onto the bridge. Whoops of air erupted between the steel struts, pounding his ears. Only the sound of the dying motorcycle, screaming toward the heart of the gorge, broke through the roar of the violent wind.

The train was in a downward run, gathering speed as it emerged from the far side of the bridge. The tracks clung to the precipitous granite escarpment above the sheer drop to the river. He fought to get his footing, his icy boots slipping and finally gripping the ladder. As he loosened his grasp on the steel rungs, skin tore from his hands, left behind on the frigid steel. The pain was excruciating. He groaned, fighting the urge to let go, to fall into the white void.

Using his forearms, he inched his way up the

ladder onto the curved roof of the car and then wormed his way toward the exhaust vent. He wedged his body against the vent and drew his knees up against his chest.

He pulled the hood of his coat around his head and closed his eyes, his chest heaving, struggling for air. His wildly pounding heart gradually slowed and the tension left his limbs. He suddenly started to laugh uncontrollably. He could feel sweat running from his armpits down the sides of his body, pooling at the small of his back. How could he sweat when he was so damned cold? He opened his eyes and squinted into the wind. Blasts of dry snow whirled up from the tracks. Complete darkness enveloped him as the train whipped into a tunnel.

CHAPTER 8

April 6, 1940

Bergen

The wharf, seven in the evening. Number 13 on the Bryggen.

The Tracteursted Tavern was sandwiched between three-story, gabled buildings, each a different color. The second and third floors were covered with look-alike windows, each seeming somehow sad in the freezing rain.

Knut and Bonnie turned off the ancient wharf into a tall archway. They stepped through a wooden gate, the countless coats of black paint glistening in the rain. Heading down the narrow wood-planked alley that led to the tavern and cook house, they dropped their bags on a pile of other sailing gear and ducked into the smoke-filled room.

She motioned toward a table to the right of the door and pulled out a heavy wooden chair for her father. "Let me help you with your coat."

"The nap was a good idea, Bonnie." Even in the familiar surrounding, his eyes still seemed distant, distracted.

She tossed their wet slickers on a chair. "I'm worried. He's late."

"He'll make it. Look at the bar," Knut said, "at the end." She spotted the German sailors immediately. "No wonder Larsen insisted we get out tonight. Ah, just what we need." A waiter placed a wooden bowl of bread and a crock of butter on their table. "Bonnie, I think I'll just have a lager, and you?"

"Two Hansas, please." The white-aproned waiter placed two coasters in front of them and wormed his way back through the crowd to the bar. "What did you say about Larsen?"

"Larsen mentioned several sightings of German warships in the fishing lanes. Warships. There's even a story going around the docks about some German sailors rescued from a sinking steamer just down the coast. When they were questioned, they said they were on their way here to protect us from the British."

"The Germans are very good at propaganda," said a quiet voice. A tall, broad-shouldered man offered his hand to the Professor.

"Ron, we didn't see you come in," Bonnie said. "I've been watching for you."

"I came in through the cook house." He shook the water off his worn yellow oilskin. "Just brought a load of fresh catch. Fishing's good considering this nasty weather."

Ron Larsen sat quietly while the waiter served glasses of beer, then leaned forward, his black turtleneck sweater disappearing into his beard, and said, "To my cargo." Over his beer glass, he watched Bonnie nervously twist her wedding band. "Did you know I have a new baby boy?"

"Yes, your father has showered us with pictures." Knut lowered his voice. "Is everything ready?"

"Lots of activity in the harbor. The kind of precautions you'd usually see before a storm. But there's no storm expected. The rain should clear by morning. Tomorrow there'll be a full moon." He glanced across the room at the Germans.

"How much longer can we wait for Olav?" Bonnie asked.

Larsen looked straight at her. "It's still early. I've just a few more things to do. Are you ready?"

"Yes, just some duffels and a small suitcase. They're out by the gate."

"Good. They're safe there. I'll be back in an hour." Larsen hesitated, never taking his eyes off

Bonnie. "I don't think we can wait much past 8:30." He pushed back his empty glass and reached for his slicker. "Jacobsen owes me for today's catch. I thought I'd stop down at the cold table and order up something for the larder. I'll have them pack it up and bring it to you." He patted Bonnie on the shoulder. "He'll make it."

After Larsen walked away, Knut asked, "What do you think of him?"

Bonnie fixed her eyes on a large marine painting hanging to the right of her father. A pretty sloop flying a Norwegian flag was cutting through the dark water. "He's such a quiet man— living for so long on the sea. Without even seeing his boat, I trust him."

Knut ran a thin, long finger along the lip of his beer glass. "Good. I think Breckkan will like him, too."

Fishermen packed the bar and deep voices resonated under the low beamed ceiling. Larsen stood next to a group of uniformed German sailors, talking with Ake Jacobsen. Jacobsen was animatedly piling a selection of cheese, meats, and dark bread for him. Ake tossed a pickled egg at Larsen. Just as Ron reached up to catch it, a German sailor reached out and snatched the egg. He tossed it to a comrade, who promptly swallowed it.

Jacobsen made a guttural comment and the German laughed. In the growing silence at the bar, the laugh seemed all too loud. Jacobsen appeared to grumble again. The German raised a clenched fist. Larsen stood very still.

"That Kraut's flirting with trouble," muttered Knut.

Larsen leaned toward the bar and helped himself to another egg, tossed it to the sailor, then turned and went through the swinging doors to the kitchen. The air, smelling of beer, smoke and resentment, slowly cleared and the murmur of voices began again.

Bonnie tapped her watch. "It's five past eight."

Knut patted her hand calmly. "He's here."

She looked toward the door and saw a man in a bulky, grimy overcoat. The bandage on his face was tinged at the edges with red. The hands that hung at his side were bluish-pink, partially clenched. His hair was matted, his wind-burned face covered with stubble.

"What happened to you!" said Bonnie.

"I need a drink." He put one arm around her and, with the other, motioned to the bartender. She kissed him, then touched the bandage. He pulled off his coat and gingerly slid into a chair.

"My God, Breckkan, you look awful!" said Knut.

"I'm all right." The color was returning to his face. A flush of red set high on his cheekbones. "Is everything ready?"

"Yes." Knut pushed forward in his chair. "Did you get what you went for?"

"For a price," said Breckkan, taking a bite of the fish the bartender had slid before him. He ate voraciously. Wiping his lips with his napkin, he said, "The Germans were waiting." He drained his beer. "Waiting expressly for me. In my lab. In my office."

"What happened to your face?" Bonnie insisted.

"A disagreement. They got rough. I'm already feeling better," he said, stretching and rubbing his neck. "I'm here and I got what counts." The warmth of the room was almost too comfortable. He focussed on the old professor and asked, "How are you? A bit pale yourself."

"A little chest pain, but I'm okay now."

Breckkan finished his glass of beer just as Larsen put a hand on his shoulder. "What happened to you, Dr. Breckkan?"

"You must be Larsen."

"Right." He squatted down beside Breckkan. "I've just heard there's Gestapo in town. I think we should be on our way."

Bundled against the sharp cold, they gathered their bags in the shadow of the archway. Larsen and Breckkan took the duffels and Bonnie picked up the small suitcase. "That's ours, too?" asked Breckkan.

"I'll carry it."

Stepping out onto the wet cobblestones of the Bryggen, they were immediately struck by the freezing rain. Larsen ducked his head and motioned for them to follow. Passing a row of darkened warehouses, they neared the end of the wharf and walked out onto the wooden pier.

Sleet mixed with rain poured in off the bay, swirling in sheets against the steep tile roofs, bouncing back with resilience and swirling up again in the wind with fresh strength. Each window facing the narrow harbor, warm with light, captured the swirl and threw the storm back at them. Each burst seemed wetter and colder. Hidden corners and protected doorways collected the frozen ice crystals as the western wind pounded the waterfront.

The mean storm smelled clean, a mixture of spring and winter. Later, Breckkan would barely remember it; Bonnie would only recall the cold wind.

"Tomorrow," said Larsen, helping the Professor on board, "after the storm, a full moon, clear skies, a promise." He could see his breath. A flurry of snow mixed with ice hit the pilothouse windows and raced down like strands of liquid silver.

The *ANNA* sat moored in the indigo shadows. She was a forty-five foot diesel fishing trawler with two masts. The forward mast carried a jib and four-sided staysail. The aft mast supported the four-sided mainsail. Two-thirds of the way aft was the narrow pilothouse, a wooden structure windowed on all sides, the single bulb casting a dim yellow light. A thin sheet of ice glazed the deck; frozen icicles had formed on the ropes and stanchions. Ice and debris swirled in the frigid water.

Tugging down his knit stocking cap and turning up the collar of his slicker, Larsen held out both arms. "Bonnie, you're next. Step on and then transfer your weight to the foot on the boat, not the dock." Breckkan boarded simultaneously, holding her elbow.

"Until we're out of the harbor, I think it's best we keep out of sight."

Trying to ignore the pain in his hands, Breckkan barely heard Larsen. The duffel straps had sliced into his raw palms, exposing tendon. I can't tell her now, he thought as he shoved his hands deep into his pockets, shivering in the drizzle.

"Professor, watch the ice." Knut shuffled in small, quick steps to the port side. "It won't be for long." He kicked the lock on the latch, breaking the ice away, opened the gearbox, and helped him into the stale recess.

The Professor hunched down, his shallow breath frosted in the darkness. Larsen handed him a blanket. "Are you all right?"

"Never thought I'd sail out of this harbor like a coward." His slim hands were shaking, but his eyes were bright. He propped his head awkwardly against the blanket. Ron closed the hatch softly, leaving the old man in the coffin-sized locker. Streaks of light from the pier filtered through cracks in the wooden hatch.

Breckkan helped Bonnie settle into the fore locker. She murmured to him, "Watch him. The cold..."

Larsen heard her and said softly, "Don't worry. Leif told me. I'll take care of him. We'll be out of here right away." He motioned toward the locker on the dock side near the pilothouse. "That's yours, Breckkan. I've got to go up to the harbormaster's office to sign us out. You've sailed before?"

Breckkan looked down at Bonnie. Her expression said it all. "Since I was a boy," he answered.

"Like all good Norwegians. The ANNA's creaky, but a good boat. You'd better get out of that wet coat." Larsen reached into the pilothouse and tossed a slicker to him. Breckkan winced as he caught it. "You'd better take care of those hands." He pulled out a first-aid kit. "Take care of your face, too. There's plenty of antiseptic and carbolized vaseline. Fresh dressings, too. We'll leave as soon as I get back." He jumped to the pier and disappeared into the drizzle.

Breckkan stepped into the pilothouse, took off his wet overcoat, then gingerly peeled the souring dressing from his face.

The pinkish-brown antiseptic rinse burned as he poured it on his cheek and let it drip from his chin. He winced, gritted his teeth, and poured the solution onto each hand, watching the yellow foam, while resisting the urge to scream. Removing the lid from the thick-walled glass jar of bacteriostatic ointment, he gingerly rubbed it on his face and hands. After wrapping both hands, he pulled on the slicker and stepped into the shadows on deck.

Suddenly, he heard shouts to his right. Straining to see through the sleet, he could make out half-a-dozen shadows under the warehouse lights. What the hell's happening now, he wondered. Damn it, where's Larsen!

A light flashed across the boat, momentarily silhouetting him. He instinctively crouched and held his breath. An automobile moved slowly past the ANNA and parked in the shadows midway down the wharf.

"Olav," called Bonnie, hunched behind the hatch door.

"Quiet." Breckkan watched the dock, wondering if it was the same car at the mountain inn. "I'm going ashore."

Suddenly aware of the whiteness of his bandages, he grabbed a stocking cap and gloves from the wheelhouse, pulled them on, and turned up the collar of his coat. He jumped from the boat, watching his step on the ice-glazed pier.

He stopped behind a sand-filled barrel, a part of the antiquated system of fire fighting on the Bryggen. The dark-red barrels were distributed along the length of the waterfront. Hunched down, he listened to hostile voices echoing in the darkness. Cautiously, he moved from one barrel to another, approaching the angry group. He kept an eye on the parked car. He could see it was empty. It wasn't the black Mercedes. Paranoia, he thought, well-earned paranoia.

He glanced past the car at the figures ahead and involuntarily shuddered. Two Germans were arguing with Larsen. A crowd of fishermen were menacingly flinging insults at the Germans. He crouched down and looked back down the wharf. Cold and quiet.

Suddenly, the harassment turned violent. He watched the dark silhouette of the uniformed sailor reach into his coat and pull out a gun. A fisherman bolted at the German, sending him sprawling on the icy cobblestones. Breckkan heard the grunt of effort as the soldier fought to stand up.

The other sailor reached for his pistol, but was too late. A kick from Larsen sent him writhing on the street. Larsen kicked him again and the gun skidded across the ice. A warning shout from within the crowd pierced the cold and the men disappeared into the blackness.

Larsen ran for the boat. Breckkan started to call out but choked back his shout when he saw the crumpled figure of the sailor scramble for his revolver. Larsen slipped and blundered past Breckkan, the German now just behind him. With his shoulders hunched and his hands low, Breckkan sprang forward, knocking the sailor to the pavement. He grabbed the man from behind and smashed him against the car. With a gasp of air, the German fell to the gutter. He heard voices shouting orders in German. Breckkan didn't look back; only motion counted.

Holding his right hand to his chest, he ran after Larsen. Both hit the deck of the trawler simultaneously.

"I hope you broke the bastard's neck. Let's get the hell out of here," yelled Larsen, jumping into the pilothouse and pressing the starter. "Cast off. I'll go aft." The cold diesel engine coughed and died. He pressed the starter again. The boat shuddered, and the engine caught. He shoved the gears into reverse and ran to the rear of the boat. Breckkan smoothly unwound the figure eight of the tether and threw the rope to the dock. Looking up, he saw the German running full speed at them, his right arm held out. Light glinted from the Luger in his hand.

Bonnie stood up and screamed, "Olav!"

"Get down!" he shouted.

The trawler was inching back, freed from the pier. As Larsen ducked into the pilothouse, two crack-like explosions spit from the Luger. One bullet shattered the front window; glass shards exploded into the cabin. The other pinged off a steel door hinge. He spun and snapped off the light, leaving only the red sea lights burning in the blackness. "Breckkan!" he shouted.

"On my way." He ran in a crouch toward Larsen. Suddenly, he slipped on the icy deck and fell hard against the forward mast, smashing his right shoulder. He frantically looked for Bonnie. Another burst sounded to his left. Scrambling up, he ran cat-like, on hands and feet, toward Larsen. "A gun," he yelled.

"Just this." Larsen shoved a canvas bag across the floor. "It's our only chance to get away!"

Breckkan grabbed the bag and jerked it open. A flare gun and two flares. He felt the trawler chug backwards. In the darkness, his throbbing, wrapped hands fumbled with the gun. He slid one of the cartridges into the barrel, clicked it shut, and wiped the rain and ice from his eyelids. With only one thought, he stood and ran toward the bow.

Another shot rang out from the Luger. He dodged at precisely the moment the bullet struck the forward mast, spraying splinters on the deck. Totally alert, he took a wide stance and aimed the flare gun at the German and pulled the trigger. There was a click. Nothing.

The German ducked into the shadow of a warehouse doorway and raised his revolver. Breckkan dropped to the deck, jerked open the flare gun, popped out the dud and shoved in the remaining cartridge.

The ANNA was a full boat's length from the pier. Breckkan stood again and aimed at the German. There was a report from the Luger, the nine millimeter bullet passing cleanly through the folded sail next to Breckkan's shoulder. He deliberately pulled the trigger. There was a whoomp and jerk from the gun. The flare hissed in a wavering line of light arching toward the German. Upon impact, a white phosphorescent flash engulfed the man as it burned its way through his belly. The thrust of the detonation lifted the man off his feet, tossing him like a fiery ball into the wooden wall of the warehouse front.

Breckkan stood transfixed and watched the kaleidoscope of horrors with strange fascination. The images repeatedly flashed before him, searing a dark memory behind his eyes. He felt Bonnie's hand on his arm and turned toward her, like a statue on its axis, his eyes fixed. He could feel the heat from the fire charging his body.

Suddenly, an explosion reached his ears. The warehouse was without a face, the facade blown away as barrels of fish-oil ignited one after another. Larsen, a dark shape against the fiery reflections on the broken windows of the pilothouse, shifted from reverse to half-forward. The ANNA slowed to dead in the water as her propeller churned the icy sea and, gradually taking greater bites, she moved forward in a slow arc away from the flaming waterfront.

Men swarmed down the Bryggen, grabbing buckets of sand from the barrels, futilely trying to control the inferno. Red walls of fire arched into the sky. Breckkan stared at the destruction, unbelieving. My God, I've destroyed Bergen! The sounds of fire sirens mingled with the crackling of burning wood. Breckkan looked away. He dropped the flare gun and covered his face with his arms. Muffled explosions continued, one after another. "No! No, God. NO. Stop!"

Breckkan lowered his arms and looked back at the fiery scene, his eyes involuntarily focusing on a uniformed figure next to the parked car. The figure was crystal clear in the white fluorescent light. The intense heat of the flames had evaporated the dense fog. The man, on crutches, removed his hat and stooped to enter the car. The door slammed, and the car sped down the wharf.

His mind whirled. Only a flash. It was insane!

The trawler moved toward the center of the harbor and all four aboard stood looking at the blazing waterfront. Yellow-white tongues of flame were everywhere. Silver and yellow light rippled across the water toward the boat. Breckkan picked up the flare gun, turned, and walked slowly to the pilothouse. Wordlessly, he held out the gun to Larsen.

"You did the right thing," Larsen said softly.

PART II

CHAPTER 9

April 7 - 8, 1940

Berlin

Colonel Richter had been overwhelmed with the vastness of the meeting room, the new Empire architecture, the austere walls and floors of enormous blocks of marble. He had heard that Hitler insisted on volume calculations of his prestigious public buildings, cubic space rather than square footage. The Chancellery alone contained 1.5 million cubic yards. The immense scale provided a suitable backdrop for the dictator, he thought to himself. He could see how the design might easily move the remote leader into the realm of self-idolatry.

It was a stage setting for tyranny.

The group had been small but elite. In addition to Göring, the High Commander of the Armed Services, and the Head of the Navy had been present. Richter had represented Admiral Canaris' Abwehr. Included also was Hitler and his special staff: Army High Command XXI.

The only guest was a representative from the Kaiser-Wilhelm Institute. The staff scientist, Dr. Berkei, began with a progress report on nuclear research in England, predicting that they were neck and neck with Germany. Unable to control himself, Berkei had broken protocol and jumped to his feet without permission and hurriedly sketched equations on a blackboard. Looking directly at the Führer, he proposed that if 1.5 tons of uranium were mixed with a ton of heavy water to form a paste, then enclosed in a sphere of a 60 centimeter radius surrounded by a protective shield of water, it would stabilize at a constant temperature near 800° centigrade.

Hitler interrupted the spontaneous presentation and demanded specific conclusions. "First," Berkei stated, "it is a brand new source of energy, easily translated to millions of kilowatts."

"Go on," said Hitler.

"But, if you released all that energy at once," he gestured with both hands, his eyes flashing with excitement, "you would generate an explosion capable of vaporizing a giant city, say Paris, into the stratosphere."

Hitler sat with his stubby hands on the table, watching the scientist. Berkei returned to his seat, aware for the first time of his breach of protocol. Everyone watched the Fuhrer, unsure if he was displeased or disinterested.

"So, Dr. Berkei, you are proposing the indiscriminate total destruction of a city, particularly one filled with exquisite architecture?" Hitler's voice was shrill, high-pitched enough to cause the scientist to wince. "A new energy source, you say. Correct me if I am wrong, but didn't you use tons in your calculations?" He sneered at the scientist. "What would Army Ordinance say about that?"

"Ordinance is aware of the problem," said Colonel Richter, opening a folder. "The only commercial source of heavy water in the world is the Norwegian Hydroelectric Plant near Rjukan in southern Norway." Richter read on, left with the unenviable task of revealing the state of negotiations with Norsk-Hydro. "I. G. Farben is part owner of the Plant. In response to Ordinance demands, the German company tried to persuade the Norwegians to ship all their existing stock of heavy water to Germany." Richter tapped the file for emphasis. "A total of 185 kilograms as of February. Further, we ordered the average monthly output of 10 kilograms be increased by tenfold. The Norwegians flatly refused. All I. G. Farben employees on site were formally asked to leave. None have." Richter closed the file. It was poor consolation that his Abwehr agents in Scandinavia were impressively accurate. "Norway's negative response is, in fact, a threat, an affront to the Reich."

Maps of Norway replaced Dr. Berkei's equations. Army High Command took over the meeting. Their message was, "The Reich shall have the Plant." Secrecy and surprise were essential. For early spring, this year's weather would be excellent— no major storms. Merchant ships with combat troops hidden aboard were already on station outside target ports along the Norwegian coast. Hitler listened briefly, then ended all discussion with the order for immediate execution of the prepared invasion plan: The Weser Hour. *April 9, 04:15 Norwegian time.*

50° North, The North Sea

Breckkan opened his eyes. He heard the sound of creaking and understood. It had awakened him, or was it the body of Bonnie against him in the narrow bunk. She shifted. "Are you awake?" he asked.

"Yes. This rolling. I'm queasy."

"Lie on your stomach. Here, put the pillow underneath you. It'll help. Keeps you from tossing." She snuggled into the pillow. In moments she was asleep.

Breckkan lay awake, looking up at the wooden ceiling of the cramped cabin. A faint ambient light filtered in through the porthole. A gray dawn was breaking outside.

Heavy-eyed, he waited for his brain to wind down, to relax. His mind was exhausted, crowded with images of the inferno on the wharf. Innocent men burning. The screams. He felt a flood of emotion sweep over him, a mixture of regret and guilt. He closed his eyes, but the giant fireballs would not go away. He wrapped his arms around his sides and shivered. Guilt. The boat shuddered, rose and fell as a sudden swell opened and closed. His neck muscles tightened and he began yielding to a feeling of overwhelming sorrow. Whether he was blameless or not, his self-condemnation was total.

A heavy wave tossed the boat; this time his mind played a trick. Breckkan stared into the light cast by the kerosene lamp swinging from a chain hooked to an overhead beam. The softness of the light caused shadows to deepen, obscuring reality. The rare shiny bits of metal in the cabin created a puzzle of bright points, waiting to be joined. His mind could not tolerate more ugliness, pain, or inhumanity. There had been good times, hadn't there been? His brain, lulled by the motion of the sea, roamed back through the years to his father's death.

Breckkan shivered. He had never felt so cold, so empty. Then he felt the pulsating throb on his face and touched his cheek. He looked blankly at his bandaged hands. At no time in his life since the tragic drowning had he been so treacherously poised at the brink of another disaster. Did he possess such a secret that the world deserved his sacrifice? His wife? His family? Was it really their duty to risk their lives to protect it? He turned to Bonnie, pulling in her warmth. She rolled over to kiss him and saw the tears streaming down his cheeks.

Kissing him on the forehead, she said quietly, "Let's get you cleaned up."

"Good idea." He peeled off his clothes and stood shivering in his shorts. He looked thinner, more vulnerable. She held out a small basin of water and a towel. He braced himself against the bulkhead and lathered his right cheek. She started to hand him the razor, but noticed the tremor in his hand and took it back.

"I'll do it." The razor scraped his jaw-line, but he didn't wince. She worried; he was naturally quiet and thoughtful, but never withdrawn. Was it the deep shadow of depression? He blinked his eyes and seemed to read her mind.

"It was the nightmare, your father again, wasn't it?" He nodded absently. "Olav, we've gone over this a hundred times..."

"It's my problem. My phobia." The boat creaked and shuddered. He went on slowly and painfully. "I despise that word and I despise myself for being afraid— afraid of water."

She watched him tremble involuntarily and ached for him. "You have no reason to be ashamed. You've conquered that fear. My God, Olav, don't you remember the Regatta, in Copenhagen? You were incredible. You dove in when von Stein attacked me and I fell overboard. Bohr saw the whole thing. The undertow was vicious, but you..."

He laughed and said all too enthusiastically, "And I am your hero. Now throw me some fresh clothes." He put on a heavy sweater, then pulled on a pair of dark wool trousers. He offered a grunt of compliance as she taped a fresh bandage on his face and expertly wrapped his hands.

"They're healing nicely. Even your face looks better."

He cupped each bandaged hand under her breasts. "Haven't lost my sense of touch at least."

The sky was overcast and a cold wind was coming from the northwest. Choppy waves rose on the low ground swell. Visibility was good. "A long night for you. Sorry I couldn't help," said Breckkan, joining Larsen in the pilothouse. Bonnie and her father sat on the forward deck, both lost in thought, looking aimlessly out to sea.

"No problem, I'm used to it. Sometimes I'm at the helm eighteen hours straight." Larsen took one hand off the wheel and ran it through his salt and pepper hair and squinted into the light. "The radio's been busy. Traffic in the area."

"What've you heard?"

"Only numbers. I'm guessing they're speed or distance. Or code numbers for bearings."

"How far are we from Lerwick?"

Larsen pointed to the chart in front of him. "About 90 nautical miles. Want to take her for awhile?"

Breckkan nodded and took the wheel. They fell into a companionable silence. He watched the Professor walk unsteadily along the deck past the pilothouse and head below. Bonnie stood at the rail, her back to Olav, her figure silhouetted against the white sky as the prow of the boat lifted in the swells of the sea.

"You married, Captain?" Breckkan asked.

"Yes, my wife and son live in Telavaag, just south of Bergen. She was lonesome when we lived in Bergen," he said thoughtfully, "so now we live with her family. My father checks on her while I'm away."

"Leif and Knut are quite a pair. They hiss and spit at each other like two tomcats."

"They're both at that age when all old men can do is..." He suddenly stopped, grabbed a pair of binoculars and stepped out of the pilothouse. He looked astern and studied a point on the horizon for several minutes. "Bring her starboard 15 degrees."

Breckkan spun the wheel and brought the ANNA to 340 degrees. An acute northern heading, he realized, away from the Shetlands. He maintained the heading, not questioning the strategy.

"Port 40 degrees," said Larsen. "All stop. Lock

the wheel and help me with the sails." They moved quickly and smoothly in unison. The mainsail billowed and snapped as it filled with air.

"There's a ship out there. She changes course whenever we do. I don't know why, but we're not taking any chances. Remember, we're a fishing boat. Tell Bonnie and the Professor to stay below, then help me with the nets. Take a look. She's closing in." He handed the binoculars to Breckkan. "Destroyer class. German insignia." He stared at Breckkan and asked, "Anything special in those duffel bags of yours?"

Breckkan hesitated, his face grim. "We think so." He turned and watched the destroyer approaching.

"Whatever it is, get rid of it!"

Breckkan touched the bandage on his face. He felt catatonic, his mind intermittently backtracking and freezing. How could they possibly know where we are?

"Move! Goddamn it!" said Larsen sternly. "They'll tear us apart if you have anything important to them."

Breckkan forced himself to open the fish locker. He shoved aside the top layer of fish and dug beneath the tarp. As he groped for the notebooks, he glanced back at the oncoming ship just 3,000 feet away, the barrels of its four-inch guns pointing straight at the trawler. He lifted the binoculars and scanned the Germans on the bridge. His breathing stopped. The foredeck gun was moving to target: the ANNA!

Larsen grabbed for the binoculars just as a flash of fire and black smoke spewed from the forward four-inch gun. Moments later a screaming sound passed over the ANNA. The men instinctively ducked, then turned to watch the geyser of water spray high in the air barely a hundred feet away.

The low decibel roar of the gun reached their ears as they watched the geyser swallowed by the waves.

"They won't miss next time," yelled Larsen. The two men exchanged glances; they both knew what they had to do.

Larsen leaped into the pilothouse, clicked on the radio, and spun the tuner to the international distress frequency. He snapped another switch, keeping the call on automatic.

Breckkan leaned down the hatch. "Bonnie, Knut, get on deck!" he screamed, then spun around to the lifeboat and clawed at the fittings. As he swung the boat out over the water, he was suddenly knocked off his feet and thrown across the deck.

The ANNA had taken a direct hit. She jerked violently, her forward deck bolted high into the air, then crashed back, groaning in the water with a convulsive shudder. Larsen's body flew through the pilothouse window and slid through the splintered glass on the yawing deck. A second muffled roar filled the air.

Breckkan rose to his knees and fought for his bearings. Bonnie crawled over to him. He had been brutally slammed down the hatch to the galley floor. Unsteadily he climbed to his feet and with Bonnie's help, they scrambled to the deck above. The Professor lay tangled in a maze of rope, clinging to the side of the fish locker, fighting the precipitous angle of the deck. Breckkan reached for a gaff and forcefully plunged the forked tip into the deck, then swung his body down towards Knut.

"Grab my legs!" he yelled. "Hurry!" The wiry professor pulled himself onto Breckkan's back just as Larsen wrapped a powerful arm underneath his shoulders.

"No time," spit Larsen, blood streaming from his broken nose. "Into the water, Professor!"

Without hesitation, Breckkan grabbed for Bonnie's hand and they both jumped from the ANNA. The frigid dark-green water swelled to meet them. Foam, bubbles, splintered wood, bits of torn sailcloth and netting swirled in the destructive turbulence of the North Sea. Larsen did a mental inventory; they were all in the water and alive, at least for the moment.

From the destroyer, the Deck Officers calmly studied the mayhem. "Captain, the lifeboat. Another shot?"

The German captain watched the strangers fighting for life in the relentless freezing water. "No, they aren't going to survive anyway. The cold will take them." He lowered his binoculars and walked away.

From the wallowing lifeboat, the Norwegians watched as the ANNA slid beneath the water. Her aft was gone, and with it, her powerful engine and propeller, gutted by a salvo of four-inch explosive shells. Glancing toward the German destroyer, Breckkan observed the arcing wake of the retreating vessel. We're all dead now, he thought with a shudder.

Only an oil tarp Larsen had managed to pull aboard protected the group from the elements. Bonnie somehow had saved her suitcase. Breckkan noticed it, but didn't ask how or why. He didn't care; it seemed to comfort her. She shivered involuntarily, clutching the case to her chest. Knut lay in the bottom of the boat, his eyes closed, his mind empty.

Larsen searched the horizon. Had anyone heard the distress signal? The ANNA sank so quickly.

Near darkness, a Scottish fishing boat found them. The single lamp on the lifeboat served as a beacon. The Scottish captain hadn't heard their distress signal.

Breckkan and Knut sat in the galley of the Scottish boat at a stained, chocolate-brown table.

Bonnie opened a tin of salted herring and set it on the table along with a loaf of rye bread. The simple meal was shared in silence.

Breckkan felt a blanket of exhaustion settle over him— after four days and nights of intense pressure, of death. He closed his eyes and spread his palms on the scarred table. Fireballs scorched through his vision. It was self-defense, all self-defense. I killed people at the Plant. Plural. More than one. Bonnie watched him, feeling his pain. She could only ease the physical part, but his mind...

Knut spoke with a noticeable slur. "It's crucial we get your information to the British."

"The data books are gone." Knut didn't seem to comprehend. "Knut," Breckkan repeated quietly, "the research, the data books are lost to the sea. No one has them now."

Knut, his hand trembling, pulled his own oilskin wrapped books from his pocket. Breckkan stared first at the small package, then at his wife. She placed her arm around him. "You can reconstruct yours; I know you can."

"This is all more than coincidence." Breckkan could almost detect the despair in his own voice. "We are being used, played with like toys."

Knut stared out the porthole. He could see nothing but blackness. "And if you're correct, what choice did we have?" he asked, turning toward Breckkan.

Breckkan shrugged. "None." Bonnie looked away.

CHAPTER 10

April 9, 1940

Lerwick, The Shetland Islands

The Scottish trawler churned out of the heavy fog bank that hovered a half mile off the coast. The leaden sky promised more rain. The harbor just ahead was crowded with fishing craft, a forest of masts swaying back and forth in the gentle swells. Hundreds of birds, gulls, auks, and gannets, were circling and screeching, occasionally swooping to the water's surface to catch their breakfasts.

The Professor sat on a storage locker, looking like a tired old man on a park bench watching the crowds pass by, watching and remembering. His pale face was tinged with gray. At one point, he looked up at his daughter, opened his mouth to speak, but seemed to change his mind and turned his head away.

She looked at Breckkan, asking with her eyes if she should join Knut. He shook his head, his own eyes dark and worried. She understood and tightly gripped the rail.

Through the mist, she could see the outline of the village. The stone cottages neatly hugged the shore as if marching in a line right out into the sea. Swirls of fog drifted across their slate rooftops, absorbing the black smoke curling up from the chimney pots.

The Scottish captain expertly maneuvered the trawler closer to the pier and then reversed the engine. Churning white foam replaced the geometric pattern of waves at the stern. "Pull her to," he called to a waiting dockhand. "Fine morning to be in Scotland."

"Aye. Lovely mornin'. Bit o' fog, but lovely," the dockhand shouted back.

Larsen and the local tied the trawler in place with heavy ropes, forward and aft, secured to the stanchions. Over his shoulder, Larsen called to Breckkan, "I'll be right back. Just want to check with the harbormaster." The Norwegian disappeared into the crowded dock side. An occasional cheerful profanity, bristling with the characteristic burr, rose out of the hubbub.

Breckkan moved restlessly; he felt uneasy. He put one foot up on the rail and leaned forward, his eyes darting.

"Here they come now," she said, pointing toward the crowd.

In stride with Larsen was a roly-poly man, his shape encircled by a thick, oiled fisherman sweater. "Come ashore. Meet Fergus," Larsen called to them.

Breckkan jumped to the pier and reached up for Bonnie. Larsen stepped forward, motioned to the Professor and gently took the whole weight of him, lifting him off the boat. Suddenly, a blast of freezing rain mixed with popcorn snow showered them and they hurried up the dock.

Ducking through the harbormaster's door, Breckkan sensed the odor peculiar to Scotland: the rich smell of burning peat. The blue plaque over the entrance was unfamiliar to him, but suggested some ancient guild of the sea. A gloomy light filtered through the narrow windows. Two chairs faced a shallow fireplace, the hearth and mantel blackened by years of accumulated soot. The vertical iron grate radiated with glowing peat. Breckkan moved in front of the fire, warmed his bandaged hands and gingerly flexed his stiff fingers.

Fergus lit a cigarette. He wore half gloves of leather, his exposed fingertips stained a nutty brown from nicotine. "A drink, Captain?" he asked. Larsen nodded. The harbormaster looked at the other Norwegians. "A whiskey? It's very fine. The best single malt. You look like you need it."

"No thanks," said Breckkan. Bonnie shook her head and sat by her father.

"Why not," answered the Professor, pulling the borrowed coat around him.

The harbormaster reached into the bottom drawer of his desk. "Island malt or Highland malt? Island malt can be a bit reeky, but try a wee dram." He poured a splash from a bottle of Laphroaig.

The Professor took the glass and sipped the amber whiskey. Clearing his throat, he said, "I suppose it grows on you. A bit like tarred rope." The harbormaster grunted and tossed back his whiskey in one swallow.

Breckkan bent over the desk, looking at a map spread on the surface covered by a scratched piece of glass. Only the dark edges of the coastline stood out; the land masses were empty. There were no towns, no roads, nothing. A sea chart. Only the entrances to harbors were marked. "We've got to get to London," he said, looking up at the barrel-chested Fergus.

"What's that?"

"We've got to get to London," Breckkan said loudly.

"Och, aye. You've been expected," said Fergus, lighting another cigarette with the burning nub of his last one. His eyes bored in on his guests. "If you can prove your identity."

"What?!" snapped Breckkan, immediately feeling the electricity generating in the small room.

"No offense, mind you. But you did arrive on a local trawler. I know Larsen explained, but..."

Berlin

Mean, spitting rain fell on Berlin. The citizens were still hard at work, most unaware of their country's act of aggression against an ally of decades. Radio and newspapers reported the "ATTACK BY BRITAIN" and the gallant efforts of the German Army and Air Force to save the Norwegians. The headlines in *Der Sturmer* read: "OSLO IS SAVED."

Colonel Richter entered Abwehr Headquarters at 76/78 Tirpitzufer, a maze of dim corridors and creaky staircases. The only advantage of the building was the direct underground access to Wehrmacht Headquarters in the neighboring Bendlerstrasse. The "fox-hole," as the staff called it, was the antithesis of the offices housing the Ministries, but Admiral Canaris liked to emphasize to his guests that the Abwehr was not a political bureau, unlike the Gestapo.

Richter averted the salute of the guard on duty, his face tipped downwards. His boots clicked rhythmically on the marble as he walked through the angular cast shadows. He chose the stairs over the antiquated elevator.

He entered his office on the fourth floor; the Lieutenant looked up from his work and snapped to attention. "Good evening, Colonel. You're working late tonight. Can I get you something? Brandy? A mineral water?"

"No. Come into my office."

"Yes, sir."

"Sit down, Lieutenant." Richter removed his tunic and rubbed his eyes with closed fists. He looked extremely weary and as if under enormous stress. "I've been closeted with Canaris all day. He even made me go with him to walk his dachshund."

The Lieutenant suppressed a laugh. "And how is Seppl?"

"Don't ask. At least his pallet on the floor is more comfortable than those metal chairs. I tried again to talk Canaris into replacing that threadbare Persian rug but he refused. I actually think we could carry out that scarred old desk of his and replace it with a crate and he'd never notice it. Seppl has better taste."

Richter crossed to the French doors, clutching his hands behind his back. Past the balcony he could make out the orderly rows of chestnuts and limes in the Tiergarten. The wet weather perfectly suited his depression. In the light of the streetlamps, he could see the lucky ones hurrying home under their umbrellas, their work day over.

"I was sure we had the right man to bring out the Norwegian's research. Our Major von Stein, that damn cold bastard, is either inept or his enthusiasm for this project is far more than I anticipated."

"Sir, we've had no reports so far."

"No, damn it! He hasn't reported back! The only reports are from the Abwehr station in Oslo, and apparently von Stein did meet up with Dr. Breckkan." Richter fell silent.

"So we can presume..."

"Presume? Never presume! It was a disaster. A goddamn disaster! Half our garrison at the Hydro Plant killed or wounded. Von Stein wounded, too. But nothing about the data or their experiments, or the scientist, Breckkan. No reports. Nothing!"

"What is von Stein's condition?"

"The bastard vanished." Richter rolled a pencil between his fingers. "Only an obnoxious message from Himmler."

"Maybe von Stein has a plan. He's inventive."

"Maybe." I sure as hell hope he knows what he's doing, Richter thought with total disgust. "Notify the Networks to watch for him. His purposes and loyalties might have been the same as ours in the beginning, but now I'm not so sure."

On the coffee table was a gift from Canaris, a

letterpress in the form of three bronze monkeys, one cupping his ear, intent upon listening, another peering suspiciously around, the third with its hand over its mouth. He picked up the logotype of the Secret Service, feeling the weight of the bronze. "As Section Chief and representative to the High Command, I have the dubious honor of reporting to Herr Borman at 10:00 tonight."

"That means the Fuhrer is watching this project personally."

"Of course. He wants the Norwegian data. Our top physics theorist has shown without a doubt that graphite won't work, whatever that means. He maintains the secret is heavy water. Von Stein has to get their work on heavy water, especially now that so many working on it have defected and escaped to England. We'll have no excuses if we fail. None!" Richter sat down at his desk. He leaned back and closed his eyes. "Go home. I'll need you early tomorrow."

Lerwick

Trust your gut instinct, thought Breckkan. Just a backward islander or some dumb son-of-a-bitch trying to push us around.

"You must be important. I've orders to call this number in London...," Fergus tapped his trouser pocket, "and give your names— if the lines are clear. The storm's building; you may have to stay the night."

Breckkan leaned forward on the desk, his hands spread out on the glass top. "Tell him, Larsen."

"I told you, Fergus. He's Dr. Breckkan. That's his wife, Dr. Bonnie Breckkan, and the man enjoying your whiskey is her father, Professor

Kittleson. The ANNA was blown out of the water by a damn German destroyer. Do you understand?"

Breckkan glared at the harbormaster. "Ring the number."

"There was a news item on the BBC this morning that might interest you," said Fergus.

"Ring the number first," said Breckkan. He pushed the telephone toward the Scot. "Believe me, sir, this is not a pleasure trip. Try the number!"

With a scruffy hand, he fished out the piece of paper and placed the call. "Lerwick here. Your friends have arrived. Aye, all are well." Breckkan straightened up, not taking his eyes off the man, but there was nothing unusual in his expression other than concentration.

"Right you are. We'll wait." Fergus winked at Breckkan and hung up the phone. "Not to worry, they're to ring right back."

Breckkan sighed loudly and walked to the window. When speaking to London, Fergus hadn't mentioned the attack by the German destroyer, or that they nearly drowned.

Bonnie moved to the fire and took off her soaked pea jacket. The smell of fish clung to her. She loosened the plaits braided around her head, shaking her hair free. The harbormaster clucked in approval. Neither she nor Breckkan seemed to notice his stare.

The telephone rang. Fergus picked it up and listened. "It's Scapa Flow," he said. "They're sending a plane."

Bergen

The black car turned left toward the spires of St. Mary's and headed down the narrow cobblestone street. The driver eased the sedan up onto the sidewalk and a tall uniformed man got out in front of the antique store. He rapped the glass panes of the door with his cane. The shade pulled up, revealing a stocky, baldheaded man standing in front of a dusty counter top. The bald man nodded and opened the door.

The uniformed man grimaced with pain as he stepped down into the shop. The officer paused to look at a collection of antique pewter mugs. He picked up the half pint and studied the rim of the tankard. "The stamped numbers...curious."

"Weight verifications. Sailors didn't like to be cheated when their tankards were relined."

"English then?"

"Right. James Yates. You've a good eye."

The officer smiled wryly. "Do you have what I asked for?"

"The identification papers were easy, of course, but the tickets..."

The officer cleared his throat and said, "A problem? I've had a hard enough time getting here."

"No, no," the dealer continued hurriedly, "your friend was most helpful. Your name is on the passenger manifest. Everything is ready."

The man with the cane was out of the shop sixty seconds later, a brown package tucked under his arm. He slipped into the back seat of the car.

Lerwick

"I can take you to the airstrip, but the ride will cost you. Fact of the matter is that petrol is scarce," Fergus said.

"We'll pay. Let's get going," said Breckkan.

They stepped out of the office onto the rain-swept street and turned into a mew. Despite his girth, Fergus moved quickly toward his car, his rubber boots squeaking on the smooth wet flag-stones. His dog, a white terrier, barked and wagged his tail simultaneously, scratching the tattered seat of the old Morriss.

Knut settled into the back seat and Bonnie slid in beside him. The Professor looked older, his white flurry of hair amplifying his sunken eyes. "I'll be fine once we get to London," Knut muttered, noting his daughter's stare.

Larsen leaned against the front door and said to Breckkan, "I'll be heading back to Norway as soon as I find another boat. Most can always use an extra hand."

Bonnie opened the window and reached out for Larsen. As he leaned down, she kissed him on his cheek and murmured, "Give our love to your father." Larsen nodded; there was an awkward silence. He pushed his hands deeper into his coat pockets and stepped away. Fergus gunned the engine, ground the gears, and the car moved slowly down the mew, turning at the first corner.

Berlin

Richter slowly folded the communique and absently looked out the balcony. So, von Stein is on the move, he thought. He has surfaced in Bergen. The antique dealer's report emphasized how effectively von Stein used his Norwegian accent. Physically, though, he was slow. His injuries apparently are quite debilitating as had been reported by the Vemork physician.

That attempted rape years ago. His obsession with genetics; his mother's disease and early death. Those grotesque embryos in his office. Of all the damn anatomic places for him to be disabled. I hope to God he's still after the data. I hope we haven't lost him, that he doesn't have his own motives now.

The waiting Lieutenant asked if the communique contained good news. Richter tore the paper into small pieces. "I don't know."

The Shetlands

The coast road to the south of the island was lonely and narrow, lined by low stone walls. They sat in silence. No other automobiles were on the road, only occasional locals on bicycles. Fergus deftly handled the Morriss with one hand, occasionally releasing the wheel to ruffle the Westie's head. As they topped a hill, the feisty terrier barked sharply, jumping at the dashboard and clawing at the windshield. A flock of sheep crowded the road, forcing them to a stop. The Westie barked furiously; Fergus held his hand on the horn. The sheep moved at their own pace, bleating plaintively. The lead sheep suddenly bolted across the field and, like a cascade of ball bearings, the others tumbled after him. Turning his head toward his passengers, he said, "You see now why I bring the little mutt along. He thinks he cleared the way."

Breckkan smiled. "Spunky little dog."

"Och, aye," Fergus replied. "No small amount of self-esteem."

I've known some scientists like that, Breckkan thought to himself. Sir Malcolm in London...there by the grace of God goes God.

The landscape was barren except for occasional windblown and bent trees; the bark gnawed away as high as the sheep could reach. Veering inland from the coast, they passed a solitary crofter house crouched low against the wind. A mound of sod squares was stacked by the squat door.

Bonnie asked, "Who lives there? It's so lonely."

"The people who work the land and tend the sheep, ma'am."

"They don't own the land?"

"Aye, they're tenants of rich English landowners. The owners come only for sport."

"That was a big stack of turf," said Breckkan.

"It's got to last the winter. Sad part that, the land goes barren 'cause the topsoil goes with the peat."

"Man seems to have a penchant for laying waste," muttered Breckkan.

"That's a bit cynical, don't you think?" asked Knut. Breckkan didn't answer.

The Morriss slowed and turned right off the road onto a muddy track, then turned again in front of a stone-based windmill. They continued over low, rolling hills scored with craggy ravines, stopping as the track ended at a large, wire-link gate. A bulldozed dirt area beyond served as the runway. It was oriented east to west, allowing planes the advantage of the prevailing winds. A high fence, topped with coiled barbed wire, surrounded the primitive airstrip. A small hut sat just outside the gate and, further on, a low stone building hugged the edge of the strip.

The car slowed to a stop and Breckkan opened his door. "I'll get it."

Fergus nodded. "You'll need these." He pulled a pair of wire cutters from his coat pocket. "Misplaced the key."

Breckkan took the cutters and walked to the heavy gate. He struggled with the chain, his hands throbbing from the pressure of the tool handle. He felt the link snap, pulled the chain free, and gave the gate a hard push.

The distraction was nearly fatal; he didn't hear the sudden roar of the motor. The car lunged forward. Breckkan's subconscious took control. He glanced back and saw the onrushing car. Simultaneously, he lunged for the swinging gate, the momentum swinging his body clear. He let go of the gate and stared unbelievingly at the Morriss. Bonnie and Knut had said nothing; it was all so sudden.

"Goddamn transmission," muttered Fergus as he ground the gears into reverse backing past Breckkan.

"What the hell!" Breckkan demanded as he glared at Fergus. Crazy islander, a wonder we made it this far.

"You almost killed him!" Bonnie said in a raspy voice. "I think we'd better walk from here."

Fergus looked at her in the rear-view mirror. She could see the image of his reddened face, his narrow eyes, their pupils darkened pinpoints. In one motion, he threw the gear into first and floored the gas pedal. The sudden speed threw her against the seat.

Breckkan saw the car bolt forward and head straight toward him. My God! He's going to hit me! He spun and ran down the muddy track. The stone building was a hundred and fifty yards away. Mud clung to his boots like weights, slowing him down. The roar of the onrushing car was directly behind him.

Wide-eyed, Bonnie fought to right herself and screamed, "Stop! Stop! What're you doing?"

The car didn't slow. She lunged forward and grabbed at Fergus' arm. He jabbed his elbow at her, breaking her grip, and throwing her against her father. The old man, too weak to help, gasped for air.

The stone building was a hundred yards away. Breckkan glanced over his shoulder; the Morriss was nearly on him. The split second look at Fergus shocked him. I'll never make it, he thought.

Bonnie struggled to get off Knut as she screamed, "Stop, you son-of-a-bitch!"

"Son-of-a-bitch, hell!" he roared. "You Brit-loving..."

Breckkan saw the ravine and, without thinking, dove for it. The world rolled wildly as he tumbled to the bottom. Long stem grass, mud, and rocks showered him. The car raced past, lurching and careening on the muddy track. Fergus turned in his seat, straining to see Breckkan.

"Look out!" yelled Bonnie.

Fergus turned back to see the stone wall. There was a crash.

Bonnie pulled herself from the floor of the car. Knut was crumpled under her. She started to shake him and cried, "Father, Father..."

"Stop it!" He slowly pulled himself onto the seat. "For God's sake, you're going to break something." Raising up, he looked into the front seat. The Westie was lying on the floor, his neck broken. The horn blared as the weight of Fergus' body pressed against the steering wheel. "He's not going to bother us anymore," said Knut. "Let's get out of this damn thing."

Breckkan crawled from the ravine and stumbled toward the car. "You all right?" he called when he saw Bonnie climb from the car. "Knut..."

"Are you all right?" she asked, clinging to Breckkan.

"I'm okay," he sighed, breathing heavily.

They looked back at the car. It had been on purpose.

They huddled against the piercing cold. The blaring car horn could still be heard in the distance over the wind. The ceiling had lowered. Where the sea met the sky, a gray infinity spread before them. Looking up, they saw a black dot emerge from the dense layer of clouds, growing in size as it descended toward the isolated dirt strip. Soon the plane was on the ground, taxiing toward them, bumping along the slick runway. A fine spray misted around the wheels as the heavy plane squeezed the water from the saturated soil. Reaching the end of the strip, the two 900-horsepower Wright Cyclone engines suddenly roared louder, spinning the aircraft around in a 180° arc. The propeller nearest the waiting car feathered to a stop while the engine on the far side continued roaring at idle speed.

The door on the right side of the plane near the tail opened, and a figure, dressed in a dark brown leather flight jacket and khaki trousers, lowered a ladder to the ground. The navigator introduced himself.

"Glad to see you," yelled Breckkan.

"Pleased to help, sir. You're to have VIP treatment. It'll be about a three hour flight," he said, reaching for Bonnie's suitcase.

As the Norwegians clambered into the drafty interior, Breckkan thought he heard the car horn stop. Can the bastard still be alive?

The navigator instructed them to secure themselves in the sling seats suspended from the overhead, then pulled up the ladder, closed the door and locked it. A young-looking pilot appeared. "Rather primitive. A bit noisy and bumpy on takeoff, but we'll have you in London soon."

"Are you carrying any oxygen?" Breckkan asked.

"A little, sir, but there'll be no need. We'll be flying at about 5,000 feet." Breckkan nodded and looked at Knut. He seemed preoccupied with the trappings of the seat.

The second propeller began moving in a balking motion, then broke into a steady roar as blue-black smoke belched from the engine. The Dakota moved down the runway, gathering speed. First the tail wheel, then the entire plane lifted away from the ground. To the passengers, it seemed as though they were suspended; there was no real sense of motion, only a slight sense of pressure pushing them back into their seats. The plane climbed and turned out to sea. The pilot took her to a thousand feet, banked and headed toward mainland Scotland. He adjusted the engines and leveled off at 5,100 feet.

Crossing the shores of the mainland, the sky cleared to a three-tenths cloud cover. The ground far below was rugged, a blend of the ancient tartan colors: soft brown, gray-green, rust and lavender. Below lay the village of John O'Groats, the birthplace of Bonnie's mother. Margee Riley, the only daughter of the postmaster of the northernmost settlement on mainland Scotland, Margee that had fallen in love with a handsome Norwegian scientist and bequeathed her golden-red hair to their only daughter, Dr. Bonnie Breckkan.

Bonnie felt a momentary calm. The constant roar of the engines and the separation from earth made her feel safe and free. She closed her eyes and fell into a hypnotic sleep. A little more than an hour into the flight, the plane encountered turbulent air over Balmoral Forest, jolting her awake. She stretched and turned to look behind at her father. She was shocked by his condition. Tearing the safety harness loose, she reached forward and grabbed Breckkan's shoulder. The Professor was ashen gray, his face dripping with perspiration. His blanched fingers feebly tore at his collar.

"What's wrong?" cried Bonnie. Knut muttered inaudibly. "Olav! Do something!"

Breckkan bent down and felt for the old man's pulse. It was barely palpable and thready. He immediately worked his way forward to the cockpit, holding on to the interior struts, and tapped the navigator's shoulder. Leaning close, he yelled, "Professor Kittleson's very sick. I think he's dying! We've got to get medical help!"

The navigator put his hand to his throat mike

and spoke hurriedly to the Captain. The Captain motioned to the copilot and grabbed the bottle of oxygen cradled behind his seat. Bonnie stepped aside as the Captain put the black rubber mask over Knut's nose and mouth. After several deep breaths, the Professor calmed, no longer agitated.

From a corner inside the fibrillating upper chambers of the Professor's heart, a blood clot had probably formed, his body demanding more oxygen because of the altitude, his heart increasing its pace. The faster flow would dislodge the clot, blocking off blood flow to a portion of the right ventricle. It seemed the worst had happened: with the sudden loss of oxygen, that part of the man's heart had died.

Bonnie wiped the perspiration from Knut's face. Tears ran down her cheeks. Breckkan held the oxygen mask in place. The stricken man was still, his breathing shallow and irregular.

The navigator tapped Breckkan on the shoulder and shouted, "The Captain said we're cleared to land in Edinburgh. About fifteen, maybe twenty minutes."

Breckkan nodded. In an attempt to reassure her and himself, he leaned over and spoke into her ear. "He'll be okay. There's a large medical center in Edinburgh. Famous."

"Dear God, please help him," she murmured, softly stroking his white hair. His eyes remained closed.

The Dakota landed smoothly at Turnhouse Airport. An ambulance was waiting on the tarmac.

CHAPTER 11

April 28, 1940

Mayfair, London

He wore an ill-fitting tweed suit and a dirty brown tie the color of dog feces, yet he felt a sense of relief when he reached Old Bond Street. Passing elegant, sandbagged store fronts, he limped to Number 21. He straightened his shoulders and entered the venerable London salon: Gieves, Naval and Civil Tailors and Outfitters. Leaning on his cane, he paused to look at a display case of regimental and school ties.

The salesman of perhaps sixty years was scrupulously polite. "We're ready for you, sir. The alterations are completed. If you would like to try them on, this way, please."

He closed the door to the fitting room, latching it securely. Balancing himself against the door, he took off the old clothes, folded and laid them on a chair. He put on the white dress shirt and expertly tied a four-in-hand knot in the gray silk tie. As expected, the dark gray double-breasted suit fit perfectly. Inspecting himself in the full-length mirror, he smiled. "Better, much better."

He handed the old clothes to the clerk and instructed him to package them, then took out a sterling-silver cigarette case and matching lighter. The English may be the world's most inept lovers, he thought to himself, but they certainly have style.

The clerk returned with a parcel wrapped in blue paper. "Dr. Erickson, your receipt, sir. We have kept your measurements on file, sir, should you need anything."

"Very good," he said, placing the receipt in his passport case. The worn passport fell open to the first page. The mauve Norwegian stamp on his picture was smudged; the name printed under the picture read: R. Erickson, Telavaag, Norway. Occupation: University Professor.

By the brass clock in the showroom window, he could see it was 11:30, an hour before his scheduled luncheon meeting at the Cafe Royal. Glancing back into the store, he saw the clerk busily stacking bolts of cloth. He limped to the corner, turned left and, moving with the crowd, crossed Piccadilly. The sidewalks were crowded with solemn, preoccupied businessmen, as gray as the April sky. He retraced his steps, crossing St. James Street and continued down Piccadilly past Fortnum and Mason. Despite rationing and shortages, the windows were burgeoning with stacked pyramids of Indian and Ceylon teas, mustards and jams. Through the glass, he could see chattering ladies queuing for the tearoom.

He stopped at Hatchard's and worked his way through the crowded bookstore. Toward the back, he passed the narrow stairwell winding to the basement where the paperback section was housed. Glad the art books aren't down there, he thought. I couldn't get down the damn steps.

Half an hour passed easily. He purchased a thin green volume of Constable's sketches. She never understood my love for art, he thought as he collected his change.

Next to the Royal Academy, he took a shortcut down Air Street and passed under the pair of neoclassic arches, and then out into Regent Street. The noontime traffic was heavy, omnipresent taxis competed with the double-decker buses. Crossing the street toward the restaurant, he was nearly hit by a motorcycle with a side car, his eye catching only the flash of a white scarf as it roared by.

The ornate lobby of the Cafe Royal bustled with an elite mixture of barristers, businessmen, and members of parliament. The entrance to the dining room was guarded by an arrogant French maitre d' who received and escorted the select few to their linen covered tables set with heavy silver and fine china service plates.

He leaned lightly on his rosewood cane and surveyed the gilt and red baroque dining room. Handing his bowler and packages to an attendant, he murmured to the maitre d', "Professor Erickson." He was taller than the Frenchman and glared down at him through his tinted glasses as the man searched the leather-covered reservation book.

"Ah, yes, two for luncheon. Please, this way, sir."

"My guest should arrive soon. I'll take that table," he said, pointing with his cane. "And bring me your wine list."

"Of course, sir."

He limped slightly as he walked to the corner table and slid onto the red leather banquette. He habitually chose corner tables, a tactical move, both to observe the entire room and protect his back.

At precisely 1:00, he looked up and saw the maitre d' escorting a striking blonde toward him. She had an elegant profile, a strictly European face. With a half smile, she sat down and commented, "How you've changed, dear." To those seated nearby, they looked like handsome lovers sipping champagne, involved in each other. "Quite respectable now," she said, running her index finger around the rim of the champagne glass. "When you left the flat this morning, I was afraid you might be picked up for vagrancy."

Ignoring her comment, he removed the silver case from his pocket and offered her a cigarette. "A good day at Whitehall?"

"My, aren't we the aristocrat," she said, staring at the case.

"As I said...Whitehall?"

"The General was busy with a crisis this morning. Delayed arrivals. Some sick old fool stranded up in Edinburgh. I was afraid I might not make it by 1:00," she said, leaning closer, her cashmere sweater and tight-fitting suit jacket clearly indicating how much she enjoyed showing off her figure.

"Someone important?"

"A Norwegian. Scientist, I think. The old fart had a heart attack and botched the schedule." She took a sip of champagne. "Erickson, don't you have a first name? The Network listed only— "

"Just Erickson." He waited a fraction of a moment. "This scientist, did you get his name?"

"No. It was classified."

Realizing no more information was forthcoming, he asked, "How's the food here?"

"Dull, but the wine is excellent, and cheap."

"Then order for us." He motioned for service and sat back. A stiff-backed waiter took their order: sea trout, pommes frites, and courgettes. How clever, he thought to himself, fish and chips. "Is my fellow countryman in a good hospital?"

"I presume so. He's at the medical college." She began eating, pushing the zucchini and potatoes onto her fork with the fish knife. He picked at his food. She was right, it was dull, but the claret was superb.

"Sad. We all took such chances to get out before the invasion and then to have the body fail," he said, watching her dispassionately.

She swallowed a mouthful of food and reached for her glass. "Well, the poor soul should be grateful that my General could get him medical care so fast. Oh, I did stop by the Free Norwegian Government

Headquarters. It's just down the hall. Their office is in total chaos." She smiled. "Did you know King Haakon and his staff are preparing to move here?"

"I presumed he would have to run soon. There's not enough room in Oslo for him and Quisling." He pushed away his half-eaten meal, the limp potatoes lapping over the fried fish.

Sonja took a lipstick from her purse. "Plans this afternoon?" she asked.

So beautiful, so stupid, such a low-life agent, he thought, glancing around the crowded room. And too casual. I caught the slip during your drunkenness last night. So Berlin is worried about me. Well, the less they know... "I think I'll take in the exhibition at the Royal Academy. I should be back at your flat around six."

"I'll fix supper in," she said, leaning forward. "Got to get back to my General. Have enough money, Erickson, or did you spend it all on Bond Street?"

"You could be a little more discreet," he snapped. "The funds are more than adequate." He rose coldly and distantly, but the woman didn't seem to notice. A passing busboy assisted her with her chair. She patted him on his pink, rosy cheek, enjoying his blush. The tall man watched; he wasn't embarrassed by the flashy blonde. He was completely disinterested.

Outside, she waved for a taxi with a gloved hand. "Tonight?" she asked.

Von Stein turned and crossed Regent Street, not looking back.

The Strand, London

Breckkan stepped out of the depressing, sooty, red-brick Victoria Station and onto the cobblestone pavement. As he joined the queue for a taxi, his eyes followed the gesture of a young uniformed man ahead of him. High above London air-warning balloons floated over distant spires. The next boxy, black taxi pulled up and the driver deftly reached back and opened the rear door. Settling back into the cavernous compartment, Breckkan placed a hand on his briefcase, and said, "The Savoy, please."

"Right, guv'nor," the cabbie said. The taxi made a full U-turn in less than twenty-five feet and entered the stream of traffic.

Breckkan closed his eyes. Events of the past few weeks flashed chaotically through his mind. Norway at war. My data lost. Already he was laboring to reconstruct pages of experimental data, the myriad of equations defining nuclear chain reactions, energy released, rates of heat exchange, the effectiveness of heavy-water regulation, particularly the usefulness, no, the necessity of super coolants both in managing the reactions and producing the essential U-235.

He had left Bonnie in a boarding house near the hospital, but only after a terrible argument. She was his only friend, only sure contact, absolutely only love, but he knew he had to leave her. He promised her she was safe and they would be together as soon on Knut could travel. The staff of the Royal Infirmary was competent, but Bonnie was agitated, obsessed with their staying together for survival. For the first time in their marriage their parting had been strained.

He reached up and pushed down the window for fresh air; the cabbie's head was obscured by a cloud of pipe smoke. They passed the Houses of Parliament. He wondered how soon the great building would suffer from a new war. As the driver deftly negotiated the roundabout at Trafalgar

Square and headed into the Strand, he was struck
by the apparent breezy attitude of the crowds.
Neither in the queues for the buses, nor in the
cocky strides of young legal aides, in their dark,
boring garb, nor in the tweed-encased matrons,
no waists visible above their sturdy brown
shoes...nowhere did he see fear. Just the ordinary
business of living. An occasional sandbagged pill-
box. A troop of young boy scouts listening to a
lecture from a white-haired Home Guard official.
He saw serious faces, earnest faces, but no fear.

In the past three weeks, he had felt fear. Terror. Sweaty panic. Mistrust. He was certain he
wasn't alone. All Norwegians must be living in the
same weak panic. What was their normal business of living like now? All major ports seized in
forty-eight hours. A King and his son, my friend,
in hiding. That ass, Quisling, thinking he can con-
demn our country to cooperation with the Germans. My God, Mother is at their mercy.

Can we ever have a normal life again, trust
anyone? No wonder Bonnie was so... He suddenly
realized the taxi driver was speaking to him. "Pay
up, mate."

A uniformed doorman patiently held the door
open. A gray-gloved hand proffered assistance.
"Checking in, sir?"

The driver stared at him in the rear-view mirror. Breckkan snapped to, adjusted his necktie and
paid him. "Thanks, guv." The taxi lurched away
down the narrow street back onto the Strand.

He headed for the reception desk, following the
attendant with his luggage. He was looking forward to a long bath and a drink when he heard
his name called.

"Breckkan! I've checked you in. You're only a
week late. Here's your key. A drink or want to

freshen up?" asked Bill Wakefield.

"A drink sounds good," Breckkan said with a tired smile. The bath could wait; a person to talk to was more important just now. How he wished it were Bonnie. He turned to the porter and held up his key, "Take my luggage to the room, please," discreetly handing the man a generous tip. He kept his briefcase.

Breckkan followed the American across the lobby to the residents' lounge to a quiet corner table. In the glow of the brass floor lamp, Breckkan studied the man. Wakefield's hair was shiny black, combed straight back from his temples and forehead. His dark suit and tie made him appear nearly anonymous, yet Breckkan was well aware that William K. Wakefield could walk into any private club and the porter would assume he was a member. He had the bearing of a moneyed personage who could make life difficult for anyone in his way. Breckkan tossed his overcoat and muffler onto an adjacent chair and then settled back on the couch, facing the room.

Wakefield motioned to a waiter and ordered two whiskeys and a bottle of seltzer water. "Good looking coat," said the American.

"A new wardrobe. We lost everything at sea. By the way, thanks for the offer to send money to Edinburgh, but luckily Breckkan Mining keeps an account at the Bank of England." Breckkan spoke quietly, withdrawn.

An unobtrusive, slim waiter brought their drinks. Splashing soda into his glass from the siphon, Wakefield said, "Your escape was impressive." Breckkan said nothing. "Like your father, your abilities are quite formidable." Lifting his glass, he tapped Breckkan's. "Welcome, my friend."

"Thanks." Just how much does this rich, well-connected American know about all that's happened?

All those connections...and I denied him his wish, marrying his daughter. Is he getting even?

"How's your father-in-law doing?"

Taking a swallow of his drink, Breckkan said, "Better."

"That was a helluva trip, even for a young man."

"Thank God for the plane. He'd never have made it otherwise." He drained his glass. "Hope I get a chance to thank the one who arranged for it."

"You just did." The American signaled for another round of drinks.

"You?"

"Yes."

Breckkan jerked his head up. "You contacted the harbormaster?"

"Yes," answered Wakefield.

"I assumed Roald did it."

"I'm afraid Roald is pretty damn busy right now. Terrible sea battles. Norway has lost four destroyers."

Breckkan leaned forward and ran his fingers along the edge of the mahogany coffee table. "Well, Norway almost lost one of its scientists."

"What are you talking about?"

"The harbormaster. The bastard tried to kill me."

"He what?!"

"You heard me," said Breckkan, staring at the table top. "Anything else I should know? Is there any good news?"

"I'm afraid not. Do you remember the name of the boat you left Norway on?"

Breckkan looked up. "Of course, the ANNA.

"I thought so. Our intelligence reported extraordinary courage shown by a Norwegian. We think it was the Captain of the ANNA."

"I wouldn't be at all surprised." Breckkan's face momentarily brightened. "What's Larsen been up to?"

"The report read that a trawler, armed with a

single deck gun, sailed straight into Bergen harbor." Breckkan's smile disappeared. The thin scar on his cheek reddened. "A direct hit smashed the Lewis gun. The gunner lost both legs." Wakefield paused, moistened his lips and continued. "And to spare the crew more anguish, he rolled himself overboard. He wasn't found."

Breckkan placed his hand in his right pocket and dropped his head. The lamplight created a vague halo above his thinning blonde hair. "And this gunner?"

"He had lost his own boat to a German warship. Her name was the ANNA."

The tinkle of piano keys merging with a trombone sounded in the distance as the dinner hour began in the River Room. "Why don't you unpack? Professor Chadwick's meeting us for dinner at Simpson's."

Ediburgh

Bonnie looked out her window at the grim castle towering above the tenements on the sheer black rock. The wind had come up and she knew rain was likely. She picked up her umbrella, glad she'd purchased a wool suit. She wound her way down the tight spiral staircase and called, "Just going for a walk, Major, and to check on Father."

Major Grey poked her head through the kitchen doorway and said in her broad Scots accent, "Not to worry, dear." She turned back into the room, softly humming a sad Scottish tune as she dried her hands on a cotton towel.

"What's that?" Bonnie asked, following her into the kitchen.

The Major was a rock-solid shape bound by her apron, with a long face topped by hair of iron.

"Oh, I understand he's much better."

"You talked to the doctor?" Bonnie asked.

"Aye, much better, he did say. Well, off you go, dear. It's going to rain for sure." The woman chattered away, breaking eggs into a bowl. "You know what they say 'bout our Edinbro' weather? We have but three days of summer...and they're not consecutive." Bonnie couldn't help but smile. "Oh, almost forgot. Picked up some daffodils for the Professor. Here you go, take 'em, dear. Give him some cheer."

A double-decker bus flashed by on Lauriston Place. She threaded her way through the traffic and walked quickly down the short block on Chalmers Street, emerging at the immense green park, rightly called the Meadows. The clouds rippled by overhead, the spaces between them rapidly opening and closing. Just like the canvases of Turner, she thought, the cloud formations in a swirling vortex over the brown earth, minimizing humankind altogether. A proper placement for humans as the globe headed toward world war.

The wind swept across the vast green park and a feeble sunshine broke through the clouds. The laburnums and copper beeches glittered, their pale green buds trembling in the light. A hazy smokiness hung over the roof tops, just above rows of black chimney pots. She stopped to watch the pigeons crowded around a dignified, tweed-clad man as he tossed peanuts in wide, sweeping arcs through the whirring wings.

Gradually, the light faded. Thunder? She saw a few lights snap on in the southern wing of the Royal Infirmary and then the hurried pull of the blackout curtains. She ran toward the main entrance, already feeling dampness in the air.

The Theater District, London

Von Stein walked down a long, sparrow-brown

street of three- and four-story houses. Rows of doorways, rows of windows, meditative and featureless. He suddenly felt as glum as the sky.

Sonja's flat was three flights up in a respectable brick building. Years of accumulated soot had streaked the red brick with dark umber stains. The district was a mix, bordered to the north by Oxford Street and its fashionable antique shops and galleries, and to the south with theaters backed up to the Chinese ghetto. Her building housed mostly the peripheral people who always seemed to cling to the theater.

Unlocking the front door of the flat, he walked from the freezing vestibule into her living room. It was a room of gauche luxury, overdone and unnecessary. Clumsy, dark wood furniture, fringed lamps, tasseled drapes, a chaise lounge draped in a discordant afghan— all intended to exude a flush lifestyle. He had hated it immediately.

She was completely unaware of his contempt.

Sonja walked into the living room from the tiny kitchen carrying a tall glass a quarter full of gin. Von Stein could tell from her gait that she'd been drinking for some time. "Hullo. Yer late. Started without you." She lifted the glass unsteadily and drained it with one swallow. "Hava good afternoon?"

"Yes," he said, removing his hat and looking at the statuesque drunk. "I'd like to freshen up."

"Sure. You just get comfortable, luv." He winced at the endearment and said nothing. He closed the door to his bedroom and undressed, immediately sorry he hadn't purchased one of the silk robes at Gieves. He took a towel, wrapped it around his waist, and walked into the hall. She was filling her glass from a decanter, her back to him. Without looking up, she said, "Wanna drink in the loo?"

"No, thanks. I'll be right out." He walked to the bathroom and closed the door. Lathering his face, he shaved and began rinsing off the remaining soap when the door opened. Sonja leaned against the doorway, clad in a white satin robe, glass in hand. He slipped on his tinted glasses and looked up at her reflection in the mirror. "If you don't mind, I'll be finished in a minute."

"No hurry, luv," she said drunkenly. "Wanna have some fun?" She moved close to him and rubbed the glass on his back. He stiffened. It was the first time in months a woman had touched him. She put her arm around his shoulder and massaged his chest. He closed his eyes. She was an expert at these things. He could feel his heart pound. She leaned her head against his back, and he could feel her long hair.

"You'd better leave."

"Com'on, Erickson. Don't waste the chance."

"I said, leave!" He whipped off his glasses. The opaque eye glistened like an opal.

She was startled at first, but stupidly intrigued. He was beautiful, no fat gut like the general. She was going to have him. "I want you, Erickson, and I know you want me." She slid her hand down his side and loosened the towel. As it fell away, she reached for him. Her hand froze. The flaccid, putty-like member rested on top of two shriveled, scarred lumps. "My God!" She jerked her hand back.

He swung around, his left eye flashing. "I warned you, you whore!" The shaving blade slashed across her throat. Her dark eyes were wide open in instant death. The glass of gin smashed on the floor as she fell, hitting the tub, her legs all crooked and wrong. He watched her blood streaming down, staining the thin fabric of her gown, running and pooling on the mosaic tiles of the floor. The smell of gin mingled with the sweet smell of coagulating blood.

He despised the smell of gin.

CHAPTER 12

April 30 - May 1, 1940

The Theater District, London

Looking down at the body, blood and broken glass, he muttered, "Damn! You fool!" His hands trembled, due to his fury at her discovery of his sexlessness. No reason to worry about that now, he thought, looking away. I'm a practical man, work out problems methodically, dispassionately. This is no time to be concerned with fleshy, unpredictable human beings. Just clean things up.

As if under the influence of an insidious anesthesia, von Stein became completely calm, numbed to his surroundings. He limped to the bedroom, took the blue package from the armoire, ripped the string away, and put on his old clothes. Yanking off the wine-red bedspread, he returned to the bathroom, pulled the body flat on the tile floor, and rolled it in the bedspread. With crude jerks, he dragged the roll into the hall.

He removed a box of Borax from under the sink and, with a wct rag, wiped down the wall, tub and floor. He wrung out the pink stained rag and felt a shard of glass embed in his palm. Cursing himself, he thought, I deserve it. All that bitch could think about was fornicating. A special brand of kinky sex would have satisfied her. He realized he was hungry as he kicked the inert, wine-red roll out of his way.

He efficiently searched the drawers of Sonja's bureau, looking for tweezers to extract the sliver of glass. In the top drawer, he found a pair mingled amongst a pile of cheap jewelry. He pulled out the glass with the tweezers and sucked the blood on his palm. Using his other hand, he rifled through a stack of lingerie and found a locked

metal box. After smoothing the contents in the
drawer, he took the box into the galley-like kitchen.

Using a carving knife, he pried open the box.
Three of her passports, one German and two Norwegian, fell out onto the floor. There was also a stack
of fifteen hundred pounds sterling and a blurred
photograph of a distinguished, white-haired gentleman, his arm around Sonja. "Older men," he re-
marked to himself. "Must have been a fixation."

He carefully folded the notes and put them in
his inside jacket pocket. Inept slut, he thought.
Any of her lovers could have found these passports. Damn sloppy for the top Abwehr agent in
Whitehall. Along with the photograph, he shoved
them in next to the money. Looking at his watch,
he was surprised at the late hour: 11:00.

Glancing around the unkempt kitchen, he noticed a skillet filled with grease, several brown eggs,
a small bag of coarse flour, and a scrawny chicken
loosely wrapped in butcher paper. The makings of
chicken and dumplings, a typical German peas-
ant dish, he thought to himself, and pushed it
aside. Then a small smile crossed his face; a chilled
bottle of French champagne sat in an ice bucket,
the only hint of quality on Sonja's menu.

Rummaging through each cupboard, he found
Greek olives, smoked oysters, a bottle of
cornichons, and a tin of goose liver pate. He took
a loaf of bread from the bread box and arranged
his rather elegant repast on the dining table. He
popped the bottle of champagne and considered
the whore's horde, as fine as a catered hamper
from Harrod's food hall.

Settling in the armed dining chair, he ate
slowly. Clearing the table, he heard laughter and
garbled song coming from the stairwell. He swallowed the last of the champagne just as there was

a loud knock at the door. He clenched the glass and nearly broke it. Who the hell is it? The pounding became more persistent.

"Ya there, Sonja?" called out a male voice. "The pubs are closed. Com'on, ya gorgeous blonde. Be a lady and do this gentleman the favah of a nightcap."

Von Stein reached for the butcher knife and slid it in front of him. He moved across the room and stood by the hinged side of the door. "Com'on, Sonja. The night's still young." The doorknob twisted back and forth. He could sense the weight of the man's body against the door. "Ya comin'? Or do I hav' ta break down the door?"

Just when he expected the intruder to break down the door, all movement stopped. He heard the man fumbling with keys and a final slurred curse as the door across the hall slammed shut.

Von Stein rubbed his face with relief and was surprised to find his forehead cool and dry. He went into the bedroom, put on his overcoat and pulled on gloves. He passed by the kitchen and gathered up the keys to the flat, pocketed them and looked at the tightly wrapped burgundy roll. "Well, here we go, lady," he said aloud. Bending down, he tugged at the bundle, lifted one end and placed it over his left shoulder. When he stood, pain shot through his groin. He gritted his teeth as he adjusted the weight and then pulled on his hat.

He limped to the door, opened it cautiously, and looked into the empty hall toward the dimly lit stairwell. He stepped out of the flat, closed the door, and locked it. Directly across the hall, he could hear the drunken actor singing along with a loudly playing Victrola. "It's delovely, it's..."

Reaching the stairwell, he took one last look to assure himself that no one was there. Breathing quietly, but deeply, he began his descent.

"Caughtcha, ya drunken, sexy sot."

Von Stein spun around, crunching the bundle against the stairwell wall. A middle-aged, stubble-faced man with greasy, slicked back hair was standing in the flood of light coming from his flat. In the back light, von Stein could barely make out his drunken grin. The man swayed and swallowed deeply from a whiskey bottle, cleared his throat, and continued, "Thought yer were Sonja. No matter. Canna help, mate?"

"No, thanks," said von Stein. "Have to leave early tomorrow. Need to load the boot now. Sorry to have bothered you."

"Na bother at all. Put down yer load." The man belched loudly. He smiled, his arched eyebrows inching upwards just like a court jester, a harlequin. "I hate to drink alone. Com'on. We'll tip a few. Have a snort wi' ol' Johnny."

Von Stein's mind was ice clear, sharp. I'm going to need his help. Damn these steps. He climbed back to the landing and followed the drunken actor into his flat. He lowered the heavy roll carefully to the floor by the door. He clenched his teeth to keep from groaning in pain and limped into the parlor.

"John's me name. An' you, sir? Com'on, 'ava nip," he said in a pure Cockney accent, ruining the consonants. He held out the bottle.

"Sounds good," said von Stein, not bothering to answer the question and walked over to his host. Johnny was awkwardly perched on a dingy stool by the kitchen pass-through opening. Von Stein reached for the proffered bottle and, as he raised it to his lips, his right fist came up sharply, crushing the man's throat. Johnny's eyes rolled and he began to fall forward, gasping for air.

He switched the bottle to his right hand and, with his left arm, forced the man's head back against the counter. He pushed the bottle into the injured man's mouth. The contents ran into the rapidly swelling trachea. With each gasp, the victim filled his lungs with burning, acidic liquor and died of asphyxiation.

He carried the body to the bedroom and dropped it on the unmade bed. With cool disgust, he undressed the dead man, then rolled him off the bed, making certain his neck and face struck the night table. He returned to the entry and dragged the wine-red roll to the bedroom. Closing his eyes to the pain, he heaved Sonja's body onto the disheveled bed.

He gathered up the bedspread, found a drawer of knives, selected one and wiped her sticky blood onto the knife. He used a towel to wipe the handle of the knife and the whiskey bottle clean of prints. Returning to the bedroom, he tossed the knife onto the floor beside the man's body and threw the bottle against the wall. He then smeared the sticky bedspread over the male corpse. He stood back and calmly looked at the carnage. Not perfect, he thought, but it will do.

Glancing at Sonja, he focused on her eyes, which were open and looked as though they were about to cry. "Sorry, dear," he said aloud. "Unfortunately, you and this poor bloke belong to that vague, peripheral mass of people whom the world will not notice passing." His eulogy done, he caught a glimpse of himself in the cracked vanity mirror. And so do you, von Stein, he thought.

He gathered up the stained spread and left, closing the door behind him and crossed to Sonja's flat. Standing in the kitchen, he undressed. He removed the pound notes and photograph from the coat and rolled the old clothes and overcoat carefully in the bedspread. He sponged off in the kitchen sink. He was almost sorry about the actor, but then John had saved him from the risky business of carrying the body through London's streets. It was 1:00 in the morning; he could still rest before catching the train to Edinburgh.

The ringing of the alarm shocked him awake. He felt rested, even invigorated. It had been a dead, untroubled sleep. He neatly made the bed out of habit.

Dressing in his new suit, he gathered up the spread, and stuffed it in his suitcase. At the door to the flat, he leaned on his cane and took one last look around. Was it her own bad taste or only part of her cover, he wondered.

With effort he limped down the street toward the Chinese District and then to Gerrard Street. He passed by the rear of St. John's Hospital, catching the corbie-step silhouette of the building against the weak morning light. In an alley to his right, he saw a large waste bin and threw the suitcase up into its center.

He proceeded to Leicester Square, passing under the budding trees and the bust of Shakespeare and on toward Trafalgar Square. Luckily, at this early hour, a taxi was just stopping at the rear entrance of the National Gallery, letting off a bespectacled academician. It was a strange reminder of his mission: get Breckkan.

After assisting the elderly occupant from the taxi, he settled back into the dark seat. The pain in his groin was acute from the hurried walk. Leaning forward, he said, "Victoria Station."

The Strand, London

In the tradition of fine English hotels, the Savoy had anticipated his every need. From his river suite he could see the Houses of Parliament to his distant right. If it comes to a bombing war, this city couldn't be more perfectly laid out; the Thames will lead the enemy down its throat. A sickening feeling settled over him. That damn Lewis gun. What a hideous thing to have happened to Ron Larsen. Was the list of horror ever going to end?

Lifting his face toward the torrent of water pouring from the fourteen-inch shower head, he tried to wash away his sadness, closed his eyes, and leaned against the stark black and white tiles of the shower walls.

He reached for a giant white towel on the steam-heated chrome rack, rubbed his hair vigorously, wiped the steam from the mirror, then slipped into a white terry robe, and opened the door to the vestibule. As expected, his polished shoes and pressed suit were there, left by the floor valet. He dressed slowly, war and nuclear theories crowded out by thoughts of Bonnie and her troublesome words of hurt and worry when he had left her alone in Edinburgh.

The low light glanced off the bay window and reflected onto the ceiling. Just like in Venice, he remembered. Had it already been a year? He would never forget the reflected light of the Canal shimmering on the ceiling of their honeymoon suite. For the first time since he had arrived in London, he smiled.

As the gondola swept under dark bridges past sepia palazzos and out into the Grand Canal, Bonnie could only murmur, "Breathtaking."

He seemed to read her mind. "We have plenty of time. Don't worry."

The gondolier skillfully turned the boat from the bustle of the Grand Canal into the Rio del Vin and docked at the first landing. A uniformed attendant stepped from the shadowed doorway and stabilized the rocking boat. "Welcome to the Hotel Danieli."

They emerged from the private dock straight into the heart of the lobby, an ornate fourteenth-century hall. As Bonnie took in the elaborate staircase to her right, Breckkan headed for the reception desk. Nervously twirling the long red tassel on the room key, he crossed the entry hall to look for her. So damn independent. So damn beautiful. He had to remind himself she was now his wife. But where the hell was she? As he scanned the enormous lobby for her, he spotted the red hair before he noticed the well-dressed man standing next to her.

"Olav, he's offered to be our guide," said Bonnie. "We can take his boat to Murano."

Placing his hand in the small of her back, Breckkan said, "First let's check out our room." Addressing the Italian, he added, "Our thanks, signore. Perhaps later."

"We don't need to unpack right now..."

"Who's talking about unpacking?" Bonnie grinned and fell into step with him as he turned away.

Breckkan watched her sleeping, her red hair spread over the pillow. He quietly climbed from bed, crossed the room to the window and cranked up the shutters. As he pushed open the two tall windows facing the Lagoon, light reflected from the shimmer of the Canal and bounced off the vaulted ceiling of their suite. "You're naked," she called from the bed.

"No one can see me except maybe the sea gulls on Guidecca. Besides, maybe I need more than one woman."

"After that?" She slid down under the sheets, covering her head. "That's not enough?" came the muffled question.

He crossed the room to her side of the bed and slowly ran his hands over the sheet-clad body. "Just kidding. Actually, I don't think I can keep up with you."

She slowly pulled the sheet from her face. "Well," she grinned, "I'm the one waddling like a duck." Breckkan laughed as he bent to kiss her. "Go take a shower, a cold, cold shower. Please!"

Though the door from the vestibule to the bedroom was closed as well as the bathroom door, she could still hear him singing over the sound of the shower. She crossed the vestibule and quietly opened the bathroom door. She could see the outline of his body through the sheer white shower curtain. The tightness in her throat warned her of how much she loved him. She reached for the curtain and began to step into the tub just as he turned around. He reached for her, but slipped just as she fell headlong against him. He grabbed for the curtain to stop his fall and heard it rip from the rod.

He was on his back and she was on top of him with the curtain tangled between them. "For Christ's sake," he yelled. "I think I've broken something."

"Not that!" she laughed, sputtering in the stream of water.

He moved his head away from the water just in time to see the bathroom door open.

A maid in a black and white uniform stared at them with wide eyes. "Signore? Signora? You rang?"

Bonnie buried her face in the shower curtain. Breckkan raised up and looked at the maid. "More towels, please."

The maid nodded and backed quickly form the room, closing the door behind her.

Bonnie lifted her head from the sopping curtain and sputtered, "What happened?"

"I must've hit the servant button when I fell. Or

you did, you boob." He collapsed into laughter again.

She sat cross-legged on the bathroom floor, hugging her sides, hiccoughing between giggles. "No way. You were the one who wanted more women!"

Despite the chill of the April morning, they sat at a table on the terrace of the hotel. Bonnie held her coffee cup in both hands, enjoying the warmth. A mist was hanging over the Grand Canal, creating a pearly iridescent haze. Landmarks across the Lagoon seemed to merge together in half-tones.

The evening before, as she laid in his arms, he had told her about the scar under his chin. Sometimes, when he spoke of his youth, she wondered how he survived to adulthood. "What are you thinking about?" she asked.

He looked up. "Mussolini's on his way."

"To Venice?"

"To the Danieli. He and his son-in-law, Ciano, are rounding out a tour of the North. They've been trying to drum up support for the Germans. We've been asked to vacate our suite."

"But I'll miss the Carpaccios at San Giorgio," she said.

"We'll be back. Besides I've thought of something better."

"And Harry's Bar."

He bit into a croissant. "Turner must've sat at this very table."

She affectionately brushed the crumbs from his face. "You haven't shaved."

"I did last night. Just for you. Let's go." He smiled and pulled back her chair. She followed him from the dining room to the elevator.

"Here we are," he answered as he ushered her from the elevator and guided her out the side door to the dock where a 12-meter sloop was moored.

"Isn't she a beauty? It's motorized. Easily managed by two." Breckkan gave her a kiss on the forehead and helped her onto the boat. "You'll love it. I promise."

As Breckkan started the four-piston engine, Bonnie slipped the rope free. He slowly increased the power of the motor and the yacht moved gently into the Lagoon. Bonnie stood next to him and watched as they crossed the Basin, passing between the islands of Giorgio Maggiore and Guidecca. He steered the boat north toward the Lido Porto after clearing the islands and, once into the Adriatic, set a course south by southeast.

She watched as Venice shimmered in the distance. He tapped her on the shoulder and said, "I don't think I've forgotten a thing. Our luggage is below and there's champagne in the ice chest. You break it out while I set the sail."

Bonnie ducked and went below, finding, to her delight, an elegant paneled sitting room with a tidy galley tucked to one side. Pulling back the chrome latch on the ice chest, she smiled: Asti Spumante. If it's as good on deck as it was in bed...

She found him stretched out on a built-in seat near the fantail. He had taken off his shirt and shoes and bunched them under the seat. The full sail pulled the yacht through the placid green water. She sat cross-legged at his feet and poured the sparkling wine. "Well, Captain, will our destination be a secret forever?"

He sat up. The breeze tousled his hair. "Korcula, Yugoslavia. My father and I sailed there years ago. I was just a kid. I don't remember much, but..." He paused, looking out at the open sea. "I remember it was his favorite. On a coast of a thousand islands."

She watched him, trying to imagine the small Norwegian boy standing by his father as they sailed the Dalmatian Coast. No wonder he's not afraid of anything. "Yugoslavia? Is this place safe for us?"

"They're neutral. Besides, it's really unspoiled. A virgin. Not like you," he said, poking her leg with his toe.

Breckkan sat alone on deck, his right hand resting lightly on the wheel. Ahead, he could make out the outlines of several islands. He steered toward the lighthouse visible on the larger land mass. We've crossed the Adriatic, he thought. Not a moment of trouble. The dark islands hovered over the silver water, then disappeared as a cloud passed over the full moon.

Suddenly, the sail undulated and snapped as a blast of wind struck from the South. The yacht veered erratically, caught in the sirocco. He responded immediately to correct the yaw just as the bow dropped into a trough. As the bow rose, water spewed across the forward deck. He stood, bracing himself against the captain's chair, and spun the wheel to a southerly course. All seas are the same, he thought. Just as you begin to trust them... The sail contorted again and he fought to steady the wheel. He felt the trembling in his hands and the sweat beading on his forehead. The wind is hot, dangerous, he thought, as he reached up to wipe the perspiration. His shirt was soaked. A wave of nausea washed over him. Not now, no, not with her. He shook his head furiously, trying to regain control of himself, but his mind whirled deeper. Deeper into the trough, deeper into the nightmare. He was on another boat. It was another storm, happening all over again, convulsing around him.

He jumped as she placed her hand on his shoulder. "What's going on? You're soaking wet." She moved around to face him. His hair was matted, his forehead glistened with sweat. She reached for him and felt his clammy skin. "Why didn't you call me?"

He shook his head and said, "I'm okay."

She reached for a towel draped on the chair. "Let me dry your face." He didn't resist, but closed his eyes and dropped his head as he sat down. He kept his head down as he reached for her shoulders. She could feel the tremor in his hands. Glancing to her right, she caught the outline of the islands scattered in the distance. "We're across," she breathed to herself, "but where?"

"I'm sorry." He paused and then looked at her. His eyes were glazed and his cheeks seemed hollow. She started to speak, but looked away, sensing the angst in his expression. He stood and walked toward the front of the yacht, shaking his head. She watched as he looked up at the sail, rubbing his neck with the towel.

He turned to look back at her. In the moonlight, she looked fragile, even vulnerable. "I'm sorry. What a helluva time for this to happen." He looked away for a moment, then back at her. "I'm terrified of water."

"What are you talking about? The Regatta. Copenhagen." He shook his head. "You dove in when von Stein attacked me and I fell overboard."

"That was different. All I could think about was saving you. Something terrible happened a long time ago. Since then..."

"Then why are we in this boat now?"

"It's my way of proving..." He looked straight at her. The wind ruffled his hair; he looked better, less agitated. "It's my way. Do you understand?"

"Not completely, but I'll try," she said softly as she reached for his hand. With the growing light, his demons seemed to have left him.

Breckkan shook his head, then realized he was

silhouetted against an open window. Quickly pulling the blackout drapes shut, he realized he badly
needed a drink and Chadwick was waiting.

Leaving his suite, he took the elevator to the
mezzanine, turned right down the wide hall, and
descended the steps into the lobby. Since his afternoon arrival, the activity had increased; the lobby
was packed. He spotted Wakefield leaning against
a sienna marble column, newspaper in hand.

"Hello," Breckkan said as he shook Wakefield's
outstretched hand.

"The weather's turned nasty. Come with me."
Breckkan followed him through the lobby to the Grill
Room. At the entrance, Wakefield greeted the maitre
d', telling him in a quiet voice he would like to save
his friend a walk in the rain. With an understated
bow, the maitre d' turned and led them through the
Grill's kitchen into a large stock room and unlocked
what appeared to be a seldom-used door.

Breckkan silently followed Wakefield through
the underground passage, only a few gas jets lighting the way. They passed through an open iron
door, then up into the bustling kitchens of Simpson's. The black-capped master chef, Arthur Moss,
waved a greeting over the din.

Noting the sign, "Men Only Bar," on the main
floor, Breckkan smiled, thinking to himself that
Bonnie would be appalled at the custom gratify-
ing male self-esteem. She had once compared the
gatherings at the smoke-filled men's clubs to that
of a dog pack: men like each other like dogs like
each other. She had dubbed the exclusive Oslo
Club, "Holberg's— a mausoleum of ossified
masculinity."

From his mahogany podium at the head of the
stairs, the Captain greeted Wakefield by name.
"Professor Chadwick has already arrived, sir. This

way, please," he said, leading the way to a green leather banquette.

Chadwick stood and reached out to shake hands with the American. "I see you've brought our guest, Mr. Wakefield."

"Let me introduce Dr. Olav Breckkan. I think you know his father-in-law quite well."

"Who in this profession doesn't?" responded Chadwick, grasping Breckkan's hand and shaking it firmly. "What do you fancy? Whiskey, champagne?"

"I believe I'll stay with whiskey."

"Pardon me, gentlemen," interrupted a waiter. "May I suggest oysters as a starter?"

Not looking at him, Chadwick said, "We'll choose straightaway from the trolley."

"Very good, sir. We're usually short of meat, but I've saved you something special. Tonight I have fine spring lamb from Yorkshire. It's from my cousin's farm, Bernard Thomas, in Holywell Green. A find lamber, he is."

"Thank you. And a bottle of your best claret," said Chadwick, waving him away. He turned to Breckkan. "All's well with Professor Kittleson?"

"The doctors are confident."

"Good. You got your work results out before the Germans invaded?" He paused only to study Breckkan's face. "Your work is in concert with ours as far as I know. It would have been devastating to hand that over to the enemy."

Breckkan reached for his whiskey and, with a calculated motion, slowly took a swallow. "I agree."

"Do you think the Germans know you have it?"

"I have no idea."

"Well, then," said Chadwick, "a more personal question. Just where are you hiding the data?"

"In my head."

"All of it?" asked Chadwick.

"Yes, all of it. Heavy water will work as a moderator, no question, but..." Breckkan drained his glass. "Professor Kittleson's work is impressive. My wife and I have considerable data to support him as well."

"You're leaning that way, toward graphite?"

"We're not counting out anything." It wasn't the time or place to defend his scientific work and opinions.

"Keeping you options open; I don't blame you. The fact is that nuclear energy is now a reality, for all sides." Chadwick half-turned to the American. "Perhaps the United States had best start helping us keep as much uranium out of the hands of the Nazis as possible."

Wakefield's expression showed no response. There was something almost oriental about his unobtrusive calm. Finally he spoke up, "I'm not naive about nuclear energy, but the problem is a political one, so far as American is concerned."

"No one asked for this war," Breckkan said intently. "That *political* naiveté will have to break down soon, Bill."

Silence prevailed as a chef in white toque and long white apron rolled a large silver-domed trolley to their table. He rolled the dome back on the hinges, disappearing it into the under portion of the trolley, revealing two beautiful joints of lamb. "Dr. Chadwick," the carver asked, "how would you prefer your meat?"

"Well done." His guests nodded in agreement. Using a heavy steel carving knife, the carver sliced portions from one of the joints, as a waiter added roasted potatoes and a wedge of cabbage to each plate. Chadwick tipped the carver and busied himself with eating.

Breckkan ate slowly, watching his host. He was

dressed in typical English manner, a baggy gray suit and school tie; the suit coat was fitted too long at the waist, emphasizing his height and gangly legs. He had appeared stooped when he stood, perhaps from an old back injury or arthritis. If he was abrupt, Breckkan guessed Chadwick was ill at ease or worse, bored, with any other subject than his own specialty.

Wakefield carefully folded his napkin and said, "I'm amazed. Times like these and such fine food."

"I agree," Breckkan said. "The best food I've eaten in months."

Chadwick wiped his mouth and motioned for the waiter. The table was cleared and the tea service appeared. "So, Breckkan, might we count on your joining our laboratory? We need your experience." There was nothing but a positive assumption in his tone. No conceit, no impertinence.

"I would be honored to work with you."

"Good. We'll send a car tomorrow to take you up to Cambridge."

"Fine," answered Breckkan, "but my wife and Professor Kittleson, they'll be joining me."

"I assumed that," Chadwick interrupted. "Now, returning to our earlier discussion, I would hope you would work with us on graphite."

"Remember, Dr. Chadwick, the bulk of my work has concentrated on heavy water, metallurgy, and cryogenics."

"Yes, however, with the Hydro Plant inconveniently located in German territory..." He paused, sensing Breckkan's sudden anger in response to his blunt comment. "Sorry. I didn't mean to be callous." Chadwick's long face tightened with worry. "We must be first to succeed. We need you NOW."

Breckkan looked away, fully realizing the impact of his work. Bonnie's voice, shaking with emotion when he left her, filled his ears.

Chadwick signed the bill with a scrawl. "Fancy a walk? We're quite near the Chinese District. I find it a rather interesting area of sorts. A physician at St. John's Hospital is a dear friend of mine. We can shortcut through the hospital."

"It's near midnight," said Wakefield, looking at his watch. "The theater crowds will be gone."

CHAPTER 13

May 9, 1940

Oslo

Petter stood to one side of the drawing room windows, catching an oblique view of the black sedan negotiating the steep drive to the forecourt. "They're here, Mrs. Breckkan." Her head tilted slightly to one side, her concentration consumed with the solemn First Movement of the Brahms Symphony No. 1. The bell rang at the entrance doors.

Petter stiffened, but waited patiently until she said, "Let them in. Don't offer coffee, tea, anything." She glanced back at the business journal in her lap, closing it at the sound of footsteps on the stairs.

"Madam, Mr. Gustave Breckkan and Major von Papen have arrived."

"Thank you, Petter. Leave the doors open."

"As you wish. I'll be just down the hall should you require anything." She felt the resistance in his voice and knew his tone of civility was only for appearance.

"The gardens are spectacular, Dora," commented Gustave, absently looking past them to the view of the Oslofjord below.

The tall German officer extended his hand. "Mrs. Breckkan, my name is Frederick von Papen." He spoke directly, his neatly pressed dark suit adding to his composed appearance.

"Excuse my curiosity, but what exactly is your military position?" Dora reached for the Florentine marble box on the side table and took out a cigarette. The German moved quickly to light it, stepped back, and settled easily onto the sofa opposite her. For such a tall man, he made little noise when he moved, and noise was one of the first things she had missed when Nic was gone. Noise, activity, vibrant movement.

Gustave sat down heavily in a chair. "The Major is highly placed; he might be able to act in our mutual interest. He's the man who can keep the company trade routes open."

"Your background, Major?" Dora asked as she tapped the cigarette on the marble ashtray. "Before the war?" she added.

"International trading. Getting things to the right places on time, that sort of thing."

She concentrated on his expertly trimmed beard, trying not to admit to herself she had no choice but to listen to the man.

"As emissary from the German High Command, I'm to oversee the productivity of your country's enterprises. It is absolutely necessary that Breckkan Mining continue at full production." He studied the petite woman. "We want to demonstrate our respect for you, therefore, your brother-in-law," he nodded at Gustave, "will remain as the company head and you, Mrs. Breckkan, will remain as titular head."

"Titular! What a ridiculous word!" she muttered, grinding out her cigarette. It wasn't hot in the room, but she crossed to the windows and threw them open to let in fresh air.

"Dora, we have no choice," said Gustave. She glared at him, totally aware of her vulnerability.

"As I said, Mrs. Breckkan," continued von Papen in the same infuriatingly calm voice, "with respect for your position, we have decided to move you and your manservant. You shall continue under house arrest, but in a safer place." Raising his voice and speaking more deliberately, he continued, "The only reason you're not going to prison as certain of your countrymen are, is that you are

American born, and fortunately for you, you continue to carry your American Passport. The United States has made the very wise decision to stay out of European business."

Dora stared unblinking at the officer. If only you knew just how Norwegian I am, she thought—more so than most Norwegians, including Gustave.

"I'm told you usually go to your island home each summer." Dora continued to look out at the grounds behind the estate. "Skatøy? Is that correct?"

She said in a solicitous tone, "That has been my habit since we bought the island." As she reached down for another cigarette, the Adagio of Brahms Fourth Movement began, exquisitely expressing her feelings.

"We will supply transportation and the appropriate escort to Kragerø. Of course, you will be permitted to take your personal belongings," continued the officer in a monotone. "I will be using your home here in Oslo. It should be comfortable lodging for visiting senior officers. I'll also be watching Breckkan Mining personally. Have you any objections?" She sat stiffly, wanting to scream. The German looked at Gustave questioningly, thinking perhaps she was hard of hearing. He repeated the question.

After several more moments, she answered, "Since this seems to already be settled..." She glanced at Gustave. "I assume you have a timetable."

"We would like to suggest next weekend. Would you be willing to receive help with your transfer on the morning of the thirteenth?"

"We'll be ready, Major. I do ask one favor, though."

"A favor?"

"Monthly reports, with briefings from Gustave." She knew the request was absurd, but continued. "I realize I have no authority, but I know how the company runs most efficiently. If the plant managers think I've turned my back on them or worse, that you have taken me away, there will be chaos. But, if they think I still have some authority..." She raised her eyebrows as she snubbed out her cigarette.

"Done," said Major von Papen.

Edinburgh

The bedroom was freezing. Bonnie lay motionless, her head barely visible under the mound of blankets. She shifted slightly, her bare foot touching the repulsive, cold rubber of the water bottle, and decided to face the morning chill. She pulled on her robe and padded to the window, looking out at the ancient tenements, an intricate maze of alleyways and U-shaped closes. Abstractly noting the line of ice on the inside of the glass, she shivered and pushed her hands deeper into her pockets. Two sharp knocks and the opening of the door turned her attention to the arrival of the Major's maid.

"Ah, yer're up, lassie. Here's a proper Scottish breakfast." She was small and dark. Her gentle voice belied any sullenness. "There's porridge, cream, Ayrshire bacon, tomatoes, eggs, and kippers. Checked meself to make sure the kippers were smoked proper. Over oak. And I put a nob of butter on top." From beneath a dark mop of hair, the soft spoken voice continued. "So, off I go, dearie. Just put the tray outside the door when yer're done."

When the girl had left, closing the door behind her, Bonnie realized she had never made direct eye contact with her. She was still thinking about the small dark woman, speculating on her place of birth, when she walked through the hospital gates and entered the maze of old turreted buildings.

The cream-colored corridors were endless, with

miles of thick pipes wrapped in blankets. The faint odor of antiseptic permeated even the countless coats of enamel paint. She followed an officious trio of nurses up the stairs to the second floor.

Coming out of Knut's room was his doctor, a robust man of sixty years with serious blue eyes and dandruff. But dandruff or not, Bonnie had liked him immediately.

Catching sight of her, he paused, slapping that day's copy of *The Scotsman* against his palm, and said briskly, "And a good morning to you, Mrs. Breckkan. Have you seen the latest? Rumor has it Chamberlain resigned and Churchill has been summoned to Number 10. High time for a decisive leader, I'd say." In a softer tone, he continued, "Not to worry, dear. The night nurse said he was in quite a temper in the wee hours. Something about her dropping trays." His bright eyes flashed with humor. "But he's sleeping quietly now. We've a new nurse to absorb his barbs. Go on in."

Bonnie pulled up a chair to her father's bed and studied him; his color was pale, but no longer ashen. He looked comfortable, thoughtful, at peace. He seemed to be seeing beyond her, beyond the room, to some private memory. Was he young and in love, sailing a small boat to the island, trying to impress his young bride, his thick blonde hair blowing in the wind? Did he remember opening the bottle of Bernkastler and tasting the spice of the pale wine? Did she like it? He seemed happy, whatever his thoughts. She turned to hang her umbrella and coat over the back of the chair.

"Why are you here?" he asked abruptly.

He was speaking Norwegian, his voice slurred. He scowled, noticing the slur; so did the nurse sitting in the corner. Bonnie replied, for her benefit, in English. "Good morning, Father. The staff seems rather amused with your outbursts."

His head turned toward the window, eyes squinting in the light. He looked back at Bonnie, his concentration seemingly fixed. "Rest, they say. I've never rested in my life." He ran a thin hand through his wild white hair. "How can you rest while these well-meaning souls poke and prod, disrobe you, and then drug you."

"Glad you're feeling better, Father. I'm sure they'll be relieved to have you leave."

"And that's not all. If it is the business of this so-called health facility to heal people, the least they could do would be to bring some proper food. Everything...and I mean everything, their pasty porridge or some pitiful pudding...everything is watery and gray. The only occasional difference is when they cover some nondescript blob with so-called 'cream sauce.'" His color was improving with the pace of his tirade. "And that Doctor! I do believe he enjoys the gift of the grape. I swear I smelled claret on his breath." The nurse's knitting needles clacked furiously. "Ah, but there is one bright spot in my day. Peggy. A wisp of a thing. She pops in occasionally to share the latest joke with me."

"And what's the latest from this Peggy?"

"Seems that everyone about here, everyone living on this side of the castle— you've seen it, haven't you? The castle?"

"Of course," Bonnie answered, exasperated with his wanderings for once. "Go on."

"New Town is what they call the other side. It's supposedly all too wide open and windy. Some boring city planner's dream. It's where all the conservative pin-stripes and flannels take roost."

"The joke, Father, please." The clacking needles slowed.

"Ah, well, Peggy swears that in New Town, sex

is what they deliver coal in."

Bonnie blurted out a laugh and heard a chuckle from the corner. The shadows on the Professor's face had faded; his peevish mood brightened. "And you, my dear lady, do you call New Town home?" he asked the nurse.

The color flushed high on her cheekbones as she defensively answered, "Goodness no, you old coot. I've a flat on Chambers Street, near the Kirk of Greyfriars. Luv'ly, even tho' the chimney pots will likely tumble down with our next great wind. Enough chatter from you now," she said, putting down her knitting and fussing with the bed linens, tucking the sheets in tightly enough to cut off Knut's circulation. "Time to rest and then another luv'ly luncheon." Her authoritative bustle indicated to Bonnie that the visit was over.

"I'm off, Father. Maybe I'll pick up something for you to eat that's neither gray nor mushy. I think I'll go take a look at Greyfriars."

"Watch yourself. The square below is full of meths at night. Drunks, all of them."

"Meths?"

"Meth drinkers. Your father's told me 'bout your training. You should know what's created by boilin' milk through coal gas. Methyl alcohol. The poor souls drink the stuff."

Von Stein shivered as he leaned against the moist stone work. The cold dampness was seeping through the wall.

He had positioned himself where he had a perfect view of the side exit and the main entrance. He stiffened as a pack of boys from the George Heriot School flashed by, giggling and screeching, then casually watched two small boys in blazers pause in the middle of their antics. He smiled grimly at them. They hurriedly finished marring the wall with their pocket knives and ran down a flight of black steps.

Bonnie stood at the gates of the Kirk, peering at the somber monuments in the graveyard. There was a sense of remote stillness in the Edinburgh spring, a northern chill draped the city. She slowly walked down the narrow, curving street, passing the doorway of a secondhand bookstore and the misted windows of a dingy cafe. An opening in the block led to a row of dank buildings; black ice glazed the darkened close.

A smoky smell permeated the layers of soot and filled her nostrils. Suddenly she felt a tug at her coat and spun around in the street.

"Crykie, dearie, giv' this old woman a kiss!"

Spittle sprayed on Bonnie's coat. The woman leaned even closer, her dank, sickening smell engulfing Bonnie's senses. She wanted to push her away, to run. She did neither, but fished in her pocket and gave the old woman a half crown. "Get some food. Some coffee."

"May God have mercy upon you. But no kisses? No kisses..." Her voice drained into a low moan. The spit from her mouth ran into soot-caked wrinkles. The pitiful soul stumbled off.

Bonnie stood rigid, feeling like she was transposed into a Hogarth canvas, a world of toothless smiles, hysterical laughter reverberating throughout the sordid darkness. Life passed quickly through their grimy fingers. She knew the process of degeneration: their life expectancy was under forty years.

A lorry rumbled downward on the cobblestone street. Bonnie shivered involuntarily, visibly shaken. She shoved a hand deeper into the pocket of her coat, clutched her umbrella and walked briskly down the curve, emerging at the edge of a broad square. The Grassmarket. Resisting the impulse to run, she instinctively headed toward the southwest corner of the square.

In the shadows of a pitch-black close, an alley as inviting as the grim entrance to a coal mine, stood a silent figure. He had made a complete reconnaissance and waited patiently near the bottom of the staircase. Five hundred years of wear had eroded the steps; the stone scars were caulked with soot and black ice.

He pulled his hat down further and raised the overcoat collar to protect his face. Out of two black holes in the white face, he had dispassionately watched Bonnie's encounter with the old woman. She's afraid, her concentration rattled. Maintaining a deadly stillness, he watched her through his tinted glasses.

Bonnie raced up the steps leading out of the Grassmarket. In her hurry, she slipped repeatedly on the ice and resorted to grabbing the frozen iron railing. Her face tipped upward toward the pale light at the top of the steep climb. She appeared defenseless, fragile, feminine to von Stein and, for a moment, he experienced a brief, unexplained sexual urge. As she came closer, he glanced up and down the staircase. There was no one.

Just as her strained climb brought her in front of the close, von Stein reached out and grabbed her arm, jerking her into the narrow, arched passage. Bonnie's eyes were wide, all pupils. She opened her mouth to scream, but there was no sound. Von Stein slapped his gloved hand over her mouth to prevent a second effort and whispered, "Don't!"

He forced her back against the cold stone wall,

pinning one arm behind, immobilizing her. With his free hand, he removed his glasses and glared at her with his pink eye. She swallowed a scream; the closeness of the clouded, opalescent eye was terrifying. "Bonnie, you could have been hurt. Why are you in this vulgar place?" he asked, releasing his grip on her mouth.

"You bastard! What are you doing in Edinburgh!"

"Let's get you home." His good eye twitched. "Breckkan must be worried about you. Besides, I desperately need to talk to him."

The mention of Breckkan precipitated a feeling of pure terror. Cold sweat beaded on her forehead. The strong odor of peat and the tightness of the passage brought on a full attack of claustrophobia. She had to get away. Now! She jerked her arm free. Von Stein reached for her.

"No, don't..." he murmured in a guttural tone.

Bonnie ignored him. Her foot touched her umbrella on the pavement beneath her. In one complete motion, she knelt, grabbed the umbrella and jabbed the handle into von Stein's groin. He was instantly consumed with agony, moaning an eerie screech. She ran.

Von Stein followed, fighting down the immense pain. Near the top of the stairs, he lunged forward to grab her coat, but something inside him snapped. The pain became total. His bladder involuntarily emptied as he fell to the sidewalk, rolling backward down the black steps.

Without looking back, Bonnie ran down Lauriston Place. Ahead she could see the meticulously trimmed hedge in front of the boarding house, but purposefully ran past it, turning down Lawson Street. She joined the cover of the crowds shopping on Lothian Road, walking for more than three quarters of an hour, constantly glancing back. Her mind raced, jagged thoughts finally focusing on a terrifying question. How did he find her?

She entered the boarding house and called out for the Major. No answer. Alone, she climbed the stairs to her room, opened the door and crossed to the window. The view suddenly didn't seem so innocent. "He wants me! Why did Olav leave me here alone!" she cried out loud. The silence was broken by the shouts of children flying a kite, running across the rooftops. She laughed shrilly and turned away from the window, shivering as she focused on the empty fire grate.

CHAPTER 14

May 13, 1940

Berlin

The Mercedes sped down the deserted streets of outer Berlin. The evening shadows deepened, only occasional blasts of deep-red rhododendrons punctuated the landscape. Colonel Richter sat silently, staring out the car window. He knew Canaris didn't include him in this meeting for any social purpose, that's for certain. I wonder what he knows that I don't. Goddamn, not a word. Every agent on the alert and still not a clue.

The young driver arrogantly skidded around a tight curve. They were entering the Wannsee Lake District, passing thickets of trees, manicured hedges and overbearing villas. The early twentieth-century buildings were done in the Wilhelmine neo-rococo style favored by nouveau riche Berliners. As the road carved its way through the woods, he caught glimpses of the fabled indigo lake through periodic gaps in the thick growth.

The Mercedes slowed and stopped at a set of imposing iron gates: Am Grossen Wannsee 56-58. Richter lowered his window and handed a guard his identification papers. Carefully looking at the Colonel and then the documents, the guard reviewed the list of names on his clipboard. Checking off the name, he clicked his heels together and gave a rigid salute. The gates lumbered open and the car proceeded onto the private grounds. The drive was surfaced with pea-sized gravel, immaculately raked.

Richter stepped from the car and ascended the stone steps leading to the massive gray stucco house. Wisps of mist, seemingly left over from the shrouded lake, floated past the second-floor windows. Greeted at the door by omnipresent guards, he glanced up at the lighted crest above the door, the German eagle with the swastika in its claws.

From the foyer, he was directed up curved staircase to a large drawing room. A wall with three glass doors led out to a terrace overlooking the lake. Touches of marble, mirrors, and crystal gave the room a jewel-box quality. A bravura selection from a Wagnerian opera echoed throughout the salon.

Ladies gowned in satin and silks moved professionally from officer to officer. Richter watched in amusement as the ladies draped themselves around the officers, spilling champagne and ashes on their custom-made uniforms.

The gaiety, the superiority, the total confidence which pervaded the room suddenly repulsed Richter. Didn't they realize that back in Berlin there were food lines waiting for scraps? The new German war machine was consuming all resources like a porcine carnival fat man.

A waiter offered him a cognac. "No, Fachinger water." Richter knew the waiters in their white vests and black trousers were SS.

"My best agent." Canaris approached him, hands clasped behind his back, his head slightly lowered. He was shorter than Richter, only 5 feet 4 inchs, and prematurely gray. His pale-blue eyes glanced up with a look of amusement. "I admire your abstinence."

"Good evening, Admiral."

"We need to talk. Alone." Richter followed him across the hall and closed the door to the library as ordered.

Taking his seat in an oversized easy chair, Canaris began. "Himmler will be here soon. The Gestapo insists this von Stein thing be resolved."

"Yes, Admiral. My people are working full time on it."

"And?"

"At the moment, nothing. But we will find..."

"And when you do, then what?" The Admiral warmed his snifter of cognac in both hands, swirling it slightly, and then drained it. "Major von Stein is your man, Colonel. Surely you were aware of his shortcomings."

Richter knew Canaris and Himmler were at odds. What's he leading up to, he wondered. How much does he know?

"That woman and the scientist he's supposed to be bringing over to us. Tell me about the incident in Copenhagen."

Richter chose his words carefully. "Doctor Breckkan asked for a sample of von Stein's blood."

"Why?"

"Von Stein is albino. Breckkan was doing some sort of genetic experiment."

"And you feel the incident was minor?" interrupted Canaris. "What about the woman?"

Richter looked past Canaris and said, "I understand von Stein was involved with her. Obviously she chose another man— Dr. Breckkan."

Canaris' pale eyes were ice cold. "Richter, your judgment stinks. It all has the smell of revenge, jealousy. They say von Stein's a genius. It has been my experience that many true geniuses aren't completely, shall we say, sane. Could this man be on some sort of personal rampage?"

"He was severely injured at Vemork."

"I know that! The doctors say he'll never be able to reproduce. Perhaps that is why it seems he's completely forgotten that Dr. Olav Breckkan is one of the world's most influential nuclear experts and that his work is critically important to our scientists. Von Stein is obviously out of control! Christ, and I have to deal with Himmler."

Throughout the conversation, Richter had remained standing. Now Canaris stood and walked slowly to a large buffet of palisander wood, reached for a decanter of cognac, and filled his glass to the top. Without looking at Richter, he said, "Sorry, there's no mineral water."

Richter said nothing. His face felt hot. Obviously, Canaris knew everything in the file. The attempted rape. Was it in fact lust or psychosexual? Is he insane? The Admiral's voice, tinged with malevolence, interrupted his thoughts.

"Come here, Colonel. The view of the grounds is quite beautiful. Look at those peonies." Staring out into the long shadows, he continued, "Today one of our London back-up agents sent a most distressing report." Richter held his breath and looked down at the garden. "Our principal operative in London, in Whitehall no less, is dead."

"My God, how?"

"Her throat was slit." Canaris drank slowly and deeply, then returned to his chair. "Sit, Colonel. There's more."

Richter took a sip of water. He had trouble swallowing and only nodded an acknowledgment. The timbre of Canaris's voice acted like a pincer. He felt the icy stare follow him to his chair.

"The scene was a hurried or careless effort to make her death look like a sexual encounter gone wrong, but the location of the body isn't important." He settled back into his chair. "There were some noticeably odd details though. For example, the bed was carefully made. We know she was a slob. A nymphomaniac. Then the wastebasket in the kitchen..."

"The wastebasket?" asked Richter.

"Yes, filled with empty tins, recently emptied. All gourmet foods. Fortnum and Mason."

"So?"

"Our agent didn't appreciate gourmet anything. She probably kept it there only for her lovers."

"You suspect one of her lovers?" He let out a grunt of distaste.

"No, we don't think so. Her passports are missing. And her discretionary, shall we say, funds are gone. Can you make anything of this?"

"Not knowing her, no. It appears the agent encountered someone who took advantage of an opportunity and then a windfall." Richter's mind swirled. Von Stein. His baronial background. His epicurean tastes. His apparent sexual fixations, his fastidious habits, and that unnerving notation in a report from Oslo. For no logical reason, von Stein had murdered an official driver at the Palace, putting his mission at risk from the start.

"Richter," interrupted Canaris, "pay attention. She wasn't just any whore." His long, narrow fingers wrapped around the snifter.

The collar of his uniform felt tight against his windpipe. "I was just reviewing the few facts you've given."

"Not so few. We've both been in this business a long time. I can guess what you're thinking. Tell me now, doesn't this sound a little like your von Stein? He was sent to her by our agent in Oslo."

"I'm not sure yet, Admiral."

"Well, until you are, isolate him. His only contact is the Norwegian, code-named Vulpes. That's the only way he can get help. Correct?" Richter nodded. "Notify Vulpes to cut him off. That will force him back to us. I believe your von Stein has changed his objectives." His voice had a vicious ring to it, half threat, half sarcasm.

Richter said nothing, relieved that the room was now nearly dark. A lone lamp provided the only illumination. Canaris couldn't see him sweating. He breathed slowly. Just that morning his Norwegian sources had confirmed that Kittelson and the Breckkans were joining Chadwick at the Cavendish Laboratory. So he still had some control. Von Stein would soon know to head for Cambridge. Maybe it's not too late. He can still get the data for the Reich.

"Richter, you've left me again," Canaris said icily. "It's your problem. Assign another agent if you wish. The Führer and the war department want the heavy-water reports."

"And if von Stein should get the data?"

"Then eliminate him."

"That's quite a sacrifice," Richter murmured, hoping to borrow time. "He's one of our top scientists."

Canaris walked to the door and placed his hand on the knob. In the darkness, Richter could still sense the pale eyes staring straight at him. "Remember, he's only provisional head at the Kaiser-Wilhelm. You decided to enlist him for this, so he's your problem." He paused for a fraction of a second, wrapping his warning in a facetious tone. "I'll see you receive the credit one way or another."

Suddenly Richter was alone in the library, standing in his sweat-soaked shirt. His mind had absorbed every inference, but von Stein had not been his choice. Von Stein had been chosen by Admiral Canaris himself, the Chief of German Military Intelligence. There was no way he could win. A nagging fear blew on the back of his neck. At any moment he could be reduced to the bunde...die an old foot guard in front of some dismal building.

Hurriedly, he made his exit, stopping once on the stairs to stiffen and snap a salute to Reichsführer Himmler. The shrill laughter of the ladies and the guffaws of Germany's leaders were now a pitched cacophony.

As the Mercedes turned from the gravel drive onto the route leading back to Berlin, Richter pulled a flask from the map pocket on the back of the front seat, removed the cap, and drank deeply. Moonlight flashed in white stripes through the pine trees.

Cambridge

Von Stein entered the busy street, leaving the tranquility of the quadrangle of King's Hall College. In conversation with several robed students, he'd quickly learned that insiders referred to the college only as "The Hall." His first instinct had been to check the chemistry departments of each college, and The Hall was known for its premier science program. But his plan to check all thirty colleges would not work; he was simply too weak. He needed a place to think, a place where a stranger wouldn't be particularly noticed.

The great pipe organ in the King's College Chapel began, announcing the twelve o'clock hour. He stopped and looked up at the Chapel. An understatement at best, for the facade was more that of a colossal cathedral. The midday sun shone through the quatrefoils of the stained glass windows. He leaned on his cane, gathering strength from the brisk air.

A trio of students, each with his college scarf jauntily tossed around his neck, passed von Stein, one accidently bumping him. You pompous bastards, he thought, in your elite, narrow world. The Germans will soon have you strangling in your precious scarves.

"Excuse me, sir," apologized the student, pausing to steady the white-haired man. "Still in a fog after my last tutorial."

"No apology necessary, the cane gets in the way," von Stein said, turning toward him. "Tell me, where's the best place to eat close by?"

"For something other than mutton and cauliflower, try The Cellar, just there," he suggested, pointing across the street. "Just a wine bar, but nice. A bit loud."

"Right, thank you." The rosy-cheeked boy could have stepped out of a Reynolds portrait, he thought; England never seems to change.

He gingerly worked his way down the stairs. The Cellar was a long room of ocher walls and a vaulted ceiling. The place was crammed with both students and dons. He claimed an empty table in a far corner, spread his overcoat across it, and headed for the bar. Glancing up at the chalkboard, he ordered the daily special.

The bulbous nosed bartender ladled up the soup and slid it toward him. "The mulligatawny will put some color in your face. How 'bout some wine?"

"House white will do. Give me a bottle," answered von Stein.

The warmth of the thick soup calmed him, just the right amount of curry. Even the dull pain in his groin seemed to subside. The laughter and loud talk served his purpose; he was at once in a sea of humanity, yet quite alone.

Where do I go from here, he wondered. The country, despite appearances, was on alert. A state of war had existed for nearly half a year. The nurses in Edinburgh had been a help, but now Breckkan might be anywhere in the countryside. These damn English and their drafty mausoleums. The titled upper classes were donating their country homes to the cause and God knows England had the lion's share of lords and ladies.

He reached into his pocket and pulled out the

photograph of Sonja and her lover. He angrily snapped the corner of the photo. *If she had only been more professional. I've got to identify the Norwegian agent. Take the chance to contact him.* He reached for his glass of wine, remembering she'd said the wine in England was cheap, but good. *Her sole legacy.*

A fresh-faced student, at the urging of friends, climbed atop a table and began delivering Caesar's death soliloquy. The crowd yelled encouragement and prepared to catch the thespian when he fell to his sham death.

"I've got it!" Von Stein was startled by the sound of his own voice. He shoved the photo in his pocket and hurriedly finished his wine. Grabbing up his coat and hat, he limped through the throng toward the actor, now in the throes of death.

Caesar would have benefitted from Falstaff's cynicism, he thought to himself as he pushed open the door. "What is honor? Who hath it? He that died on Wednesday," he murmured out loud.

Cambridgeshire

Top down, the two-seater MG rumbled down the country road. Bonnie paid little attention to the vociferous driver. Any other time, she would have reveled in the low-slung car and probably asked to take over the wheel, but today the feeling of anxiety increased with each passing mile. They had left Cambridge ten minutes ago and the road seemed to close in on them, growing more and more narrow, bound by stone fences. She ducked as a low tree branch whipped at her face.

The lab assistant took a hand from the wheel and pointed. "Just over there."

She turned to look as her scarf wrapped around

her face, blocking her view. She clutched at it and held the ends tightly. The car lurched as they crossed over a stone bridge and bumped onto a seldom-used grass path. They were going down-hill, but more slowly. There sat a low, white stucco cottage, its slate roof disappearing into the dark foliage. It appeared totally deserted. The assistant cut the motor and reached for the hand brake. "Here we are." He opened her door then unstrapped two suitcases from the rear of the car. "Belongs to an old widow. She has a brilliant mind for codes. She's at Bletchley Park and was glad to lease the house. Said to tell you the soil is luv'ly. You can easily have a fabulous garden."

Bonnie spoke for the first time. "It's so far from the city. I expected something closer."

The assistant led her down a randomly placed stone walk edged with day lilies and iris. He set down the luggage, unlocked the door, and man-aged to get the bags inside the narrow doorway. "Mind the step, ma'am," he said, holding the door open. The hall had low beams and a floor of gray flagstone. A window seat was to the right, flanked by geraniums in need of water.

She slowly removed her scarf and shook her head. The red hair fell loose and full. Pushing the hair away from her high forehead, she turned and caught the young man gawking. She smiled briefly, reading his thoughts.

"I'll be going now," he said, feigning a cough.

"Thank you. Do drive carefully."

She was just beginning to move from window to window, pulling back the drapes, when there was a sharp rap at the door. Involuntarily, she jumped and cursed her own skittishness. Open-ing the door, she stepped back as the keen-faced man ducked his head and said, "Nearly forgot. Your husband will be late."

"Late? But he did know when I was arriving?"

"Not to worry. I rang him up while we were at the convalescent home with your father and gave him directions. He shouldn't be long." He climbed back into the car and raked the gears, gunning up the narrow drive and disappearing over the hill.

Bonnie walked through the small, dank rooms, feeling the chill. Above the wide fireplace was a collection of Blue Willow platters and the mantle piece was lined with antique Toby jugs and a Staffordshire bust of John Wesley. Hanging to the left of the fireplace was a wide-brimmed hat, and, neatly arranged below, a pair of clogs and battered Wellingtons. Running her fingers along the carved wooden mantel, she traced an inscription: two sets of initials and a date. Probably an anniversary, she thought, feeling a tightness in her throat.

She returned to the window seat and gazed out at the sloping hillside. A gathering mist hung over the meadow. A sense of profound isolation spread over her. The strain of waiting. Why wasn't he at the station to meet me? It's been a month!

Wrapping her arms around her shoulders, she realized how terribly she missed Olav. For a moment, her mind drifted; the memories were as fresh as the spring winds. Children flew kites and ran on the beach. They had met that day at the Copenhagen Spring Regatta. She'd known immediately she would love him. He had proposed in forty-eight hours. She needed him now!

Raindrops spattered on the stone walk and soon a punishing deluge struck, dragging her back to the present. The downpour on the slate roof was deafening.

The muffled sound of a car door closing caught her attention and she hurried to the door. Through the downpour she saw a figure striding up the walk, a tall shape in the rain. Olav! She was holding him in a split second.

He held her tightly, then drew back to look at her. Her drenched hair clung to her face and coat. He wasn't sure if the water streaming down her cheeks was rain or tears as he gently touched her face. "It's okay. I'm here. I stopped to see Knut before coming," he said softly. "Look at you. What are you hiding under your coat this time? Let's get inside and find out." She abruptly pulled away and ran inside. "What's wrong?" he called as he ducked through the door. She was shaking out her raincoat. He reached for her hand and frowned. "You're cold. A Norwegian, cold?"

"Frozen."

"Well, my pyromaniac, build a fire. I have a surprise for you in the car."

Her green eyes brightened a little. "What is it?"

"No. Build the fire. I'll be right back."

Bonnie could still make out the tender red line of the scar on his face. She shivered again.

Wood was stacked neatly by the fireplace. The dry kindling lit quickly, burning steadily. She snuggled back into the deep corner of the sofa and slipped off her shoes, drawing her knees up under her chin. She tucked her skirt around her bare feet and watched the fire blaze. The logs wrapped themselves in flame.

Breckkan ducked through the door and winked as he headed for the kitchen. With the demeanor of an aristocrat, he returned bearing a tray, two glasses, and a tall green bottle. With flair, he filled the glasses with the bubbling liquid. "Champagne," she murmured.

He raised his glass. "To us. Skoal."

He settled into the sofa facing her and untied

his wet shoes, dropping them to the floor, and entwined his legs with hers. "Bonnie, are you okay?" She looked at the fire. "Knut looks good," he said for a change of subject. "He was complaining about everything." She sipped the champagne. "What's this about your moving into his hospital room last week? I didn't know about that." She stiffened and held out her glass for a refill, avoiding his eyes. "Well, what happened? The hostel wasn't that bad."

She could no longer suppress her feelings; the encounter with von Stein had been too terrible. The full force of the terror surfaced and she recounted the episode to Breckkan in frenzied spasms. She felt her heart pounding and a growing tightness in her chest. Her wet green eyes were fixed on the door behind him. The black steps, the German, the blank eye, the panic. She tried to smile when telling him about the umbrella, but, to her surprise, her voice caught and she quickly swallowed more champagne. Ending her story, her voice trailed off in a vague murmur.

Breckkan didn't move. He drank nothing, he said nothing. The muscles in his jaw were set. At first, a sickening feeling of deja vu struck him, all horribly familiar. But then he retreated, his mind functioning in an impenetrable sphere.

Suddenly it seemed so obvious. He cursed. The gut feeling he'd had in the lab at Vemork. Why hadn't he thought of it?! He spoke in a low monotone. "Albinism usually causes no mental aberrations, but when that genetic defect is severe, circumstances like encounters with drugs, or any number of things could radically alter brain function. That guy was sent by his government to collect all our work. But, after he saw me at the Palace, his motives went personal. The useless murder of Roald's driver was just his first acting-out."

"You're saying he could be insane?"

"Medically, the seeds were there."

"Then he's stalking me." She stood up and tossed a small log onto the fire. Her back to him, she sensed the fury in her husband's silence.

Breckkan looked at the amber glow of the backlight behind her hair. "Bonnie, please, come here." She laid back against his chest. Gradually her muscles relaxed as she rested her head against him. "There's something I need to tell you."

Sitting up, she said, "Dora!"

"No, I haven't heard anything. I did ask Wakefield if there was a way for me to write her."

"And is there?"

"Yes, and not through the Free Norwegians. I sent the last message that way. Got word to her about Knut."

"What is it?"

"Larsen. He sailed back to Bergen, became part of the Resistance." There was no other way to say it. "He's dead."

The sound of rain awakened her. She stretched her arms and kept her eyes closed. She remembered. She reached for Olav, but found the bed empty. Her eyes popped open. More rain. Then she heard splashing coming from the bathroom.

When she pushed the door open, he looked up from the tub. "You're awake. Thought you might sleep all day."

"You undressed me and put me to bed?"

"At least I remembered the nightgown. What a pity."

She leaned over to kiss him and dropped down on the cotton mat beside the tub. Breckkan leaned back and took her head in both hands. "A long time." He suddenly took her shoulders and, with one motion, pulled her over into the tub.

"You bastard!" She clung to him. He lifted the gauzy, wet nightgown over her head and licked the water from her hard nipples. In their intense love-making, the terror and loss were momentarily forgotten.

They stood in the middle of the bathroom, a towel pulled tightly around both of them. Neither wanted to let go. "Ole, don't leave me again. Please, can't we stop? They don't need us. Can't we just let the whole damn world destroy itself? They don't need us." He kissed her gently. The intimacy was broken by the ring of a telephone. She whispered a curse as he went to the parlor to answer it.

"Bill Wakefield," said the voice. "Hope I'm not interrupting."

"No," mumbled Breckkan, readjusting the towel with his free hand.

"We've been asked to meet with Churchill on the fifteenth."

"The Prime Minister?"

"Yes, all of you."

"Why us?"

"Lots of reasons, not the least being the first clear reports from Bergen are coming in. Some goddamn Gestapo officer is trying to make a quick reputation for himself." Bonnie brought him a robe and helped him into it. Wakefield continued, "But we have heard your mother's okay. Probably because of her American papers, but she and her manservant are under house arrest."

"Where?" asked Breckkan.

"Oslo. They didn't get out of the city."

"Breckkan Mining? What's happened to it?"

"The Germans took it intact, but the Resistance has already managed to disable some of the operation."

"Listen, something's really worrying me. Bonnie was attacked in Edinburgh."

"What! No one reported anything to me. Is she all right?"

"Physically."

"Can she describe the attacker?" asked Wakefield.

"He's very pale, maybe sick. Uses a cane."

For a moment, Wakefield was quiet. "Goddamn it! Someone of that description has been asking questions around here."

Breckkan ground his teeth. "By any chance was he wearing dark glasses?"

"Matter of fact, yes. Do you know who it is?"

Breckkan's eyes lost focus. He realized Wakefield had known all along that Bonnie was in Edinburgh.

"Breckkan, are you still there? You and Bonnie stay put; get some rest. I'll send a car for you the day after tomorrow. Five o'clock p.m. Be careful!"

Kragerø

The small motorcade turned on E-18 and followed the coastline south. The somber green fjord was a constant companion on the left. Major von Papen had been most amenable, agreeing with Dora's suggestion of the more scenic route to Kragerø. Absorbed in the view, she thought of Nic, of how he had loved Skatøy. Her throat tightened at the memory of his death. The worst time of her life. She looked up as they sped through the quiet streets of the village of Larvik. The worst until now, she thought. Is this where it will all end?

They pulled to a stop behind Major von Papen's car at a German military checkpoint. His driver passed over their travel documents and pointed to the luggage in the back seat and then back at Mrs. Breckkan's car. The two motorcycle escorts left their cycles and approached the checkpoint guard when they heard Major von Papen's voice rising in argument.

"Trouble?" asked Dora, looking at Gustave in the front seat. Gustave rolled down the window but said nothing. Major von Papen turned from the young officer in charge of the roadblock and walked back to their car.

"Officious bastard," snapped von Papen in a low voice. "He's going by the book. Not an original idea in that little head. They want your ID papers, too. Give them to me. We'll never get to that damned island."

Dora and Petter passed their papers forward. The Major tapped them against his open palm, waiting while Gustave searched his topcoat. Finally, with a grunt of effort, he pulled out the rumpled papers. "Thank you," Von Papen condescendingly murmured.

After a perfunctory check, the motorcycles roared through the checkpoint with the two staff cars close behind. Dora and Petter settled into the large back seat of the black Mercedes sedan. "Comfortable, old man?" Dora asked. Petter looked straight ahead. "It will be good to be back on Skatøy." They drove on in silence.

Leaving the E-18, the motorcade slowed and turned eastward toward the sea. On the outskirts of Kragerø, they passed a small churchyard, a sobering reminder of the dangers of seafaring life. As the cars accelerated through the narrow streets, Dora searched waiting for a glimpse of the water. A sharp turn to the right, down a steep hill and below lay the bay. They descended the narrow main road, directly past the Victoria Hotel and stopped twenty-five yards from the first dock. A white boat boasting a wide blue stripe rolled gently in the water. Two gangways, one forward, the other aft, acted as lifelines to the ferry.

Dora immediately opened her door and started to step out. "No, wait," called Gustave. She ignored him, swung her legs out, and walked toward the boat. Her walk was steady, even stately.

Petter was beside her immediately. "Are you all right, Mrs. Breckkan?"

"I'm fine. I just need fresh air."

Gustave opened his door and, with both hands on the door frame, pulled himself from the seat. "A boat hand will help with the luggage. You wait here," called von Papen.

An old man in a stained wool sweater began unloading the first car, stacking the sealed crates and steamer trunks on the dock side. The man glanced at Dora and walked toward them.

"What do you want?" asked Major von Papen.

"Checking to see if there's more luggage in this car, sir." Offering his weathered hand to Dora and then to Petter, he said, "Good to see you, Mrs. Breckkan. Moving to the island a bit early this year?"

"Yes," Dora answered, looking steadily at him.

"You've brought the sun with you. Anything else..."

"Three pieces of luggage in the trunk. Please be careful with them."

"Ah, you can trust Kristian, ma'am," he said. "Wood is stacked, and the house has been aired."

"Your papers again. My apologies, Mrs. Breckkan, one more check." Gustave reached into his coat pocket and produced his document case, but von Papen stopped him. "No need. You're not staying." The comment came too late as a sudden gust sent the packet skidding across the stone walkway.

Dora bent down and snatched up the card wedged under her foot. She handed the official German pass back to him. Gustave turned to kiss her goodbye, but she was already walking along the granite dock.

She stepped carefully over untangled nets left out to dry and made her way toward the gangway. The old sailor strode by her, balancing a steamer trunk on his shoulders. Adjusting the load, he said quietly, "Don't worry, everything is cared for."

"Kristian," called the ferry captain. "Is that the last of the cargo?"

"Aye, sir. Ready to go."

Dora pulled her black cape around her and turned to look at the dark water. The weather was cold and breezy. The sun cut hard edges on the profile of the lighthouse on the promontory.

"Farther north than Berlin, but more temperate," called von Papen from the dock. "I can see why you come here, Mrs. Breckkan." She forced herself to remain quiet and swallowed a retort as Petter took her arm.

Standing at the rail, they watched the German Officer and Gustave get into the back seat of the staff car. The motorcycle guards kicked their starters and bursts of black exhaust fouled the air. The ferry gave a small jolt and began to pull away. In the distance, Dora caught a glint of sunlight off the black cars traveling in tandem. Fools, self-important fools.

The boat cleared the harbor and steered an east-southeast course. Skatøy was barely visible on the horizon.

PART III

CHAPTER 15

May 15, 1940

Cambridge

Wakefield, noticeably agitated, paced the cottage. Though usually meticulously dressed, he had pushed his hands deep into the pockets of his suit coat, stretching the fabric out of shape. His white collar was moist, not from heat, but anxiety.

Bonnie stood quietly in the corner setting up a tray of cocktail glasses.

"Where is he?" blurted Wakefield. "I told him to stay here, damn it."

"I tried to keep him here, but he wanted to do something at the lab. He needed to..." Her eyes darted around the room, focusing on an umbrella stand. Among the jumble was a cane. The image of von Stein's dark shadow flashed through her mind. His face just inches from hers, his hand caressing her face, then briefly her chest. To keep from trembling, she ran her hands over her tightly bound hair and fussed with the braid, removing and replacing the hairpins.

Wakefield peered out into the growing dusk, slammed the door shut, and walked back to the cold fireplace.

Bonnie heard the car before he did. "Here he is," she said, hurrying to the door. With long strides, Breckkan walked toward the cottage. She ran to him. "You're late. I was repeat afraid..." He grabbed her with one arm and lifted her into the air, doing a complete turn.

"Bonnie, we did it! The graphite experiments are working. We're right! All that work for something!"

"Ole," she interrupted, "you've been drinking."

"Right. Chadwick took the lot of us to a pub to

celebrate. Come on, you're not mad, are you?" He gently lowered her to the ground.

"We have company."

For the first time, he noticed the camouflage-painted Rover parked to the side of the house. "Bill? He's a day early." Now what is he pulling, thought Breckkan. I don't like him always changing plans.

"He's very upset about something."

Ducking through the door, he greeted Wakefield with a handshake.

"Hello," said Wakefield quietly.

"A drink?" asked Breckkan.

"Not now. I think you ought to hear something first."

Breckkan walked over to the hearth and began building a fire. "What is it this time?"

Wakefield leaned against the back of the sofa, both arms outstretched, his head down. "The worst. Goddamn it! And it happened in our embassy."

"Which embassy?" asked Breckkan, turning around.

"The damn American Embassy! Excuse me, Bonnie, but..."

"What exactly did happen?" she asked.

"This is top-secret, and you're directly involved." His fingers drummed rhythmically on the sofa. "I'm so goddamn mad. All the safeguards, all the precautions. Yesterday, one of the clerks in our embassy was arrested. The bastard's been leaking correspondence between Churchill and Roosevelt."

"Jesus Christ!" said Breckkan. "How long has that been going on?" He loosened his tie. Let's just see how he explains this one.

"We don't know yet, but by the time our people finish with him, we damn well will." Wakefield clenched his fists; his knuckles went white. "The bastard passed the stuff to some Russian émigré, who in turn got it to the Germans through some Italian diplomat. A ridiculous chain of transfers, but it doesn't really make a helluva lot of difference. We have to assume your presence here is known in Berlin. More important, your work. We've got to get you out as soon as possible."

Bonnie walked to the corner cabinet and selected a bottle of Glenfiddich, nearly knocking over the seltzer bottle. "Are we going together this time? Or, are you leaving me behind again?"

"Together," snapped Breckkan. He took the bottle from Bonnie and splashed the whiskey into three glasses. He handed one to her, then turned to Wakefield and asked, "Soda?"

"No, straight," answered Wakefield in a voice subdued with concern. "The latest reports admit the Nazis have made a clean sweep to the Channel. Britain is being routed, pushed back into the sea." Wakefield emptied his glass in one swallow.

"My God," Bonnie whispered.

"Now you understand our situation. There's no time left. I've got to get you off this damn island. And for now we can't use official channels. Ambassador Kennedy is even under suspicion. He's such a goddamn blind pacifist, just like Chamberlain. We've been instructed to keep him in the dark about things. FDR doesn't think he's all that trustworthy." Wakefield put down the glass. "I've got to go. Lots of arrangements to make."

"Bill, I still have my US Passport. And it's current," said Breckkan.

"I know. We checked. Now, stay here. No more trips on your own. And don't use the phone. I've got to get you seats on a plane out." As he walked to his car, he called, "Be ready to go at a moment's notice." Wakefield didn't look back.

Breckkan closed the door and walked over to

the tray of liquor. Without asking, he refilled both their glasses then wearily sat down in an easy chair and leaned his head back. Wakefield certainly had a way of wording their options. Here we go, he thought. The sacrificial pawns, their cat's paw, being pushed around again. And nothing we can do about it.

Bonnie heard the gunning of an engine and dropped the plate in the sink. Breckkan bolted for the door.

The yellow MG spun itself deeper into the mud track at the top of the hill. Breckkan ran toward the car, recognizing his lab assistant's car. The driver turned off the engine and climbed from the sports car.

"Looks like your MG will be staying awhile," said Breckkan.

"Sorry, sir. Turned too sharp. Slid off the track."

"What's going on?"

"Your research." Breckkan stared at the man blankly. "Sir, your data. It's been stolen!"

Breckkan paled; a wave of nausea swept over him. How could this happen? It's von Stein. I'm sure of it. No, can't be. It's paranoia. Get control of yourself! He leaned against the car, his mind spinning ahead. "What experiments were taken?"

"All the heavy water data."

"When?"

"Either last night or this morning. Had to be during working hours. No evidence of a break-in."

"Anyone see anything?"

"Dr. Chadwick told the authorities he had noticed a stranger, at least a stranger to him. About 8:00 this morning."

"What did he look like?"

"All I heard was something about an old man. White hair. A cane. That's why Dr. Chadwick didn't pay much attention. He assumed security had checked him out."

"My God, man! Von Stein..." Breckkan felt a crushing heaviness in his chest, a constriction in his windpipe, just like in the lab at Vemork. Von Stein so close again. How does he keep doing it? Who's guiding him?

Bonnie sidestepped the slippery mud and pulled her sweater tight around her shoulders. She could see the tautness in his jaw-line, the thin scar red against his pale skin. Something was horribly wrong. "What is it, Olav?"

"He got my data. Can you believe it! He got my goddamn data!" Breckkan looked up abruptly and snapped at the assistant. "Let's get this car out of this mess and get back to the lab."

"I'm sorry, sir. I was told to inform you of the robbery and insist that you stay here. I'll get help back in the village." He backed away a few steps, then turned and disappeared over the hill.

Bonnie reached for Breckkan's arm and walked slowly back to the cottage. Breaking the silence, she asked, "Who do you think did it?"

"Von Stein." It was a statement of fact.

"How can you be so sure?"

"I just know. The son-of-a-bitch got it all."

Bonnie hesitated momentarily, "What about the graphite project?"

"He said he only took the work on heavy water."

"Well, then the Germans, or whoever...have the wrong information, don't they?"

Breckkan nodded affirmatively. "Yes. The wrong data." He started to laugh. How terrible the price. How ironic. How damn disgustingly funny!

Oslo

His mind withdrew to England. His departure
had been covered by the chaos of the Dunkirk retreat. Pretty spectacular, von Stein had to admit.
Never had he seen so many boats and so many
varieties of boats working together for one cause.
Get Britain's army home! There suddenly was no
front for Britain, no foothold, just the frigid channel at their back. With an energy that even surprised himself, he had easily stolen a small, motorized boat from the marina and joined a new wave
of fishermen frantically engrossed in the rescue
efforts. Once away from the shore, he had purposefully drifted east and north, distancing himself from the ramshackle armada. Alone in the
choppy waters, he set course for Norway, crossing
without incident to Oslo.

It was all so easy. He made contact at once
with a Nazi agent, code-named Vulpes.

Though surprised to see him, he quickly made
von Stein comfortable in an opulent guest suite.
Vulpes asked only for a chronological report of his
activities. "For my own files," he promised.

Von Stein sat back and smoothed the silk robe,
thankful to see his hand was steady. Though physically tired, the morphine had freed him of pain.
"Breckkan was sloppy."

"I beg your pardon," responded Vulpes.

"Breckkan let the old professor slow him down.
Was late making contact with Chadwick. Recall
we both anticipated he would join the Cambridge
group. Breckkan felt safe there, lowered his
guarded, but my compliments go to British Security. I nearly didn't get into the labs. I almost got
caught. But the Norwegians have disappeared
again. My situation is compromised. The Network
is falling apart. London has too many reckless

agents. So I decided to fall back to you. Only you."
He reached into the pocket of his robe and removed
a small, leather-bound notebook. He flipped
through the pages; the writing was cramped but
legible. The equations that would buy him the location of his enemy. "Here, Breckkan's research."

Vulpes nearly lost control. "You got it!"

"For you." Von Stein leaned back, enjoying the
spectacle of Vulpes rushing though the pages like
a starved carnivore with a piece of fresh meat. "The
handwriting is hers in some places, but the equations are all there, I assure you. Now I want you
to help me."

"You made a wise decision. I have ways of working outside the Network. I'll find Breckkan for you."
He stood to leave, then said politely, "I think you
need medical help, so I've made an appointment
with a specialist." Von Stein shot a look of distrust
at Vulpes. "Don't worry. He's a professional. Totally discreet. But only if you approve, of course."

Hours later, over a leisurely lunch at Blom's,
Vulpes was able to appraise von Stein of the
Breckkan's relocation. He further explained that all
cruise services had come to a halt. All that remained
in the area were the still neutral American liners,
the sister ships *Washington* and *Manhattan*. He had
arranged for passage on the next New York run. It
seemed Vulpes had limitless resources.

Looking up from his plate, Vulpes's attention
turned to a tall, tired-looking man at the door.
"Right on time. Major, the physician is waiting.
And I believe that bag he's carrying will have an
ample supply of painkilling drugs."

The noise of the crowded restaurant drowned
out von Stein's reply as he pushed back his chair
and reached for his cane.

After examining von Stein, then making sev-

eral discreet inquiries, the physician explained that
research programs dealing with storage of certain
chemicals under extreme cold were in progress at
the Vemork Plant. He deduced that it must have
been nitric acid, stored in the liquid nitrogen tank,
which had burned through von Stein's uniform
and melted away the skin of his penis and contents of the scrotal sac.

Von Stein trembled, his strained face flushed.
Those bastards! Develop more and more explosives,
chemicals that, without discrimination, maim and
destroy. Hypocrites. And the biggest of all was Mr.
Nobel. That fortune of his made from the discovery
of TNT, then to endow a peace prize. A peace prize.

"Major." The physician cleared his throat. "Major, your injection is ready."

CHAPTER 16

May 15, 1940

Cambridge

Breckkan watched the olive-painted Rover Saloon emerge from the mist and brake to a stop in front of the cottage. "Bill's here. Let's get going," he said, picking up their suitcases.

Wakefield gave a half wave and opened the trunk. "Rain's letting up, but still heavy clouds," commented Breckkan. He buttoned his tweed coat and looked at the sky.

"All the better," said Wakefield.

"You've found something already?" asked Bonnie.

"Wasn't easy." He shifted gears and steered the car up the drive. "Every available transport is needed at Dunkirk. The situation is deteriorating rapidly. But I managed to thumb you a ride on a courier plane."

"Courier plane?" Breckkan asked.

"Direct pouch from Churchill to Roosevelt. There's no time to waste." Wakefield turned down the main road.

Breckkan instinctively glanced behind them. No one followed. As they swung into a roundabout and exited on a road headed west, he noticed the signposts were missing. The countryside bore a subdued air. There were few cars on the back roads, even fewer than normal, because of strict gas rationing. Beside a crumbling Norman church, he caught a glimpse of a stone wall bearing a WWI memorial. Each soldier's name was obliterated. For the first time, he felt the consuming anxiety of an England at war.

"Bill, about the stolen data..."

"It's going to good use, Breckkan."

"What do you mean by that!"

"That leak I told you about."

"You mean your lousy security!"

"Breckkan, we've passed the word; we consider the theft a massive loss, the project has been completely compromised."

Breckkan suddenly understood. All his early work and all the hours reconstructing it from memory, and for what purpose? Disinformation!

The American glanced at his friend, suspecting what he was thinking. "You've bought us the time we desperately need."

Breckkan ignored the comment, instead asking Bonnie to give him a scrap of paper. "Bill, will you get this note to Dora?"

"I'll take care of it." Wakefield tucked the message in his inner coat pocket. "Trust me, Breckkan. This turn of events had made a real difference."

Breckkan grimaced. Suddenly this non-scientist American had shifted tense. No longer was he speaking abstractly, but rather after the fact. Big decisions had been made and he, as usual, was not a part of them. Had he become Wakefield's son-in-law would things be different? "Is the courier plane we're taking part of your plan, too?"

"I don't get your point," said Wakefield.

"What I mean, to be simplistic, is if you guys are using my data, or Bonnie's and Dr. Kittleson's, for catch-a-spy bait, are you planning on getting us killed to make the story even better?"

"I've no more to say about these things than you." His voice was extremely quiet. "You and your family are being given priority. That's all I know."

Breckkan, already agitated, fully realized he again had no control over his own life. Were they sticking his hand in the fire? He looked at Bonnie, but her eyes were concealed by her hat. He continued in a strident tone, his words coming fast, military-like. "We have a right to know where we're being sent." The scar on his cheek reddened.

"Take it easy, Breckkan; your father's temper is showing."

"No, you take it easy, Bill. We're being chased! I've nearly been killed. Bonnie's been attacked. Knut's sick as hell." Breckkan's next statement seemed to cast a gray pallor over the peaceful green fields. "I know the son-of-a-bitch who's after us." He paused and took a deep breath. "And someone, someone close is manipulating the whole thing."

"Manipulate is a sinister word."

"It sure as hell is," snapped Breckkan. "And, by God, I'm sure as hell concerned. That killer is after me. Me, personally."

Professor Kittleson methodically traced his fingers around the rim of the homburg in his lap. He looked out the window, his gaze appearing to be focused on the countryside, but the word "sinister" drew his attention to Wakefield. He stopped fidgeting with the hat and reached up to smooth his unruly white hair. Bonnie sensed his disapproval and placed a hand on his arm, tapping him softly.

Wakefield cleared his throat and said, "Look Breckkan, I've got three of the brightest physicists in the world in this car. The decision makers, no matter who they are, no longer look upon atomic power as academic." He fixed his eyes on the road. "They, and I mean the Germans, the British, and now the Americans, are committed to building this damn weapon, and with your knowledge, your help. Anyone after you is doing it for the same reason— to use your knowledge. Not for some paranoid personal reason. Now get control of yourself."

"Bill, you don't know what you're talking about. You don't know what's gone on in my life, Bonnie's life." Breckkan was convinced that Wakefield had Roosevelt's ear, but he wasn't convinced his motives were all that high-minded. "I'm about to just sit back and watch you all blow each other to hell! I'm much too busy keeping that sick killer away from us."

"That's enough!" Knut snapped. "That's all I'm going to listen to." He leaned forward and looked directly at his son-in-law. "Now you two listen to me. All of us are in this up to our ears. There's nothing personal. It's the kind of work we do." His eyes flashed at Breckkan. "We all chose to be in this field, and we all knew or at least suspected the risks ahead. Despite that, we've enjoyed the special privileges this new science has brought."

"Privileges, hell!" interrupted Breckkan. "You're right though about taking risks. We're just pawns in the big boy's games."

"Just a minute, young man, let's get your thinking straightened out right now. First, while you were yachting with your royal friends and, secondly, while you were attending the premier schools in Europe, being tutored by the great minds of our time, and finally, vacationing in the lap of luxury, where the hell do you think the workers for your family's company were?" Knut plunged on, not allowing an answer. "I'll tell you. In the mines, setting off unreliable explosives. Loading ore by the tons. Now just exactly who's been taking all the risks?"

Breckkan sat silently, glaring at the landscape speeding by. The reprimand though unsettling was not as hard to take as the fact he'd been through it before, only then with Dora.

The Professor leaned back in the seat; his speech was thick. "Breckkan, you're not just a gentleman, but a gentle man. My God, I let you marry the only person I love on this whole earth."

He glanced at Wakefield's reflection in the rear-view mirror. "Breckkan, you know you have to carry on. Now make it easier for everyone."

On the western horizon, a roll of blue-gray clouds was developing, heavy with rain. They passed through a small village; a white-haired man was tacking a poster on the door of the local pub, "Support the Bedford Militia."

Nearing a black-topped turnoff, Wakefield downshifted the Rover and squeezed onto the side road. "Welcome to Kimbolton. It's an old RAF base upgraded to bomber class."

The vague steepled outline of a church rose in the mist above the treetops. They approached a broad meadow, quartered by transecting strips of black-top enclosed by a perimeter track. Hastily built prefabricated huts dotted one side of the field to the right of the runways. A squat brick building at the far end of the field served for the control tower. The highly visible runways were the only parts of the Kimbolton base that seemed out of balance with the soft-edged English landscape.

Kimbolton RAF

Bonnie's heels clacked on the concrete floor of the metal building. The corrugated steel hut resembled a ribbed half-pipe, the support struts exposed. Wire mesh over the light fixtures cast cross-hatched shadows through the cigarette smoke on to the curved walls.

At the far end of Operations Center were nautical, geographical, and meteorological maps, and a large chalkboard. Columns of ID numbers were listed vertically with the aircraft code-names, followed by the names of the crewmen. Numerous erasure marks were smudged in the last column labeled "Mission Progress."

"Colonel Reed, sir," called the Sergeant above the hubbub. A stiff-backed officer stepped down from the platform and walked across the room.

"Right on time, Mr. Wakefield," he said crisply, shaking the American's hand. "You can be sure we'll get your friends to America. They'll be flying in a fine aircraft, but I'm afraid it's not built for comfort." A small, keen-eyed officer joined them. "Captain George Archer, your navigator. At times other than these, he'd be addressed as Sir George," Reed said. Breckkan and Knut both shook the Captain's outstretched hand.

Colonel Reed looked at the handsome woman beside them, then hesitated. "I've just received a report from Norway. You didn't get out any too soon. The enemy has broken all bounds of decency. Because of the help our ships received from the people of Telavaag, the Germans took a terrible revenge. Telavaag was completely destroyed." He continued in a monotone like checking off a list, keeping the inventory straight. "The houses, more than three hundred, were leveled. Livestock was either taken away or destroyed. Their entire fishing fleet was sunk. The Navy has confirmed the entire male population between the ages of sixteen and sixty-five has been deported to Germany. Many were randomly selected for torture and then shot."

Bonnie fought back tears. Breckkan's pale eyes fixed on Knut. They all knew Telavaag was home to Ron Larsen's wife and baby boy.

Colonel Reed pointed to a large table where an immense map was laid out. "Your route tonight, Archer," he said briskly, "will be the northern one."

"Hazardous, if there's bad weather," said Archer.

"Yes, but on balance, the safest for this trip. Your route will be via Iceland through Labrador, then on to Montreal. It avoids most of the enemy's observation posts, but unfortunately, the trip will have to be a little longer tonight. Go north to Carlisle before turning to sea. Get above the 56th parallel as soon as possible. Then direct to Iceland, and straight for Goose Bay." Captain Archer raised his eyebrows. "Naval Intelligence reports German ship sightings above Dublin and on the West Coast near Torry."

"They're watching us from Donegal, too?" asked Archer.

"We can't take chances. Besides, you'll have civilians in the gun turrets."

They moved to a weather map where an enlisted man was entering new data on the plastic overlay. "Looks good," said Colonel Reed, tamping out the butt of his cigar. "Thick ceiling to the west at 5,000 feet, halfway to Iceland. Winds, 30 knots."

"How far do they extend, Corporal?" asked Archer, taking notes on his clipboard.

"To 17,000, sir."

"You'll have plenty of fuel," said Reed in an almost chatty tone, "since you're not carrying any bombs."

Dressed in a leather, fleece-lined flight jacket and trousers, a Mae West, three pairs of socks, and fleece-lined boots, Bonnie felt like a child stuffed in a snowsuit.

"You may feel hot now, gentlemen,"said the Sergeant, flushing as he glanced at Bonnie, "and ma'am, but temperatures can drop below zero in the plane." He passed around packets of cheese, crackers, and chocolate.

The door to the hut opened and Wakefield

stepped inside. "Ready?" he asked.

A military truck with blackout-dimmed head-lights lumbered to a stop outside the door. Mud oozed up over the edge of the tires where it parked. Twin ocher tracks led away toward the barracks.

Colonel Reed saluted them as they climbed aboard and settled on the benches. "Safe trip. Godspeed." A Sergeant heaved up their parachutes.

Wakefield waved at them. "I'll be back in the US in a few weeks. We'll be investigating the inci-dent at the lab. We will take care of the man with the cane." Bonnie glanced at Breckkan.

In the darkness, only small yellow and red bea-cons glowed around the RAF base. They drove with-out lights, making a slow arc eastward along the perimeter track, passing a dimly lit hangar where a team of mechanics swarmed over an aircraft. Behind the blackened engine, rivulets of charred oil stained the wing.

The truck crossed the end of the main runway and suddenly she loomed above them, parked in a cul-de-sac by the fence. Breckkan's eyes followed the sweep of the giant wing span. Saber-like gun barrels projected from the plexiglass nose and tail pods, lending a sinister quality to the plane.

Captain Archer jumped from the truck and hur-ried toward the stepladder, disappearing into the aircraft through the open bomb-bay doors. Moments later he returned with a trim, blond-headed man who carefully positioned his peaked cap while he walked toward them. Captain Archer made the in-troduction. "Your skipper, Major C. W. Stephens."

The skipper offered his hand. "The co–pilot, Captain Robert Jones, is checking things out with the ground crew." He pointed to the plexiglas pods. "The men will take the gunner positions."

"I'll take one, Major, " interrupted Bonnie.

Before Knut could object, Breckkan gestured toward the ladder. "There's no time to argue. Remember, you trained her."

"With shotguns," growled Knut.

"With any gun," snapped Bonnie. Knut seemed to accept her testiness; Bonnie's sensitivities had been stretched beyond their limits. Trained as an equal to both himself and her husband, she still was doomed to a life of waiting. Breckkan left her in Edinburgh to watch over him. Breckkan met with the top scientists in all of Britain, leaving Bonnie to be accosted by the one stinking man she reviled in all the world. No, he wasn't going to question her capabilities tonight, and yes, she sure as hell could shoot.

"We've been briefed," said Major Stephens. "If Mrs. Breckkan feels up to it. She'll have a fine view come morning."

The Professor sat strapped into a sling seat, listening to the checklist litany called off: oxygen, parachutes, receivers, transmitters, flare gun, code book, intercom mikes. A dim red light bathed his face and the empty bomb racks next to him. Captain Archer sat below and forward, hunched over a fold-down desk, studying the glowing instruments and making last minute calculations.

The headsets suddenly crackled with static through the open intercom. "Ground control says you're ready," came a voice from the tower. "Turn them over."

The port engine began whining, rebelling, then settled into a rhythmic roar. The starboard engine caught and the skipper came on line. "Welcome aboard Britain's finest, the Mark V Armstrong-Whitney. We'll be flying at 15,000 feet, speed 230 miles per hour. First stop: Iceland."

The tower broke in. "You're clear for takeoff, Trailblazer. Repeat, Trailblazer, 2100 hours. Cleared for takeoff."

The plane vibrated as the skipper pushed the throttles, shaking the chill loose from its walls to settle on the passengers. Objects beside the runway whipped by in blurred flashes. The co–pilot called out the airspeed, "Hundred 'n ten..."

Breckkan, seated in the tail pod, watched the runway lights grow closer together and pressed back in his seat. "Hundred 'n twenty..." The plane climbed, turning to a northerly course with the tail wheel lifted beneath him.

The intercom crackled and the skipper said, "Okay, Rob, time to move Mrs. Breckkan up to the nose seat."

"Roger, Skipper."

The bomber broke from cloud cover at 10,000 feet and leveled into cruise altitude. Condensation pouring back from the heated exhausts formed contrails in the cold. Archer came onto the intercom. "Navigator to whomever wants to know. We're leaving the Coast." A chorus of "Rogers" followed.

An hour into the flight, Trailblazer was north of the Irish Sea, over the North Channel. "We have two new gunners aboard," said the skipper, "and I believe a first for Kimbolton's 379th: a beautiful redhead in the nose seat. Time to test fire the guns."

Breckkan released the safeties on four .303-inch machine guns. Bonnie released the safety on her single gun. The sound of machine gun fire ricocheted through the hollow war machine. "Secure," came the voice from the cockpit. The smell of spent shells and smoking breech clung to the air. "Settle back. Hopefully no interruptions to Iceland."

The crew fell into complete silence, more penetrating than the cold.

Trailblazer completed her first leg in six hours. The refueling in Iceland was uneventful, except the Professor had refused to walk around with the others. He remained on board, engrossed in his journal.

Droning west by southwest on the leg to Goose Bay, the bomber encountered heavy turbulence. "We'll be climbing up out of this," the skipper announced. "Try to find some smoother air. Keep your oxygen masks on at all times. If you have to leave your station, don't forget to switch over to the portable oxygen bottle."

60° North

The plane suddenly made a sickening drop then stabilized. The page of his journal flipped backward. Knut reread a passage. The words seemed lofty, arrogant, part of youth. He flipped ahead, searching for the passages recounting the unspoken communication between two lovers, when there are no secrets.

I can't believe my feet are so cold, he thought, not with three pairs of socks and fleece-lined boots. His legs were leaden. The oxygen mask felt like a clammy hand grasping his face. Another sudden fall interrupted his annoyed discomfort.

"Sorry, folks, but up we go again. We're at the leading edge of a storm." The plane rocked as it climbed, leveling at 18,500 feet. Ice crystals formed on the plexiglas. The skin of the plane radiated a metallic cold.

Knut wiggled his toes. Nothing happened, not even a tingle. He thought his feet were frozen. If I could only get my boots off, I'd massage them. My hand, it won't move.

His right arm did not obey. What's wrong? He tried to push forward in the sling seat; only the left leg moved perceptibly. He tried to purse his

248 JACOBS

lips and whistle. A breathy sigh developed.

My God, I'm paralyzed!

Suddenly the plane made an acute turn. His head spun. The noise of the engines increased, becoming unbearable. The bomber dove, arching carelessly through the air. We're crashing! What's wrong with the pilot? Level out! Level out! No, turn up the oxygen, I can't breathe. I'm falling out of my seat! The bomb-bay doors are opening. I'm falling!

The plane rolled crazily. Light in the fuselage and bomb bay brightened. The space was like bright daylight. God, I can see the clouds. We're flying into the sun!

No, Bonnie, you mustn't go outside, it's raining. Stay here with your mother and me. Don't you like the greenhouse? See the rivulets of rain on the panes. No, no, over there. He pointed angrily as he jerked off his gardening gloves. Now go, help your mother, I must tend my orchids.

This one, isn't it beautiful? He held out his hands, cupping the vivid purple flower. I don't recall this much red in your throat. Did I hurt you? Tears came to his eyes. I promise I won't cut you. I'll nurse you to health. Now, where's the light switch? The light switch. I'll turn it off, then the bright red in my dear orchid's throat will fade. Now, isn't that better? Beautiful deep violet, only a touch of pink in your throat. Look at you. Soft. Perfect.

"This is the skipper again." Bonnie awakened from a light sleep. "Rob will be making his way through the plane. He has your passports. When we land, agents from MI-2 will be boarding."

His instructions were interrupted by violent turbulence. After the skipper stabilized the craft, Archer explained, "MI-2 is Canadian Military Intelligence. They'll brief you on the final step. Everything's been arranged for you to enter the United States. You'll receive appropriate instructions when the time comes. I hope to— " He was cut off.

Bonnie gazed out the plexiglas' in the nose seat as Trailblazer flew into the sun. Fragments of rainbows refracted from the ice crystals. In the sunlight, she felt a rush of elation.

There was a muffled discussion, indecipherable over the intercom. Shortly, the skipper came back on and said, "Tail gunner, come up to the flight deck, please."

The skipper's request jarred Bonnie. Why Olav?

Breckkan connected his oxygen to his portable bottle and detached the intercom. Then he saw the co–pilot taking the Professor's pulse. The plane's attitude changed; they were descending.

Bonnie pressed her mike button and asked, "Major, is there a problem?"

"Not certain yet, Mrs. Breckkan. Just asked your husband to help Rob. Will try for some smoother air lower down."

Breckkan knelt beside the co–pilot at Knut's seat. "My God!" The old man was strangely still, his eyes wide open, opaque. The left side of his face sagged; his tongue protruded from his mouth. Slowly, Breckkan reached out and closed Knut's eyes. "Must be a stroke. The altitude..."

He unstrapped the lifeless Professor while the co–pilot pulled out a blanket. They wrapped the body, leaving only the face uncovered. Breckkan gently molded the disordered face, trying to make it appear more natural.

"I've got to talk to the skipper," said Jones, backing away.

Breckkan crouched and worked his way forward to the nose gunner compartment. As he placed a hand on Bonnie's shoulder, she involuntarily jumped. His expression said everything. She shook her head slowly, tears welled up in her eyes. He held on to her tightly and headed back to the body.

"Father, Father..." She knelt at his side, running her hand over his unruly white hair. His expression looked like he'd just remembered something, something important. She touched his lips; they were a dusky gray. You dear, wonderful man, you gave me everything. Taught me everything. She choked, and a sob froze in her throat. Tears ran silently down her face.

She looked up at Breckkan. "Ole, it hurts so much." She began to cry uncontrollably. He rubbed her shaking shoulders, but said nothing. His throat felt constricted. He loved the man too; worse, he was powerless to lessen her pain.

The skipper emerged from the cockpit, his mask hanging to the side. "I'm so sorry."

Clearing his throat, Breckkan said, "Major, what do we do now?" He helped Bonnie to her feet and wrapped an arm around her.

"We've a terrible dilemma, Mrs. Breckkan," the skipper said grimly while looking at the dead man's face. "We simply can't land in Canada with a deceased passenger."

Bonnie squeezed Breckkan's arm. "Yes we can!"

"No, Mrs. Breckkan," he said solemnly, realizing the cruel decision he was forcing her to accept. "This is an ultrasecret mission. I'm carrying extremely sensitive communiques directly from Churchill for the President of the United States. We can't have anything drawing attention to us or your presence. You'll soon be entering the United States, a neutral country." He hesitated. "Your father would never want to expose you to more risk."

Bonnie reached out and grabbed the Major's flight jacket. "You don't know a damn thing about what he would want! I'm his daughter and I don't even know what he would want." She released his coat and buried her face in Breckkan's chest.

Breckkan held her tightly, then whispered, "We must do what he says." He looked up at the ceiling, trying to regain control of himself. "I can't even imagine what you must feel."

She pulled away from him and looked at her father. Stooping down, she gently caressed his face and her eyes filled, their green melting into tears.

The brake-like action of the open bomb bay doors slowed the somber flight. Sunlight glistened off the green-black swells of the Atlantic, fifty feet below. Bonnie held Breckkan's hand tightly and stabilized herself by gripping a steel strut. She didn't take her eyes off the sewn bundle.

Major Stephens closed the Bible and looked up at Breckkan. They moved the body from the bench to the open doors. The Major gave a slight nod and the bundle was gently slid from the aircraft. The body conveniently sank beneath the sea's rolling surface. The bomb bay doors closed.

Several moments passed before Bonnie turned and moved to the bench where her father's body had been. "I'd like to be alone for a while."

Left to herself, she stared across at the empty seat. He was so unselfish, so generous, the very traits she saw and adored in Olav. She couldn't bring herself to think of his being dead. As she let her head drop, her eyes caught sight of his journal under the seat. Opening the book, the journal fell open to a crumpled page. Her eyes focused on the carefully hand-printed poem. She read it over and over.

Lightly now
When I first loved
I gave my very soul,
utterly swerved
to love's control
But Love deceived me,
stole my youth away,
and turned my sunshine
into tear-stained grey.
So I, this little while
ere I go hence,
Love very lightly now,
in self-defense.

CHAPTER 17

June 20, 1940

Aboard The *Washington*

Through a break in the curtains, a thin stream of early morning light interrupted the darkness. The man stood in the cramped but efficient bathroom, illuminated by a single wall-mounted lamp. Black liquid ran in rivulets down his forehead. He watched in the mirror as the transformation took place, the hair color gradually turning midnight black. He reached for a jar of paste-like material and dug out a glob and rubbed it through his hair.

Draping a stained towel over his shoulder, he stood back from the mirror. That's it, he thought. He stepped into the darkened stateroom and padded over to a heavy barrel chair in front of a built-in table. He snapped on the lamp and picked up a small silver-framed picture, looking at it passively. The rakish, black-haired figure in the photograph, arms wrapped around two young innocents, wasn't in real life quite what the image projected.

Vulpes secured passage for him on the American luxury liner for the eight day transatlantic sail to New York. The *Washington* was built to carry twelve hundred peacetime passengers but now carried three times that number on the westbound trip. When they departed Oslofjord, Luftwaffe streaked overhead, harassing the American liner despite clearly marked neutrality emblems along both sides and upper deck.

From the anonymity of steerage, he had surveyed the mostly American passengers and crew. Leaning quietly on his cane, his back to the rail, he studied every gesture, movement, and habit of the Americans, patiently developing a plan to disembark with a new identity, new credentials.

Late on the fifth night at sea, he watched as a man stepped from a cabin on AA Deck, First Class. A lady reached for him, her silk robe open, exposing her breasts and more, but he reluctantly removed her hand from his crotch. Von Stein followed him down the stairwell to B Deck, noting his stateroom number.

From there it hadn't been difficult to learn about the man. His name was Ted, an American, and he was a "host" for the ship line. In reality, he was the ship's paid gigolo, given an unlimited expense account to ensure the happiness of the single, occasionally not, women during their crossing. Very hospitable of the Americans, even on a ship pressed into evacuation duty, thought von Stein. Ted was rarely seen by day, preferring to present himself in one of the crowded cocktail lounges when darkness fell. Handsome, flashily dressed, and wearing too much cologne, he moved smoothly from table to table, speaking intently, leaning forward, intermittently appearing fascinated or playing the role of the confidant.

Von Stein placed the photograph back on the table and glanced at his watch. Seven-thirty A.M. They would be docking in less than an hour and he had one thing left to do. Ted's luggage was packed and outside the cabin door, ready to be picked up, and transferred to shore with the rest of the rated crew. Von Stein would claim it after Customs, since employees received cursory examination by the officials. He reviewed the passport and the faded photograph of Ted Smith, born in Joplin, Missouri, USA. The cosmetic changes are passable he thought as he slouched, trying on the new personality. Interrupted by a rap on the door, he straightened. "Yes," said von Stein in an upper-crust English accent.

"Ted, it's me," answered a male voice.

"Just a second," he snapped off the light and opened the door. A young man in a crisp white uniform grinned at him. He mockingly saluted, balancing a tray with his left hand.

"A hangover from another busy night, Ted? All those extra passengers. Damsels in distress," wise-cracked the steward.

Von Stein forced a thin smile from the shadows. "Do you have it?"

"As promised. And breakfast as usual. Want me to set it up?"

"No." Von Stein spotted the numbered curser's manila envelope beside the dome-covered plate. He crossed quickly to the desk and set down the tray.

"Understand we're going to the Mediterranean next. Try my luck with those French and Italian women, " said the steward. "But I'm not paid as well. See you ashore."

Von Stein grunted, his back to him. "Close the door." Nosey little jerk, at least he didn't seem to notice anything unusual. Buy why should he? He smirked as he glanced back at the photograph of the gigolo: his fake English accent, false shoulder pads, tight-crotch pants, elevator shoes, dyed hair. Everything about him was false.

He removed the dome from the breakfast plate. Globules of fat laced the cold bacon and eggs. With disgust, he pushed away the tray, leaned back, and opened the envelope. Shaking the contents onto the table, he took the set of keys and fingered them, noting the Bronx address on the tag. A thick wad of bills was bound with string. He untied it and counted out Mr. Smith's cumulative assets. US currency amounting to a grand total of $9,000, but his mind was hardly concerned with money.

He reached down and opened the suitcase, his sweaty palms feeling for the fabric pouch. Despising his tremor, he gingerly arranged the glass syringe and steel box on the cloth. He stared at the white powder in the small glass vial before setting it on the desk. Opening the metal box, he removed the hypodermic needle, which was bathed in alcohol, slid it on the syringe, lit a match, and watched blue flames engulf the needle, burning away residual alcohol. He snapped the top off the glass vial and, using the needle, mixed a clear liquid with the white powder. He placed the full syringe on the black cloth and rolled back his left sleeve, slapped his wrist, and expertly slid the needle into the blood stream of a bulging vein. He seemed to freeze for a moment, then already in better control, he systematically stored the paraphernalia in the pouch and leaned back in the chair, closing his eyes.

His anxiety, his self-doubt vanished as a profound heaviness filled his body. Slowly, his extremities became light, his mind cleared, and a sense of well being flooded over him. Morphine was no longer required for pain, it was a needed friend. With the help of the euphoria, he fell into a recurring fantasy; he stroked Bonnie's soft skin, touched her lips, kissed her green eyes.

He had been right to wait, to assume Ted's identity just hours before docking. His right hand rested on his crotch. No fornicating duty to perform for those lonely bitches. Pure disgust rose like acid in his throat. Breckkan, you son-of-a-bitch! The gigolo's tight pants chafed against his crotch as he stood. He groped for the photograph and hurled it across the room, the glass shattering on the carpet when the frame struck the wall. "Shit!" he breathed through clenched teeth. He grabbed the arms of the chair and squeezed them viciously, shutting his eyes against a burst of visual images framed in hatred.

It had been four A.M. Ted had performed well on his last night of duty. He leaned over to kiss the hand of the middle-aged lady before closing her door. Her mussed hair, her smudged lipstick, her silk robe. A shower of pink feathers floated to the floor from the feather-adorned cuffs.

Ted was drunk, very drunk. Timing his approach with a calculated bump, von Stein offered a slurred apology. He caught the smell of champagne and leaned closer, suggesting a bit of fresh air. Humming an indistinct tune, the gigolo walked out onto the fantail. Von Stein quietly walked up behind him and plunged his knife into Ted's neck, ripping through vocal chords and blood vessels and killing him instantly. As he struggled to remove Ted's keys, the ship rolled unexpectedly and the body slid from the deck, disappearing into the foaming wake. Furious, von Stein regained his own balance. His knife was lost, buried deep in the gigolo's throat.

His thoughts were interrupted by an abrupt scurry outside the stateroom door. Porters were collecting the baggage piled in the corridor. He heard the creak of partitions and bulkheads and knew they would be docking shortly. He limped to the porthole. "Land of opportunity," he murmured aloud as he flexed his stiff leg. His head throbbed. I don't need a country, a career, a family. He felt a shiver at the nape of his neck. The thought of family unnerved him. Dear Maria. What would you think of me?

There was a sudden blast from the ship's horn. A flotilla of Moran tugs churned slowly by the *Washington*, all blowing their deep, wailing horns, water guns shot giant streams of water into the air to salute to the American liner. He felt the vibration in the deck when the ship slowly crept into her berth on the north side of Pier 90.

Von Stein put on the garish checked sport coat, the gigolo's choice of disembarkation clothes, and fingered the hat. A nicely shaped crown, excellent silk lining, expensive, he acknowledged to himself as he pulled down the brim. He adjusted his dark glasses, then stepped into the hall and made his way through the crowded public rooms out onto the deck.

The sun was bright, and the tall buildings of Manhattan glistened against the clear blue sky. The cool breeze had a distinctly fishy smell. Gulls lazed in slow, broad spirals overhead, circling the two squat smokestacks of the American ship. To his right, at Pier 88, the magnificent *Normandie* was berthed, creaking as she shifted in the changing tide. She seemed strangely lonely, looked after by a skeleton maintenance crew and a security team. With no empathy, von Stein gazed at the silent French ship, stranded in New York, another foreigner, dispossessed from home.

He shifted his weight from his cane and leaned against the rail, looking down at the cobblestone pier. With studied casualness, he began testing his memory of Ted, comfortably assuming an arrogant, offhanded manner, appropriately bored. As he turned to sidestep a scurrying child, a passenger next to him gestured toward the deck above. "A lady trying to get your attention. Up there." An elegantly dressed woman stood waving at him. The woman with a penchant for pink feathers now sported a bright yellow suit.

"Ted, darling," she called down to him. "Beautiful morning, isn't it?" Von Stein waved, moving his cane close to his leg. "My car can take us— "

She was interrupted by a deafening blast of the ship's horn.

Von Stein nodded affirmatively and merged into the milling crowd. The woman waved a gloved hand in acknowledgment, then lowered it reluctantly as she lost sight of him.

Winnetka

The indigo Packard sped north along the lake shore. The car slowed when they entered Evanston, crossing the community on tree-lined Sheridan Boulevard. The woman had been asleep, her head resting comfortably on her husband's shoulder, ever since they had safely crossed the Canadian border at Windsor.

The driver caught Breckkan staring at the scar on his neck. It ran conspicuously from the tip of his earlobe toward his Adam's apple, disappearing into his collar. Looking up at him in the rearview mirror, he ran his index finger along the course of the scar. "Little rough in the twenties." His right eyebrow lifted permanently and he smiled only out of one side of his mouth. He frowned, then smiled and cocked his head. "I was a pretty wild kid."

Breckkan lifted up his chin and pointed to his scar. "Me, too."

The driver seemed accustomed to dealing with special clients. Bill Wakefield had reminded Sam that the United States was not at war; regular law enforcement agencies could not be approached for protection. In fact, the police couldn't even be told of the Breckkans' problem. Obviously, Sam had been carefully selected.

"Your English. You both speak it perfectly, sir."

Bonnie shifted, blinked, then looked up at Breckkan. He rubbed her shoulder and planted a kiss on her forehead. "My mother is American. My wife has a great ear; she can mimic anything."

"Mr. Wakefield has you in a gem of a house. By the way, Mrs. Breckkan, we're on Green Bay Road now." Catching Bonnie's eyes in the rear-view mirror, Sam continued. "This'll take us to your new home in Winnetka."

Breckkan searched for something familiar. He was just a child when he and his parents last visited Wakefield. Nothing looked the same. He pulled Bonnie closer to him, understanding the confusion in her face. Home. The word meant nothing. Nothing familiar. His voice was soft as he nodded at the passing store fronts. "You're going to like the Americans, Bonnie. They're self-assured, energetic." And insulated, he thought.

Sam gestured toward a long building constructed of half timbers in an Old English style. "That's the main train station— the Chicago-North Shore Electric Train."

"That's how we'll go into Chicago?" asked Breckkan.

"No, Doctor, I'll be driving you."

"No need. We can..."

"Sir, that's my job." Neither Breckkan nor Bonnie ignored the subtle admonition.

The Packard turned off Elm Street and wound its way east toward the lake. The grounds surrounding partially hidden homes were sprawling, immaculately tended. As they drove through the massive iron gates and onto the narrow driveway, Breckkan immediately recalled the security, the insulation. Wakefield's home was perfectly situated. Looking where the drive curved to the left, he saw the main house. Memories began to emerge.

It was built in a style unique to Chicago: a three-story structure constructed of blocks of rough-hewn gray granite, balanced architecturally. The weight of the stone was relieved by wide-arched windows and doors and a great long portico.

Sam abruptly turned right, passing the main house and followed the drive toward the lake. A gardener bending over rose bushes looked up from his work at their approach. Sam gave him a wave, and in return, received a discreet nod. "The walls surrounding the main house were built by the original owner. The only unfortified boundary is guarded by the lake."

The road continued downward, curving to a stop in front of a stone building. A paved walk, bordered by rhododendrons, wrapped around the right side. The second-floor clerestory windows faced west over the garages.

Sam shut off the motor. "The guest house is yours. A beautiful view of the lake. I've checked it out: only entrance is by those stairs." He pointed to the white staircase at the end of the walk. "They creak nicely."

He opened his door and leaned back to add, "I'll be at the main house." He grinned one-sidedly, his smile merging into the dark shadows under his eyes. "You take Mrs. Breckkan upstairs. I'll bring your bags."

New York City

The gangway was in place on the pier at the foot of West 49th Street and 12th Avenue. A smartly uniformed band began playing Sousa marches. Limousines, taxis, and porters' carts crowded the dockside. Von Stein worked his way to midship, then down the steps to F Deck and the gangway. He waited a fraction of a second, then crossed the pier with a large group of passengers and, ignoring his limp, walked briskly to the brick building housing Customs and Immigration.

His heart pounded erratically as he neared the control booths. The Customs officials went about their ritual, surveying each passport bearer, stamping the documents. Von Stein felt sweat trickling down his spine. Too slow, too cautious, he thought.

He stood rigid while the Customs Officer reviewed the data on the front page and then stared at him. Finally, the official reached from the chrome seal, stamped the passport and said, "Welcome home, sir."

Winnetka

Breckkan looked out the bank of windows in the living room. Two old oak trees stood their ground like an honor guard between the cottage and the lake. A light summer breeze was gathering strength. A sudden gust rounded the corner of the building and he turned his attention to the far window. He could see the entire network of terraced gardens working down the slope. A band of lush green lawn visually separated the flowering beds from the main house. His eyes followed a series of paved steps threading down the terraces and disappearing behind a dense hedge. Through a break in the hedge, he could glimpse a swimming pool. Something new, he thought.

The wind buffeted the house again and he smelled rain in the air. He took off his suitcoat, loosened his tie, and paced the room. On a desk by the bookcases, he spotted a leather binocular case. Adjusting the magnification of the 8x30 power Zeiss, he turned toward the windows and focused on the lake. In the distance, he could see an object motionless in the water. Initially, he thought it was a large boat at anchor, but pulling in the image quickly, he realized it was a permanent structure built of brick at least two or more miles from the shore, he calculated, fingering the exquisitely made German instrument. He felt Bonnie's presence beside him.

"Can we unpack later?" she asked.

"Sure." He could see the fatigue in her face as she removed the comb, loosened her hair, and shook her head. Her glistening red hair covered her shoulders and back. Behind her, a weak ray of evening sun refracted through the rain-spattered windows. The light caught her moist eyes as she turned back toward him. She blinked and swallowed. He tilted her face toward his and kissed her. Then he held her. "Are you all right?"

"Just tired. I think I'll take a long hot bath."

He watched her walk slowly away and turned again to the windows. He resisted the instinct to close the drapes and instead watched darkness close in over the water. He frowned, visualizing his father's face in the darkened windowpane. How many times had Nic warned him of the danger of accepting anything at face value? He suddenly, profoundly understood his father's dictum: consciously or unconsciously, all men spend their lives striving to be free of anxiety. Remember this, Nic had said, and you can anticipate anyone's most obscure motives. And what of Wakefield's?

He roughly jerked the drapes shut and walked back to the desk. As he turned on the lamp, he noticed a letter addressed to him. The Savoy address was crossed out, replaced by the address of the Cambridge Laboratory. He stared at the cancellation stamp on the envelope: Copenhagen. He opened the letter, read, and reread the handwritten text:

21 May 1940

Dear Breckkan,
    ...Precarious as it may be, I insist we stay to-
gether as a family. I did mail two letters to you,
though. I learned my lesson in WWI and sent you
one copy by air, the other by surface, hoping one
will reach you.
    The night you put me on the train to
Copenhagen, my countrymen were to awake
to total Nazi occupation. The government,
right or wrong, believed heroic suicide
would accomplish nothing. But we are not
blind in Denmark, we do have some common
sense. Ole Chievitz, you recall him?— my
closest friend and Professor of Surgery—
has insisted all Danish hospitals be equipped
to treat gas poisoning. Believe me, from what I've
seen, those Nazis might try such an outrage. He developed a "nose catheter" for supplying a stream of
oxygen to a victim of such an attack. No factory here,
since the press of the war, could undertake an order
to make such tubes, so I volunteered the Institute.
My God, after all, my staff does have the know-how
to make such apparatus. Even I helped on the production line. Within one week, we made 6,000 tubes
and shipped them to stockpiles in our hospitals...

    He imagined Bohr writing quickly, deliberately,
his lucid commentary describing apocalyptic possibilities. My God, why didn't he get out when he could?
Does he have any way of knowing we have confirmed
the most feasible moderator for the weapon, that we
are on our way to making a giant bomb? What is
mankind coming to? His hand trembled as he returned the letter to the envelope.

CHAPTER 18

June 21, 1940

New York City

Von Stein waited to cross 59th Street, furious that he was twenty minutes late.

In their telephone conversation, the agent said he would be in the bar. Look for a turquoise box on the table. He would wait precisely one half-hour then leave. If they didn't make contact, the next scheduled meeting was in two days.

Glowering at an arrogant young Wall Street type who cut in front of him, he entered the revolving doors to The Plaza Hotel. He threaded his way through the packed lobby, dodging rows of luggage and the social-business elite of Manhattan. Keeping his dark glasses on, he stopped momentarily, allowing his eyes to adjust. He ground out his cigarette in the sand of a lobby ashtray, obliterating the imprint of the back-to-back P's and headed for the Oak Bar.

A small man, nearly bald, was seated at a table in the middle of the room, directly in view of the entrance. Von Stein hooked his cane on the back of a chair. "Good afternoon, Kessel."

The Professor half stood and offered a moist hand, his face pale, tinged with gray, like a spoiled oyster. His yellow teeth resembled a lemon wedge sourly set against the pallor. Von Stein reluctantly took the chair with his back to the entrance and stretched out his stiff leg.

"I see you have today's paper," Kessel commented. "The Republicans have a candidate, after five or six ballots. Wilkie will be a good President, don't you agree?"

"Yes. Seeing that nonintervention in the European

war is his slogan." He watched the Professor, hoping to catch some subtle response of satisfaction.

"May I help you?" interrupted a waiter.

"Scotch, no ice," answered von Stein, immediately realizing he'd made his first mistake.

The Professor seemed to ignore the faux pas. "I'll have another of your marvelous martinis." The waiter nodded and placed a bowl of cashew nuts on the table.

Kessel tapped the table with the tips of his fingers, his little finger spread pretentiously. With the berating voice of a lecturer, he said, "The only place whiskey is taken neat in America is in cowboy movies." Von Stein glared at the bald head with two wiry tufts of gray hair above each ear. "As you asked, I've brought you a little gift." He pushed the shiny turquoise box toward von Stein. "The Tiffany look, classic...don't you think? And here's some things you might find interesting." He placed an envelope on top of the box. The oyster face grinned and chewed a nut as the waiter served their drinks.

Von Stein reached for his glass and took a sip, then opened the envelope. Its contents revealed:

1. Giant Cyclotron being built, University of California.
2. Contract issued, construction of a Heavy Water Plant at Trail, in British Columbia. Not yet started.
3. US Government purchase of thousands of acres in Tennessee. No significant water power in the region.

Von Stein exhaled through clenched teeth, then took a sip of scotch. Of no concern to me, he thought, the mission is accomplished. Shifting in the hard chair, a spasm of pain shot through his pelvis. The morphine was wearing off.

Kessel leaned forward and ferreted out several cashews. "I understand you're quite fluent in a number of languages, Doctor von Stein."

He grimaced. With total nonchalance, the vain little man had actually used his real name. Von Stein had made certain to use only the assumed name.

"Von Stein, to be precise," pronounced Kessel, spitting it out "Ssch-tein" with a German accent. He continued, "Our friends at home will be pleased to know you're here."

Von Stein looked around the dark paneled room saying nothing. Why should they be pleased? Vulpes had given him the contact, presumably outside the Network.

Kessel continued as he leaned forward and whispered intimately. "The Colonel will be most pleased."

Something's wrong. He felt suddenly agitated with this vulgar little man. Richter wants something. "Well," von Stein replied, taking the initiative, "perhaps you know the whereabouts of our colleagues?"

The Professor sat back, clinging to his vital piece of information like a child with a treasured blanket. "Compton's lab."

"Compton's?" said von Stein, removing his glasses and rubbing the bridge of his nose. "I would've guessed Princeton."

"No, the University of Chicago. Rather good gin here, you should try it. You're in luck; your Chicago contact is a lieutenant in the police department. Nice touch, eh? Petrusini. Oak Street Precinct. Speak to him in Italian. You do recall some of your Italian?" Von Stein chose to ignore his insolence. "First talk to him about Fiesole. He'll have your orders from Berlin."

I'll bet he will. You, little man, are too cowardly to do the job.

Kessel stared, fascinated with the scarred eye. "Perhaps your glasses?" he said, closing one eye for emphasis.

Von Stein immediately replaced his dark glasses, fighting his temper. You perfect ass! Until now I couldn't justify my revulsion for you as a reason to kill. "Thank you," he said dryly. "Two mistakes."

"You'll learn," said Kessel. The anemic smile returned to his face. He folded his white cocktail napkin in small squares and flattened the wet paper under his empty glass. "I must go. My next class is at 2:00. You know how to reach me." He hoisted his pear-shaped body from the chair.

"And your specialty, may I ask?"

"Political science. Isn't that a farce?"

Von Stein grunted in agreement. It seemed to him that all politics were a farce. "Isn't that why they call it the mother of tyrants?"

"How clever. I'll use that in my lecture. You'll take care of the bill?" he added, placing a pudgy hand on von Stein's shoulder and pointing at the turquoise box. "Ciao, my friend. Don't forget my little gift." Von Stein shuddered at his touch.

Von Stein followed shortly, after another scotch, this time with ice.

He sat on an empty bench at Grand Central Station and waited for his train. It had only required two days to complete his plans. He noticed a flashy newspaper next to him on the bench and started to push away the scandal sheet when his eye caught a lead line in the upper right corner. "Columbia Professor Commits Suicide." The picture accompanying the article showed a bald man hanging by his tie from a toilet stall in one of the university men's rooms. The perfect tribute, von Stein thought as he casually pushed the newspaper aside. He fought a sudden urge to wash his hands.

Chicago

From the street, the western stand of Stagg Field had an almost imposing air with its medieval ivy-covered corner turret. But within the structure under the football stadium, there was little to please the eye. A vague effort to disguise the utilitarian atmosphere had been attempted with stretches of green and white paint on the block walls. Naked bulbs hung from electrical cords draped across the massive concrete support beams.

Angry voices rose in argument from behind a closed door. The scientists in the room were not discussing the complex equations chalked on the blackboards, equations concerning fission regulators: helium, hydrogen, graphite, and heavy water. The discussion had degenerated into an argument over the question of secrecy.

The entire Uranium Project was hanging in the balance.

Compton struggled to gain order among the scientists. Bill Wakefield and an army colonel sat at the back of the room, watching the heated exchange. "Gentlemen, please, gentlemen," called Compton. "Quiet! The question of secrecy is one we have to deal with, NOW!"

Dr. Enrico Fermi looked back at the industrialist and the Colonel. "It appears a decision has already been made."

More voices rose in anger. "Not true," said Compton. "Now please! All of you." The scientists grudgingly took their seats on the scattered lab stools. Compton rubbed the back of his neck with a handkerchief and looked down at a piece of paper. "We've lost a colleague today. One of our best theoreticians has resigned, the cause, secrecy, or rather the lack of it."

Breckkan assessed the feelings of the group, knowing in his own mind he adamantly believed in the necessity of total secrecy. But there was Fermi and his assistants. Compton had to try to please a room full of egos. Then there was the Colonel, whoever the hell he was, and Wakefield again. The accusations became more bitter. Friends were suddenly hurling unfounded charges, becoming condescending, acting irrationally. Breckkan perceptively shook his head in sadness. What better divisive instrument than the specter of developing a world-altering instrument of war? Yet, for himself, the pain and sorrow already wrought was very personal— the loss of family, the loss of home.

"I know that Dr. Breckkan worked with Bohr, and we all know Bohr's feelings on this subject," said Dr. Fermi.

Breckkan rose to his feet and looked around the room. "Bohr has always felt secrecy would subordinate science to the political system, causing a race among nations."

"How naive," said another of the scientists sarcastically.

Breckkan ignored the comment and continued, "Because of what he believed, Bohr and his wife are trapped in Denmark."

"Okay, now," came the full voice of Wakefield. "Dr. Compton has been charged with a terrible task." Moving to the front of the room, Wakefield continued, "Your job is by direct order. None of you are here by accident." Breckkan's mind already was entertaining that notion. "The President of the United States has a personal interest in this project and, I might add, Henry Stimson, now that he's Secretary of War, would like nothing better than to enlist every one of you in the army."

"Just let him try!" snapped Fermi.

"Please, no more inflammatory comments," said Wakefield loudly. "The Uranium Project is now top-secret. Those who can't live with the arrangement had better quit now."

The scientists slowly filed out of the laboratory, each quiet, deep in his own thoughts.

Dr. Compton shoved his hands into his lab-coat pockets. "Breckkan, wait just a minute, please. You're desperately needed here; I hope you know that." His voice was serious, but gentle. "The breakthrough for a nuclear weapon will come, that's a fact. Here, Princeton, Berkeley, London, or, God forbid, Germany. We MUST be first."

Breckkan pushed back his lab stool, sweat ringed his armpits. "An awkward predicament," he murmured finally. "I've trained all my life for this."

"Circumstance, Breckkan. We're all caught in it."

"Does that explain away everything? Is that to be our excuse?" Breckkan tapped his files.

Compton removed his gold pocket watch. "I'm sure you aren't the only one facing a moral dilemma, but you handled yourself well. It's late. Go on home." He paused at the door and said, "At least Hitler doesn't have an exclusive on the nuclear race. We have you, Breckkan."

Breckkan watched the Nobel laureate physicist walk away, then reached for his files and placed the data in the safe, spun the lock, and flipped off the light. He heard typing in the secretarial pool and the sound of a saxophone on the radio. He headed down the hall towards Bonnie's lab. As he pulled on his suitcoat, he tried the knob. The door was locked.

He hurried straight toward the main entrance

and flung open the double doors, calling out, "Sam? Where's Bonnie?"

Sam turned from the Packard parked at the curb. "Mrs. Breckkan left over an hour ago. About 3:00. I assumed you..."

"You let her go alone?" said Breckkan, sliding into the back seat.

"She had me call a cab. A friend of mine picked her up. He's already checked back with me. He's waiting for her now."

"Where?"

"North Michigan Avenue."

"Get going!"

Berlin

The air was oppressive. Richter unbuttoned the collar of his tunic, his mind cataloguing his suspicions. He was tired and it wasn't even noon. He leaned forward to tap his driver's shoulder. "Pull over."

The dark sedan drew to the curb, stopping near the entrance to the Tiergarten. Addressing the driver, the Colonel said, "Take a walk. Feed the pigeons. I'll signal when we're ready." When they were alone, Richter pulled a leather pouch from the map pocket on the back of the front seat. "Lieutenant, you've been most observant. This information isn't just worrisome, it's a goddamn catastrophe!"

"Yes, sir, I was afraid of that. I brought it directly to you when I saw the contents."

"Has anyone else seen it?"

"No. I had just arrived at Tirpitzufer when the priority delivery came in. I checked it in. No seals were broken and..." The Lieutenant glanced through the back window and nervously wiped the beads of perspiration from his upper lip with his hand and said nervously, "The SS Liaison Officer wasn't in the dispatch office. I signed his name and took the pouch."

Richter removed his cap, took out his hand-kerchief and wiped the sweatband. "Good. You did exactly the right thing." He knew Himmler's goddamn smart asses, those reptiles, would love to rub his nose in this. He held up a newspaper clipping picturing a bald man hanging by his tie from a toilet stall. Snapping the clipping with his fingernails, he continued, "No great man, but Kessel was capable, and a key player in the Net-work. A real loss." He pulled out a white envelope. The postmark was New York City. "Kessel's last report," said Richter as he opened it and began reading. High on the top margin was penned: "Did our lover of Italian art assume another identity?"

Richter sat stiffly and studied the text of the letter. A body had washed ashore just north of New York harbor: six feet tall, estimated at 175 pounds, blue eyes, black hair, Caucasian, in good physical condition.

Was Kessel right? Is this von Stein's work? If so, he's in America. Richter stared ahead at the car's domed instrument panel, then forced his attention back to the letter. Suddenly, he broke into laughter, then read aloud: "The deceased was employed as entertainment director aboard the neutral American ship *Washington*... Our man von Stein would be a great entertainer without his balls!"

The Lieutenant grinned and gestured crudely. "He still has fingers."

"That's disgusting," snorted Richter. Then he once again read the coroner's description. Richter pointed to the sentence referring to the cause of death; a knife had been found, still deeply lodged in the victim's neck. "Remember that freezing morning at the Kaiser Wilhelm Institute?" The Lieutenant turned ashen. It's von Stein; he's killed again, thought Richter. No matter how great a genius he is, those drugs are rotting his brain. He's getting reckless. Richter loosened his tunic, then reread part of Kessel's last report: "It seems the only person who will be able to prevent our man from succeeding is this Breckkan. Von Stein has found him several times, yet the Norwegian has managed to evade him, even terribly wound him."

"Klaus, I'm no scientist, but our man is. He'll locate Breckkan again, find the main research center in America. You watch and see. We'll just have to sit back and wait." He paused, reviewing the report.

The interior of the car was like a pressure cooker, the moist heat nauseating, but neither rolled down a window.

"He's like the black hare in the pack, and maybe he doesn't trust anyone, but I don't think he's left us. He's still a German. Yes, I think he'll do it."

"That will save us, Colonel."

"Only if he reports directly to me." Richter suddenly experienced the familiar feeling of paranoia invading his entire being. He was certain Himmler would crush the Abwehr at the first opportunity. He removed his dark glasses and wiped them, squinting in the noon glare. There seemed to be no shadows, only the merged edges of intensely bright shapes moving in time with the shimmer of the heat. He replaced his glasses and tied the string around the flap of the pouch. I can trust no one, he thought.

Richter turned in the seat and murmured to the Lieutenant, "The driver...he's Himmler's. To him there's a line between the Waffen SS, the Gestapo, and the Abwehr. And for him, only Gestapo counts. Watch him!"

"I'll get rid of him."

"No. We know what he is. For now, it's safer that way. At the High Command Meeting yesterday..." Richter's eyes narrowed. The driver, hands behind his back, was standing by the huge fountain quite a distance away. "Yesterday, Himmler announced the solution, as he called it, for over one hundred Belgian prisoners his Waffen troops had taken. There was nothing civilized about it. Nothing professional."

"His solution?"

Richter spoke dispassionately, "Slaughter. A mass execution of Belgian officers, businessmen, clergymen, writers, artists, anyone who fit the category of an 'intellectual.' Himmler's a beast."

"Did von Stein ever work with the SS?" asked the Lieutenant.

"No, he learned evil on his own. Actually, I'm beginning to think he was born to it." Richter called out for the Gestapo driver.

Chicago

Sam accelerated smoothly into the traffic on North Michigan Avenue approaching the Allerton Hotel. "Insistent one, your lady. Didn't want me tagging along. Said it was a surprise."

"You shouldn't have left her alone."

"Like I said, my cabbie friend called in and she's fine. He's waiting for her."

Breckkan leaned forward, his hands on the back of the front seat, watching the crowds. "Did she look all right?"

"Stunning."

Despite the cautions of Wakefield, Sam had allowed her out of his sight. Why hadn't he checked with him? Why hadn't she checked with him? Breckkan was losing his temper.

"There's the cab," Sam said.

"Pull in."

"No space."

"Then double-park, damn it!" He jerked open the door and yelled at the cabbie. "Where is she?"

"Inside," he answered, pointing at a nondescript five-story brownstone.

Breckkan sprinted across the wide sidewalk and pushed through the revolving glass doors, finding himself in a sedate marble foyer. He spotted a directory just past the elevators, and quickly running his eyes down the list of firms, noted law offices, accounting services, and a notary public on the upper floors. The second floor housed a medical laboratory and doctors' offices.

As he punched the button for the elevator, he heard the sound of high heels clacking on the stairs to his left. He turned to see Bonnie descending the steps, checking her watch, her face flushed. She appeared excited and beautiful all at once. "Bonnie!" he called. She looked down at him. The elevator doors opened and a crowd surged around him. He called, "Are you all right?"

He moved to join her and then pinned her against the wall with a stiff outstretched arm. "You scared the hell out of me. I can't believe Sam let you out of his sight."

"It was important. I had to be sure first." He looked at her questioningly. "You're going to be a father," she said quietly.

Mystification, exhilaration: Breckkan felt them both.

"The doctor says about five and a half months."

He felt clumsy, stupid, and could only think of holding her. He wrapped his arm around her and glanced at the growing crowd in the lobby, all flowing toward the exit. "Let's get out of here." He kept an arm around her waist and propelled her into the street. "You're sure you're all right?" he asked again.

"I promise. Let's celebrate."

"That's my girl."

Sam was standing at the curb waving to his friend as the cab pulled away. When he saw Bonnie he quickly stepped to the street and opened the rear door of the double-parked Packard.

"Sam, wonderful news. Mrs. Breckkan is expecting a child!"

"Your first born, American." A horn blasted behind them.

"Take us to the best place in town," said Breckkan, slipping into the back seat.

"Yes sir, the Cape Cod Room, just down the street."

Breckkan held her tightly with one arm around her shoulders and kissed her lightly on the neck. Bonnie beamed, oddly proud of herself. Father would be pleased. Yes, she thought, American born, but conceived in Norway.

CHAPTER 19

September 21, 1940

Chicago

Snipping carefully, he trimmed off the last of the dyed hair and flushed it away. He crossed the room, cracked the door an inch, reached down for the newspaper, then slammed the door shut. The *Chicago Daily News* headline read: "Unseasonably Cold Weather— First Day of Fall". He tossed the newspaper on the bed, walked over to a small built-in counter, and poured a mug of coffee from the pot on the electric plate. Settling back into the only chair in the room, von Stein reached for his cigarettes. He rubbed the sterling silver surface and snapped open the case. Stretching to pick up the book of matches, he tensed, suddenly racked with pain. Sweat welled in the small of his back and his face twisted. He grunted as he reached for the whiskey bottle and splashed a generous amount into the cup.

He had injected the last of the morphine hours ago. Too risky to steal more now, he thought. Besides, without the repeated shocks of pain, his mind drifted into long periods filled with jagged fragments of trivia; only occasional flashes of unnerving truth managed to register. For him, the end was near and he knew the syndrome. His mind was failing.

He sat hunched on the mangy chair and sipped the whiskey. As the liquor dulled the throbbing, his eyes wandered from the antiquated bath to the sagging mattress. The dinginess of the room suited him. The Washington Hotel was located on Commercial Avenue in the heart of South Chicago's retail district. Just like he sometimes savored the pain of his wound, he was oddly attracted to the decaying area, melding effortlessly into the seamy neighborhood.

Stretching his stiff leg, he absentmindedly thumbed through the Art Institute catalogue. Abruptly he jabbed at the floor plan diagram. Gallery 30. The gallery had been packed, but he couldn't have missed the red hair. Had they exited into the main hall, we would have walked into each other. It was all so easy, he thought.

As he was about to strike a match and light his cigarette, there was a sharp knock on the door. "Want your fresh sheets?" called a gravelly voice from the hall.

"Leave them by the door," said von Stein, picturing the moustache over her lip.

"Well, don't forget to leave the dirty sheets by the door or I'll charge you." He didn't respond.

Later, he kicked the stack of sheets into his room, wincing at the sound of a screeching streetcar stopping directly in front of the hotel. Perfect access to the CTA. He watched a rough-looking crowd elbow their way aboard. Rude bunch of immigrants, like that arrogant Italian bastard. His mind drifted again. The public rest room. Kessel. Despicable, but a provider of valuable information and yet another piece of the Network.

The cop had set the time for five in the afternoon at the Oak Street Beach. During the brief telephone conversation, he told the police lieutenant to bring a detailed city map, the type issued especially to patrolmen.

Von Stein purposely arrived a half-hour early, and from a crowded bus stop watched the police car pull to the curb. The heavyset passenger, dressed in civilian clothes, slammed the door, adjusted the brim of his hat, and patted the handkerchief in his breast pocket. Von Stein watched every step the Italian made from the concrete curbing onto the sand.

The wind coming off the lake was brisk, the water agitated. Small waves broke with a low roar a hundred feet from the shore. Von Stein turned up the collar of his coat, adjusted his dark glasses, and surveyed the beach area. The rumble of the breakers merged with the cacophony of the traffic on Lake Shore Drive. The Lieutenant, one of Chicago's finest, stood alone at the water's edge, glancing first at the deserted beach and then out at the breakwater.

"Reminiscent of the Italian lakes, isn't it?" von Stein said in Italian.

The man turned quickly, surprisingly agile for his weight. "You know the Lombardy Region?" he asked with deliberate enunciation.

"Yes, but I miss the cypress of Fiesole."

The Lieutenant was a full head taller than von Stein and easily fifty pounds heavier. From southern Italy, he thought, none of the finer features of the North. "I expected a uniform."

"Off duty," Petrusini answered, fingering a gold pocket watch on a heavy chain. "I'll make full detective soon."

"I can't help but be curious. If you have such a bright future here, why are you helping me?"

The Italian laughed harshly. "My family stayed in the old country, retreating into the past. It's pathetic. A man can have many loyalties. Were you followed?"

There was silence. Von Stein opened his cigarette case, aware Petrusini was looking at the silver case. Removing a cigarette, he asked, "Did you get what I asked for?"

"I got it."

Von Stein leaned away from the wind to light the cigarette. "Give it to me." With a large, gloved hand, the Lieutenant took out a thick, accordion-folded map. Quickly, von Stein located the North Shore section, studying each quadrant as he unfolded the map. Police substations, hospitals, commuter train stations, university buildings, power substations.

Suddenly he stopped, his attention focused on a particular map: a schematic layout of the city water works. Chicago's water source: concrete and brick towers two miles offshore. Each intake building was connected to the shore by a five foot tall brick-walled tunnel sixty feet below the lake surface.

"Cold as hell out here." Von Stein backed away from the foam of a small, dying wave. "Let's get out of this wind." Suddenly the Italian reached out, clasping his hand on von Stein's shoulder, and propelled him forward. Petrusini jerked him to a stop by a high retaining wall, well out of sight of the busy street above.

Petrusini relaxed his grip. "A directive from Berlin, from Colonel Richter to you, Stein. For your sake, you had better get it right this time." A smirk crossed the huge man's face. "Seems you let yourself be duped; the data you stole was nothing but junk." Von Stein ground his teeth together. "You, the great German scientist." He pushed closer, forcing von Stein against the concrete embankment. "Colonel Richter orders you to immediately find a way into their lab here. Stagg Field. Get the real stuff and this time get evidence of the progress of their research, where they stand. You will not transmit the information yourself. This time you'll bring it directly to me. Understood?"

Von Stein eased himself away from Petrusini and stepped back, careful of his footing in the sand. He flicked his cigarette to the ground, watching the Italian's hand slide into his coat. Von Stein instantly grabbed for his revolver wedged in the small of his back and dove to the ground. The .38 police special exploded; the bullet whipped over his shoulder, and tore into sand just behind him.

Enraged, von Stein deliberately aimed his gun at the policeman's head and watched the back of his skull shatter. The man's brains splattered onto the retaining wall and the lifeless hulk crumpled to the sand. I'll get what they want from that goddamn Norwegian, and do with it what I wish.

He braced himself with his cane and brushed the sand from his suit, then stuck the revolver back in his waistband and coolly walked away. A blast of frigid wind struck him when he stepped onto the sidewalk. He tipped his cane toward the waiting patrol car in a salute and crossed the street.

Berlin

Richter took another sip of mineral water and, almost as if speaking to himself, said, "What's happening in Chicago? Not a word. Two months since the only report. Cryptic as hell, a football field, in the heart of Chicago. Something special is going on at this Stagg Field." He stopped talking aloud. Von Stein will get in, I'm certain of that...but will he report it to me?

The Lieutenant spoke curtly, giving orders over the telephone, then slammed down the receiver.

"Give me your best guess, Lieutenant. Do you think he's broken already?" Richter was interrupted by a knock on the door.

The Gestapo clerk clicked his boot heels. "The US files, sir. By what authority?"

"Mine," snapped Richter.

"You must sign..."

Richter interrupted him, grabbing the files. "You're dismissed!" He waited until the Lieutenant slammed the door behind the clerk, then sat down wearily at his desk. "Typical of his kind. Self-important bastard." Shuffling through the bulky file, he asked, "Now, where the hell is that latest report from Petrusini?"

Winnetka

It was a depressing evening, the sky overcast, a sooty gray. The lake and sky appeared to merge. Breckkan stripped to his swim trunks and anxiously dove into the steaming water, forcing himself to swim at a fast pace. All sound disappeared; everything seemed distant. A flock of ducks flew overhead, pointing south, and it started to rain. Ignoring the drizzle, he pounded out the laps, trying to drown the nightmare. Reaching the deep end of the pool, he shivered in the water and thought he heard a voice, words echoing indistinctly in the water. Then he saw her standing at the pool's edge and swam toward her.

"Are you all right, Ole?" she called from under the umbrella as she held out a towel. She moved around to face him. His hair was matted, his forehead glistening with sweat. She reached for him and felt his clammy skin. "Why do you do this to yourself?"

He shook his head. She wrapped his robe around him. He didn't resist, but closed his eyes and dropped his head. She could feel the tremor in his hands. Glancing toward the lake, Bonnie saw a thick bank of fog rolling inland, swallowing the lake house.

"It's the only way I'm ever going to get over it." He looked up at her. "The water." His eyes were glazed and his cheeks seemed hollow. She started to speak, but looked away, sensing the angst in his expression.

He rubbed his neck with his hand and planted a wet kiss on her cheek, then patted her on the rear and took the umbrella from her. "Those steaks cost me 35 cents a pound. They'd better be perfect," he said as they walked down the sloping lawn to the lake house.

Climbing the steps, he held the umbrella over them both and breathed on her neck. "I'll grab a sweater. Then I'll fix you the finest dry martini this side of Harry's Bar."

"I never made it to Harry's, remember?"

"A fact you'll never let me forget." He ducked his head through a navy crew-neck sweater and ran a hand over his damp hair. "For the record," he began his lecture, "the recipe from Giuseppe Cipriani himself, the Venetian champion: a bottle of good English gin and one of dry white vermouth. Pour one part of the vermouth and five parts of the gin into a carafe. Mix carefully, then chill." He opened the refrigerator with flourish and held out a frosted glass to her.

She took a sip and leaned her head back, then flashed a goony look at him. "Perfect. I can feel it going all the way to my stomach and exploding." He laughed and lifted his glass to his lips and took a sip.

"I've got a surprise for you." She lit a candle on the small table by the bank of windows. He caught the reflection of the candle flame in her green eyes and felt a familiar ache. The simple pleasures of an evening together. He could almost forget the guards outside.

Pulling back the starched white napkin from the platter in the center of the table, she said, "The gods have smiled on us. Look what Sam found." She served him a plate of silken, delicate gravlaks. "As good as Dora's," she said.

Breckkan cleared his throat and swallowed another mouthful of salmon. The rain had intensified; he could make out only the bare outline of the golden foliage of the oak trees. "Doesn't the weather remind you of Skatøy?"

"Don't make me homesick." She placed the steaks on the table. "Sam also instructed me on the simple virtues of bistecca alla fiorentina, a Florentine specialty." She stabbed a perfect bite of beef from his plate and popped it into her mouth. His always seemed to taste better.

"You're eating for two; what's my excuse?"

She kissed him and stroked a damp strand of errant hair back into place. The telephone rang. Both jumped involuntarily. He moved to answer it as Bonnie muttered a muffled curse.

"No, Bill. Just finished. Tonight?" He glanced at Bonnie and pointed toward the drapes, motioning her to close them. He hung up the receiver. "Wakefield's back from Washington. There's trouble."

Chicago

Von Stein removed the Browning pistol from his belt, his gift from Kessel, and balanced it in his hand. He played with the ring at the base of the butt and pried it off, inserting the magazine and pushing it firmly home with the heel of his palm. Gripping the slide by the retraction grooves, he pulled it back as far as it would go, then released it slowly. As he rotated the safety catch, he smiled, strangely excited. The obvious had suddenly struck him. After two weeks of dead ends, it seemed so easy.

Following them hadn't been difficult, although his sleazy identity had more than once nearly gotten him in trouble walking the streets of

Winnetka. Petrusini's map made it so simple, he thought. He had detested the dank environs of the northernmost water tunnel, but it was perfect: two miles offshore with a clear view of the Wakefield Estate. He had studied the routine of the guard and realized they were as neurotic as any guards: all animals of habit. A paroxysm of pain shot like lightning through his leg. Those sudden moves at the beach. That goddamn murderous Italian. The pain lessened and his mind cleared.

The perfect place was where he first spotted them. Tuesday. Every Tuesday at the Art Institute. He sighted the pistol at the alarm clock on the night table. A well-placed shot and a crowd to witness Olav Breckkan's death. He had one more errand. He owed it to himself.

Winnetka

Wakefield had refused to say anything more on the phone; Breckkan agreed to meet him and had left immediately, leaving her alone once more. Trying to concentrate, she checked the last set of equations in the notebook. Sliding the data into the desk drawer, she pulled out her letter to Dora, and wrote quickly closing it with small talk. She leaned back and capped the fountain pen. A bitter wind blew from the North, hurling rain against the French door.

Leaning heavily on the desk for support, she rose slowly to her feet and placed her hands on her abdomen. The Doctor was concerned with her sudden increase in weight. Her blood pressure was high and bed rest, a lot of bed rest, was advised.

Bonnie shivered involuntarily and pushed back the chair. She hated watching Olav trying to confront his obsession: water. The Regatta, Copenhagen. How did he ever manage to save me? The undertow was vicious, but his grip was strong, pulling her to shore.

She wrapped her arms around herself and went into the bedroom. As she reached for a sweater on the closet shelf, she accidently kicked the small suitcase. She fingered the tag, barely able to read the address: 4 Fjeldsgaten, Bergen. Memories of her father in his greenhouse, bent over his beloved orchids, rivulets of rain streaming down the windowpanes and the lights of the Bryggen sparkling below.

Tears ran down her cheeks as she picked up the suitcase they had so carefully guarded. She carried it into the living room, pushed aside the letter, and lifted the case onto the desk. Slowly, she unsnapped the latches and opened it, revealing dozens of packets wrapped in tissue paper and tightly packed layers of cotton wool. She ran her hands over them; nothing seemed broken. Carefully, she removed the large one from the center and unwrapped it and felt her face flush with emotion. Through wet eyes, she caught the glint of light from the hand-blown figure of Saint Nicholas, one of her earliest childhood memories. Now you will delight another child.

"Damn the world," she said out loud as she touched her stomach. She leaned back on the desk for a moment, then gently rewrapped the Christmas ornament, replaced it in the case, and snapped it shut.

A blast of rain hit the door and she suddenly felt very alone. She sat down at the desk and picked up the letter. Dora, she thought, I'm sorry to burden you, but I need to talk to you. I'll be damned if this pre-eclampsia is going to get me. Enough self-pity. She closed the envelope.

A soft rap on the door jolted her. Looking at

her watch, she smiled. She crossed to the door and opened it. "Ole..." Her throat froze.

"Good evening, Mrs. Breckkan." He stood motionless in the rain. His white hair was soaked and plastered to his head. One eye stared unblinking at her, the other was fixed and clouded. "The rain on the glass produces an amusing kaleidoscopic effect," he said in a flat, conversational tone. "Your red hair seemed to dance around your head. I've always loved your hair."

She tried to slam the door, but he shoved his foot over the threshold and flung the door wide open. "What do you want!" she screamed. Von Stein lifted his cane and touched her skirt, then moved the tip of the cane slowly up onto her abdomen.

He's going to kill me, kill the baby! "I have nothing you want," she said without inflection. There was no comment from the strained, intent face of the German. "What do you want?" She stifled a scream. The tip of the cane pressed harder on her stomach. "Please, for God's sake!"

Abruptly, he withdrew the cane, stepped back, and stared at her through the rain. "I wanted you." He glanced at her pregnant belly. Suddenly he reached for the doorknob and, with one smooth motion, pulled it shut, leaving her alone.

She rubbed her abdomen where the cane had touched. Her eyes blinked rapidly, confused and terrified. She jerked the door open and stepped out into the storm. The needle-like drops struck her face. "You bastard!" she screamed hysterically. "You bastard!"

Backing into the house, she slammed the door and locked it. She fought for breath. How long had he been there?

Skatøy

The sky over Skatøy was the color of slate. Dora gave a last short wave at Gustave on the departing ferry.

"You know, Petter, there's probably not a man in Norway who wouldn't sit down and have a drink with Gustave. Maybe it's those sad dog eyes of his. I don't know how, but he's keeping the company alive. It's hard for me to admit, but we owe him for keeping the hope alive that we can somehow, someday, return to a normal existence. But it's taking its toll...did you notice his suit pants were shiny? And he's lost weight. Not that it isn't good for him." She raised her hand to her forehead to shield her eyes from the wind. "Talk to me, old man."

"He's in a terribly compromised position. I don't know how he keeps his sanity. Did he tell you about the labor camps north of Oslo...mostly old friends..." Petters' voice trailed off, caught by the wind.

"Yes, he mentioned a few names, but then it seemed to hurt him too much. He said Oslo isn't a city at war. It's worse than that...a city of terror." She threaded her hand around his bony arm and turned back toward the cottage. A jagged crack of lightning illuminated the scene. Dora's hand trembled as the roll of thunder filled her world.

Chicago

Vulpes, I've met with our friend, wrote von Stein, glancing over at his cane propped against the velvet chair. The cold rain hadn't helped; he still felt aroused. *She's damaged goods; that child should have been mine.* He reached up and dabbed at his forehead and wet hair with the towel draped around his shoulders, then swallowed a gulp of whiskey.

She's pregnant, he continued. *The first funds ar-rived safely. However, allowing for this new devel-opment, may I suggest the payment be doubled. I shall wait for your answer before proceeding.*

Signing off, he laughed out loud. They're dead anyway, he thought, but it's worth a try. And the secret of Stagg Field is not for you, friend. When I get it, Vulpes, there will be a much higher bidder.

CHAPTER 20

September 23, 1940

Chicago

Breckkan looked blankly out the window while the Packard moved with the early morning traffic toward the city. He paid no attention to the sights; his thoughts were focused entirely on von Stein. He had made up his mind. The Norwegian shifted restlessly in the rear seat, fidgeting with the keys to the lake house, then leaned forward. "I'm not hiding anymore and I'm not going to sit on my butt waiting for him to make the next move."

"Mr. Wakefield's upset, too. He's really beefed up security." Sam accelerated as he passed a slow moving garbage truck.

"I don't give a damn. I'm taking care of this myself. He's after me...so now I'm after him. I'm going to need some help, just the kind I think you can come up with."

"Dr. Breckkan, you're not going to do anything. Leave this to us."

Breckkan sat back and looked at the reflection in the mirror, studying the scar on Sam's neck. "That's not what I want to hear."

Breckkan thought back to the Copenhagen years with von Stein. The German was unpredictable. Very sure of himself, yes, cocksure. His infamous genetic theory: he had insisted the combination of redhead genes would purify his. A child, conceivably theirs, would be free of albinism. She had ridiculed him. That man doesn't give a damn about Germany, science, a bomb. This is so damn personal. Bonnie rejected him. In his crazed mind, she denied him a future, a heritage rid of his defect.

He broke the silence in the car. "Sam, this

von Stein, I know him very, very well. He's insane. Crazy people have crazy reasons for doing things. But they still have reasons." Sam only nodded. "There's got to be a way to figure him out, a way to anticipate his next moves. So, you see, you and your people..."

"My people?"

"Your connections," said Breckkan, sliding forward in the seat. "You've got to help me find him fast or I'm dead. Bonnie too."

Sam's eyes narrowed; the dark shadows around them intensified. He said nothing.

* * * *

A lone light reflected on the damp sidewalk under the corner entrance to the western stands of Stagg Field; the overgrowth of English ivy glistened with moisture. The University of Chicago had long abandoned dreams of great football teams for scholarship. Von Stein limped across the empty street past the entrance, noting the armed night watchmen just inside. Keeping to the deep shadows of the old masonry building, he worked his way down the street. Petrusini's maps detailed a complex drain and ventilation system installed underneath the stands, with several entrances designated on the playing field side of the stadium. He pushed his way through a thick hedge and onto the field, cringing as lightning pain shot from his pelvis into his leg. Crossing the open grass, now bathed in cold pink light, he found an exposed shelter area, once used by opposing varsity teams.

He checked the map. With his shoulder he shoved aside an old, upturned wood platform, exposing a ventilation entrance. He pushed open the mangled, rusting grill and was immediately engulfed with the smell of excrement and rotting debris. Covering his nose with the back of his hand, he flashed a light into the tunnel. Others had been here, he realized, Chicago's homeless, the poor bastards. He dropped to his knees and crawled into the filthy concrete passage. He clawed his way along the labyrinth of narrow twisting tunnels, trying to position his legs in an effort to relieve the torrents of pain.

Stopping to rest, he suddenly became aware of a low-pitched hum. It seemed to come from somewhere deep beneath him. When the pain finally subsided, he pressed on, faster now, moving closer to the reverberation. His right hand reached forward with the flashlight to find the next turn. Nothing! He jerked back, trying to keep from pitching headfirst into the void and dropped the flashlight. Cursing himself, he clung to the edge of the crawl-way, mentally counting aloud. The clang of the flashlight reached his ears just as he said, "Five." Fifteen to eighteen feet, he calculated. Peering down the shaft, he saw the beam of light from the metal flashlight. The shaft was probably three feet square. Steel loops projected from one side, forming a ladder.

Carefully, he lowered himself on to the first rung. Damn! His shoe slipped on the thick layer of ocher-colored slime mold covering the rungs. In no time, his hands glistened with the cold wet slime. One good thing, he thought, it will be easier to climb out, getting this crap off the ladder now. At the bottom, he jarred open a narrow panel and, hunching down, peered into the room. A row of 25-watt bulbs illuminated a maze of generators, furnaces, and pipes. He swung his body into the room, crossed to the door, and inched it open. Naked bulbs cast a flat light down the hall. Walls painted with stretches of green and white extended in both directions. Except for the hum of the pumps behind him, there were no other sounds.

Moving cautiously along the corridor, he stopped at a set of large double doors marked: "KEEP OUT! EXTREME DANGER!" Using his knife blade, he slid the latch back, releasing the lock. The room was pitch and his flashlight revealed only more blackness.

The risk had to be taken. He snapped on a large toggle switch and banks of high-intensity floodlights suddenly lit the room, momentarily blinding him. As his good eye accommodated, he surveyed the large room, estimating the ceiling to be twenty-five, maybe thirty feet above him. In the center of the huge room, where Petrusini's maps and floor plans had labelled a room as "double squash courts," was a giant pile of "bricks" arranged more or less in the form of a doorknob. The equator of the structure was at least a fifth again larger around than the poles. Trying to develop a visual image of its size, von Stein estimated the entire structure to be the size of a two-car garage.

He audibly gasped, "Graphite. Goddamn it, it's a graphite pile!"

He had to have tangible proof. Just as he began to jot down the numbers which were carefully painted on each layer of graphite bricks, a shrill siren screamed overhead. In one stride, he reached the light switch, then stepped into the fully lit hall. Without bothering to look, he raced for the equipment room. As he slid the dead bolt home, the hall filled with sounds of running footsteps. Dangerous though it was, he cracked the door and peered into the hall. Guards, too many to count, and a tall blonde man in a lab coat were running toward the former squash court.

Von Stein touched the pistol in his coat pocket. He was just feet away from Breckkan! He could kill the bastard, but the information... Another time, he swore under his breath. Now, move!

Fighting to remain conscious from the convulsive explosions of pain in his groin, von Stein reached the grass of Stagg Field and ducked into the thick hedge. He fainted.

The sun was high in the sky when he awakened. His clothing reeked of excrement and slime mold. He wiggled his toes; his socks felt spongy. A smile crossed his face, he knew their secret. The smile faded. He reaffirmed his promise to himself; Breckkan, you're dead.

Your widow will soon be mine.

* * * *

A group of girls in tartan uniforms passed them in a flurry of giggles. Sam stepped to one side of the marble staircase and let the next pack of children pass. "Crowded like a schoolyard today," he muttered, nodding graciously at a trio of nuns. "You sure you'll be all right? What did the doctor say?"

"I'm fine, Sam. Go on. We'll meet you back here in an hour. Ciao." She offered a small wave as he walked away.

Breckkan bounded up the last steps to the second floor and held out a guidebook. "Where's he going?"

"Didn't you read the paper yesterday? The Gauguin show opened on Sunday."

"Sam likes Gauguin?" asked Breckkan. Bonnie nodded, absorbed in the guidebook. "Think we have a voyeur for a chauffeur?"

Bonnie ignored the innuendo and opened the museum floor plan.

"Southeast corner, Galleries 30 and 30A," said Breckkan.

They walked hand in hand. Reaching the entrance to the Renaissance Collection, Breckkan glanced into the room. It was filled with children, all listening to an Art Institute curator deliver a lecture.

"Let's move on for now," he said. "The Flemish Collection, that marvelous Breughel." They rounded the corner and entered the adjacent Galleries 28 and 29.

The children were not alone with Miss Mackenzie in Gallery 30 and 30A. A man stood in the far corner, his shoulder against the wall, leaning on his cane, wondering if the children really gave a damn about Berenson. The pain in his leg was pure torture. He glanced at the Gallery entrances to his right and directly across the room. They wouldn't backtrack to his left, entering to his left. He was positive. He knew how many steps to the far end of Gallery 30, just as he knew where their favorite work of art hung.

When the lecture ended, Miss Mackenzie motioned to the children to follow the nuns. "No running, girls."

Finally, the handsome couple entered the far doorway, half in silhouette, pausing to look at a tiny Vermeer. Now moving into Gallery 30A, the man whispered something into the redhead's ear.

Von Stein reached under his suit coat and slid out the pistol tucked in his belt. It felt strangely cold to him. Ignoring the pain in his leg, he took several long strides, pushing children aside as he moved toward the couple. There, forty feet away, stood the personification of all he despised. He lifted the weapon into firing position and spread his legs solidly as he sighted straight at Breckkan. I have your secret, and now I have you.

The children milling in the center became a blur. Sweat beaded on his forehead. He sensed moist heat flooding from under his collar onto his neck. Ringing in his ears blocked the sounds in the room. Suddenly a burst of lightning pain shot through his groin. Muscles in his index finger involuntarily tightened, and the gun responded with a deafening report that echoed through the galleries and down the marble corridors.

Bonnie, as if in slow motion, turned toward the gun, her left cheek covered with blood.

Breckkan spun toward her, his eyes wide with disbelief. His mind sped, comprehending the flashing images. He immediately saw von Stein with the gun in his hand. "You insane son-of-a-bitch!" he roared, then grabbed Bonnie, roughly forcing her to the floor.

"Sam, goddamn it! Sam!" Breckkan shouted over the cacophony of children's hysterical screams. Looking at her blood-stained face, he cried, "Bonnie, no!"

"I'm not hit!"

Suddenly a deep sick feeling engulfed him. He cautiously raised his head and looked around. There beside him lay a small girl, dressed in a tartan jumper with a blood-stained large white square collar. Her eyes were wide and glazed. She didn't seem to feel the vicious tear in her neck. She blinked slowly. An expression of confusion and noncomprehension clouded her face. The eyes remained open as life left them.

Von Stein stood looking at the hell he had created. He watched Breckkan shift to his knees and cradle the dying child, the nuns crowding toward him.

The screams and sound of running feet penetrated his brain. He became nauseated by a white-hot pain. Unable to set up a clear shot, he backed away from the tragedy, picked up his cane, and limped away, avoiding the guards and Sam as they rushed in from the corridor.

Winnetka

Bonnie turned on her side and pulled up her knees. Breckkan adjusted the sheets and leaned over her, kissing her softly on her pale cheek. As he smoothed her hair, the Doctor murmured, "The sedative will take effect shortly. You'll be able to rest now, Mrs. Breckkan. If you should need anything, I'll leave my number."

"Sam will show you out. Thank you for coming," said Breckkan.

"Mr. Wakefield is a long-time friend," said the physician, shutting the bedroom door quietly behind him.

Breckkan turned to the window and looked at the western sky. The afternoon light was changing from golden to mauve; he guessed the time to be around five. He glanced back at Bonnie and could tell she was asleep.

Closing the drapes, he walked into the living room. "Good, you're still here, Bill."

"Of course I'm here," he answered, all too aware of the agitation in Breckkan's voice. "Sam, why don't you go now. I need to talk to Breckkan."

Sam looked intently at Breckkan. "I'm okay, Sam. Go on."

Wakefield poured two glasses of whiskey and handed one to Breckkan. "To Bonnie." Breckkan lifted his glass and drank without comment. Wakefield sat opposite him and waited. "Why? Why is he after you?"

Breckkan searched for words, then slowly said, "Stein is brilliant...in some ways maybe even genius. But he has a fatally flawed mind." He hesitated again, then continued as if talking to himself. "I took away the one woman he believes could have given him a normal child, a chance to cleanse, to reestablish the von Stein lineage. Maybe even his place in society.

"The guy's crazy! A little girl is dead, for Christ's sake. You know, Bill, back at Vemork, when he was in Nazi uniform, I thought he was..." Breckkan shook his head, his eyes sharp. "A brilliant mind turned cruel, evil. But he doesn't give a damn about science or the Reich. He's completely devoted to himself."

"If you're right then, where has he gotten his cash, his identity papers? He had to enter the US somewhere...and a place to hide? He's either very lucky, knows you well, or he's being fed information regarding your every move." Wakefield's body language was unusually animated. "You may have more than just von Stein after you."

"Before you go any further, get me a gun. I do have dual citizenship, so it certainly shouldn't be illegal."

"Okay, Sam will have one for you before the day's over. Breckkan, who do you think is helping von Stein?"

"What are you suggesting?"

"I don't know. Maybe it's someone here, someone in the lab. What about that man Compton reported?"

"What man?" asked Breckkan, completely blank.

"The scientist with the shortwave radio."

Breckkan laughed harshly. "You mean one of the other foreigners you brought to the lab?"

"You know those shortwave sets are banned under the Secrecy Act. Besides, that one was short range."

"It's got to be more sophisticated than that,"

snapped Breckkan. "It's been going on since Bergen."

"Well then, maybe the source is in England. Or Norway. Who knew about your departure?"

Breckkan set down his glass and began to count on his fingers. "In all, five. The pilot and copilot. You do remember the RAF Crew," he said sarcastically. "And don't forget Sir George, that's three, and of course there was that Colonel Reed...and yourself."

"A good list. Let's take one at a time." Wakefield leaned back on the sofa, hands clasped behind his head. "Colonel Reed first. He's been moved to HQ in London. Busy with bomber runs over the Lowlands. Not likely he would have access to your every move, would you think?" Breckkan shook his head negatively. "Now, the pilot and copilot, they're flying missions over the Continent. Because of the Brits' heavy losses, no more regulars are assigned diplomatic duty. How could either learn of your or Bonnie's activities?"

"I guess they could, but that's stretching."

"Sir George, not surprisingly, is back in London and works directly with the PM." He turned and stared at Breckkan through half-closed eyes. "If Churchill trusts him, I think I will."

"That leaves you," Breckkan said quietly.

"That it does. Let's put aside the fact that I've known you all your life. Certainly, I knew your every move. But," he paused for a moment, "give me one good reason why I should try to destroy you after I've baby-sat you from Norway on."

"I can suggest several reasons. For one..."

Wakefield loosened his hands. "Let me finish. Why wait until now to order your death? That's a little like scratching your right ear with your left hand. It would have been a helluva lot easier to get rid of you before you got to England, don't you think?"

"Say you really don't give a damn about me. Remember Vienna? What you're really after is my research, my connections in Europe, lots of things. Why not let me bring all of it to you?"

"Good argument," Wakefield answered tersely.

Both men sat in silence, avoiding eye contact. Abruptly, Breckkan said, "Stein first showed up at the banquet. Only days before the invasion." He stared at his empty glass. "Someone in Norway."

"Such as?"

"Well, he would have used his own people to trace me to the Hydro Plant. But only Bonnie and Knut knew about the boat. Everyone else involved with the ANNA is dead."

"How about someone at the harbor? Or Professor Kittleson's secretary at the Institute? As I recall, the Germans allowed her to leave." He rubbed his forehead, then absentmindedly fingered his cuff links. "What about your Navy friend, Commodore Duun?"

"Damn it, Bill! He was picked for that spot by the King! Roald's been my friend forever."

"Right, right. Take it easy."

"Besides, he wouldn't have had an opportunity to do anything anyway. He's in London with the exiled government." Suddenly Breckkan was speaking in a rush. "The harbormaster! What about him? Hell, he did his best to kill all of us."

"True. And we've now proven he was a Nazi sympathizer. But he's dead. He hasn't been around to tell anyone anything for some time now. Keep thinking. We're narrowing the list." Wakefield refilled his glass.

Breckkan placed his face in his hands. "God, this brings out the worst in me. I'd even have to list my own mother. We've purposefully kept her aware."

Wakefield stood, walked over to his friend, and

placed a hand on his shoulder. "Does anyone read your mother's mail besides her?"

"I don't know. We channel mail through several routes. Don't know exactly how it gets to her."

"Well, keep thinking." Wakefield walked to the door and turned the knob. "For now, you're safe. We've sealed this estate up like a sardine can."

Breckkan sat in a slump, feeling both vulnerable and exhausted. "How in God's name are we going to find..." He looked up, but Wakefield was already gone.

Berlin

Richter closed the latest report on the US agent. He leaned back, staring at the bronze monkeys and muttered a curse. What in the hell is von Stein thinking? Goddamn bastard's a killer. He'll probably manage to get the Chicago information out and give it to the SS or the Gestapo! This is like a snowball rolling down a hill. He jabbed at the report. What basic motivation still pushes him? Hate. Love. Lust. Pain. He went to battle, but for whom? For what? He should never have been let out of his lab full of rats. He's hasn't a thread of loyalty to anyone. What did I set in motion?

Chicago

Sam handed Breckkan the Smith & Wesson .38. "Plenty of these around. And I have two of my best men staying in your apartment tonight."

Breckkan took the gun and slid into the front seat. "Talk to me. Where are we headed?"

"I don't like this one bit, Doctor. It'll be my ass."

"It's my responsibility. Enough. What have you found out?"

"One of our people spotted him going into the

BRECKKAN 303

Washington Hotel this afternoon. He's still there. It's a sleazy flophouse on the South Side. With some persuasion the desk clerk told us he's on the third floor. Room faces the street."

"What are we waiting for?!"

"Dr. Breckkan, why don't you leave this to me?"

Halos formed by the mist around the street lights. "If it was your wife and your life, what would you do?"

A soft rain continued to fall as the Packard cruised south and stopped at the intersection of Commercial Avenue and 92nd Street. Breckkan looked out at the three-story building on the corner. The Coca-Cola sign at the side of the building glowed iridescent red on the wet pavement. Surveying the building, he could see three lighted windows on the third floor. "Which one?"

"Nearest the corner." Sam reached over and placed a hand on Breckkan's shoulder, gripping to the point of pain. "This is no country squire's weekend shoot. So far, because I feel for you, I've done everything you've asked for. Now you'll do things my way. Understand? I've seen too many good men die because they were consumed with hatred. I'm not going to let that happen to you. Stay in the shadows of the doorway of the Walgreen Store. Watch for me at his window. Then get ready; he'll be on his way out."

Breckkan closed the car door quietly behind him, then crossed the street to the drug store. He didn't see Sam leave and was surprised when he looked back and saw the car empty. He turned up his collar and tucked his chin down in an effort to stay warm. The red neon sign flashed rhythmically through the drizzle.

Suddenly, the calm of the night was torn by the harsh clang of a fire alarm. Moments passed and a figure filled the window. A hand waved, and Breckkan reached into his pocket for the .38.

Men and women rushed from the hotel, many trying to protect themselves from the rain with jackets or hotel towels over their heads. Breckkan stared intently at the figures running from the building, each momentarily lit by the entrance lights. A streetcar screeched to a stop in front of the hotel.

Breckkan jumped from the doorway and ran toward the streetcar. A woman saw his pistol and screamed. The trolley clanged across the intersection, barely missing two fire engines arriving on the scene. Breckkan spun around, looking quickly up and down the street, and then ran to the corner.

"No use," yelled Sam, running up behind him. "He's gone."

"What do you mean, gone?"

"Spotted him too late. Chased him down two flights of stairs. The bastard dove headfirst down a laundry chute. By the time I got to the basement, he was gone."

"Goddamn it!" yelled Breckkan.

"Come on, Doctor," called Sam, grabbing his arm. "Let's get the hell out of here."

The Packard pulled away from the chaos. "He'll be back. We'll get him." muttered Breckkan.

"He's not coming back here," said Sam flatly.

CHAPTER 21

Late September, 1940

SKATØY, NORWAY

Dora stood at the top of the steep path leading down to the inlet. The air was crisp, the light pale. The radio had issued a weather alert; a storm was approaching from the North, gathering strength over the Hardanger Plateau. Already the water at Skatøy was choppy. White caps spasmodically struck the granite dock.

From his second-story window, Petter watched Dora gather a shawl around her shoulders. Her soft blue skirt whipped at her legs. Looking across the water, he sighted the perky blue and white boat rounding the far promontory. He knew it would be several more moments before she could see it. He watched and gave a sour grunt, hoping Gustave was enjoying the invigorating weather.

When the boat pulled alongside the white-fenced dock, a deck hand jumped to the pier and expertly wrapped a rope around the stanchion. Gustave appeared on deck, his hand clamping his hat down on his head as a gust buffeted the boat. He made the jump to the dock and then leaned unsteadily into the wind. Following the deck hand, he took short, cautious steps, sliding the leather soles of his polished shoes on the smooth stone.

"Good morning, my dear," called Gustave, his face appearing at the top of the steps. He pulled up his coat lapels trying to block the cutting wind, and paused to catch his breath.

"Good morning, Gustave. Kristian, just leave his bags by the door," said Dora. "And Petter will need to put that wooden crate in the cold house, I imagine." The deck hand nodded. Dora leaned closer to him and shouted against the wind. "Does the Captain think you'll be able to stay on schedule? The radio…"

"Not sure, Mrs. Breckkan. Afraid we'll be heading back to the mainland any time now. Keep your radio on."

"Looks like your stay may be longer than expected, Gustave."

"Damnable weather you're having," Gustave said, taking her arm.

"Nic always liked it. Invigorating, he used to say."

"Mrs. Breckkan," said Petter at the front door to the cottage. "I don't like the sound of your cough. It's nasty out there. I should've met the boat."

"Don't look at me like that, old man. Same cough since I had pneumonia in 1925. Now, get us some coffee."

"My coat, Petter," said Gustave, shrugging off his chesterfield, but the manservant was already in the kitchen. "Testy today, isn't he?"

"He's more eccentric than ever. Must be the isolation." Dora turned on a brass floor lamp and reached for her cigarettes. "Sit down, Gustave." She sat stiffly, her small head tilted to one side, twisting the loose rings on her thin fingers. She adjusted the rings back into place, her hand trembling slightly as she picked up the lighter.

"Let me do that," said Gustave. When he leaned close, she noticed the tiny broken vessels on his nose and cheekbones and was positive they weren't the result of laboring outdoors. "Don't you ever get lonely?" he asked.

"Sometimes. Melancholy might be a better word. But there's a grandeur here. I've never been anywhere quite like these islands."

Gustave settled himself into the deep cushions of the sofa and unbuttoned his tweed jacket. "Well,

I must say the cottage is more darling every time I come."

"Darling nothing!" she snapped and exhaled a thin stream of smoke. "It's adequate. And it's solid."

Gustave ignored the cutting edge of her comment. "It's best that you're here, safe and away from the Germans."

"How very stoic of you."

He leaned back, his large hands clasped behind his head, a trace of a smile on his lips. "What is Petter up to?" he asked, noticing the rich smells coming from the kitchen.

"I believe he's managed a seafood chowder. At least we get plenty of fish. Have you brought us any staples? We're low on everything."

"Of course." He rose to warm his hands before the fire, glad for the change of topic. He was beginning to feel his hangover. "I've brought oranges from Madeira. And I was able to bribe the Senior Supply Officer from Command Headquarters, greedy little bastard, into selling me a fine leg of lamb. Lamb, mind you, and not just any lamb, but one from the Netherlands."

"For God's sake, Gustave," interrupted Dora, "lamb is either lamb or mutton, not some national prize."

Turning his back to the fire, he said, "I don't think you appreciate the strain, the complexities of the situation in Oslo."

"And I suppose I should be grateful," she said, her eyes flashing with bitterness. "Grateful for your powers of persuasion. You've always been good at exploitation, but without my company...you do remember that Nic left me Breckkan Mining?...you would be shoveling snow on some prisoner brigade with the rest of my friends."

Gustave felt his face color, but coolly said, "With-

out me, dear Dora, you would have no company."
He reached for his briefcase and fumbled for some
papers. "Here are the latest company reports."

Petter entered the room carrying a large wooden
tray. Gustave straightened his tie and returned the
glare of the manservant. Stirring two cubes of sugar
into her cup, Petter asked, "Will you need me?"

"No, that will be all," she said and took the
cup. "Gustave and I have business to discuss."
The radio crackled, fading in and out. Through
the static, the meteorological report confirmed
gusts of 45 knots and issued small craft warn-
ings. Gustave switched off the radio and walked
to the east window. The horizon vanished into an
infinite grayness. He was trapped.

"The ferry won't be back today."

"Godforsaken place," he muttered, not turning to look at her.

Ignoring the remark, she said, "Breckkan's
room is made up. You can sleep there." Dora looked
up from the August ledger. "Come here, Gustave.
Explain some of these entries."

"Which entries?" he asked, continuing to stare
out into the enveloping grayness.

"It's not any particular entry, rather it's what's
missing."

"Missing?" He seemed bored. "What are you
talking about?"

"To begin with, WKW Industries. Aren't we
doing business with them?"

"No."

"Look at me!" she snapped and stood up.

He turned and said with an expressionless face,
"We aren't doing business with WKW. It's that
simple."

"It's not simple at all. Nic and Bill were the
closest of friends. You certainly remember that."

He gestured with a superior movement of his hand and said, "Dora, dear Dora." He crossed to the fireplace, put his hands on the mantel, and studied the painting which hung above. "The Grand Canal, Venice. Canaletto, I believe."

"A gift from Nic." She despised the self-officious tone in his voice.

"But I don't recall it hanging here."

"It hung in my bedroom in Oslo." Her eyes fixed on the back of his neck. "And it will hang there again. Gustave, answer my question. WKW?"

"It's tied with the vagaries of war. I don't want to bother you with details. Tell me, how is Bonnie feeling?"

"Bonnie's fine." She fingered the cameo at her neck. "Don't keep changing the subject. Bill Wakefield was indispensable to me after Nic died."

He sensed the alertness in her delicate, intelligent face and ambled over to the desk. "Aren't you impressed with Wakefield's connections? Some of the finest of Chicago's underworld protecting them...and your future grandchild."

Dora's mind screamed, her suspicions were right after all. She retreated to the desk chair and stared at the pages of the open ledger. With a sudden motion, she shoved the ledger toward Gustave. "Gustave, once again, WKW? What's going on?" She reached for a cigarette.

Grabbing the heavy lighter from the desk with a doughy wet hand, he flicked the flame. The flame flared inches from her face. "Well?" His eyes leveled with hers. "Put the damn cigarette in your mouth." With great self-control, she deliberately moved the cigarette to her mouth. After she exhaled the first stream of smoke, he snapped the lighter shut and dropped it, marring the desk. "Your friends at WKW are up to their ears in munitions production. Their pyrite quota took the bulk of our production. The authorities were going to force us to cut them off."

"You mean you cut them off, and didn't make the Germans do it?"

"I told you, Dora, you wouldn't understand."

She pushed back the chair, brushed past him, and walked to the window. "Oh, I understand."

Gustave slowly closed the ledger. "It's all beside the point because Wakefield closed his offices in Oslo." He looked aimlessly out the window past her. "You Americans thought that so-called neutrality would pay off handsomely, but instead it's cost all of you half the world market." She glared at him and ground out the cigarette, ignoring the insult. "By the way, more of your dilettante friends have been put in the internment camp outside Oslo. Want to know the names of some who have already died?"

He began to walk toward her, but stopped. She raised her hand, and with a thin finger, pointed at the ledger. "Page four is always the same. The heading is FOX, no account number. What or who is Fox?"

"Some German company, I presume."

"You presume? Gustave, enormous amounts of money are bound up in these transactions. Aren't you the least bit curious?"

"Dora, there's simply nothing to it."

She shifted in her chair; she was flushed, her eyes wet but intense. "When you moved me here, I recall your speaking to that young German officer who accompanied us. You had handed him your identification papers. He glanced at them briefly, saluted, and then left us alone. Now," she took a deep breath, "tell me about Fox!"

"My dear, there's nothing to be said." He pressed back into his chair and studied the frail woman across the desk.

"Well, I didn't think much of the fact that there wasn't a number on that page, certainly not at the time. Perhaps it would soon be explained."

Gustave laughed out loud. "So, an account has no number. So what?"

Before Gustave could continue, she stopped him with a raised hand. "The nice gifts you bring. The box with the lamb from the Netherlands, for example."

He looked at her, his pupils fixed. Where is she going with this?

"All the boxes have been stamped with an official German seal."

"We're an occupied country, my dear."

"No, Gustave, it's the handwritten German script on the line in the seal. Always the same 'foks,' but often smudged. It could be "vulp"-something. What does that mean?"

"I've no idea," he said with acerbity. "An interesting way to occupy your time."

"You should've been more clever." She moved to the fireplace, measuring her pace. Now's the time, she thought. "How did you know Bonnie was pregnant?"

"You told me, of course."

"No, Gustave, I didn't tell you. I made up my mind I would tell no one. It would be safer for them."

"Perhaps Petter mentioned it to me."

"Hah! He despises you and you know it!"

Gustave jerked to his feet and shouted, "Why, you ungrateful bitch!" He strode to the window. The fog obscured everything, even the promontory beacon. Only the sound of the crashing waves rose up over the cliff. Suddenly, he spun around and thrust an accusing finger at her.

"Don't lose your composure now, Gustave. You've put on an extraordinary performance. A perfect front, man. How fortunate for you. A war, just the thing, am I right? Nic always felt you were incompetent, an upper-crust degenerate, but he was wrong. You're extremely competent...competent at manipulation, exploitation, using anyone and everyone. You want Breckkan Mining."

"Perhaps a bit of truth in that, my dear one, but don't mistake my intentions. How in that antiquated, privileged little head of yours can you explain how your children made it to safety? Their friends? With Roald at sea and Bill Wakefield at Whitehall! I was the one who covered their butts and was able to get them safely to Windsor and on to Chicago."

"You answered that one tidily. My, how you lie well under pressure. I never grasped the scope of your malignancy. How did you know they entered through Windsor?"

"Go ahead, Dora. Quit playing; tell me what you really think."

"You know, oh, how well you know what Nic called men he didn't trust." She paused to watch his reaction, but there was none. "He called them foxes— clever, self-serving, untrustworthy. Your own brother described you as a fox more than once. Gustave, even in choosing a code name, a goddamn fake name to embezzle from my company, you couldn't be original." She crossed to a side table, opened the drawer, and removed a carton of cigarettes. No more doubts. The label was stamped on the box; the word written across the seal was smudged. "Take a look for yourself. The script is so intricate. Is it 'foks,' German for fox, or is it 'vulps?' I'm guessing it probably is the latter, vulpes. Fox in Latin." She looked at him and could smell his fear, see the hatred in his sneer.

"Always so self-righteous. So smug." His eyes narrowed. "So secure with all of Nic's money, my money. Look at you, a snivelling old lady, your only companion that pathetic little servant." His voice was hoarse with bitterness as he continued. "All around me, men are sleeping soundly, the so-called guardians of our society. In fact, my dear, they're more hypocritical, more deceitful, more subtle than you can imagine. What the hell do you think Nic was up to! Your fancy friends! That son of yours! Oh, I know about your informant, Kristian, that messenger assigned by Roald."

"You ass!" Dora hissed, glaring at the man's impassive face. "There's nothing you won't do."

"You're quite right." He reached for the heavy gold lighter, balanced the weight of it in the palm of his hand and started toward her.

She dropped the cigarette carton and reached into the open drawer. There was a sharp crack followed by a dull thud. A bullet from her .32 Walther PPK tore into him, searing a path into his right lung cavity.

The lighter fell from his hand as he looked at her through incredulous eyes. She pulled the trigger of the semi-automatic again, aiming this time at the left side of his chest. Blood from a severed large artery quickly filled the chest cavity, drowning him.

Looking down at the motionless body, she murmured, "Dear Gustave, why was it so terribly hard to give, even a little of yourself? You have jeopardized everyone."

She sat perfectly still, barely aware of Petter's approaching footsteps. He stood in the shadows of the room and said, "Mrs. Breckkan, lunch is served."

CHAPTER 22

October 15, 1940

Winnetka

Von Stein descended the slick wet stairs into the water-intake building. He pulled the corroding metal door shut, and looked around the grimy room, grunting in disgust. The walls glistened with moisture; green and black mold grew in profusion on the aging brick walls. He sat in the green glow of a control panel and glanced at the fogged lenses of the water meters. Carefully, he set a pair of binoculars on a metal workbench, then leaned against a pressure valve and rubbed his inflamed shoulder. Thank God he had realized the Packard seemed out of place. That bodyguard, despite his size, had been agile and quick. Time has run out. Reaching into his satchel, he unwrapped a sandwich and took a long swallow of whiskey. Dull the pain. He would have to move quickly.

He touched the bruise on his temple and felt the heat. Momentarily he stared at a date chiselled in the concrete floor. Fiesole flashed into his mind— a marble crypt, his mother's name chiselled there. He reached down and traced the Roman numerals. All so long ago, another life. He barely remembered her.

Suddenly: claustrophobia. I can't take this place any longer. He tossed the half-eaten sandwich into a corner and watched a rat scurry to eat it. He pried open a large tub of lubricating grease. Gouging a handful of the thick, sticky material, he rubbed it on his face and hair, then wiped his hands on his coveralls. It will cut the cold, he thought with a shiver as he slipped off his shoes. He picked up the binoculars and moved to the small window for a final look. Carefully focusing, he spotted a guard wave an all clear sign toward the main house, then turn from the shore, disappearing behind a tall hedge.

Berlin

"No alternative," they had told Colonel Richter. Himmler and Canaris had both impugned his wisdom and ability to control the Network. Richter questioned that they ever gave a damn about any of the Network, just the fact that his Major von Stein was lost. All channels of communication broken. A new effort was to be launched to obtain information on the progress of atomic research being done in the United States, and they had no alternative but to reassign Richter.

Not a bad place, he thought. Lake Como certainly enjoyed better weather than Berlin, though it was quite out of the way if an officer wished to advance his career.

At least von Stein hadn't succeeded and transmitted any findings to Himmler. That would have surely meant his death. Recalling his meeting with Canaris when the whole scheme was proposed and the subsequent early morning visit to the Kaiser-Wilhelm Institute that put it all in motion, Richter realized things were never right from the offset. There were two facts that kept coming back to him from the files: Breckkan is no quitter and he loves his wife. He should have realized von Stein didn't have a chance after all. Somehow, that fate seemed fair.

Winnnetka

Breckkan nervously glanced at his watch: 4:00. The Doctor had stayed nearly an hour, concerned with her blood pressure. Trying to appear relaxed, he walked back to the bedroom.

She leaned back against the pillows and set aside the newspaper. "I see the United States is going to get involved in the war after all."

"I heard some of the graduate assistants at the lab talking about it." Breckkan took the Smith & Wesson .38 from the top drawer of the dresser. He spun the cylinder and snapped it shut. "They're all fired up, ready to enlist, but I wonder what they'd do if they knew there's a German assassin in Chicago right this minute, and he's already killed an innocent child in a public place." He walked around the bed and placed the pistol in the night table drawer. "Who's helping him? Who's leading that bastard right to our door?" She leaned across the bed and reached for him. "It has to be someone highly placed. Someone well-connected. Norwegian, or American..." He broke off, letting his thoughts run their course.

Bonnie sat quietly, rubbing his shoulders, then finally said, "I've been writing your mother..."

Suddenly, he stiffened, slowly shook his head and turned to look at her, his face distorted with a mixture of revelation and fury. "Gustave! It's so damn obvious." He managed a low laugh. "That son-of-a-bitch! That's how he manages all the fresh produce and meat, even delivering them to Skatøy."

"Breckkan, he's family. Besides, the letters were to Dora."

"Oh, I'm sure he maneuvers her into reading parts to him. The pompous prick always acts so interested, loving every detail. I never thought he really gave a damn; he just couldn't bear to miss out on anything."

"Slow down. Your uncle's holding the company together for us. He can't be working for them."

"He damn well can!" Breckkan stood up. "All those sentimental speeches about family, his affectionate compliments. That's his real talent, using people. He loves his connections, prestige." The deceit. The very thought of it. "You know, he's never really created a damn thing; he only takes. Now, that's a real art."

Bonnie fought to control her voice. She said in a flat tone, "If you are murdered..." She swallowed and then pressed on, "And if the baby and I are killed..."

He finished the thesis. "Then only Mother would stand in his way. He'd have it all. I'm going up to the house to talk to Bill. Somehow, I've got to warn her." Bonnie felt his hand grow ice cold.

Von Stein wiped the blood from the knife on his coveralls and looked down at the guard crumpled on the floor. The body involuntarily convulsed; the dead man's chest heaved. Glancing quickly around the cramped service room, he sidestepped to the door. He cursed as it creaked open. The hall was empty, also the servants' staircase leading to the second floor. And the master suite, he guessed, remembering the lights coming on in a bank of windows as he had crossed from the pool to the main house.

Ignoring the pain, he took the stairs two steps at a time, then looked back. All was quiet. He walked silently in his bare feet down the carpeted hall, hugging the wall, and stopped at the pair of walnut doors. He turned the large brass ball knob and inched the door open. He could hear a fire crackling and the occasional rattle of a newspaper. A man was seated in a leather wing-back chair facing the fireplace. Von Stein slid the knife from his pocket and slipped into the room. He gulped as the newspaper flapped in the breeze from the open door. Von Stein quickly shut the door, holding the knob to prevent it from latching. The man shifted, then turned the page. Von Stein moved closer to the figure. His heart thumped against his chest as he reached the back of the chair. He caught a glimpse of the editorial headline: "Should We Become Involved Again?"

He lifted the knife and drove it into the back of Bill Wakefield's neck, severing the spinal cord. The stunned body slid awkwardly to the floor face down.

One brief glance and von Stein was no longer interested; his attention turned to the fireplace. He removed the screen and then rolled the newspaper into a cone. A torch. I've got to draw him to me, he thought. He limped from window to window, lighting the drapery afire. Then he returned to the fireplace, picked up a brass kettle and sniffed the kerosene. He rolled another torch and lit it. Hurriedly moving down the hall, already feeling the waves of heat, he poured a trail of the flammable liquid. At the bottom of the stairs, he dropped the burning newspaper to the floor. With an explosive burst, the flames leaped upward. The greasy odor of kerosene filled his nostrils as he quickly closed the outside door against the billowing smoke.

Instinctively crouching down, he caught a glimpse of two guards running for the front entrance. Chaotic shouts reverberated inside the house. Von Stein slipped behind a hedge and worked his way through the shadows toward the pool. The lake house was just below.

Breckkan pulled on his jacket, walked to the night table and removed the pistol. "Here. You know how to use it."

"Breckkan..." Her voice trailed off as he left the bedroom. There's nothing anyone can do for Dora. Her thoughts were suddenly interrupted by the crash of the front door against the wall.

"My God!" shouted Breckkan. "The main house is on fire!"

Bonnie jumped from the bed and ran to the living room. Breckkan stood on the landing, his eyes fixed and wide. The second floor of the main house was ablaze. The lakeside bank of windows exploded, sending a roar of fresh fire toward the roof. Muted cries and shouts mingled with the brewing storm and muffled roar of the flames.

"Stay here!" he yelled, bounding down the stairs. It was cold, but he didn't feel it. He ran up the lawn, jumping the tiered rock steps. Ahead of him, steam rose from the pool, misting above the hedge, swirling with the black smoke. He burst through the hedge onto the flagstone deck. His peripheral vision caught an object at the edge of deck behind the diving board. Shoes, brogues? Crossing to the object, he recoiled. The shoes were on feet.

Kneeling, he frantically pushed aside the low-lying branches and tugged at the crooked body. The guard's face wore an expression of surprise; his head lay in a pool of blood, the throat slit. "Damn it, Goddamn!"

"Self-defense," came a calm, cold voice behind him.

Breckkan whipped around. "Stein!"

Von Stein stood just in front of the trees, a tall warped figure, his face and hair covered with grease.

"You're not getting away this time, by God."

"Wrong," whispered von Stein. He moved closer, his limp accentuated from the long swim.

Breckkan's eyes flickered from von Stein's face to his right hand. He caught the glint of a knife; the blade had a serrated edge. Now! Move now! He spun and lunged for von Stein. But at the same moment, von Stein, with a jolt of adrenalin, dove for the pool, plunging deep. Oh God! No!

Breckkan's mind raced. The water! A bolt of light-ening split the sky above him. The image burned: the tangled body, the freezing water, the sudden flash of lightning, white light filling his world. NO!

Some higher brain center took control of his actions and forced him to dive into the pool. Dark water swirled around him. Momentarily he lost ori-entation before striking the bottom of the pool. He fought back toward the surface and heard the muffled splash of von Stein. Damn! Where?

He spun toward the splashing and watched in amazement as von Stein's powerful arms propelled forward. In the mere seconds it took von Stein to cover the distance, Breckkan realized his mistake. In the water, von Stein's body gained strength. I'm trapped! He shuddered violently. The German's face was inches away.

Breckkan dove deeply, tearing at the water, fighting for an edge. He tucked his knees, flipped over, and propelled himself up from the bottom of the pool, aiming his head at von Stein's torso. Suddenly he was twisted violently as von Stein grabbed his arm. With a vicious kick, he freed him-self, lunged upward, and reared high up out of the water. A constricted scream broke from his throat. "I'll kill you!" He struck out through the spray, then plunged deeply again. The bottom, he thought. I can spring. Get him again!

But von Stein was too fast. Keeping his head up, he grabbed for Breckkan, locking his neck in the crook of his arm.

Breckkan struggled blindly, his lungs heaving. I've got to get free! A loud clap of thunder deafened him. His mind locked in the past: ropes from a cap-sized boat reached out for him. He clawed at his neck, choking, then felt a huge weight pressing him under. The knife! Get the knife! Thrashing in the water, he managed to elbow a solid blow to the German's abdomen. Von Stein's face contorted with pain and he slackened his grip. Breckkan wrenched free. He kicked to the surface, gulped for air and, with a burst of energy, forced his body back toward the bottom. As his shoulders disappeared below the surface, he felt a sudden, terrible, downward thrust. Von Stein savagely lashed out with his knife, burying the blade in Breckkan's left shoulder.

Instantly he felt an exploding pain. His inner ear registered the gnawing, ratchet sound of the serrated blade sawing into his shoulder bone. The dark water enveloped him. He kicked viciously, fighting the paralyzing pain, found the handle, and wrenched the knife from his shoulder. His body spiraled toward the bottom, bubbles bursting from his mouth. Warm blood from the jagged wound mixed with the water, and pink clouds swirled upward.

Von Stein broke to the surface, his face distorted by the effort. He reached out through the steam and cupped the bloody water in his hand. Breckkan, your luck just ran out, he thought. Always the big winner, not this time. Breathing heavily, he watched the water drain between his fingers.

Bonnie shoved the pistol into the pocket of her robe, ignoring the shocks of pain in her abdomen as she raced down the stairs. A horrible scream of pain and outrage reverberated in a blinding flash of lightning. She lurched onto the deck, her eyes momentarily clouded by the swirling steam and smoke. Then she saw him through the mist. Von Stein's white head lunged out of the water, his hair plastered to his head. His clothing clung to him, the wet fabric hanging in gyrating furrows. Suddenly a silver flash disappeared into the water as if chasing the shoulders of her husband. She understood immediately.

"Olav!" Von Stein saw her and started back paddling. "Help! Someone, help!" she screamed.

Using his powerful shoulders, the German dove deeply. Breckkan clutched the terrible knife. Through the bubbles of his silent scream, he felt the force of water from von Stein's approaching strokes. Have to get air, Breckkan thought. With a final thrust, he sprang toward the surface. Von Stein's body slid past just above him.

The two bodies struck each other, Breckkan thrust out his right hand and jabbed the serrated knife deep into the soft flesh of von Stein's abdomen. With enormous strength, he locked onto his body as they fought violently for the surface. Breckkan's head broke through the water, his mouth open, gasping for air and choking uncontrollably. Bonnie frantically clawed for the pistol in her pocket. The two bodies slid back under the water.

Hearing the shouts and screams, Sam bolted from the main house and ran for the pool, his pistol in hand. Just then the two men exploded to the surface, locked in a vicious stranglehold. Sam dropped to one knee and raised his gun.

"Shoot, damn it, shoot!" screamed Breckkan.

Sam shook his head, his eyes frozen on the tangle of the blood-covered bodies. Von Stein screamed in outrage as he tried desperately to wrench free.

Bonnie knew there was no time. She lifted her pistol. "God forgive me," she whispered as she fired.

There was a violent splash, arms loosened and flailed in the water. The bullet struck Kurt von Stein in the head. He froze, his head suspended above water, staring at her. Suddenly, he roared, "I loved you!"

His words echoed in her brain. In that moment, she saw his soul. His body slid under the surface.

Sam ripped off his shoes and dove into the water. He grabbed Breckkan around the waist, pulled him to the shallow end of the pool, and eased him onto the deck. She relaxed her hand, and the gun fell to the deck.

Breckkan's eyes were wide as he lay there, his breath coming in shudders. His head tipped sideways and he spit up water. In an agonized whisper, he managed to say, "You got him." His eyes flickered as she cradled his head in her lap. He tried to focus on her face, but couldn't. The wail of arriving sirens jolted him to consciousness. "You all right?" He lost consciousness before she answered.

"I'm fine," she whispered, gently smoothing his wet hair.

As the ambulance headed toward the Evanston Hospital, she looked back through the small window. The attendants were busily working on him, adjusting the flow in the intravenous tubes. With a shiver she realized only moments before she had risked killing Olav when she shot von Stein.

The ambulance swerved through oncoming traffic. Distracted, she rubbed a trembling hand across his blood on her robe. "He'll be all right," she whispered to no one. "It's over."

About The Author

Kent Jacobs, a practicing physician for over twenty years, lives with his wife, a professional painter, in southern New Mexico.

His interest in writing began during the early years of his career while a full time academician, with the publication of numerous scientific papers and articles in popular magazines.

His contemporary fiction writing springs from his affiliation as a trustee for the literary journal *Puerto del Sol* (New Mexico State University) and his position as a Regent for the sprawling Museum of New Mexico.

WATCH FOR THESE NEW COMMONWEALTH BOOKS